The Lion
Unleashed

J. M. Barlog

BAK BOOKS
San Diego, California

ISBN 978-0983145356

Printed in the United States of America
OPM 0 9 8 7 6 5 4 3 2 1

To Mary, for always believing

1

Isaac the Jew steered his two-wheeled hay wagon around rocky ruts as the last of the three-wagon caravan. Every muscle in his withered old body ached. His calloused hands grew numb from clutching his reins so tightly. The afternoon breeze swirled through Earlham Forest, jostling his gray beard and thin white hair. His stomach grumbled; his red-rimmed eyes burned from lack of sleep. But Isaac sat vigilant, erect in the midst of an escort of six fully caparisoned knights and an equal number of mounted soldiers. The knights wielded shields emblazoned with the lion rampant of King Richard. The soldiers carried spears or maces. All wore the scarlet and white of Richard's reign.

Isaac acquired his name from his friend, the king himself. Years prior, Richard had rescued Isaac from a violent throng bent on stoning him for being a Jew. In that moment of terror preceding his demise, when lesser men cower and cry, Isaac stood stolid, shoulders proud, staring down the black eyes of Death. His courage so impressed his king that Richard no longer called him Isaac, a Jew—he became Isaac the Jew, representing the soul of his people.

In time, the king realized Isaac wielded a gift for communicating. So secretly their friendship grew, despite Isaac's age being ten and one years the king's senior.

Isaac made Richard laugh; he always encouraged his majesty, regardless of the endeavor, and all the while, he allowed his king to feel as if he had developed the answers he sought for himself. Counseling a king was tricky business Isaac excelled at. Yet the Jew also displayed a talent for offering up the right words to appease his lord. The simple man had his king's ear... so long as he did not bend it the wrong way.

Richard turned to Isaac when he accepted the crosier for the Third Crusade into the Holy Lands. Wars were expensive undertakings, and Isaac assisted his king's insatiable demand for funds to prosecute the invasion.

Now, after years of inactivity, Isaac ventured from his safe haven in the dense forests of Northumberland, where the Jews collected in relative obscurity, since even the king could never quiet the bitter disdain English nobles held toward their kind.

With a rising hand, the lead knight halted the caravan, forcing Isaac to rein his beasts abruptly. The response jolted Isaac off the delicate balance he maintained on his mounded hay. The jarring movement shot agonizing pain ripping up Isaac's already aching spine. He swallowed a groan of agony.

"Why must we stop," the old man muttered under his breath. His brown eyes scanned dense foliage encroaching around them. The ominous silence spread a foreboding chill through the Jew.

Isaac's fear grew exponentially as tense moments elapsed without motion. He repositioned himself atop the hay stuffed to overflowing in his wagon.

One wagon held the purpose for their journey, a second provisions for the men, while the third hauled feed for their horses.

Panic invaded Isaac's throat, releasing an acrid fluid onto his tongue the longer they remained stationary. They could only reach the safety of Londontown if they kept moving! But the knights were busy surveilling the forest.

Isaac reminded himself that days stood between them and the comforts of Queen Eleanor's castle. Once safely there, he would eat well and sleep in a warm soft bed. Fifty and four was too old to be traveling. But his queen called; nothing would prevent him from delivering on his promise.

Nothing.

Thwack!

The first quarrel buried its four-pronged tip into the soldier accompanying the second wagon. A second followed immediately, piercing the lead knight's shield.

A third quarrel took the soldier beside Isaac. Blood sprayed like a mist as the man rolled off his thrashing mount.

Screams erupted from every direction.

Horses shied violently.

A trio of mounted knights flailing broadswords broke over the rise attacking the caravan's right flank. The escorts readied for the onslaught.

Isaac's horses surged, pounding hooves into the soft dirt to gain speed quickly. The wagons rumbled forward as the knights fanned out to allow them through, while they themselves fortified defensive positions against charging brigands.

Five more knights entered the charge from the caravan's opposing flank.

Isaac trembled. A fourth quarrel whipped wide of its target, thunking into the timber side panel of the second wagon.

The clangor of fierce battle threw Isaac's heart into his throat when the lead knights engaged the first wave of assaulting brigands. Blades thudding shields like thunder drummed into Isaac's brain. He drew his dagger, knowing full well a sword would run him through long before he might be effective with such a meager blade.

Each wagon driver understood exactly their response to such an attack. They strapped the reins with all their force, demanding speed beyond what their beasts could deliver. As the knights engaged the marauders, the wagons broke through at full gallop, pounding the dirt down the forest path to escape the foray. They were to run full pelt until they reached the safety of Londontown, regardless of how long that might take. Under no circumstances were they to stop now. Fighting men could be sacrificed—the wagons, with one in particular, had to reach the castle.

Isaac slapped and cursed as much speed as he could from his pair of chestnut chargers, hoping to keep pace behind the other wagons. As they thundered past, two more soldiers fell to the fighting.

Minutes later, the three wagons reached their quickest speed exiting the forest into a sun-drenched meadow. They desperately needed a woodland maze to aid them. Ahead, another ridge of pines waited. The drivers feared the openness—they became easy targets for arrows. But they had no options at the moment. They needed to rely on the traveled path until they reached the mouth of the next encroaching woods.

Isaac fell further behind. And when he craned a look over his shoulder, four knights thundered in his wake. They were pursuing them! Their escort was meant to prevent attackers from launching pursuit.

A crossbow quarrel zipped past Isaac's head, freezing his heart. It missed him narrowly, within an arm's length. His hands trembled; his mouth went bone dry. White-eyed, the terror of death consumed him. He struggled to manage the reins, needing more speed from his lumbering beasts.

A desperate shriek erupted from his throat. He was only heart-beats away from death.

The wagons ahead gained on him. He was the weakling—the most vulnerable—the sacrificial lamb to spare the others. The brig-ands would encounter him first. It was up to Isaac to disrupt their pursuit long enough for the others to escape.

He would die if he failed to act.

Shouts came from the wagons. The drivers' lives depended now on their horses outlasting the knights in pursuit. Since the pur-suing chargers carried men weighted down with armor, the wagons held a slight edge. The brigands' animals should tire before a pair of stout stallions drawing wagons. That, however, mattered little to Isaac at the moment. Glancing back, he spied ruthless eyes through helmet slits closing in faster than anticipated. The extended sword came within a score of horse lengths of him.

One more breath before death took him.

He had to act immediately!

Isaac veered from the path, angling toward a ridge of stacked beech trees on a course leading away from the other wagons. He prayed his last-ditch strategy might save him. After all, the riders sought the chest not the hay.

He sliced into the forest at a crease running perpendicular to the path of the other wagons. He begged his God to aid him. With His help, his maneuver might spare his life. If it failed, he was mo-ments from dying.

A single knight broke from the pack to pursue Isaac.

The Jew's heart swelled into his throat, clogging his breathing. He risked a hand off his reins long enough to position his dagger. He would, at least, try to remain alive for as long as possible.

Then the knight slowed, realizing Isaac would disappear in the forest before he might overtake him. As a result, the brigand wheeled his charger back to rejoin the pack, spurring his beast into a full charge.

Isaac drove his lathered animals at breakneck speed along a narrow path guiding him amongst branches intertwining overhead. Ducking and weaving sent agony up his spine, but minutes later, the forest camouflage swallowed him up.

He had survived... at least for the moment.

2

Dusty morning light beamed into the great hall of King Richard's castle in Londontown. Much was astir this day, resulting in a cacophony of voices saturating the air.

Delphi, scrawny for a twelve-year-old, dodged this way and that, eluding the grasp of two pursuing guardsmen as he snaked around a crowd exiting the keep into the castle's main courtyard. From the fear and desperation on his sweated impish face, it would appear the lad's quest was a matter of life and death.

But undaunted, Delphi dashed toward the great hall, where he could only hope he might find what he so fervently sought.

"Stop, boy!" the lead guard growled. He lunged, only to miss the lad's fluttering hempen cowl.

Delphi would have laughed at the soldier's feeble attempt—if he weren't so terrified. He had to succeed. It meant everything to him to reach his destination. He could not allow a guard, or even a knight for that matter, to prevent him from reaching his goal.

"Grab that boy!" another called, hoping to snare a passing soldier's attention when he neared a crossing corridor.

Too late.

By the time the soldier spun about, Delphi slipped elusively past by pressing against the sidewall to evade a wildly outthrust arm.

Then the towering main doors to the great hall opened. They were still twenty paces beyond Delphi's reach. He could see the glaring light, hear the voices of throngs of people within. Defeat clouded him at the sight of the tightly packed bodies.

But he was almost there. If only he could squirm through everyone in his way.

A fist closed around his flapping cowl.

Delphi screamed!

He surged forward, sliding to his knees to break the grasp the guard had upon him.

None of the men in fervid pursuit knew why they were chasing Delphi, or even why he was running. They had no idea the motive behind the lad nearly kicking a guard in his privates when the man detained him at the entrance to the castle's royal wing.

Serfs were forbidden in the royal wing without proper authorization from someone in authority, usually a baron or archbishop. These were dangerous, uncertain times, and it became imperative all be queried prior to standing before any of the royal family. Children in particular were isolated from the royals, since most were little thieves dispatched by desperate parents to steal or beg for whatever they could return to their family. Oftentimes, only stealing staved off famine and destitution in the kingdom.

Persons having properly cleared business with the queen or Princess Joanna gained entry. Joanna's past experience against her brother John forced her to trust only those she became personally familiar with, or someone vouched for by a person she trusted. By king's law, anyone could request an audience with the queen, but the requesting party must acquire a sponsor to speak in their behalf before being granted entry.

Eleanor and Joanna knew John's minions infiltrated their castle at every level, and as such, they might have uncovered secrets the prince was never meant to know. Try as they might, both women knew the prince had gathered intelligence concerning their plans regarding Richard's imprisonment. John would do whatever he could, and rally whomever he might to his cause to prevent Richard from ever returning to his beloved England. The deposed king proved no threat to John as long as he remained Henry's captive.

Ten more paces and Delphi would be there. The lad crawled every which way, squirming around fat legs and thin, male and female. Women invaded screamed when he slid between their legs. He sucked in a breath and closed his eyes when two soldiers blocked his way. Yet determination had brought him this far. He would not fail now.

Before the two soldiers could react, Delphi wedged his arms between the two to peel them apart. He then pressed forward into the core of the great hall.

Success!

Delphi spun. She had to be there. All his effort would go for naught if she were absent this day.

Then Delphi spotted her. Princess Joanna. The most beautiful woman he had ever laid his young eyes upon. Her milky white skin exuded a near angelic glow in the light beaming from above. Her lapis-colored eyes sparkled the way the sun plays upon a summer pond.

The princess' lips arced into a smile when their eyes met.

Delphi's heart almost stopped beating at coming before his princess. If he had a mother, surely this was what she would look like. But she still seemed so far away, and now four soldiers took up pursuit.

"They would never harm a child," he muttered over and over, flowing against a rush of men. They would never throw him in the dungeon, he convinced himself, even if he were taken.

"My lady!" he yelled at the very top of his lungs when a pair of steel-like hands clamped his shoulders.

He was caught. He had come so close to her only to be dragged away and kicked into the square.

"You'll get twenty lashes, boy!" the soldier grumbled, firming his grip on Delphi's grimy, tattered shirt.

The lad squirmed. He refused give up. He wouldn't. Not now. Not when he was this close to her.

Delphi snapped his shoulders down then away from the clasping hands. He broke free, flattening to his belly to squirm like a snake through the legs of a bishop. On the other side, he popped up.

Princess Joanna smiled, towering over him.

"You are quite the determined young lad," she said.

Her wonderful words fell into his ears, almost bringing him to tears. She had addressed him, directly! He could almost reach out to touch her silky hand. But he refrained, knowing that would get him in even more trouble than he currently brought upon himself.

"Grab that little..." the soldier scowled, reaching in to yank the lad by his flopping honey-colored hair.

Tears blurred Delphi's eyes; intense pain flooded his brain.

"Release him!" Joanna commanded.

The anger in her voice matched the anger in her eyes, conveying immediate obedience.

With a grim face, the soldier reluctantly complied.

"My lady," Delphi squeaked out, whisking away the tears dribbling down his cheeks. He must never allow the princess to see him cry. How would that look to her? She would think him nothing more than a child when he was so much more.

"Tell me what brings such a persistent young man before our queen this day," Joanna said. Her smile brought immediate cessation of Delphi's tears.

"My lady, I heared the king in the German demands a ransom for the return of our king," Delphi announced.

"Yes, that is true. But the affairs of kings need not concern one as young as you."

Joanna lowered to one knee so she could be eye-to-eye with the boy. Rynhawker, standing beside her, set his arm to steady her descent.

"Then I come before my queen this day to offer this to bring our king home," Delphi said most proudly.

He unfurled a fist to two half farthing pieces in his dirty palm.

Joanna's eyes traced from the boy's open hand to his eyes. Her smile wormed its way into young Delphi's heart. Then her face turned grim and serious.

Had he done wrong? Was what he did not proper?

"How did you come by these?" the soldier near him interrogated.

Joanna's tight lips and hardened eyes silenced the man. Then she returned her attention to Delphi in a non-threatening way. Delphi's expression suddenly revealed he felt offended—and frightened—at the same time.

"He stoled them, my lady," the soldier jammed into the silence before Delphi could respond.

"Nay, my lady. I sold a peahen to the farmer Calenwell. He gave me these two half farthings. Ask him. He will tell you I did not steal the coins."

Joanna glanced at Rynhawker, smiling at the boy's tenacity.

"He lies," the soldier pressed.

"I tell the truth."

"Where did you get the peahen then, boy?" the soldier pressed.

Delphi paused. He had hoped his tale would not progress this far. He looked into Joanna's wonderful eyes, finding comfort. He knew what he must do.

"I stoled it," Delphi confessed, tearing up, as if his heart were breaking.

The soldier grabbed Delphi's shoulder to drag him away. This time Rynhawker stepped in to remove the man's hand from the lad.

"You are a fine young man to offer what you have to free our king. But I am afraid the King of Germany will only accept gold and silver in exchange for our king's freedom."

Delphi's eyes dropped to his meager, and now meaningless, offering. He had risked everything to come before the princess to help his king, and now it was all for nothing.

The disappointment in Delphi's eyes tore into Joanna's heart. Beneath the grime and despair of living a serf child's life, Joanna detected the heart of a gentleman.

"Perhaps I shall take one half farthing to help in the ransom and convince the King of Germany to accept what we have to offer him," Joanna said.

Her smile wormed into Delphi's heart. He had succeeded. He was helping his king.

"For the other half farthing, I command you to buy back your peahen, so that your family might share a meal worthy of one who has worked hard in support of his king. Tell this farmer Calenwell that I command him to sell you the bird at the half farthing you offer."

With that Joanna returned to her feet with the aid of Rynhawker's arm. Yet Delphi remained rooted where he stood, his eyes steadfast on her face, his hand clutching the single half farthing.

"I have no family, my lady," he said.

The words came without the force Delphi had used earlier, as if shame laid heavy upon his heart.

Something about the boy, though, snared Joanna's interest. Something in his innocent eyes captivated her. Perhaps she saw her brother the king when he was the same age as those eyes.

"What is your name, boy?" she asked.

"I am Delphi, my lady."

"Do you wish to be of service to the princess in order to help your king?"

"Yes!" he chimed.

His grin spread across his face. Delphi's eyes alighted at the words. He had never dreamed he might be able to remain this close to her. His only desire up to this point was to come before the princess to offer his help for his king. Now he would be beside his heart's strongest desire.

Joanna motioned Althera forward, her servant in attendance, to lead Delphi away.

"You will remain in the castle in the service of your princess. I will have many important tasks for you. Will you help me?"

"Yes, my lady. I am at your service."

Delphi bowed clumsily.

Joanna turned to Rynhawker and Thomas standing nearby. Her eyes revealed that something had come to her mind, something to aid them in their quest.

But before she could speak, a bishop called out at the door.

"My queen, messengers from the court of King Henry request an audience with your majesty."

The hall came to immediate silence. Eleanor looked to her daughter, who shared her concern.

3

Eleanor wasted no time vacating her throne to be escorted from the great hall. A mélange of emotions raced through her head. Was this good news or bad? Joanna followed by a step with Rynhawker and Thomas no more than three paces trailing the princess.

Minutes later, Eleanor sat in her chambers, an anxious Joanna at her side. The queen's heart pounded with expectation. Rynhawker and Thomas remained stoically in the background.

"Speak what you have come to say, whoreson," Eleanor growled with fire flashing in her eyes.

She anticipated nothing but dire news would come from the friar and soldier who now stood before her. Only the friar lifted his eyes to meet the queen's. The soldier stared at his feet.

"My king awaits your response to his demand," the friar delivered in a voice fraught with fear.

Silence consumed the room. Anger seethed inside the queen's chest. Eleanor narrowed her eyes, contemplating her response.

Joanna leaned close to gain her mother's ear.

"Silence breeds fear in our enemies," she confided.

Eleanor required no counsel; she knew exactly what she must deliver.

"Your king shall receive an answer when I deem he shall need to know. Until then, tell your bastard king he will rot in hell for his sin against what God has ordained."

Eleanor spate the words like snake's venom.

The friar swallowed, bowed as he would before his own king. Both men knew in order to leave this castle with their lives, they must do nothing to anger the queen more than King Henry had already done.

"Your majesty, I am instructed to inform you if you wish your king to breathe beyond Candlemas, you will deliver to Henry's court the ransom he demands forthwith."

"Forthwith!" the queen raged.

Joanna turned to gauge her mother's reaction. Henry tightened his stranglehold on the English Crown. He could do whatever he wished to Richard once he informed the English Crown of his conditions.

Strategically Henry had chosen the second day of February to end his patience with the queen. With the dead of winter his ally against an English invasion, the queen would be unable to delay an assault until spring.

Eleanor rose, flipped a hand up to dismiss the men. She hastened her departure, extending her back to them as her answer.

"Queen Eleanor, what words do I return to my king?" the friar begged.

Eleanor stopped short. She snapped about to glare at the friar. So many vicious words clamored inside her head she could think of nothing that might make sense to the lowly clergyman.

"Richard will return to rule his England. You inform your bastard king of that!" she stammered.

The queen marched from the chamber while Rynhawker and Thomas escorted the men into the corridor. Both sighed, relieved they had lived to deliver their king's message. Now they could return home to safety in their own lands.

Joanna knew how Henry intended to squeeze the queen into submission. The first days of fall approached. He would allow her no time to amass her army so she might launch an invasion. Winter was an imposing time for war, best to launch an assault in the spring. Henry's execution threat now excluded that.

But would he follow through on his threat? Or was this merely his desire to intimidate the queen? Could her mother risk inaction to find out? Delay was the one option Henry stole from her. The princess vacated the chamber considering what course they should follow based on Henry's latest demand.

4

Richard knelt in putrid straw with Baldwin crouched a few feet from him. Only their fierce hatred had sustained them in this dungeon. A few feet away, Hugh curled in the fetal position, placing his back to the cell door.

Each man knew exactly what to do. Each had waited months for this moment. It would take everything they had to make this plan succeed.

They waited. Seconds seemed to last forever. Richard and Baldwin stared at the door, hoping for that telltale flickering of light around the frame to forewarn them.

The Lionheart had carefully cataloged the guards' patterns for weeks. He planned and replanned this night in his head a hundred times before revealing the details to his comrades. He believed Baldwin could fight, but he held concerns regarding Hugh. So Hugh would be the diversion providing Richard and Baldwin the opportunity to act.

An hour passed. Baldwin's legs ached from holding his statue-like position. Their locations had been precisely selected to allow them to strike without requiring more than a single step.

But the king was the lynchpin of their success. He would attack the lead guard, leverage the man's own weight against the second guard, while relieving the first of his blade. Baldwin would launch a step behind his king to wrestle the second guard's sword free before he might levy it against Richard. In their minds it seemed a viable plan.

But would the guards cooperate?

In the lightless gloom of their cell on previous nights they rehearsed until each man could execute exactly as Richard commanded.

Hugh's heart pounded his chest the way the smithy hones a broadsword with his hammer. The longer they waited, the more Hugh perspired. He dared not wipe his palms, fearing that would be the precise moment the guards entered, rendering his deception void. If he failed his king now, he would never forgive himself.

Baldwin shifted slightly, firming his stance. He had practiced launching at least fifty times. He knew exactly how far he could go, and where the guard needed to be before his launch. If he acted prematurely, he would miss the second guard, leaving his king vulnerable to the man's blade.

Richard held perfectly steady. His mind raced through the steps, examining all possible outcomes from the guards. If the same two guards appeared, Richard felt sure they would succeed.

But their assault inside their cell was only the first action in a more complicated and daring scheme to gain their freedom. The next action in the king's plan required more effort and cunning, but by then they would be armed and capable of fighting.

More time ticked away. Fear crept into their bones. Nothing moved inside the dungeon cell nor outside in the corridor.

Richard silently prayed this might be the night. He needed God's help. Perhaps God was still angry over his failure in the Holy Lands, and as a result, He intended to disappoint him.

Hugh wished to speak. But he knew their ruse could be destroyed if he did. His faith quickly waned. This may not be the night for them. They would spend another miserable day in this stinking hole littered with human excrement.

Then flickering light seeped through the cracks. Guards shifted outside.

Richard sucked in a breath. Their moment arrived. He balled his fists instinctively. Then his brain countermanded his instinct, ordering them unclinched. The slightest gesture could expose their intent to their captors. Absolute surprise was vital.

The charged moments seemed endless.

Keys jangled. Then came the turning of the lock holding them prisoner. A bolt slid back. A moment later, the iron-bound timber door creaked open slowly. A hulking guard crowded the frame. He was not the one from previous nights. He shouldered more brawn than Richard expected. And he assumed the dominant position, entering the cell ahead of his comrade. But unlike the previous guards, this one left the hilt of his sword uncovered in a show of arrogance. He had entered unprepared for an onslaught.

That haughtiness would cost him.

The second smaller guard followed, shifting to the first guard's right, a water bucket in one hand, bread scraps in the other. His sight almost induced Baldwin to smile.

Richard's racing heart choked his throat. He held his hands perfectly steady while he waited. He needed them advanced one more step to gain their optimum advantage.

"You in the corner, come about," the first guard growled.

Hugh remained silent, lifeless.

Nothing moved while the guards waited for a response.

Then the first guard took that fateful step. The second followed as Baldwin spoke.

"He's dead," Baldwin offered without moving.

At the moment Baldwin spoke, Richard launched into the first guard, seizing the man's arm before he could reach his sword to clear it from its sheath. The man retreated to brace himself, which sent him into the second guard as Richard had predicted.

Baldwin launched from his squatting position to throw his weight into the second guard. The water bucket toppled. The bread fell away while Hugh rolled about to spring into action.

Richard slammed a brutal fist into the hulking guard's jaw. The man's larger size, however, allowed him to maintain footing against the king's initial strike.

Baldwin whacked the second guard's face while the man groped to draw his sword. The king's comrade quickly swiped the guard's sword arm to knock the emerging blade away.

Richard struggled against the larger guard. The man successfully withdrew his blade against the king's resistance, but another driving fist to the face sent the guard reeling, allowing Richard to seize his blade and wrestle it free of his captor's hand.

But their struggle also created telling noise, which was very bad at that moment. They were ill-equipped to fend off more armed men rushing in to help.

Richard levied the sword to the first guard's throat, forcing him to circle to the rear of the cell.

"Speak not, lest I open your belly here and now," Richard commanded in the fiercest whisper he could master.

The second guard surrendered his blade to Baldwin, backing without resistance to stand beside his comrade.

"How many are out there?" Richard commanded.

Neither spoke.

"Tell us," Baldwin scowled.

Hugh scrambled to collect up the bread scraps so they might eat, giving them strength to fight.

"You will never escape," the first guard offered plainly.

"You will be our shield," Richard responded.

The first guard stared into Richard's eyes.

"They will strike me dead with a quarrel before they allow King Henry's prize freedom," the man said.

The guard watched his words slowly seep into Richard's brain. If he could destroy their confidence, he might be able to save his own life. The guard was, in his own way, pleading for his life in this exchange. No good could come from their actions for any of them, including the guards.

Richard knew in his heart Henry would do whatever he must to keep his prisoner in his charge. Allowing Richard to escape would mean a lost ransom. Richard's success would also make the King of Germany a mockery to his subjects. But Richard had no time to contemplate the matter. They had to move.

The tense moment between guards and captives lingered. Richard understood the guards were at risk as well as his men. What would Henry do to Hugh and Baldwin if they failed? Richard had already witnessed Henry's black heart on the tournament field. One or both of his faithful might die if this ran afoul.

So far, no men came running to aid the guards. Outside the cell, all remained quiet.

Maybe too quiet.

"My lord, what shall we do?" Baldwin asked in a voice fraught with doubt. Could they possibly have a chance of escaping their prison? Baldwin lost faith that their actions would lead to anything but death.

Richard shoved the guard into the corridor. He moved directly behind him, his sword at his prisoner's back. Baldwin pushed the second guard out before shifting behind him. Hugh, unarmed, remained at the rear.

They advanced no more than a dozen strides when two soldiers sleeping at the table bolted up. They drew swords to fight.

"Advance and your man dies," Richard shouted like a command.

He needed the men to know they would seal their comrades' fates if they charged.

"Relinquish your swords, and all will live to see the next sunrise. You have my word," Richard pressed when the men vacillated.

"Do as he commands!" the first guard offered.

The soldiers remained hesitant, holding fighting stances.

Certainly, some would die in a fight with the king. None of Henry's men believed themselves capable of defeating the King of England. And they well knew the penalty for any who inadvertently killed their king's prize.

Baldwin shoved his prisoner closer to the front, placing both the men between the soldiers and his king. Above all else, Richard had to be protected if the soldiers attacked.

First, the soldier nearest Richard lowered his sword. With the tip toward the floor, it lingered before the man finally released the hilt. The second soldier followed, setting his weapon to the floor soundlessly.

"Hugh, take the sword," Richard ordered.

In that moment all three of Henry's prized prisoners became armed and controlled the dungeon.

"What now, my lord?" Hugh asked.

He harbored fears that his king's plan had not been formed further than escaping their cell. The dangers yet to come were unimaginable at this point. For all they knew, a dozen armed and armored knights awaited their next move.

Sweat trickled into Hugh's eyes, stealing his vision. He wiped it away, lowering his guard momentarily. He had to force himself to breathe, he was so scared.

Richard could sense from the tensing of his prisoner's shoulder that the man hoped for an opportunity to retaliate.

The king would deny him.

"Take all but him to the cell, lock them away," Richard commanded, indicating his prisoner would remain. Trying to manage more than a single human shield could cause too many problems, so Richard opted to keep the largest of the group.

Hugh responded without retort, frantically leading the soldiers to their cell, where he shoved them in before locking the door. Exhilaration ran through him at the power he wielded over those who treated him brutally.

"Set me free," someone called from further down.

For a brief moment, the three took a breath. Now firmly controlling the dungeon, they could analyze their next move.

"I command all prisoners to sound off," Richard called with firm authority.

They waited. No other sounds came.

"Hugh, open the cells," Richard commanded.

Hugh moved quickly unlocking and throwing open the doors in an offering of freedom. No one appeared. All but three of the sixteen cells were empty. One revealed a man so beaten and weakened from starvation that he could never walk on his own.

"My lord, what am I to do?" Hugh asked.

"Leave them. Lock the doors. We will find no aid from other prisoners."

Richard and Baldwin exchanged a look of grave concern. They had hoped to hide their escape amongst other prisoners fleeing the dungeon. Now they were alone in their quest for freedom.

5

"Come, we must hurry now," Richard said.

Hugh unlocked the dungeon door, allowing the four men into the corridor. They dashed the hundred paces to the spiraling staircase leading to the castle's ground floor.

It was too soon to smell the sweetness of freedom, but it was far better than the stench of their dungeon cell.

Richard had been led up and down the staircase at least a dozen times since their captivity in this place. He recalled easily the route to exit the castle once they had reached ground level.

With a forceful nudge, Richard shoved his prisoner slowly up. He realized as the light descended to greet them, they had poorly timed their plan. Instead of escaping under the veil of night, they were moving up the staircase to a sun creeping over the horizon. From their cell they had no way of discerning night from day.

To their misfortune, the castle would be awakening. Knights and soldiers would be rousing in search of food. They would be less alert at this moment, but still the king had hoped they might have darkness to aid their egress.

"My lord, what shall we do?" Baldwin asked, realizing their chances of fleeing became slim once the soldiers and knights learned of their escape.

Richard stopped everyone midway up the staircase. Though the worst possible place to pause to rethink his plan, he had no other choice.

The portcullis would rise with the sun, as would the drawbridge lower, allowing serfs into the castle square. Soldiers would tend livestock and perform duties on the castle grounds. Knights would be about commanding the others, or they might remain in the knights' hall.

They needed a way out of the keep undetected in order to reach the stables and secure mounts. As long as no one sounded an alarm, the portcullis would remain up and the drawbridge down. If, however, someone sounded their escape, they may become trapped inside the inner or outer bailey, and all would be lost. It was impossible to fight their way to freedom once the portcullis came down.

But Richard understood there was no turning back. They had made their move, and they had to see it through to its conclusion, even if it meant one or more of his men were struck down.

Hugh's hands trembled clasping his sword in both of them. He would have to fight—he knew that for certain. But could he fight? Could he hold his own against one of Henry's soldiers? Or worse, could he defend himself against a knight?

"My lord, allow me to lead," he found himself saying. He swallowed hard at the thought.

Richard did not countermand his request. Instead, he allowed Hugh to advance to come beside him, replacing his hand on the shoulder of their human shield.

"We are all going to die," the guard muttered softly as he waited at the lead of the pack.

Angry at the man's words, Baldwin whacked the back of his head hard with the hilt of his sword.

"Then we make certain you die first," he added.

"My lord, command me," Hugh offered, trying to hide the cowardice emerging in his voice.

Richard motioned them to advance. Just before coming around the final turn into the dim morning's light, they paused once again.

Faint voices fell into their ears.

Hugh's gut turned to stone. His throat convulsed. They had reached that critical moment. Once they entered the main floor, they would have no choice but to fight their way out.

Moments passed. They waited. The voices faded, yet the men still clung to the tenuous security of the staircase wall.

Richard nodded to leave the staircase into a quiet, seemingly deserted corridor.

Their paces were quick but measured, silent as they eased to the end of the corridor. The further they progressed from the staircase, and the closer they came to escaping the keep, the greater became their chance for success.

Richard shoved the guard when the man intentionally slowed, hoping someone might encounter them before they exited the keep.

"Hold your tongue if you wish to live," Richard reasserted.

They entered a crossing corridor. God's hands were cradling them, as it seemed few people were astir this morning. Though failing to gain darkness their ally, they had the early hour in their favor.

Emanating from somewhere close by, the aroma of baking bread found them. They desperately needed more nourishment, but the risk of exposure proved too great to attempt to locate the source.

Richard became confused at the intersection of two corridors. He had always been taken right—a path to the throne room, where he stood before King Henry.

So he chose the corridor to their left.

"Give us the quickest way out," Hugh commanded of his prisoner.

The man said nothing, merely whisked a slight smile at the thought. They would find their own way, or they would die.

They advanced painfully slow in the corridor. But they kept moving. Movement favored freedom.

"Who goes there?" sounded from what seemed a far distance behind them in the corridor.

They inadvertently left their backs exposed.

Baldwin glanced over his shoulder to a soldier taking sword to hand, quickening his pace. But the distance remained their ally.

Hugh shoved his prisoner hard, forcing him to run. Richard followed a step behind, thrusting further to force more speed from the reluctant runner.

Baldwin, however, knew what he must do.

"Which way, my lord?" Hugh spat in panic.

They reached the corridor's end. It offered a left or right pathway.

Richard had to think on the run.

"The kitchen," he muttered.

They reached their critical juncture before Richard could think his decision through. There would be people in the kitchen hard at work. He also realized all kitchens had doors exiting the keep onto the castle grounds.

Richard pressed his brain. How far did they have to run to reach the stables? Stress kept him from retrieving an answer.

Good fortune rewarded them. The aroma of roasting capons assaulted their noses upon rounding the corner to their right.

Hugh so wanted to discard their prisoner; the man was working to defeat their escape. Could he still be of value to them? Richard was less willing to abandon one with at least some worth remaining.

Baldwin retarded further, came about in anticipation of a fight. His difficulty in running meant he could never keep pace with his king. He could help them more if he could drop the soldier.

Baldwin backed around the corner last. The kitchen lie ahead. He knew they could escape the keep through that expansive room. He also realized the soldier would overtake them before their exit.

A dozen strides into the new corridor, Baldwin stopped. Here he would fight to save his king. He levied his sword and waited. He determined what he would do. He could only pray the soldier's sword skills were inferior to his, since his leg would prevent him from...

"Baldwin, come," Richard scowled, seeing his comrade about to sacrifice himself.

"You must go!" he yelled. "Hugh, keep our king safe."

Hugh stopped in his tracks at the words. He came about to view Baldwin's back, his comrade poised for the fight. It was the worst action Baldwin could take.

The soldier dashed around the corner, sword frantically flailing, anticipating their clash.

Baldwin's position gave him an additional few seconds to fortify his stance before the soldier's assault.

Their blades locked with a horrible clank that reverberated through the corridors. Anyone within a hundred paces would have heard.

They had only moments now before others would come clam-oring to overpower him. Baldwin had to take him quickly.

"Go, my lord. You will be free," Baldwin yelled while he thrust, forcing the soldier toward the intersection of the corridors.

Baldwin's strength served him well. His blood pumped power into his arms. He pressed his advantage, hoping to slay his opponent before anyone could assist him. Baldwin surprised himself with the skill with which he battled back the assault. It had been so long since he had worked a sword, he thought he would fall at the first conflict.

Richard stopped. He refused to leave his man behind. He had to aid Baldwin, though at the moment, his comrade held his own against a man half his age, but equal in size and stature.

The callow soldier knew not when to press his attack, nor when to retreat to fortify his footing. Baldwin used that to keep the man from advancing.

With a driving slash, Baldwin relieved the soldier of his blade. As it clanked harmlessly to the floor, the soldier retreated down the corridor.

With a faint smile, Baldwin rejoined the others.

Moments later the four spilled into the kitchen to face a dozen sweating servants busy at four blazing hearths. The men broke for the door to the courtyard a dozen long strides away.

No one spoke. No one yelled. Women and men alike merely slid from their path so they might pass unabated. And once they passed, the servants returned to their duties preparing food for awakening knights and nobles.

In his frenzied haste, Hugh lost his grip on their prisoner when the door leading out came open. Feeling opportunity at hand, the guard twisted free to dash for the safety of a storage room opposite their exit.

At that moment Hugh could think only of freedom. He had allowed the guard to escape in an instant of inattention. He prayed it would not cost him his life.

The unanticipated turn of events caused Richard to pause. To his right came the morning sun. To his left, the human shield they might still need. Should he allow the guard to escape? Or risk remaining inside the kitchen until he recaptured the man? They had no time left to consider. They had to get free of the keep.

Outside, Hugh felt the first rays of sunlight upon his grimy face with the harsh morning sun initially blinding him. They had not considered that would happen. All three had to close their eyes until they stumbled into the shadow coming off the inner bailey wall.

But a moment later, Hugh reversed his direction to pursue their prisoner. Without that shield they would have to traverse two hundred paces of open courtyard to reach the stables. They needed the man, though doing so increased their risk of recapture.

"Leave him," Richard commanded.

They would proceed unshielded from here—returning to the keep could mean never reaching the stables.

Baldwin joined them, the last out the kitchen door.

Covered in the filth of their imprisonment and emitting the stench of human waste, with hair mangled and unkept, the three matched the pace of knots of peasants flowing about the castle square.

People roaming the square meant the castle gates were open! They could ride out into freedom.

Richard breathed the first fresh air into his lungs. He swallowed his smile—they were far from free of this dreadful place. They needed mounts to make their way through the baileys and the barbican.

But they were outside the keep and moving in the direction of the stables. A few serfs offered strange looks without comprehending the identities of the three marching beside them.

Richard's stature towered over most in the square, which would make them easier to locate amongst the crowd. To compensate, the king hunched forward like a hobbling cripple, making himself less visible amongst the locals.

"My lo..." Baldwin started.

He caught himself.

Addressing his king would alert others to their identities. Soon more soldiers would spill out that same kitchen door after them.

Hugh pointed to the stables a distance away, constructed to the right of the castle square. He could smell freedom now.

There would be men in the stables tending the animals, possibly soldiers preparing mounts, maybe even knights departing for a day's ride.

The three men adjusted their pace to match others moving about the square. If they walked too quickly, they would stick out. Only if they reached the stables unnoticed would they have a chance of seizing horses to make it into the forested countryside.

But they licked that wonderful taste of freedom on their lips. A free wind brushed their faces, jostling their hair. Their stomachs rumbled in hunger, their throats parched from lack of water. But none of that mattered now. Only the sweetness of freedom mattered.

Richard led to the stables, but they dared not enter through the two main doors. They needed a way in that went unnoticed by any inside or they would never get far.

The castle stables abutted the inner bailey wall at the rear with an overhead loft to store feed. Richard scaled the distance with his eyes. Neither Hugh nor Baldwin could make the climb. Richard might succeed, but then he left his comrades unguarded.

Amid a cluster of peasants flowing toward the barbican, they reached a door situated at the far side of the stables. It allowed them entry, as it was used primarily for dumping dung from the stalls.

Gruff voices across the stables caught their attention. But one by one they slipped in to find secluded refuge in a lightless dusty corner. So far, their movement had gone undetected.

Richard breathed relief. They need only secure mounts to ride out the castle gates. As long as no one noticed, they might succeed.

Freedom.

That single thought swam inside Richard's head. They were moments away. Once beyond the gates, the forest would swallow them up; it would take days of diligent effort for Henry's knights to hunt them down.

Richard motioned each into a stall, secure a horse. The king waited with sword poised to defend all three if anyone approached.

The voices across the stable seemed to fade from their ears. Only the sounds of waiting horses entered their brains.

Hugh breached the nearest stall housing a chestnut stallion, which turned to face him but made no sound.

Baldwin eased further along. The next stall in his path came up empty. He paused before the third when a man exited a stall at the far end. The man, however, continued away, oblivious to Baldwin pressed against the inner wall.

Once clear, Baldwin slipped into his stall. A tethered black charger waited. The beast whickered, but it made no move to shy away. He quickly located a bit, fitted it into the horse's mouth in preparation. Only then did he risk sucking in a deep breath. He could hardly believe they were this close to being free.

Both Hugh and Baldwin waited inside their stalls. They needed to hold until all three could ride out together to have the best chance of escape. Anyone lagging could easily be recaptured.

Only then did Richard emerge from the shadows. He had to move the furthest to reach a ride. He would be the one most at risk of exposure.

He advanced only five long, quick strides when the stables' double doors swung open wide. Daylight flooded in to illuminate Richard during his final strides for the next occupied stall.

Roger de Argenton stood akimbo in the center of the opening. A dozen knights flanked his either side. Arms and armor filled the gateway from the stables.

No one spoke. But then words were unnecessary, futile.

They had failed. Richard could make a dash for a stallion, and he might possibly fight through the men barricading his exit. But the portcullis would crash down before reaching the barbican.

"A noble attempt. I applaud your courage and cunning, Crusader King," Roger called in.

Richard saw only silhouette, but he knew the voice too well.

Roger made no attempt to enter. No one ever knew what to expect from the Crusader King. He knew from reputation, though, that coming too close to the Lionheart when armed could cost him his life. At the moment, Roger had no way to assess Richard's state of mind. Would the Lionheart fight to the death to remain free of the dungeon? Could he be that foolish?

"My archers along the parapet will strip you from your mounts before you reach the outer bailey," Roger added when no sounds came in response to his first calling.

A stall door opened. Hugh edged out; defeat filled his eyes. He awaited instructions.

All was lost. They could do nothing to help their king now. Baldwin exited next, taking his place beside his king.

"I know you are armed... and desperate. But no men need die this day. Cast down your weapons and advance," Roger offered, absent any arrogance in his voice to gain the Lionheart's trust.

Now was not the time to gloat, which could spur them to fight and sacrifice Henry's treasure.

Richard looked at his comrades. They knew exactly how far they had yet to go to reach freedom. They understood what they faced if they tried. Richard searched his mind for a way out that would not result in death to either of his comrades.

"Command me, my lord," Baldwin whispered. "I will die if it means you gain a chance at freedom."

"No blood has been shed this day. My word no English blood spills if you surrender here and now."

His spirit crushed, Richard capitulated. Freedom was not to be theirs this day.

Three swords thudded into the dirt.

Only then did Roger enter to retake his prisoners.

"The king shall never hear of this. I promise your men will be spared from punishment," Roger conveyed in a whisper while moving Richard from the stables.

Seeing defeat in his captives' eyes, Roger favored that King Henry need never learn of Richard's transgression, since his attempt failed without forfeiture of life. Even Roger secretly harbored sympathy for the way Henry treated his prize.

6

Under the veil of midnight Joanna met with Rynhawker in the castle. While everyone slept, they strode with purpose quietly and swiftly through the corridors. So many ideas rushed through her head that Joanna failed to keep hold of a single one. Bits and pieces of a possible course of action drifted by. Now she sought to pluck and assemble those pieces in a way that served their need.

Everything they did had to be performed with grave secrecy— John's spies pervaded every corner of the queen's stronghold.

Torchlight flooded the small chamber with its table and two chairs. Joanna and Rynhawker entered John's secret alcove. Her body stiffened. The hairs on her arms rose while her insides knotted up. Her breathing came in gasps of terror. The horrors of that night flooded her head as if she relived them in that heartbeat. John had vowed to kill her in this very chamber. She had uncovered John's secret hideout, and that had cost her dearly. Disjointed images flashed like lightning across her mind's eye. During that terrible moment she had believed she would die at her brother's hand.

Now to their benefit, John had fled the castle in a flurry that fateful day when he failed to usurp the crown, forcing him to abandon what he held in his secret place. It was unlike John to lack a contingency for failure. At the time, he must have believed his success to be so certain that nothing could go awry to warrant flight without what he needed most.

Joanna had changed all that.

Now all she uncovered here became hers to use against him to help the king. And she would employ every scrap of information to aid Richard. She could only hope she might find here what she needed most.

At the sight of her ashen face, Rynhawker took her arm in silent concern. He understood the terror she would be experiencing at that moment. He vowed on his life never to allow anyone to threaten her again.

"This was the place," he whispered for confirmation.

Joanna nodded, stripped away the tears overflowing her eyes. This was where... Priscilina's face bloomed in her mind. The price her servant paid for her loyalty wrenched Joanna's heart. A surge of bile hit the back of her throat. She choked it back down.

"No one shall ever hurt you again," he added to reassure her.

Somehow words fell far short of comforting her. She knew John. He would use whatever he could to get even with her for her acts against him. She had robbed him of his play for the throne. He would never forget, nor forgive, for that interference. Women were never to meddle in the affairs of men. She was never supposed save the crown for their rightful king.

Joanna crossed to the shelf holding John's parchments. She prayed she might find something to help her.

"What do we seek? John is no longer the threat he posed before the coronation," Rynhawker asked.

"Anything useful against our enemies," she replied, never allowing her eyes to stray from the rolled stacks before her.

One by one she transferred four parchments to the table. There she spread the first one open. It was a map of England marked with all the castles. Beside each John had recorded a letter indicating loyalty to either Richard or John. At the time of the markings, John had strong-armed the support of most barons and dukes in southern England. However, many northern castles still remained loyal to Richard. The fight for the throne would have been a bloody one... had Richard returned to England.

Joanna also realized from the number of castles, and the numbers annotated beside each, that John once commanded a formidable army to march against his brother. What remained uncertain now was how many marked on the map still turned against their rightful king.

"John should have lost the support of those under his command once the word spread Richard was still alive," Joanna muttered.

She unrolled the next parchment, placing it over the first. Discerning no value in what she saw, the princess drifted away to stare at the shelf, hoping for anything of greater value.

Rynhawker retrieved one that he unrolled over the previous two. A pair of burning candles served to keep the parchments in place while they examined them more closely.

"Philip's fortifications," he commented, disregarding the information as unimportant to their cause, since they believed King Philip to be Richard's ally.

When Rynhawker removed the candles to allow the parchment to roll itself up, Joanna stopped him.

"Wait," she commanded, choosing to suspend her examination to look more closely at the one on the table. Knowledge of French fortifications could be important to them.

"There is little we can learn from this," Rynhawker insisted.

"Everything could prove meaningful to our cause," Joanna corrected.

She examined the parchment more carefully, focusing along France's northern boundary. She couldn't know why at the moment, but something told her to understand the locations of Philip's northern fortifications. Castles meant soldiers and knights, and though she failed to comprehend it at the moment, they seemed important.

At first, she overlooked the most significant detail on the map. Then she realized exactly what she was seeing. John had redrawn the boundaries, adding a substantial portion of Aquitaine to King Philip's domain.

"John has leveraged English lands to gain Philip's loyalty. He turned France against us," she muttered.

John and Philip were in league against the Lionheart, despite an alliance of years between the kings. The union gained John vast power over the queen. Eleanor could never keep the prince from the throne with Philip's might behind him.

Joanna paced.

"I must learn to fight," she voiced more to herself than to Rynhawker.

She returned to retrieve a parchment she had abandoned earlier. Unrolled, she placed it over the one Rynhawker had spread out.

Fragments of that night still haunted her. Had she been able to fight off John or Griswalt when they trapped her here, her servant Priscilina might still be alive. She realized she needed to be as strong, and as determined, as any man if she were to have any chance of success.

"My lady?" Rynhawker queried. The words seemed unfathomable. What was she asking?

"I will take up the sword to save my brother," she said with an unshakable confidence.

"That is not possible."

Rynhawker cast his eyes askance. He wished to avoid angering her, but what she implied would be foolish and impossible.

"I will. You will teach me to wield the sword."

"That will never be possible."

"No! You dare tell me no?"

"I will never allow harm to reach you. To provide you a sword is to place you at risk of dying. That I cannot do on my oath as your protector."

Rynhawker stalled for a long moment, leaning over the parchment. He could see in her eyes nothing he might say would deter her from the foolishness of her desire. He would have to find another way to convince her.

So he removed his sword, laying it over his forearm for her to accept the hilt.

"Here. This is what you ask," he said. His face remained smileless; his eyes narrowed in the dim light of the candles.

Joanna never hesitated. She accepted the blade out of defiance for what he had said, and the way he now looked at her. At first it felt light in her hands as she lifted the tip skyward. The honed-edge blade felt right in her grip... but not for long.

"I can do this. I will do this for Richard," she stammered.

It took only a few moments before the true measure of the broadsword's heft began to wear on her muscles.

Rynhawker retreated two steps to stand at the shelf, allowing her ample distance in the space.

"Swing it," he ordered. Anger slipped into his words as if he were commanding a squire.

"You think a woman cannot fight?" she snapped in equal anger.

He was mocking her with the look on his face. He said nothing, nor did he smile, but his eyes told her he refused to believe her.

"Swing it!" he commanded, this time more insistent, revealing for the first time a coldness in his eyes and along his furrowed brow.

Joanna swung left to right as hard as she could. The tip careened off the rock wall, drooping as the weapon's full weight played upon her arms.

"Again," he commanded.

She came back with all the strength she could muster. An unintended groan escaped from the strain tugging at her arms. The blade became an anvil in her hands.

"Now lunge at me."

She hesitated.

"Lunge at me now!" he scowled at her.

She complied, raising the tip chest high while forcing the blade to arm's length with everything she had.

Rynhawker seized the slow-moving steel in both hands.

"You think you can defend yourself against a trained knight or soldier," Rynhawker said calmly, relieving her of the sword to return it to its sheath.

"I will use a sword of less weight," she countered.

"Your enemy will snap the foible with his broadsword. You must fight equal to equal."

"Then I will become skilled with a dagger," she countered.

The fury of their confrontation built inside her. He sought to make her feel incapable of defending herself. She had to prove him wrong. She would find a way to fight for her brother's freedom.

"We shall have no more talk of fighting. We must concentrate on gaining information to help our king. Let your cunning mated with my sword allow us to aid Richard."

Feeling defeated, Joanna brought the next parchment from the shelf to the table. She unrolled it, but at first glance she concluded it offered no value. Then, upon closer inspection, she realized exactly what they stared at.

A rush of excitement filled her head. Her eyes met Rynhawker's. Her lips turned a cautious smile.

"King Henry's castles!" they both said aloud with a glimmer of surprise in their words.

For moments, neither spoke while they assimilated the markings on a map outlining Henry's domain.

"Richard is in one of these castles," Joanna said.

Rynhawker knew from her inflection that this map had sparked something critical in Joanna's mind.

"This could help us locate our king," she added.

The exhilaration in her voice spilled over into the knight. Rynhawker so wanted to reach out to take her hand into his, but instead he surveyed the map from end to end. Charcoal markings annotated more than a dozen fortifications. However, all that was discernible from the map were their names, locations and shapes; along with the region's topography. No one had indicated the innate strength of the fortifications, nor the numbers of fighting men that might be there, or if the structures were deemed vulnerable to attack.

"If we determine which castle holds Richard..." Joanna said.

Her eyes studied each marking, taking in every nuance that could be gleaned. Lines marked paths of rivers throughout Henry's domain. That triggered in Joanna's mind the realization that rivers offered her a way to navigate her enemy's lands.

Silent moments passed. Determining which castle held Richard could allow her to find a way to reach him and thus free him. Dare she allow Rynhawker to know her thoughts?

"If you were Henry, which castle would hold your greatest prize most securely?" Joanna pondered.

Flickering candles ticked off time in anticipation. That question's answer became paramount.

"The one most defensible," he replied.

"Exactly. Then which appears most defensible?"

"We cannot know for certain," he replied.

How could charcoal markings on parchment reveal such information? Yet Joanna realized to a certain extent they could.

"No, we cannot. But can we eliminate any?"

"Yes. These four to the north," Rynhawker responded, now understanding her line of inquiry.

"Why?" Joanna pressed.

She desperately needed a lesson in strategy from her knight.

"They are vulnerable to invasion from the sea. Once Richard held the ports, he would seize the castles in succession."

Joanna probed for a greater understanding of the military mind. She must become as cunning as her king if she wished to succeed.

"And what of those three there." Joanna indicated castles isolated in the remote eastern woodlands.

"No. They lack moats. Castles without moats and natural terrain barriers fall quickly to siege craft. Henry is unprotected in any of those."

"Then which are the best?"

Joanna's mind assembled disjointed fragments of a nascent plan to aid her brother. Bold and daring it would be, but it might be possible to free Richard.

"Yes, my lady, castles with the best natural defenses would be where I would secure the king... if I were Henry," Rynhawker said.

He realized the tenor in what he had said. To even suppose to think like a king would be an insult to a royal. He expected some punitive response from Joanna for his statement. Yet so deep in thought was she that she disregarded the spirit of his words.

"And which ones are those?"

Rynhawker pointed out three.

"Strigaarde castle here. Trifels castle to the south and Brucken castle to the east. Their foreboding landscapes make it near impossible for an army to penetrate. I see no way to bring siege craft close enough to Trifels castle to be effective," Rynhawker instructed.

Her brother the Lionheart had gleaned meticulous intelligence about his enemies, recording their strengths, along with every weakness. If Richard developed this map as a battle plan against

King Henry, then Joanna would find a way to use it for her purposes.

"They also gain the advantage of the river which allows Henry's forces to counterattack invaders."

The princess now had to stitch together her collected knowledge to determine the best course of action to help her brother. But could an invasion free her king, or merely bring about the death of too many English knights and soldiers? They had sacrificed so many lives in the Holy Lands. Another invasion might decimate Richard's army, leaving him vulnerable to attack from France, or worse, an uprising from John. Besides, Henry would be wise enough to prepare for any invasion.

Rynhawker waited silently while Joanna studied the etchings on the map. He could not fathom at that moment what thoughts churned inside her head. But he knew the determination of the woman beside him. She would be undeterred in her efforts to find a way to free her brother.

Henry would no doubt keep the king in his most secure fortification. If England chose to rescue their king by force, Henry had to assure himself his army could withstand the invasion long enough to renegotiate a new ransom. The last thing Henry wanted was his army destroyed and surrendering his prize without something for his suffering.

"We lack sufficient force to invade, but... if we knew Richard's location, we could breach their security to rescue him," Joanna muttered more to herself than to the knight.

"How might we accomplish such a feat?"

"First, we motivate Henry to do our bidding."

For a time Rynhawker gazed into Joanna's eyes as she contemplated her options. She needed to induce Henry to act in a manner beneficial to her.

"My lady?"

"We use continued silence to induce Henry into moving our king to one of those castles."

"How will that work?"

"By refusing to succumb to Henry's ransom demand, he will believe an invasion imminent. That will compel him into our wishes."

Rynhawker risked taking her hands into his, gazing into her eyes. She was serious. She believed they might find a way to achieve something most would conclude impossible.

She moved into his arms without thinking, without allowing anything rational, logical, or ethical to destroy the moment eclipsing between them.

Rynhawker welcomed her. He touched her face. His arms took her, welcoming her warmth, along with the softness of her skin.

He knew in his heart what he desired at that moment was against all that was right and good. In his soul, he knew he was unworthy of the princess, yet he needed to hold her the way he had held Merewen. He wished to comfort her, to allay her fears of the future of their king.

With candlelight dancing in Joanna's eyes, they shared a gentle kiss. The triumph of the moment brought their lips together— the burning desire in their hearts kept them there.

7

Prince John had been busy in the three months following his failure in Londontown. He had come so close. Had it not been for his meddling sister and that fool Baron Griswalt, he would be sitting upon the throne instead of his vile mother. He would never forget how Joanna turned on him. No one needed to die. No one needed to shed blood for John to seize the Crown. Now a river of blood would flow through the queen's castle.

For the present he had lost, but the battle between he and his mother and sister was far from over. As long as Richard remained King Henry's prisoner, the prince had a chance to seize the throne. And with King Philip of France at his side, along with his secret plan in motion, he could patiently wait for that day to arrive. But John's patience rarely extended beyond his next meal. He must continue to oppose his mother and sister at every turn. He must guarantee Richard never wore his crown again.

John sought refuge in Dernsley castle, a near impregnable fortress located five days ride from the queen. The fortification offered him safe haven, advanced warning should the queen dispatch men after him, and a sycophant duke easily molded to his will. There he began rebuilding his splintered army for his next endeavor. There remained a chance he might steal the Crown, though by now word would have reached even the furthest castles that Richard was alive and the prisoner of King Henry of Germany.

Duke Laroque entered to find John pacing uneasily in his chamber near a tall window.

"My lord, your men have returned," the duke reported.

He spoke quietly so as not to disturb the prince in his thoughts. Nary a day expired without John raging at someone for some minor infraction of his wishes. Lately, Laroque's stomach wrenched each time he needed to present the prince news that might displease him.

"Bring them immediately," John ordered.

Dernsley castle proved particularly clever for the prince, since Laroque had been one of Richard's staunch supporters and one of the first to pledge his loyalty to Eleanor in her quest to free her son. But Laroque was spineless, hiding behind a short grizzly beard and darting green eyes that avoided direct contact. He was also easily manipulated into doing the prince's bidding.

Once word spread Richard was indeed still alive, barons and dukes rode at breakneck speed to Londontown offering support, both material and spiritual to the queen, though few offered the requisite gold and silver.

John had made himself the black mark on the Plantagenet family, which caused his support to wane. But those fools had no inkling of the plans John placed in motion. Soon they would regret their decisions to align with the Lionheart. Once John seized power, they, too, would line up to pledge their loyalty to him.

Laroque, however, quickly realized what the opportunity presented. John could still succeed in taking the throne if anything happened to Richard in captivity. Bloodshed may never become necessary for John to win against his brother. And Laroque reasoned the men closest to the prince for the longest would rise to the highest power rung in the new regime.

Since John's very presence in his castle remained a guarded secret, only his chosen would know he had turned against his longtime friend and the rightful king. And if, per chance, Richard should return, Laroque could simply imprison the prince before turning him over to the rightful king without delay.

A bountiful surrounding forest provided John's dwindling army with food, water and vital harborage. What was once hundreds of soldiers and seven score knights had dwindled to half. Now John dispatched roving knights and soldiers to prey upon any loyal to the queen and harass her attempts to collect the needed ransom.

To fend off his rising number of defections, the prince offered a prized bounty to the man, or men, who cast the lifeless bodies of Sir Rynhawker and Sir Thomas at his feet. Every fighting man studied the knights' coats of arms and prayed they encountered the prize beyond the safety of Eleanor's castle.

John came to accept that he could no longer mount an assault on the queen in the hopes of seizing the throne by force. Eleanor's guard would be sufficient to repel any attack. With Joanna at her side, his mother could strategically launch a counterattack to decimate his army even further. No, John had to be more cunning, more skilled in his next attempt at the throne.

The prince ceased pacing to sit at the table closest to the vaulted windows looking south. A refreshing sea breeze flooded across his face, jostling his shoulder-length hair.

Moments later, a rap came at the door.

"Enter," John barked.

Two knights marched in, ragged and sullied from battle and their arduous ride. Two soldiers followed, lugging a locked chest twice the length of a man's arm between them.

John's eyes alighted at the sight. Another contribution to the ransom destined for Londontown came into his possession. His men had succeeded in intercepting more gold and silver.

He almost laughed out loud at his cunning. He had outwitted his mother yet again.

"Open it!" he demanded, shifting around the table to better view the contents.

The soldiers set the chest between them while the first knight pried the lock with his sword. Afterward, the second knight kicked the chest open, overturning it in the process. A feeble collection of gold and silver implements spilled from inside.

Disappointment clouded the prince's face as he mentally tallied the meager holdings. No more than a dozen pieces of gold and twice as many pieces of silver splayed onto the floor.

"Seems someone had little to offer our queen," John commented wryly.

"Which is now yours, my lord," Laroque quickly added.

"Tell me you have killed all the men bringing this to my mother," John commanded of the closest knight.

"My prince, we came upon the caravan in Earlham forest. They attempted to escape, but we overtook them. We killed the guards and chased down the wagons. You have what the wagons held."

"Then they are all dead. No one can lay blame for this on me?"

"As you commanded, my lord," the knight replied.

The knights bowed while John returned to his chair.

"Feed them well. Give them anything they wish."

The soldiers made their way out first, with the knights a few paces behind.

Laroque remained with his master, though he feared now he might become the recipient of John's irascible temper. How could so meager an offering help the queen in her need to raise the ransom Henry demanded?

John rose to stare out the window at a raging sea battering the rocky coast.

Laroque remained dutifully silent.

"On the morrow you are to ride to Londontown with your most trusted knights. Request an audience with the queen."

"My lord, for what reason?"

"Offer her this in support of the king's release."

"I do not understand?"

"This pittance will prove more valuable in leverage. Reaffirm your loyalty. Offer to remain in her service until Richard returns."

John turned to face his servant. Through the shadow that darkened his face, Laroque detected the telltale glint of John's sinister smile. The duke saw the conjuring of further treason in the prince's eyes.

"For what purpose?"

"Watch and listen in the queen's court. Then dispatch your trusted to report what you learn."

"As you command, my lord."

Laroque smiled.

"I am moving to Tonnewick castle without delay so I may be close enough to strike against my mother or Joanna should they move to gain Richard's freedom."

"Then you have a plan, my lord?"

"The queen must transport her ransom. Why accept this pittance when I can have it all and seal my brother's fate for good."

"As you command."

Laroque bowed before retreating quickly and quietly from the chamber. Much to do before departing Dernsley castle.

Two knights summoned Queen Eleanor from her bedchamber at the first rays of dawn. She deplored being disturbed so early. No one would inform her of why, but it seemed the queen was needed without delay.

When Joanna received word of the queen's summons, she raced from her bower to seek Rynhawker before meeting with her mother in the great hall.

Rynhawker bowed before his queen then rose to stand beside Joanna. He could see from the concern in Eleanor's eyes that yet another disaster had struck the kingdom. At first, Rynhawker thought the worst: King Richard had been killed or had died before they could free him.

Worried eyes traced from the queen to Joanna. Rynhawker knew she shared his concern. Joanna's hands trembled as she tried to soothe them in a clasp.

"What call brings you out of your bower so early this morn?" Joanna asked.

She knew in her heart the answer was about to be disturbing. She could only hope the worst had not come to pass while they plotted a way to save her brother.

The Archbishop of Rollinshire stepped forward to bow before his queen as she sat upon her throne. Her heart raced ahead of her thoughts. She sought to read the archbishop's eyes. Something in his look unsettled her when she first laid eyes upon him.

"My queen, my news will sadden your heart, I am afraid."

"Then speak and keep me on tenterhooks no longer, damn you!"

The queen's outburst tore at the archbishop's nerves.

"I have learned..." he started but paused. He knew how important the news was to the queen and her daughter. And what it meant for the future of the Crown.

"My queen, marauders attacked the caravan carrying Isaac the Jew. All perished."

The archbishop had been the go-between for her majesty, arranging for Isaac's transportation and protection while monitoring the Jew's progress from the north.

The words crushed Eleanor.

Instinct drove Joanna's hand out for Rynhawker's. She needed his touch, his warmth and comfort. But she knew better.

Tears rimmed Eleanor's eyes. Isaac the Jew had been a special friend. Though her heart ached from the news, Eleanor pushed herself erect to deal with yet another tragedy come her way.

"What does this mean?" Joanna pressed in a whisper.

"Leave us now," Eleanor commanded, her voice a pained breath.

The archbishop bowed, after which he silently and efficiently retreated from the hall.

Only after sentries sealed the doors did Eleanor release the words that so trembled inside her throat.

"Isaac carried gold and silver for Richard's ransom," she announced with a heavy sigh.

Joanna read the defeat in her mother's words.

"You are saying we have lost the ransom for Richard's release?" Joanna asked.

"Our resources remain insufficient to meet Henry's demand. Isaac was our last hope. He promised to deliver what he could from Northumberland."

Joanna cast her fear to Rynhawker.

He read her eyes in a glance, knowing what it meant for their cause. The danger increased tenfold as a result of Isaac's tragedy.

"John is behind this. I know it in my heart," Joanna stammered through clenched teeth. "His contempt drives him to do everything in his power to prevent Richard's release."

Eleanor wiped at her tears. Isaac had been a faithful servant to the king. He would be missed.

"We have no proof John was involved," Eleanor responded.

"I need no proof. I know my brother. I know what he is capable of. Who knew of Isaac's journey?" Joanna demanded.

"Only the archbishop and myself. The archbishop would never betray me."

"Well, if John is involved, then someone has betrayed you."

Rynhawker refused to hold his tongue any longer.

"My lady, if what you say is true, then John now has the gold and silver. I beg thee to allow me to ride after the guilty men. I will return the ransom," Rynhawker said.

His words momentarily derailed Joanna's thoughts. If John and his minions had perpetrated this treason, it could take the entire queen's army to hunt them down and wrest free the resources necessary to save the king... if they could even succeed. If they failed, they might lose their men, along with the treasure for the ransom.

"It is too dangerous at this time. Mother, we must proceed with the plan I have put together. You must find a way to gain us time to locate Richard."

Grief kept Eleanor from separating the myriad of thoughts rumbling through her mind. John's treason, the lost ransom, her son's freedom and now Isaac's death had all jumbled together. She could find no way to extract them so she might consider more clearly what must be done.

"Henry will expect a reply soon. The longer we delay, the more likely Henry is to do something terrible to our king. Henry never was a patient man," Eleanor replied.

Both understood the gravity of the situation. If Henry lost patience, he would make Richard pay for the queen's indecision.

"Then we will advance more quickly."

Joanna bowed before her mother, and absent a further word, marched to the doors at a determined pace. Rynhawker quickly bowed his dismissal so he might catch her in the corridor.

"We as yet have no way of locating our king, let alone the men and the strategy to gain his freedom," he said, stopping Joanna in the corridor.

"You will have all the answers you require," Joanna shot back. She snapped her arm free to stomp away down the hall.

9

Iyewebas sat alone in the near darkness of a forest hollow. Storm clouds and the thickly entangled crown canopy hid the fulgent moon. Each morning for the past three weeks he would leave the forest to trek to the castle beyond the trees in the hopes of learning if this fortress imprisoned his king. Then each night he returned to these woods where he would sleep. All he knew for certain was they moved his king from the last castle after he had located him.

After days of following the tracks the best he could, Iyewebas suspected he may have discovered his king's new prison. He heard said three days past King Henry was in attendance here, which Iyewebas hoped meant the whoreson king dragged his prize along.

As yet, Iyewebas had spied neither his king nor King Henry in this place. But he believed patience would be rewarded.

He leaned closer to his meager fire to warm him if only slightly from the chilled autumn night. He prayed for a night without rain. He spent the last three sleeping under a makeshift tarp to remain dry. Alone and hungry, he grumbled to himself while waiting for sleep to overtake him. His rabbit snares set in the surrounding forest had failed him again. He would hope for better luck in the morning.

Knowing he might be within range of reaching his king brought solace and joy to his heart, yet he had no idea what he would do once he made contact with his lord. Should he smuggle Richard a dagger? If Richard had a weapon, surely he could fight his way to freedom, and Iyewebas could be there to provide horses and a way out of the castle.

"Why do you wish this upon me?" he risked calling out to his God. He expected no answer. Why should God care to speak to him.

It wasn't that he blamed the Lord for their misfortune; he just wished the Almighty might shed some grace upon him in his quest to rescue his king. They were right and good to march into the Holy Lands in the name of His church. They did what they did for God. Surely He saw that and understood the sacrifices they had made.

Snap!

Iyewebas sprang alert, but he remained in his squatting position near his fire. His surging heart constricted his breathing. His hands trembled at the thought he was no longer alone. He remembered the last time he encountered men in the woodland. The pain he endured buoyed to the surface of his mind. A silent prayer sprang from his lips.

Iyewebas eyed an arm's-length formidable tree branch a few steps out of reach. Its heft made it a suitable club. Could he reach it in time to use it as a weapon? In his mind's eye, he envisioned a glistening blade cleaving off his hand before he reached it.

Yet the surrounding forest returned to silence. No one breached his small clearing in the night. Had he actually heard something? Maybe his mind merely tricked him. Very slowly, Iyewebas turned to gaze upon the dark fringes of his little haven. Surely no one would know he was here. He was always careful to prevent others from following him. A deaf mute was invisible to most in the kingdom. No one cared whether he lived or died. He owned nothing. He held nothing anyone could want.

Then encroaching movement caught his eye. It came at the flank of his firelight. Someone skulked about in the trees. Iyewebas knew not how to react in that moment of solitude that remained.

A tall man, clad in a black cloak with only a hint of a face beneath the cowl showing, entered the clearing. His sword remained sheathed. He stopped inside the ball of light, maintaining a safe distance from Iyewebas to avoid frightening the little man more than he seemed to be at the moment.

"Hail, friend, I mean no harm. I wish only to share your fire's warmth this cold night," the voice said.

He paused with hands on his hips away from his weapons, allowing Iyewebas to feel unthreatened by his sudden appearance.

Iyewebas eyed him with suspicion. He grunted and motioned to his ears, conveying in gesture his malady to what he believed was a wandering knight. Certainly the fine sword at his hip indicated a noble.

"Perhaps some ale will warm us both."

The man's smile lessened his grotesque scar's sinister appearance in the firelight.

Iyewebas forced a weak, uncertain smile. He saw no other option but to allow the man to share the little he had to offer.

Rothbane interpreted Iyewebas' smile as agreement. He retreated from the clearing to retrieve his ebony warhorse, which he had tethered to a tree limb deeper into the night forest while he investigated the fire. Returning with both beast and a flask from his saddle, Rothbane extended the vessel in offering as he approached Iyewebas, who rose in response.

The thought of quenching his prolonged thirst danced in Iyewebas' head. Could he be so fortunate as to have found someone willing to treat him like a man? Iyewebas' smile conveyed his acceptance of the knight's kindness, and with a wave of his hand, he offered Rothbane a place beside him in exchange for a drink.

Iyewebas guzzled down the ale without delay, the yeasty liquid dousing the rumbling of his empty belly, along with quenching his parched throat. It had been so long since he had been able to indulge in drink. He consumed only water he could find in a passing stream or from an inattentive farmer's trough.

"You hear not, nor do you speak?" Rothbane asked.

Iyewebas nodded, returning the flask to his guest. Hoping the man might have some food to share, he motioned to his mouth with clinched fingers, but Rothbane shook his head in response.

Iyewebas smiled nonetheless, settling closer to the fire, but avoiding eye contact with the knight. His mind warned something was amiss, though at the time, Iyewebas could find nothing to substantiate his ill feeling.

"You are alone?" Rothbane queried oddly.

The question frightened Iyewebas. Why did he ask it? What was he planning? Worry twisted Iyewebas' mind into knots. Might he be in danger from the man sitting beside him?

Reluctantly Iyewebas nodded affirmatively.

Rothbane sprang to his feet, levelling his sword at Iyewebas.

Iyewebas' hands shot up in surrender.

"For a man who does not speak, why did I hear someone say 'why do you wish this upon me' coming from these woods?"

The words pummeled Iyewebas off his guard. He stared at Rothbane, knowing the knight had uncovered his clever ruse. One foolish moment cost him dearly. Could he continue the deaf mute play and still keep his head? Iyewebas considered he might not.

Rothbane extracted his dagger.

Iyewebas backed away.

"Please, do not harm me," Iyewebas spoke.

The words felt wonderful rolling out of his mouth. He had tried so hard to maintain his deception, but that single moment of inattention had foiled his plot.

"Why make people think you cannot speak when you can?"

"You are a Brit?" Iyewebas ventured.

"As are you," Rothbane replied. "Both enemies in this land."

Rothbane lowered his sword, returned his dagger to its sheath then indulged in a long drink from his flask before handing it over to Iyewebas.

"How did you come to be in this land? Are you a returning crusader?" Rothbane pressed.

Iyewebas returned to the ground, where he waited for Rothbane to settle once more across the fire. Then he revealed his story of the shipwreck with his king. He explained that he traveled from castle to castle in search of his lord, who was now Henry's captive.

In all aspects of Iyewebas' story Rothbane uttered mock surprise. He waited patiently while Iyewebas divulged all the secrets the knight had sought. This man was a fool to reveal all to a passing stranger; then again, plying his tongue with ale had brought more than Rothbane could have hoped for.

"Then you know where our king is held?" Rothbane queried with astonishment.

Iyewebas' face turned a frown.

"I did... until four weeks past. Henry has moved our king from the castle on the river."

"What do you intend once you locate our king?"

"Find a way to free him, of course," Iyewebas offered proudly.

He had no idea what he would do, only that he would give his life to save his king.

Rothbane laughed.

"Laugh you may, but a deaf mute moves easily within the king's castles. Few care about someone unable to speak or hear."

"Unless foolishly he utters in err," Rothbane corrected.

"I believed I sat alone in this forest."

"And you were, until I spied your flames."

"Why did you approach me?"

"Simply for warmth. I, too, am a returning crusader who chose to travel over land. I despise the sea and all her dangers," he lied.

"As do I. But I was in the service of my king," Iyewebas said.

"Can you fight?"

"I will... if I must," Iyewebas offered, lacing his words with his uncertainty.

He always told himself he would die for his king. But would he? Could he fight if the moment came when he must? He did nothing more in his life than aid the knights before they marched into battle in the Holy Lands. He never once brought a broadsword, or even a dagger, for that matter, against one of his king's enemies.

Later, Rothbane returned the empty flask to his saddle strap then settled to enjoy the fire. It had been more than a fair exchange for the knight. In return for his ale, he gained not only warmth, but also the most valuable asset he could have stumbled upon for his quest: Someone to help locate the Lionheart.

"I offer my sword in your quest to free our king," Rothbane said, all the while his face absent a smile.

The words raised a skeptical brow on Iyewebas. He should have been elated at the thought of having a knight with a blade to assist him. But he wasn't. Something about the way the man spoke settled uneasily upon Iyewebas' mind. He wished he could understand exactly what made him suspicious. But something about this Rothbane caused the hair on his neck to stand.

Why should this one so easily fall into his aid? Certainly he understood the extreme peril involved in attempting to rescue a king. But on the other hand, he was a Brit, sworn to Richard the Lionheart, making him duty-bound in any way possible.

Rothbane removed a strip of dried venison from his belt.

"Here. Eat. We both need strength if we are to save our king."

Iyewebas smiled.

Food, glorious food.

10

On the night of the full moon, as she had been instructed, Sabine feigned illness to take her leave from the service of the queen so she might retreat to the solitude and safety of the servants' bower.

Margray grew suspicious of Sabine's sudden illness, but she knew better than to ever speak against her. For reasons unknown to Margray, the queen held Sabine in higher regard. So Sabine felt secure in the knowledge the queen would never suspect her of what she was about to do.

Sabine calculated her departure to allow her to secure a horse in the stable then exit the front gates before the guards lowered the portcullis and raised the drawbridge for the night. If she failed to execute precisely, she could miss the last chance to leave the castle. If she missed her opportunity, she must wait until the next full moon. Her master would be angry with her, but she would perform for him and that would arrest his anger.

Sabine covered her head with a low hanging cowl to allow her to leave the queen's wing of the castle undetected. Few paid attention to servants scurrying about the castle corridors. Only the knights and nobles drew attention in the halls. It seemed everyone else turned invisible to those who mattered.

Undetected, Sabine departed the keep, moving with purpose into the stables. She could see the first glimpse of the moon rising into the twilight sky. Time was of the essence. To delay would be troublesome for her now.

Once in the stables she bridled the horse in the closest stall, and without saddle, mounted the beast to proceed out into the open market square. Only a few straggling peasants remained, pulling carts toward the castle gates, while others mounted donkeys to return to their farmhouses for the night.

Sabine rode slowly, measuring her pace so it seemed neither hurried nor retarded as she weaved amongst the men flowing out the castle gate over the drawbridge. No one even looked at her as her palfrey clopped over the wooden timbers. Only a handful of men remained on the bridge as she crossed the moat for the ancient road leading into the southwest forest.

Her heart beat faster at the thought of what this night would bring. Only then did she allow her smile to grace her face, though no one would detect it in the dim light. Her most difficult task had passed without incident.

Once well beyond the pedestrian flow, Sabine kicked her palfrey into a bounding trot. The hour was late. Behind her, the portcullis lowered with a horrible screech. Moments later, the clanking drawbridge chains sealed her fate for the night. She must remain outside the castle in the forest until the first morning's light, when the castle opened to allow serfs into the market square.

Within the hour, Sabine breached the forest fringe where the river entered tightly packed trees. She abandoned all the remaining light of a red sun settling below the horizon.

Before long, two knights on horseback galloped up. Without speaking, they wheeled their mounts about to escort her deeper into the forest. Their presence made her feel like royalty herself. She knew not where they were going, nor how long it would take to reach the rendezvous.

The three riders pressed deeper into the dense pine clusters that reached out at them like tentacles of a monster known only in childhood nightmares. Her palfrey slowed to pick its way around fallen branches cluttering the path leading toward the very core of the forest. Only there would they be safe; only there could they meet without fear of reprisal from the queen in her castle.

Then the acrid scent of burning wood flooded her nose. A sharp snap from a crackling fire broke the silence. Did she see the flickers in the distance? She couldn't be certain. She steered her mount in the direction she believed led to the fire's light. Once the light appeared through the mesh of trees, she advanced alone, secure in knowing knights remained close by to protect them from harm. As yet, she glimpsed only flashes of the silvery shards of moonlight penetrating the canopy.

As her palfrey slowed, she saw the fire's full brightness. It was what she hoped and prayed for.

Her heart leapt into her throat at the thought that he would be waiting for her. This night would not be cold but warm, not alone but with him. She would be filled with excitement and pleasure. She was now so very happy she had risked her ruse with the queen. She knew well the dangers she faced; she would receive a terrible punishment for what she was doing, but she also knew this was what she wanted most in her life. This made her feel special. Here with him she was no longer simply a servant to the queen. Here she was someone who was loved. Or at least so she told herself as the fire grew brighter and the trees thinned into a glade at the very center of the forest.

A lone double-belled wedge tent awaited her when she breached the edge of the clearing.

As she had seen on previous excursions into the night forest, four horses remained tethered to nearby branches. They would not be alone; there were always armed knights in close proximity.

Prince John emerged from the crease when Sabine's palfrey luffed at her arrival. Her smile shone as brightly as the flames of his meager fire. His, however, appeared more subdued, yet he offered her a smile, nonetheless.

He came to her with welcoming arms to assist her from her mount. She wrapped hers around his neck to kiss him, but he resisted, instead whisking her away into the seclusion of his tent. Once inside he secured the flap immediately, so that he could lay her on the rich furs rolled out to make a bed.

"My wonderful lord, I have missed you," she whispered the way a lover seduces her mate.

She understood that John was never her lover, nor her mate. She was a servant; he was a prince. He would have her for his pleasure, and she would relish every moment his hands worked her body. But ultimately, he would pledge his heart to another noble, after which, she would be discarded, or at the very best, kept secret for use when he tired of his wife.

She accepted that arrangement as the best that one of her station could hope for in life. Besides, the prince had chosen her to give him pleasure. That counted for something special in her heart.

John lay close, bringing her against him in the subdued light filtering in.

"What news do you bring?" he whispered.

His hand worked up her dress to touch between her legs. She wanted to close her eyes, to immerse herself in the pleasures he provided. Talking only stole the ecstasy swimming inside her.

He probed her deeper, hungry for more of her.

"Tell me," he whispered more harshly.

Sabine drew the prince closer, clutching his hip.

"You like this, don't you," he said.

"I do, my lord."

"Then I stop if you remain silent."

Sabine sucked in her breath. In one more moment of his pleasure she would be unable to speak, but that would anger the prince.

"The queen raged over losing her ransom from the Jew, I heard tell," she burst out, hoping he would continue to pleasure her, so she could remain silent long enough to drink in every ounce of his effort.

"Then you have heard," he whispered next in a more demanding tone. "Good."

Sabine fumbled with her hand until she found him ready for her. She wanted her attention to force him into silence, but her efforts brought only angry eyes in the darkness.

"I do not know any more, my lord," she replied.

He withdrew his fingers slightly from inside her.

She responded quickly by forcing his hand back.

"Please, my lord." She was breathless now.

"Tell me what Joanna intends. What have you learned about her?"

John's words conveyed heightened anger. The pleasure she so sought was turning into pain. John shifted to use his position inside her to force her to speak rather than to pleasure her.

"Lady Joanna is very secretive, my lord. She never speaks to the queen when I am nearby. I can learn nothing."

"You must find out!"

"I promise, my lord, I will learn what you wish to know. But the queen mostly excludes her servants when she meets with her daughter."

"Have you seen new faces in the castle? What men come to see the queen or my sister?"

Sabine didn't want to speak. She wanted what she wanted. John, however, wanted something more than she had expected of him.

John thrust his hand deeper and harder, trying to inflict pain inside her.

"Joanna frequently meets in private with her two favored knights. They are her constant companions. I have never seen her alone," she offered, hoping to appease her lord enough to cease his painful thrusts.

"Does she speak to the queen about her intent? Has she revealed any other sources for their ransom?"

Sabine bit her lower lip at the wild excitement dancing up her spine, spilling into every corner of her brain.

"Tell what you've heard!"

John jabbed at her, vanquishing the ecstasy taking over her mind.

"My lord, you hurt me," she whimpered, hoping to coax him into stopping.

"I will give you what you want when you provide me with information I can use against my mother and sister. I must know exactly what they intend to do. Have they spoken about me? Have you heard my name mentioned in their presence?"

"No, my lord, they never mention you. I will do everything I can to listen well, my lord. I promise. But my treasonous actions would see my death if the queen learned of them."

John stopped. His eyes turned cold and mean.

"You will do my bidding. Or you will remain the worthless servant of the queen for the remainder of your miserable life."

Sabine shed her dress so he might partake of her breasts. His smile and the way his eyes alighted said she had pleased him.

She waited in anticipation of her pleasure while he indulged her flesh. Then she accepted him when he could resist no longer. The throbbing of sheer ecstasy lasted long after he finished inside her. She knew in her heart she would do anything for her master— even risk her very life, if he demanded it. The prince could command her. She would face treason to do his bidding.

For a long moment he curled beside her silent, unmoving. She thought for a time he had fallen dead asleep, but she knew better, since no snores erupted in the night quiet.

"Duke Laroque is now in the service of the queen. He is one of mine. Seek him out and convey your information to him. He will relay it to me."

Sabine swallowed uneasily. She felt secure meeting her prince secluded in the forest distant from the castle. Now he pressed her to possibly reveal her treason to her queen. It would be more dangerous to maintain their secrecy moving about inside the walls.

"On the other matter, tell me what progress you have made," John said as if he were speaking to the night rather than to her.

Fear wormed up her spine. Her breathing grew erratic as she contemplated her future. What if her queen or Joanna uncovered her secret against them?

11

Joanna sat with Annalise corralled in her lap on the lawn of the queen's private courtyard. A white chaupal tent shaded her from the harsh afternoon sun. Six young lads circled her, all smiling and staring with rapt attention. Delphi knelt beside her, stealing quick glances until the princess noticed. He blushed when caught, revealing his infatuation.

Just as each of their previous lessons had started, Joanna began singing the song she learned from her mother at the age of ten. Eleanor insisted each of her children know the song by heart. The lyrics extolled the Plantagenet family story, which held special meaning for the royals. Joanna's father grew tired of hearing the song so often, but Eleanor persisted, requiring each child sing it in perfect pitch, never erring in a single syllable. It was to be their way of passing their family story on to future generations.

Now Joanna sought to pass their song on to the six lads in her attendance. Some were quick learners—singing it without fail. Delphi proudly sat amongst that group. There were a few, the younger ones, who seemed to experience continued difficulty reproducing the song in the exact manner Joanna demanded. This their third week of training required Joanna to extend her patience despite the varied mistakes her younger students committed. She quickly came to realize only a few could serve her need.

"I think that was perfect. What do you think, Annalise?" she said when the lad finished.

Annalise clapped approval, smiling at young Delphi, who patted her hand.

When Rynhawker and Thomas entered the courtyard Joanna rose, surrendering Annalise to Althera's care.

"It is time she eats," she instructed her servant.

Althera accepted the child, delivering her into her father's waiting arms for the few moments spent waiting for the princess.

"Delphi, your turn to sing," Joanna said.

"But my lady, I just fin..."

A waving finger silenced the lad before he could complete his thought. He swallowed, standing before the others for a third time this day. His words came out weak at first, grew stronger as his confidence bloomed.

Once she felt Delphi was in control, Joanna strayed from her students to join her knights in private. However, she remained silent until Annalise returned to Althera's custody and the two departed the courtyard.

"Have you seen to what I ask?" Joanna pressed the moment they were isolated.

"Yes, my lady," Thomas replied.

"Good."

"But why do you summon three friars?" Rynhawker asked.

"For now you must trust in what I am doing."

"My lady, time withers away while we wait for news which may never come," Rynhawker pressed.

He had held his tongue as long as he could. He risked his words might anger the princess, but he had to speak. No one, it seemed, was doing anything to help free their king.

"Our time is best spent learning what we can about our enemies," Joanna replied plainly.

Her response would do little to quell the anger seething inside the knight. So many months had passed inactive, and still they had no information from the continent that they could use to determine where Henry had imprisoned their king.

"Would you rather we cross the channel only to face the wrath of Philip, or worse, Henry's armies?" she added, responding to his anger with her own.

"Who *are* our enemies in this?" Thomas asked.

"More importantly, who are our allies?" Joanna shot back.

She paused for their answer. They remained silent.

"They are all enemies now. Henry stands directly between us and Richard's freedom. But Philip and John seek to oppose us at every turn. John would make a much better ally to France than Richard. Have no doubt that Philip will use his army against us when he deems the time ripe for a conquest," she said.

Joanna diverted her attention back to her students in the circle on the lawn. A different lad now stood amongst the others. He flawlessly recited the song. The words brought exhilaration to Joanna's heart. Confidence grew with each little success that her developing plan might succeed.

"My lady, I do not understand," Rynhawker pressed.

"Soon you will," she replied.

Her smile sought to reassure them, though Rynhawker had little confidence any plan they might devise could help them.

Joanna's attention swung to a soldier marching at a determined pace to reach them. He stopped paces short of the princess before speaking.

"My lady, the queen summons your presence immediately," he announced.

"Inform my mother I will join her shortly," Joanna replied.

"My lady, the queen has instructed me to remain until you attend her presence in the throne room."

"For what purpose is this insistence?"

"My queen commands me to bring you to the throne room without delay."

It seemed the princess had no choice but to accede to her mother's every forceful whim. Concern swarmed Joanna's face. Her mother only became fervently demanding when a situation turned dire. Could yet more ill infect the queen's court? Joanna did not wish to think of what terrible thing had induced such a panicked request.

12

Eleanor sprang from her throne the moment Isaac entered the room. Ragged and filthy from his perilous quest, yet he was the most magnificent sight for the queen's eyes to behold.

"You have survived!" Eleanor chimed, unable to contain the joy of seeing him in the flesh.

They hugged graciously, Isaac using care to prevent his grime from soiling her majesty.

"They informed us your caravan was waylaid in the forest, that all were killed," she said.

"My queen, I am saddened to say I am the only survivor."

"Come, tell me everything."

An angry Joanna pushed through the doors with Rynhawker and Thomas at her sides. What could her mother want that demanded she be treated like an insolent child? Surely she could respond to the request without the nagging of an escort on her heels.

"We praise God," the princess muttered, seeing Isaac standing tall beside her mother. He turned to her with a smile that sent shivers of joy across her skin.

Joanna rushed to him to share a hug. She could not at first believe her eyes. Isaac the Jew was alive!

"They said all were killed."

No one expected Isaac to have survived. No one believed anyone could have survived the attack.

Over the years Joanna had come to know of Isaac, but never as well as her brother and her mother. But she knew how much Isaac meant to Richard.

"I feared I would never see either of you again," Isaac said.

"Bring us wine... and food. And prepare a soft bed for our guest," the queen ordered of Sabine and Margray standing in attendance.

"Yes, my queen," Margray offered, bowing as both her servants exited to complete the queen's orders.

Eleanor waited until her attendants vacated before she risked speaking of more. Only she, Isaac, Joanna and the two knights would hear the report of what happened to their caravan.

"Tell me all," Eleanor insisted.

"I only narrowly survived, my queen. It seems the marauders were only interested in seizing the treasure, which allowed me to escape."

"How were you able to evade them?" Joanna asked.

Every detail she could glean could help in her cause. Whatever successful tactic Isaac employed might also become useful to her.

"I broke from the caravan when the attackers went after the treasure wagons. That allowed me and my hay wagon to gain safe refuge in a forest."

"We learned the wagon carrying the ransom was destroyed," Eleanor said.

"That it was, my queen. I remained hidden in a ravine for three days following. I prayed with each sunrise that I might survive to reach you. Only afterward did I chance to leave the forest to make my way to Londontown."

"Did they bear a coat of arms?" Joanna asked.

"Nay, my lady. Rogue shields with no heralds."

Joanna looked to Rynhawker. Rogue knights could be under the prince's command.

"The day following I came upon the burned wreckage of the other wagons with the remains of our guard. All were slain. They took the chest carrying your ransom."

"They knew what they were after," Eleanor said.

Her brow furrowed in concern. Someone had divulged their secret. Or maybe John had taken to attacking anyone bearing the Lionheart herald. Either way, her gold and silver was lost.

"John is behind this. Who else knew you transported gold and silver?" Joanna said.

"I told no one, your majesty. I kept even the men in escort unaware of the purpose of our journey."

"Only three in this castle knew."

"Then one may be a spy for John," Joanna said through gritted teeth.

"The lost ransom places our king in dire jeopardy. We have failed to raise the requisite gold and silver to meet Henry's demands," Eleanor said.

Isaac read despair in her eyes.

"My queen, all is not lost. They absconded with your treasure, that is true, but they gained only a portion of what I transported."

Eleanor and Joanna stared at him. What did he mean?

"How can that be?" Joanna pressed.

"My queen, in these troubled times I chose to trust no one, not even the men tasked with escort. On the night prior to our departure, I wrapped and hid most of the treasure using the bottom of the hay wagon I drove. I left some in the chest, in case of attack. They have taken your chest, but they failed to gain the full ransom."

"You are saying you delivered the ransom to us?"

"As promised, my queen, gold and silver sits beneath the hay. Perhaps these knights will assist in retrieving it for your majesty."

Joanna threw her arms around Isaac. He spared them from certain ruin. A chance remained for freeing Richard, if there came no other way to bring him home. No one desired to pay the king's ransom, but without Isaac's ingenuity, they would have forfeit that option altogether.

"But I am afraid my offering remains less than what I promised."

13

The absence of the queen's response sent Henry into roving fits of anxious depression. He fully expected Eleanor would dispatch messengers promptly agreeing to his demand. What other options had she?

So why does she remain silent? He wondered.

Henry scowled at any, and all, who came before him for mediation. He grew weary of dealing with the petty squabbles of serfs in his realm. He had more at stake than the disputed ownership of a cow or the right of one serf to draw on the king's water from a creek crossing another's shire.

Roger did his best to arbitrate those issues the king wished to avoid. Yet he could see as each day wore on with silence from the queen that his king grew more irascible. So Roger tried diligently to avoid his king at moments of extreme agitation. He was glad he had withheld the Lionheart's escape attempt, as that would have only angered his majesty and made him more prone to inflict suffering on those around him.

"Perhaps we should do something to improve the king's favor," Roger chanced to offer on a day when Henry felt like he had reached his last thread of patience.

"Shall I dispatch another messenger with our demands restated?" Henry posed to his closest aide.

"My lord, the Queen of England may be playing your impatience. She will surely leverage any sign of weakness against us," Roger offered after carefully considering his words.

"You think me weak now?"

"Nay, your majesty. But the queen may be attempting to force a renegotiation of terms before she succumbs to your demand."

"Could she believe she actually has any leverage against me?"

Roger pondered. One wrong word might find him locked away in the same dungeon as the king's prize.

He waited while Henry weighed his own words.

"Perhaps you are right. The queen has little choice but to bow to my demand. After all, paying the ransom is the only way she will ever see her son again."

"My lord, should you give due consideration to alternatives the queen may take against you?"

Henry raised a curious brow, believing he left her no alternatives.

Roger read his king's face, uncertain of whether his words had brought favor—or disfavor—upon his lord.

For a long moment Henry considered Roger's question.

"Bring me wine!" the king scowled as he thought.

In response, a slender young servant woman, whose comely face snared the king's fancy, scurried forward with a goblet, filling it hastily with a trembling hand.

"Leave us," Roger commanded politely to the maiden.

She bowed on her retreat, never looking directly at her king as she left the chamber.

Roger settled into a nearby chair. He had motivated the king into considering his words, which was good and necessary, should the queen refuse his ransom demand.

"As I see it, my lord, the queen has but two choices concerning her son. Pay as you demand, or apply force to free the Lionheart."

Henry paused his drink to stare into Roger's eyes.

"She will pay what I demand," Henry scowled, tightening his grip on his goblet to restrain mounting anger.

"Let us, for the moment, merely consider the opposing alternative. Suppose she fails to raise sufficient gold and silver to meet your demand. She resigns herself to force in order to free her king."

"Or she sends a messenger to negotiate a better price? If mine remains beyond her kingdom's reach."

"Do you intend to negotiate for Richard's release? My lord, you have indicated no such option to the queen."

Henry considered for a moment. His demand may seem inflexible to Eleanor.

"Suppose there is another case, my liege. Suppose she chooses to keep her gold and sends men instead to return her king."

Roger paused. He needed the full gravity of his words to settle upon his king's mind. Like it or not, Henry must prepare for an invasion, the only other alternative to the ransom. If he failed to prepare, he might lose more than he had ever hoped to gain by imprisoning the Lionheart.

"My king, it is vital we execute defensive measures to safeguard your prize."

"What do you suggest?"

"Secure your treasure in your safest castle. One the queen's knights will fail to sack. Only there will both kings be safe."

"Where do you suggest?"

"Certainly, Trifels and Strigaarde can repel any siege the queen might mount."

"What of Brucken? I favor Brucken castle."

"My lord, Brucken's northern face is vulnerable to siege craft. It would fall to a joint invasion."

"What then? We are hidden from our enemies. Who will command my army to counter their assault?"

"I will, my lord. I will ride into battle to spare our kingdom from ruin and safeguard your treasure."

"Do you think England capable of mounting a sustained invasion against me?" Henry asked.

"Alone no, your majesty. But with King Philip of France..."

The words forced Henry to consider the worst.

"Philip and Richard were allies before the crusade. Perhaps he will align with England against us," Henry added.

"Would it not be better for the Queen of England to offer a portion of your ransom to Philip, rather than deliver it all to you... if together they can free the Lionheart?"

On that, Henry thought for many moments.

Roger swallowed the smile rushing to his face. He had successfully induced his king to consider the reality of war. He had but one more point to make in the matter of the Lionheart.

"What else can we do?" Henry asked.

Now Roger's slight smile emerged. His tensed muscles relaxed. He feared his king would fail to agree with him.

"My king, you must order a grand tournament. Allow our knights to sharpen their skills in preparation for a battle against the Brits. There is no finer way to hone your defenses than a tournament to rally our men."

On that point Henry thought long and hard. A smile came to his face at the idea of presiding over a grand tournament. All would get to see him, and those who came to participate would swear their allegiance. Without divulging his real intent, Henry could organize his army to defend his kingdom against an invasion—one all hoped might never come to pass.

"A tournament would be fitting, Roger."

"Indeed, it would, my lord."

Seeing Henry's brightened face, Roger concluded his latest idea had pulled his king from his latest depression. A tournament would bolster the spirits of all, including the king and his nobles.

Roger bowed before his king.

"I will order the arrangements. We will send the call throughout the realm for knights. Your generous prize to the winner will guarantee participation. Then we rally the finest of your knights to winter with us in the castle where you hold safe the Lionheart until the ransom matter is resolved."

Roger had pleased his king.

"Even if the queen invades, she will be met with carnage and death. And all the while, Richard remains safe within your walls until the she realizes only delivering the ransom will free her son."

14

A lone hay bale sat in the midst of an open meadow, staunchly out of place against the low rolling landscape. The sun had since floated across the apex of the sky drooping slowly toward the night.

Blackbirds glided in on the air currents to roost on the hay, plucking at strands protruding this way and that.

A moment later the birds launched into frenzied flight when a quarrel whizzed high and wide of its mark.

Ensconced beneath the canopy of entangled beech along the meadow's edge, Rynhawker watched the quarrel disappear into the high grass a hundred paces beyond.

"Remember everything I taught you. You must cease your breathing the moment before you release," Rynhawker said, as a patient knight would instruct his callow squire.

But it was not a squire under his tutelage.

"I executed exactly as you instructed," Joanna shot back with an angry edge to her mounting frustration.

Rynhawker stoically accepted the proffered crossbow, cocked it again then clicked a new quarrel into the channel.

Joanna rose to her knees to accept the weapon, after which, she lowered to the prone position against the forest floor. She set the crossbow on the low of a rotting log. Busy ants scurried onto her hand, distracting her. Rynhawker narrowed his eyes in displeasure when she frantically brushed them away.

"It is not the ant to fear against a charging enemy."

Joanna gazed at him in disapproval. Then she returned to her crossbow lesson.

"Steady first your aim, then check the wind, and only once you are certain, cease your breathing to release the quarrel. You will never hit anything unless you do as I instruct," Rynhawker drummed out, holding his mounting anxiety in check.

He insisted this was a fool's quest, and that what she proposed might never work. But as the princess, she commanded Rynhawker, and he became duty-bound to teach her the crossbow.

Rynhawker suspected this would never come to pass. Yet he must never refuse the princess in any request that did not directly place her in danger.

He waited while Joanna settled in behind the loaded weapon. She concentrated on keeping her aim true upon the dead center of the distant bale while she steadied her hand. Even persistent ants no longer distracted her.

"Never allow your eye to stray," he whispered.

Joanna stopped.

His words fractured her concentration. She set her cheek against the crossbow stock, followed the quarrel off the channel to the bale. She felt in her mind she had lined the shot up correctly.

Joanna inhaled, letting air fill her lungs.

She squeezed the trigger.

Her finger tightened in reflex, sending the quarrel harmlessly left of target.

Rynhawker shook his head, reaching down to accept her hand. He wanted this lesson to be finished for the day. Instead, Joanna handed up the crossbow for cocking.

"Again. I will do this."

"Perhaps we should defer to another day."

"Perhaps we should use the benefit of what sunlight remains to continue," she commanded in return.

Rynhawker dutifully cocked the weapon. Afterward, he sighted down the channel before inserting the next quarrel to confirm its aim held true.

"I can do this," Joanna convinced herself in anger as she studied her target while Rynhawker readied the weapon for her.

"Wind is slight... off your right," he remarked.

She wasted no time, nor movement in setting the crossbow on the log. Settling her trembling hand, she slipped her face beside the oak stock. The wood gently caressed her cheek as she sighted down the channel. The center of the hay bale remained central in her sight. It all made perfect sense—it should be a simple enough task to strike her mark.

This time Rynhawker settled alongside her on the ground, easing his muscular frame against her, so he might sight along the crossbow channel with her. His warmth spread over her. His breath brushed her cheek. Then his hand covered hers to steady it on the crossbow.

Joanna suddenly could think of nothing but the knight. His touch stole away all that she thought about. Having him close stirred urges inside her that she had given up on years before. Feeling his mass tempered her concentration to the point she knew she had no chance of accomplishing the shot.

"Elevate the stock slightly as you aim down the..." Rynhawker whispered the way a lover conveys feelings in bed.

"I know," she whispered in response without realizing her tone matched his, which he might misinterpret to mean something more than it did. Or did it? Did she whisper wanting him to know she felt exhilaration at his closeness?

Rynhawker said no more.

A second later Joanna ceased her breathing. She curled her finger gently around the trigger to let the quarrel fly. The iron tip thumped into the hay bale to the right and above the center.

But Joanna hit the bale!

After twenty-seven failed attempts on this day alone, Joanna hit her target. Now if only all her enemies held the girth of hay bales, she could bring them down with the crossbow.

She screamed her excitement into Rynhawker's unprepared ear.

"Hurry, cock it again," Joanna commanded, forcing the knight to his feet to prepare the weapon.

Joanna accepted it with a snap, settled into her position then raised the stock slightly as Rynhawker had commanded her previous. This time her quarrel found the center of the bale!

The princess sprang to her feet. Her excitement so overwhelmed her that she hurled herself into Rynhawker's arms. When she raised her eyes to his, she so wanted him to kiss her; but Rynhawker remained loyally stoic, the moment passing unfulfilled.

"I trust it is not a bale we intend to hit," Rynhawker corrected with hollow confidence in his voice.

"I will get better, you will see," she chimed.

"How will you cock your crossbow when I am unable to assist you?"

Those words forced Joanna to pause. As hard as she tried, she lacked the requisite arm strength to retract the string enough to engage the trigger.

"You will devise me a way to cock the crossbow so I can fire as many times as necessary."

With that, Joanna triumphantly handed Rynhawker the weapon before marching proudly into the open field to retrieve the spent quarrels.

"We must believe John will find a way to act against whatever we attempt in the service of our king," she said on their stroll to the bale.

"If the prince believes we intend to pay the ransom, his next move is to steal it before it reaches Germany," Rynhawker offered.

"Or attempt to kill our king once he is free, and before he reaches the safety of the English court," she added.

Both situations required due consideration as Joanna developed her plan to free her brother.

"We can protect him once he is free," she said with resounding conviction. "We demand only English knights escort the king once released. No one will be allowed to approach him until we restore him safely upon his throne."

"And if King Philip is in league with the prince? Can we stop his army?"

Joanna paused. Rynhawker's words sparked a new concern. The safest way to restore Richard to his throne was to execute her plan under the veil of secrecy. If no one knew, then no one could mount an offensive against them. Maybe there was a way to accomplish what stirred uneasily inside her.

"We move on winter's onset. No one will expect it."

"Then you have a plan, my lady?" His voice rose at the very thought of freeing his king.

"Indeed. But I require knights with the finest fighting skills."

"I will do thy bidding. Command me, and I shall see it done."

"Collect up the quarrels," she said, stopping before the bale to admire her accomplishment. Her smile proved as bright as the golden dying sun.

"My lady?"

"I will retrieve these."

Rynhawker crisscrossed the meadow locating errant quarrels while Joanna remained at the bale, thinking. She watched him while he located each of her shots. Her growing desire for him dominated her mind.

When he returned, Joanna forced down the sudden urge rising in her throat to kiss him. She so wanted to throw her arms around his neck so she might feel his frame against hers. But she resisted. She had to be especially strong now. She had to focus on helping Richard. The fancies of her heart deserved no place in her mind at this time. Yet she had lost the power to drive them from her thoughts.

Their hands touched when she handed her quarrels over. She refused to draw hers away, choosing instead to cling to Rynhawker's touch.

In the ensuing pause, the moment of desire between them passed unabated. Joanna decided she must find a way to display her affection for him, thereby allowing him to reciprocate to her.

"I bid you to ride into the countryside to solicit swords to our cause," she whispered.

She remained close, forcing herself to release his hand. Then they returned to the forest, where tethered mounts shuffled.

"How many knights?"

"A small number is best suited for my plan. Four or five," she replied in a stout voice. "We cannot trust more than a select few."

The size threw concern into Rynhawker's mind. They would need at least ten times that to face any of Henry's forces.

"How will they serve their king? They will ask."

"That, you will not be able to disclose. Tell them the Crown will grant each a grand reward for their service. But warn them truly, this is to be the most dangerous quest they have ever undertaken for their king."

"My lady, what do you intend?"

"Sir Rynhawker, I have full faith in your loyalty to our king, but even you must remain unaware of my intent. We must protect ourselves from John's evil at all costs."

"Who then shall watch over you while I am away? John's minions could discover you unprotected."

On that Joanna pondered. She needed Rynhawker close to her, wanted him more than he might know, but he was the one she could trust to accomplish this task vital to their success.

"Sir Thomas shall watch over our queen and me."

"You will only improve your aim with the crossbow if you continue to practice as we have today."

"Then Sir Thomas shall advance my training."

15

Two days hence, in that faint glow that precedes the dawn, Joanna watched from the ramparts as Rynhawker trotted over the drawbridge before spurring his stallion into a gallop through the meadow leading to the western forest. She lingered there for hours afterward, despite the blustery wind tangling her hair, convincing herself he would return safely to her.

Before departing the rampart, she tightened her cloak to make her way down the staircase to the keep. Her heart sank at the thought of Rynhawker being away. But she refused to shed a tear.

Sadness and fear competed to consume her.

She found great difficulty in asking Rynhawker to journey on her behalf to recruit knights for their quest. But she had to do it for Richard. Already her heart ached at Rynhawker's absence. She knew deep in her heart that everything she felt for the knight was improper. She understood her station as a royal, and the duties she must accede to for the good of the realm. Understanding that, and serving her king faithfully, did not make the pain any less.

She could find no rationalization that allowed her to sin the way she desired. She spent most of her waking hours, and those wonderfully peaceful moments before drifting off to sleep, thinking about her knight. She wondered if he felt the same way toward her. Rynhawker had entered her life at a time of great tempest. His strength and courage brought tranquility to her heart and mind. Now he would remain there. Joanna knew there was nothing she could do to remove him. Nor did she wish to withdraw him from her mind or her life.

Returning to her bower, Joanna sat at her window with Annalise napping in her arms, staring out in the direction Rynhawker had departed. When she closed her eyes, she returned to that moment when he carried her in his arms to safety in Griswalt's castle. How close she had come to death she could only surmise. Certainly John would have rejoiced had Griswalt delivered on his deed. Even then she realized Rynhawker would be someone special to her.

What if she kissed him? What would be the harm of such an act of passion? Surely God would understand the desire she harbored in her heart. There can be no sin for being in love with someone. Was it not God who placed the power to love in their hearts in the first place?

She wished now she had taken that last moment together before his departure to kiss him. To feel his lips against hers, with his arms holding her close, would have been sufficient to carry her over until he returned. She would see his face in her mind's eye at every turn of the day, and allow the image of his smile to lull her into her night's sleep.

Annalise stirred, thrusting an arm against Joanna's breast, but she remained asleep. Holding the child helped Joanna feel closer to her knight. She gazed at the innocent smiling face, knowing the life the child would now face brought a pang to Joanna's heart. No child should grow up without her mother. Yet this one would. Joanna hoped in time she might know her as her mother.

A part of the princess emerged from hiding, scolding her when her thoughts turned to the possibility Rynhawker might never return from his quest. John's men watched for opportunities against any of Joanna and Eleanor's loyal knights. Her heart raced at the thought of harm coming upon him. Her hands tensed. She wished more for his safety than his failure. He must come back to her. And when he did, she must overcome all restraint so she may welcome him with a kiss. That would make the moment of his return special for both.

Her heart returned to a quiet rhythm when she convinced herself Rynhawker was a seasoned, accomplished knight. He could fight, and he could endure to return. He had fought with Richard in the crusade and survived to come home. Now he would survive again, this time for her.

Hours passed, Annalise awakened to be turned over to Althera for care, and yet Joanna still stared into the kingdom beyond her window. She wondered at that moment about Richard's fate. Was he being treated like the king that he was? Or was he in the villainous throes of Henry's dungeon, with all the fear and dread that notion conjured in the mind.

The more she thought about her brother and his dire circumstance, the angrier she grew. She found her hands gripping her armrests so tightly that her knuckles paled. But anger fuels resolve, her resolve to rescue him. She must cease her adolescent daydreams about Rynhawker and a love that may never be, and instead focus on her plan to bring her brother home.

However, her struggling plan depended on Rynhawker's success. She needed strong, committed knights to lead them into their enemy's den. Yet to succeed, they needed more. They needed to be more cunning than the man they were opposing.

Henry would never suspect Joanna bold enough to come after her brother. That fact, she realized, gave her the edge over her adversary. Now she must find a way to exploit her advantage.

Or would Henry expect a rescue attempt?

Joanna pondered her questions until the last rays of a drowsy sun fell upon her face. Her stomach growled in anger for ignoring it for so long.

A soft rap vibrated her door. At first the sound escaped Joanna's notice. She had wrapped herself in her thoughts the way she wrapped her slender body in fur on a cold winter's night—wishing no one to force her out.

The rap grew louder yet not more insistent.

"Enter," she called at last.

"M'lady," Althera said softly, entering Joanna's bower but stopping just inside the door.

"Is the child asleep?"

"Yes, m'lady."

"Good."

"M'lady, our queen requests you sup with her in her private chambers," Althera conveyed.

Her heart besieged with conflict, Joanna would have preferred continued solitude in her bower. She wished to allow her mind to remain with her thoughts of Rynhawker and her brother and how life will be in her future.

Could Rynhawker love her? Would Richard even allow such to exist? Then again, must she even tell her brother she loved a knight and desired to be with him?

"M'lady, what answer shall I provide the queen?" Althera pressed when Joanna failed to respond.

"I shall. She may expect me within the hour."

She knew she must abandon her thoughts for now. She would indulge her mother. She would speak with her on matters that only concerned the fate of the realm and her king. She would hold her most treasured feelings safe inside her heart, where no one could see them except her and the man she loved.

In time she would find a way to be with him, if he would have her. Maybe she was a fool to think Rynhawker would wish to be with her against the wishes of their king. If Richard forbade their love, which then would Rynhawker choose—her or his oath to his majesty?

Would any of it matter? Richard may never be free again. John may ultimately find a way to seize the throne and destroy both her and her mother. Maybe only in death might she and Rynhawker be together. That thought clung to her mind as she lifted herself from her chair.

After dressing in a golden gown suited for dining with the queen, Joanna exited her bower in the wake of her servant.

16

Joanna exited her bower to Thomas patiently outside her door. He stepped off at a laggard pace behind her.

"I am supping with the queen," she said.

"Yes, my lady, I am aware," Thomas responded.

"Then we must walk faster, lest I anger her with tardiness."

"Yes, my lady, I am," Thomas replied.

Two guardsmen stepped aside the double doors to the queen's private chambers on Joanna's approach. She was expected; she needn't be announced. Thomas took up his position paces to the right of the doors once Joanna entered the chamber.

"Good evening, mother," Joanna said as she approached the queen seated at the head of the table. Joanna was late. Her frown revealed disappointment when she saw a man flanking the queen's left, the Archbishop of Canterbury beside him and another, younger man on her queen's right. Joanna would not be supping with her mother alone. Suspicion crept in as she studied each guest. Rarely did the queen entertain guests in her private dinners, especially in these difficult times. Something felt amiss, though Joanna had no way of assessing her sudden ill feeling.

A servant approached promptly to assist Princess Joanna to her chair beside the man to the queen's right.

"I thank you for attending this evening, Joanna. There is someone I wish for you to meet," Eleanor said.

Her smile seemed genuine and innocent enough. Why did she wish her daughter to meet these two?

The man beside her rose with a broad smile gracing his bearded face. His gaze seemed captivated by Joanna's beauty. Yet his eyes descended rudely below her neckline.

"Duke Laroque hails from Dernsley castle to pledge his service and loyalty to King Richard."

"My lady, may I say you look exquisite this evening," Laroque said while his eyes drank in more of Joanna's sinewy form. Laroque was easily ten years her senior, with thinning black hair that made him appear older. His meticulously maintained jawline beard presented a visage of noble distinction.

"My princess, may I introduce Baron Faulknor from my duchy."

Joanna politely smiled across the table as he rose.

"It is my pleasure to come before our gracious queen and her most lovely daughter," Faulknor said with a smile equally as bright and as bold as his duke's.

Once they returned to their seats, three servants prepared plates along a side table. The queen's came first, though she waited until the others were served.

Suspicion grew as Joanna stared at the man across from her. Flashes of the Baron Griswalt played across her mind. She tightened a fist around her knife as if it were a weapon. That terrible moment when Griswalt violated her crept across her mind. She shook it out to return to her plate.

"My lady, you are feeling not well?" Laroque inquired at the sight of her suddenly colorless face.

"I am fine," she replied.

"Duke Laroque offers us men for our bidding," Eleanor said with a gracious smile.

Now Joanna understood why they graced this table. It also explained why she felt so ill-at-ease around them—a duke parting voluntarily with his knights to help the king.

Once all were served, the guests waited until the queen took her first bite from her pigeon pie. Only then did they begin to enjoy the roasted capons and suckling boar consuming the major portion of their plates. Stewed beetroots and onions loitered about. Laroque nudged the vegetables aside, along with the pigeon pie to focus all his interest on the meat.

"We thank you for your sincerity," Joanna commented. The words sounded shallow, trite, but she could think of nothing more profound at the moment.

"I do believe this is the first time I have tasted this spice," Laroque offered in compliment to the queen.

"It is cardamom," her majesty replied with a smile. "One of Joanna's favorites."

Could either of these two be trusted with the queen? What was their real intent in coming before the crown at this particular moment? What did they know that brought them here?

And why had the queen graciously accepted to dine with them. Certainly their lower station in the kingdom would not warrant such attention from her majesty. If Richard were here, he would have ignored these two sycophants in favor of men who were more deserving of his time.

"Duke Laroque has brought a contribution to the ransom for our king," the queen added.

Laroque smiled proudly at his deed while attempting to maintain humility.

"It is a small token, I realize, but we intend to make every sacrifice necessary to bring our king home."

"And we fully appreciate your generosity," Joanna said, forcing herself to return a smile.

"We have drained our coffers in the service of our king," Faulknor added, much to Laroque's dismay.

Joanna raised a brow. Most nobles hid their valuables from the queen. Why would these two voluntarily part with things most precious to them?

"In these dark times, every sacrifice made for our king will be rewarded fivefold when Richard returns to our soil," Eleanor said.

The queen's words silently angered Joanna. Why should these two be rewarded fivefold? They have yet to prove their loyalty to their rightful king.

"To King Richard. Long live the king," Laroque said raising his wine goblet. Faulknor followed with his, after which came a less enthusiastic archbishop.

Eleanor took up her goblet after the men had finished.

"To freedom for our king," she offered.

Joanna raised her goblet to drink, though she watched Faulknor's eyes across from hers. His very look set the hairs on her arms tingling.

"My lady, I have pledged two score knights from my barony to the service of our queen," Faulknor offered, when it seemed something was expected of him. He bore neither gold nor silver for the ransom, but he could provide men freely in its stead to please her majesty.

Joanna smiled politely, thanked him for his generous offer then picked at the boar on her plate. She would no sooner trust a knight from his barony than she would trust that the duke's offer of gold and silver was heartfelt. She could explain not why she felt that way, but she suspected their presence came at Prince John's behest.

"Twenty of my finest knights have accompanied me here, and we shall remain in the service of our queen until she no longer feels our presence benefits the throne," Laroque added to reinforce his commitment to the crown.

"Your men-at-arms are well appreciated, though I doubt King Henry would place our lands in jeopardy," Eleanor said.

"The affairs of my queen are none of my business... but I pledge every fighting man I command should her majesty decide to return our king through the force of arms," Laroque added.

His words gave Joanna pause. Was the duke seeking to influence the queen's decision? Or was he fishing to discover her intent? Either way, the queen's smile was all he received in return for his offer, along with a nod that revealed nothing about what churned uneasily inside her mind. She would say nothing to anyone outside her small circle of trust.

Even Joanna refused to glance toward her mother, fearing that innocent gesture might reveal clues to the queen's intent. No doubt one, if not both, would race from Londontown to where John hid like the coward he had grown to be, to reveal everything uncovered in the presence of the queen.

Joanna would prefer these nobles depart the queen's fortress with their men to return to their own castles. Here they could uncover information to feed to John. Yet she knew circumstance compelled her mother to accept and allow them in her service until she could conjure a good reason to release them.

A terrible thought seeped through Joanna's mind causing an uncomfortable shudder. Through a few men at a time, John may be infiltrating the queen's security inside the castle, installing his own force capable of overthrowing her guards. The dread of such a cabal sent acid into her throat. She set her knife to her plate noticing her hand trembled at the thought. Was the queen in grave danger? What if that were John's intent all along? When the time came ripe for his assault, his men might already control the fortress.

"When will your majesty reveal her intent concerning our king?" the archbishop asked when the silence begged relief.

"We seek every avenue to bring our king home. I must safeguard the Crown at all costs. Only when we have assured our king's safe return, shall I announce details," Eleanor said wryly.

Even though polite conversation continued to flow around the table, Joanna heard none of it. Her mind reeled over the implications of what she considered. How could she risk leaving her mother unprotected in the castle? If she followed through with her plan, she might save her brother only to lose her mother to their bastard brother. It seemed at the moment she had no way to free Richard while simultaneously sparing the queen, if John still intended to seize the Crown before Richard returned to Londontown. John could keep Joanna out of play for Richard's freedom if fear for her mother trapped her within the queen's castle.

17

Each morning since Rynhawker's departure Thomas positioned himself close to the princess as she conducted her business. Since she spent part of each day with the queen, Thomas could provide protection to both. At least that is what he convinced himself.

He also spent hours with her in private while she sharpened her skills with the crossbow. He deplored the duty, since his time went to retrieving spent quarrels and cocking the crossbow over and over, so she might randomly hit a makeshift target.

But Thomas did come to enjoy the time Joanna spent with Annalise each day. For a few hours, usually in the afternoon, Annalise would sit with Joanna. Together they would stare out the window of her bower at the countryside below. Or they might play together on the floor with a bit or piece that had caught the child's fancy. For Thomas, seeing Annalise brought back the searing memories of Merewen and that terrible day that forever altered his life. He hoped someday the hurt in his heart might fade. But for now, it had failed to abate even the slightest.

Thomas also found it more and more difficult to contain his growing excitement for Sabine whenever he came into contact with the queen while her servants were in attendance. Especially since Sabine had shown him more and more interest with each passing day. He convinced himself it was his knighthood that attracted her and nothing else, since his meager shoulders and his beardless youthful appearance did little to turn young ladies' heads his way.

Sabine shyly averted her eyes each time she found Thomas gazing upon her, for fear Eleanor might see the desire there and know what had developed between her and the young knight. Her heart fluttered each time they came into contact, even if it were only across the queen's private courtyard. She so hoped the young knight would speak to her. At least that would bring them closer.

Later that night, after the queen and Joanna had supped and the servants were dismissed to their bowers, Sabine diverted her return so she might cross the path of the young knight.

She smiled at him, indicating with her eyes that he should follow her. Thomas complied, maintaining a safe distance so as not to become obvious in his intent.

Her heart pounding anxiously inside, Sabine journeyed through the quiet castle halls until she arrived in the kitchen. Once there, she accumulated discarded meat scraps from the platters returned from the knights' hall. But rather than consume the food herself, she moved quickly to the kitchen door, which she pushed out to the small, concealed courtyard beyond.

Both intrigued and excited, Thomas followed seconds behind, believing Sabine and he might share what she had collected.

Once outside they were alone, save for five mangy dogs hoping to scavenge scraps to stave off starvation for yet another day.

The animals pawed at Sabine as she tossed the scraps of poultry about, so that each might have some to him or herself. The smallest of the dogs vied desperately for her attention directly, since every time she dropped a morsel, larger dogs swarmed, forcing the two smaller ones at bay.

"I hoped you would follow, so we might have this time alone together," she confessed.

Sabine scooped the smallest dog into her arms, handfeeding him to make certain he had something to eat. When he finished, he licked at her nose, which brought Sabine's lilting laughter. Her smile captured Thomas' attention when she turned into the light.

After wolfing down their food, much the way knights in the castle devoured their meals, the dogs all gathered politely around her, allowing her to pet and scratch their ears.

"I, too, hoped we could be together," Thomas replied.

He hesitated to reach out for her, fearing the door might burst open at any moment. Thomas had no idea if their budding interest was considered proper.

"I have not seen your knight for some days," she said, casting her eyes to meet his.

"He is on business for the queen," Thomas lied.

He cast his eyes toward the kitchen door, and when it remained closed, he took Sabine's hand.

Their contact sent waves of exhilaration through both.

Sabine clutched his tightly, wanted to make certain he understood how she felt about him. Neither knew the right words to say, yet both knew the right actions to convey their feelings.

She came into his arms quickly, pressing her soft cheek against his. At that moment, she debated about how she should feel. She only knew his touch felt wonderful, and she wanted more.

A thrill beyond compare coursed through Thomas' body. It was the first time he had felt a woman pressed against him. That contact sent excitement spilling into his brain. The warmth and softness of her skin against his sent chills scurrying along his spine. Sabine was truly the most beautiful woman in the kingdom to him, save for Princess Joanna. He savored their contact, hoping no one would destroy this moment by intruding. Even the dogs sensed their intimacy, retreating to provide them their secret moment.

"I wish we could spend more time together," she whispered.

"I wish we could spend an entire day without being apart," Thomas replied.

"Our queen would never allow that," Sabine said in a scolding sort of way, as if Thomas had defied and angered the queen with the very thought of Sabine being away from her charge.

"When will Sir Rynhawker return?"

"Within the next fortnight he has instructed me."

"What takes him from his responsibility to safeguard our queen? Her majesty trusts only you and he to keep her safe."

The kitchen door opened. Thomas jerked himself clumsily away. A serving wench tossed a platter of bones out to the dogs' benefit.

They immediately pounced, vying for a meager scrap to gnaw, with Sabine and Thomas completely forgotten.

18

Iyewebas bolted awake in a darkened corner of the stables. He grew tired of sleeping in the forest in the dreadful fall rain. Unaware of what had forced him awake, fear shot into his head, forcing him upright. He spun to make certain he was alone. Maybe sneaking into the stables for a dry night's sleep was a bad idea after all.

Voices drifted his way from across the structure. Iyewebas had intended to rise before anyone else, so he could slip out into the inner bailey without being discovered. A dozen chargers awaited brushing while tethered to rings on the walls. Luckily, the beasts shuffled between him and the voices. But the terror of being discovered swam through him nonetheless.

He squirmed to become invisible by curling into a stinking mound of hay and dung piled in the corner.

That, however, failed.

Three soldiers appeared, stopping beside a dappled gray charger shuffling near Iyewebas' feet while he feigned sleep. He held his breath, somehow hoping that might help.

"Up, vagrant," a gruff soldier scowled.

Iyewebas remained stone still, though he heard every word.

A second soldier kicked the little man hard in the boots. The strike inflicted intense pain, along with stirring the man from his fake slumber.

Iyewebas sprang to his knees, clasping hands in supplication, delivering grunts in place of words to convey he begged for his life.

"What are you doing here?" the third soldier pressed, using his drawn sword to prod Iyewebas in the ribs.

Iyewebas recoiled from the mean jab, asking mercy with his eyes, while remaining on his knees. He had allowed the blade to prick his skin, fearing if he dared seize it, he might find it next piercing his belly.

"Speak!" the first soldier growled, shoving Iyewebas back into the mounded hay with his boot.

The men laughed.

Iyewebas gestured he could neither speak nor hear. Afterward, he crawled back to his knees.

"Worthless dung, be gone," the second soldier ranted.

"What goes?" Gerand, captain of the guard said, advancing upon his men.

Of the four towering over Iyewebas, Gerand stood tallest, wore the meanest face behind a grizzly beard. The scars disfiguring his cheeks and neck tallied the same number of the many battles he had survived.

Disdain swarmed the captain at seeing Iyewebas on his knees. He initially decided to make an example of this vagrant, lest other beggars seek the same in his stalls.

Gerand's men snapped sharply erect. None spoke. Not one of their stares drifted while standing before the man who ruled them.

Iyewebas determined in that moment that the men feared their captain more than Iyewebas feared them. He, then, should be the one Iyewebas sought to please.

"Found this foul-smelling vermin sleeping in the hay," the first soldier reported.

Gerand peeled his soldiers apart to inspect Iyewebas still kneeling with hands clasped.

"What is your name?" Gerand demanded with a stone face.

Iyewebas felt his heart creeping into his throat. Who must he fear more? The soldiers or the captain.

Iyewebas grunted, motioning to his ears.

"He is deaf and dumb," the second soldier offered.

"Then cast him out. He is no use to us."

Two soldiers yanked Iyewebas up. Their clumsiness, however, forced Gerand to take a step in retreat, placing his boot into newly dropped steaming horse dung.

Anger spread across Gerand's face the way lightning crosses a stormy night sky. He stared at his soiled boot.

Iyewebas surged at his opportunity. Believing this could be the very break he longed for, he jerked free of the soldiers, but instead of running to escape, he dropped to his knees. With his bare hands, Iyewebas scraped the horse dung from the man's leather.

"Perhaps you are good for something after all," Gerand said, chuckling in ridicule while Iyewebas worked the dung from his fingers into the surrounding straw.

"My captain, with the king's tournament near, this one may be of use cleaning out the stables," the third soldier ventured.

Iyewebas shot glances back and forth between the men as if attempting to read their lips. Then he smiled in recognition and nodded in excitement. The men gathered before him had no idea of the opportunity they had just afforded the little beggar.

"Fine," Gerand said, restraining his smile. "He remains in the stables. If he performs well, feed him kitchen scraps... after the dogs are fed."

Iyewebas once again angled back and forth from one man to the next, as if he sought to understand what they had said. Then he reached out his hands in thanks.

Gerand snapped his away before Iyewebas could contact them. Dismissing his men, Gerand marched from the stables.

Iyewebas bowed in respect to his new master. He was in! He had found a way to position himself inside the castle and thereby closer to his king. Now he must worm his way inside the keep to learn the location of the dungeon. Once he located his king, he would find a way to help his majesty escape. Rothbane would be pleased with his new station in life.

Two of the soldiers drifted away while the third, the one who had jabbed him with his sword, remained.

"You will best earn your supper before you receive it," the soldier growled.

Iyewebas bobbed his head in gratifying agreement. He surveyed the stable to locate a pitchfork with which to begin his new job. Retrieving the tool, he went right to work separating horse dung from hay, piling it neatly into a corner.

After only a few minutes, the soldier tired of monitoring the beggar. He wandered off to the opposite end of the stable. Iyewebas returned to being alone while he diligently cleared away dung while contemplating his next move.

A tournament. Was there another opportunity to be had? He would report what he heard to Rothbane in the hopes it might lead them closer to their king.

After a while Iyewebas paused to wipe the sweat from his face, depositing horse dung smears in its place. Only after confirming he was alone in the stables did he risk uttering any words. And he spoke them so softly that only he could hear them. In a weak moment he succumbed to his need to herald his excitement. He wished he could have sung out a cheer, but he knew a soft whisper was all he might risk.

"We shall become good friends," he muttered, though only the charger shuffling beside him heard what he had to say.

19

After four days of relentless riding, Rynhawker reached the small house where he and Merewen had shared their lives. It sat abandoned for the past months. Rynhawker could never bring himself to bare the memories of that place. Until now. Just the approach brought tears, along with a harrowing pang in his heart.

In those moments, seeing the thatched roof and timber door, he relived that fateful day when he returned from his training with Thomas to witness Merewen take a quarrel to her chest. He felt her weight in his arms as he cradled her into her last breath, along with the blood that soaked her clothing. He remembered the look in her eyes as she whispered her loving good-bye. And when he had whispered he loved her, so she would take those final words with her to Heaven.

If only he had returned a day earlier. If only he had remained at home to be with her. He had hated being apart from her, but he knew he must honor his duty to his king. Above all else, he had to abide by his oath of knighthood at whatever cost. But the cost he bore that day was too great for any knight to endure.

He wished now he had kissed her more, that he had held her in his arms more often, and that he had told her how much he loved her. It seemed so terrible to allow those moments to pass unrequited knowing the outcome of that day.

He dreaded facing those memories again. His scream of agony from that moment reverberated inside his brain. He had blocked it out for so long. And now it all flooded back into his mind. The softness of her touch, the gentle kiss she bestowed upon him before his departure.

I will count the days until we are together again, she had told him on his departure.

"I miss you, my lady love," he whispered, somehow hoping she might hear his words from wherever she had gone.

Surely she was watching from Heaven. Would she be angry at how he felt about Joanna now? But they spoke the vows of death do they part. Still, guilt stomped like an angry child about his mind as he neared the door to their home. He decided he must honor her memory for as long as he could.

He dismounted before drawing his reluctant charger through the door into the darkened house. He would sleep in his home for one night, beside the warmth of a fire in the hearth and indulge in hot food to quell his rumbling belly.

He imagined Merewen's angry face at the thought of him concealing his stallion indoors. Her lips would be locked tight across her face, her arms wrapped one over the other at her chest with her brows furrowed. But she would remain, as always, dutifully silent. By midnight the house would reek from animal waste, but Rynhawker could nay afford anyone discovering he had returned, even for a single night.

Then on the morn he would resume his journey. He was close now and could only hope his travels would prove fruitful for the princess and their cause.

England spiraled in disarray. Few knew whose side to take. Align with their absent king, or fall in behind the prince? If Richard never returned, then John would take the throne and dole out harsh punishment to those who opposed him. But that spoke of events yet to come. There was still the chance Joanna could save her brother and restore him to power.

How would other knights feel about the state of their realm? Would Rynhawker find friends or foes in his quest to recruit for Joanna's cause?

Alone, before the flickering flames of a small fire in the hearth, Rynhawker relived the happy moments of his life with Merewen. He saw her smile when he closed his eyes, felt her touch brushing his skin. They had sat together side-by-side so many nights before that day arrived in which he journeyed out with Thomas.

Fatigue overran his thoughts. He at last fell fast asleep, dreaming not of what was, but rather of what might be. Joanna stole his sleeping mind. Her radiant eyes played across Rynhawker's dream sight during his hours of restless slumber. He dreamt about something he might never have. But at least he dreamt.

At the first glimmer of the rising sun, Rynhawker saddled his stallion. Anxious to begin, yet cautious of his surroundings outside, Rynhawker peeled the door open a crack to scan the meadow. This would be the last time he would come here. It would provide the last memory he would carry of his life with Merewen. Annalise was all that remained from their love. He would treasure her all the days of his life. He must make certain she never forgot her mother.

"Good-bye, my dearest love. Do not hate me for being a man," he said with a voice laced with guilt that barely reached a whisper. Only she would hear his final words to her.

Though he would never return to this place again, he would never forget the woman he loved with all his heart and the mother of his only child. But he could never face the agony of reliving the day that destroyed his life forever. It was not a smile on her face as the last thing he remembered of his beloved Merewen—it was the suffering of a villain's quarrel.

Rynhawker drew his skittish stallion out. It seemed even his beast wished to remain.

Then he spotted them. Two riders, fully armored, breaching the forest fringe from where he had come the day previous. They were tracking him.

Seeing Rynhawker emerge, they drew blades, spurring their chargers into frenzied gallop.

Rynhawker slapped his beast to get it moving. As it pulled away, he swung himself into the saddle. Wheeling the beast westward, he kicked horseflesh frantically to gain more speed.

The knights were closing in fast. He had to reach the encroaching forest fringe or fall to them. He could spin around to fight, but the two might unhorse him before he might even the odds.

The riders halved the distance by the time Rynhawker found a crease in the trees to penetrate the forest. Having lived there for a decade, Rynhawker knew every fold and crease in the forest land surrounding his manor. Now he needed that to elude his pursuers. No doubt they were John's men hunting any loyal to the Lionheart.

A hundred strides into the forest the trees swallowed Rynhawker up. He retarded his pace working his way through a dense thicket meant to discourage pursuit. Only then did he shoot a glance over his shoulder. The forest remained silent and still, save for the forced breathing of his mount and his own pounding heart. Threading his way through an entangling maze of pine, he descended into a shallow gully, where he held his beast in check while waiting with drawn sword.

He could launch a charge once the men came within range. If he were lucky, he might slay the first before the second could reach him. His location gave him a first-strike advantage.

A handful of crows fluttered overhead, indicating the men might have abandoned their chase. Delaying another hour for safety, and now satisfied the men had moved on, Rynhawker picked his way out of the gully to resume this journey.

Rynhawker's day of riding wore on uneventful with night overtaking him before he left the forest for a small glade alive with flowing grasses. Churning white smoke drifted from the humble stone house perched at the meadow's edge. The structure stood half the size of Rynhawker's, making use of a lean-to as a stable for a lone dappled charger.

Rynhawker approached with reins in hand instead of his sword. He would be welcomed in this place. He expected to find a friend inside. Halting before the door, Rynhawker dismounted.

"Hail, friend!" he called, expecting a jovial response.

When none came, he advanced to the door, where he pushed it open. It was unlatched. Rynhawker's hand went uneasily to his sword, but he made no move to withdraw it.

"Duchard, you drunken fool," he called into the light coming off a fire in the hearth. The insides smelled of earth and decay.

The interior appeared in use. Discarded clothes lay about. A pot bubbled on the hearth. The enticing aroma of roasting game assaulted his nose. He was famished, but he knew better than to advance further without invitation.

A shattering war cry rose behind him. Before he could spin about, a broadsword's edge fell across his throat.

"It is Sir Duchard!"

Rynhawker made no move to extract his weapon.

"You levy your sword against your best friend?"

Rynhawker's arms went up in surrender.

Duchard's smile broke through his burly black beard that hid jowly cheeks and was speckled with snowy remnants of his dinner. He stood eye-to-eye with the knight.

"Is anyone a friend anymore?" he replied plainly.

Duchard lowered his sword. His smile remained only reluctantly. He had not seen his friend since that night in the forest when he agreed to attack Rynhawker's squire to test his efficacy.

"We have fought side by side against the king's enemies. Does that not make us friends?" Rynhawker said.

"I withdraw my sword."

Duchard stabbed the blade into the dirt.

The two men clasped forearms in a hearty shake.

"What brings you to me, my friend?" Duchard asked.

Rynhawker detected an uncertainty born out of distrust in his friend's eyes. His face conveyed his doubt for even his comrade in arms. John had sown these seeds of mistrust between knights. Now only Richard could restore true honor to his kingdom.

Duchard moved past his friend to the hearth to stir his pot.

"Surely not the aroma of my cooking."

"Yours would be a welcome improvement over my own," Rynhawker laughed.

He leaned in to glimpse the state of Duchard's supper. Hedgehog roasted on a spit. As expected, it was overdone, charred at the edges. But it was meat and it was hot.

"I see your hunting skills have improved little since our last meeting."

Rynhawker indicated the slow cumbersome animal that yielded a vile, stringy meat desperate for spices to make it palatable.

"And still alone," Rynhawker added.

He took a chair at the small table in the center of the one-room home—that being all Duchard required for contentment. His pallet bed in the far corner turned out to be the only other furnishing in the place, aside from Duchard's armor and assorted weaponry of spear, mace and battle hammer, which proudly adorned his walls.

"Then sit and tell me of your travels while we eat," Duchard offered, retrieving a few stewed beetroots from his bubbling lentil pot, transferring them to two metal plates.

"You always were lousy with the bow," Rynhawker commented as he piled his plate with hedgehog.

"I figured you would have starved yourself to death by now," Duchard laughed.

Hunger sent Rynhawker tearing meat from bone. As distasteful as it was unseasoned, it was still food.

"Yet you appear plump. Tell me how that can be."

For minutes neither spoke, choosing instead to indulge in the meal, albeit prepared by a man inept at cooking.

"And what of your young squire? I swear he soiled his breeks at the very sight of me."

Duchard chuckled.

"Thomas was knighted by our queen," Rynhawker offered proudly, the way a father speaks of an accomplished son.

Duchard raised a proud smile at the words. In his own way he had contributed to the lad's success.

"To the knight!" Duchard boasted, raising his goblet of ale.

"And how did that come to be?"

"A story we shall share when our time arrives to give up our swords."

"Then a fine knight he will grow to be under your tutelage."

Rynhawker employed the crust of stale barley bread to clean the plate of the savory fat left from the hedgehog.

"You always greet your friends with your blade?" Rynhawker ventured after a while had passed.

"Do we have friends anymore? In *these* troubled times. The prince hunts those he suspects remain loyal to Richard."

"John will relent in his play for the Crown. This never ends until Richard returns to his throne," Rynhawker said as a way to ease into the purpose of his visit.

"If he returns. I have my doubts."

Duchard pushed back from the table to wipe greasy hands across the front of his tunic.

"So we must band together to protect ourselves against them. You remain loyal to the Lionheart, do you not?" Duchard said.

But Duchard raised a suspicious brow. He had not seen his friend in many months... many months of chaos and uncertainty, months when a weaker knight might align with the prince to escape reprisal.

"I have fought for my king, Richard the Lionheart; I will die for my king," Rynhawker assured him. "Tell me you will do the same."

"To my dying breath."

Still Duchard remained unwilling to accept the words of his errant friend. Yet he did stare deeply into Rynhawker's eyes to uncover what he believed to be the truth behind what he had said. They had never lied to each other in all the years they fought together, either through the deserts of the Holy Lands or on the countrysides of England.

"It is Richard that brings me to your manor this day," Rynhawker said after a pause.

"From all told, Richard is lost. There is no ransom to free our king."

"Is that what they say in the taverns and inns?"

"The queen has taken all there is, still she fails to meet Henry's demands. That is what I hear."

"That is not true," Rynhawker lied.

Duchard showed surprise at the knight's words.

"And how do you know the truth?"

He tossed bones from his platter to the corner.

"I know because I come from counsel with the queen. Her words have reassured me. My words are meant to reassure you."

Duchard laughed a sort of cruel, mean laugh.

"A knight in counsel with our queen. Now you think me a fool."

With the bones having missed their mark in the corner, Duchard kicked them to their final resting place. His face turned suddenly serious—suspicious of his friend.

"Duchard, you still require a woman to clean after you."

"And you refuse to answer my question. Is our king lost?"

Rynhawker paused. Could he trust his friend? Could he trust anyone in the realm at such a time? Was this all folly set in motion by a woman?

Yet he knew he must recruit knights willing to fight for their rightful king. So he must first take a chance on his friend.

"I seek fighting men... for our king," Rynhawker finally said.

"I will wield my sword against any who dare bring harm to him."

"Then you will join me?"

Duchard gazed about his little home.

"And leave all this?"

"Only if you must," Rynhawker offered with a smile.

"For my king, for my friend, I will."

"Unquestioning?"

Duchard's face turned grim. He narrowed his eyes. How was he to respond to such a request?

"If what I heard was true, then the queen has but one way to save our king: Go to war. If what you say is right, then she pays the ransom to bring our king home."

Now Rynhawker took pause. How honest could he be with his friend? Would Duchard join him if he knew the truth? Would nay any knight join him knowing what was destined in their future?

"We are rallying a force to oppose Henry. Your sword would do well to aid us," Rynhawker ventured.

"Then you have others?"

"You and I, my friend, and Thomas."

"And together we three ride against Henry's army to smash through his castle gates and free the King of England from his shackles!"

Duchard's boisterous laugh forced a disquieting clog in Rynhawker's throat. Some of what Duchard had said would be true, but most would be out of the question.

"We shall recruit others to our cause," Rynhawker added.

"Be very careful, my friend, lest you recruit your enemy in the process."

At the moment, Rynhawker had little faith in the statement he delivered. Where would the other knights come from? For now he had no idea. But they had to seek out others willing to fight if they were to have a chance of success.

"And where shall we find these men willing to raise their swords against Henry in defense of their true king?"

"Is there not a knight you would trust?"

Duchard settled back into his chair, releasing a small sigh of contentment from his meal. He took a flagon to refill their goblets.

"Perhaps there is," Duchard said with a glint of a smile.

"Then we ride together?"

"For our king!" Duchard chimed.

"For our king!"

They raised their goblets, thrusting them together with such voracity that they clamored, spilling ale on the both of them.

They downed their drinks.

"God help us all," Duchard said.

"God help us all," Rynhawker joined in.

20

Over the following six days, Rynhawker and Duchard rode from shire to shire in search of knights willing to fight for the rightful king of England. They found no takers. It seemed all were tired of fighting and bloodshed. Their bitter defeat in the Holy Lands had drained them of spirit. Most wished only to be left alone to live out the remainder of their lives in peace. Even impassioned pleas failed to rally men to their cause.

Duchard argued with all his soul for their aid, despite the uncertainty of what would be expected once they reached Londontown.

Rynhawker knew soon the prince would learn of their attempts and launch a counteroffensive against them.

On the seventh day, fortune turned in their favor. Rynhawker and Duchard recruited Alwain, a knight five years Duchard's junior, but one who had fought beside him in numerous battles prior to the crusade. Alwain wore his straw-colored hair to his shoulders hoping to attract younger women; his green eyes revealed nothing but distrust for those he encountered.

At first, Alwain questioned the efficacy of a handful of knights against King Henry's forces. He had received no call to arms from the queen, so he became suspicious such a tactic could be used to bring the knights to Londontown.

The queen's call to arms was the formal edict directing all fighting men loyal to the king to the king's palace. The absence of such implied Eleanor had no intention of amassing an army to return the Lionheart by force. Freedom for an imprisoned royal usually came through negotiation. Alwain had expected to remain in his hamlet for many years to come, and thus avoid the chaos and bloodshed likely to erupt between brothers fighting for the Crown.

But over the course of an evening of stout ale, overindulging in roasted boar and recounting tales of daring times past, Alwain succumbed to his friend's call. He agreed to take up his sword and ride to Londontown to learn more about the nature of Rynhawker's request.

He made it clear, however, through his drunken slur that he had not accepted the quest. Only that he would journey with his friends to learn the true reason behind the desire for his blade.

The following morning, despite uneasy stomachs and heads throbbing in misery, the three departed the village of Penworthy, their return journey estimated to be five days.

On their second day, after sleeping in a forest clearing absent the warmth of fire, they ambled single file down a forest path in the late afternoon. Hunger gnawed in all their bellies as they had forgone breaking the fast to begin their trek at first light.

As they rode, Rynhawker considered their position. Four was certainly an insufficient number for any quest. Joanna would need at least three times that for anything she might attempt. Rynhawker decided he would return to the castle to allow Joanna to determine their next move.

Most all the knights they approached, and there were more than twenty, had quickly and categorically denied joining their undisclosed cause. It seemed Prince John's reach extended far into Richard's lands. Rynhawker worried that any one of them might reveal what he had been told to the prince, which might propel John to plan an assault against the queen. Rynhawker had been cautious to reveal nothing strategic.

Duchard led, clopping slowly a full twenty strides ahead of the other two. Alwain came next, uninterested in closing the gap between he and Duchard. Rynhawker trailed but kept within a few strides of Alwain. They would reach the halfway point of their journey in the next few hours and all remained quiet.

Upon entering a hollow in the woods bathed in late-day sunlight, Duchard pulled his stallion abrupt, twisting to his left.

Something spooked him.

Alwain failed to notice Duchard's sudden stop, narrowing the gap between them.

"What is it?" Rynhawker asked, halting his stallion to maintain distance between them. He peered through the surrounding growth unable to identify any cause for alarm.

Duchard drew his sword, leveling it to fight.

Alwain responded likewise.

"What do you see?" he pressed in a harsh whisper.

Duchard indicated a thicket of pine.

Rynhawker held his palm on his hilt, still unconvinced of a need to brandish steel. He had yet to identify any threat from the surrounding forest.

"To my flank!" Duchard commanded Alwain, who complied without retort, covering Duchard's left while positioning himself to protect from a sidelong attack.

They came like thunder shuddering through the trees. Four knights emerged from the forest thick, no more than a hundred strides distant.

Rynhawker drew his sword, took up his shield, advancing to Duchard's right flank. Duchard's shield came up ready to protect him. Alwain was the last to gain his shield. It had entangled in his straps, refusing to come free.

The marauders closed, swinging blades with unblazoned shields.

As the four knights neared, Duchard shifted his fighting position to protect his friend. Alwain abandoned his shield, bracing instead for the closest knight's attack.

Seeing Alwain vulnerable, two knights veered right to gang attack. Two could take him quickly and easily without his protection.

But Duchard reined his stallion left, placing him in position to thwart one of the knights before he could reach Alwain. With a violent backswing, Duchard struck the third knight in the advance the moment he fell within reach. Duchard's maneuver neutralized the marauders' attack on Alwain, which afforded his friend time to fortify his own defenses.

With a vicious slash, Alwain found a way inside his attacker's shield. His sword sliced the man's side, cutting through the mail at the ribs. But his thrust proved glancing, and though his blade came away bloody, the opposing knight remained mounted.

"Stand your ground," Duchard growled to Alwain, so he might provide his friend the protection of his sword.

A second later, Duchard spurred his stallion forward, Alwain lunged left, which allowed distance between he and his comrades.

The swords clanked as each man engaged a marauder. When one came within Rynhawker's reach, he jabbed fiercely but found only shield. With a backhand slash, he stopped the opposing knight's sword before it could reach his throat.

As steel clashed and driving horseflesh ground into each other, Rynhawker sliced at his opponent to divert the man's charge, which sent him reeling in a tight circle to his right.

Duchard wasted no time blocking his opponent's thrust before angling into the man's sword arm with his own. His blade cut flesh, and once injured, the man's thrusts became impotent. Duchard's next thrust jolted the man askew on his mount.

The black knight abandoned his shield to remain atop his charger, with that err becoming fatal. Duchard's blade brutally hacked the knight's opposing shoulder. With blood spurting from his neck, the man attempted one more swing of his blade; following his missed strike, he dropped headfirst from his mount.

Rynhawker was less fortunate with his opponent, as was Alwain. When Alwain came around to attack his foe, the man leveraged his shield to ram him, plummeting Alwain into soft earth.

Shieldless, Alwain turned vulnerable on the ground—he would be easily sliced up. He needed protection. He wasted a precious second spinning in the hopes of locating one from a fallen knight.

Then he ran out of time.

Alwain spun with a mighty blade swing to hold off the next charging knight. But before the mounted marauder could reach him, another knight charged from the trees! Alwain was certain all was lost as he whirled frantically around. He was out of position to defend himself from the latest brigand's charge.

But the emerging knight attacked the marauder rather than Alwain on the ground. When the mounted marauder came around in surprise to defend himself, the rescuing knight sliced deeply into the man's thigh, severing his artery. As the marauding knight fell away from his sword, the knight thrust in again, only withdrawing his blade as the man fell dead away to the ground.

The fight between Alwain's foe and the new rider had distracted the knight battling Rynhawker. When that knight tilted his shield to witness the other foray, Rynhawker slipped his blade in over the top to sever the base of the neck. Arterial blood sprayed Rynhawker's face as the marauder toppled.

The hollow in the woods fell deathly silent, save for the gasps from the survivors.

Duchard, his face and chest blood-splattered, Alwain and Rynhawker stared uneasily at the horseman poised across from them with his blade still ready but making no advance against them.

Moments of tenuous silence hung between them.

Then the man removed his helm, revealing his identity.

"I thank you for coming to my aid," Alwain said, retrieving his sword before whistling for his mount. The beast had strayed clear of the foray but dutifully remained at a safe distance.

"At the least, it should have been a fair fight," the knight offered.

"I would have defeated him myself," Alwain added.

Duchard laughed, which forced Rynhawker to laugh, while it in turn brought a smile to the unknown knight's face.

"What is your name, friend?" Duchard asked, still with suspicion in his voice.

"Sir Brayson," he offered.

"And who do you hail loyalty to? John or Richard?" Rynhawker added.

Since none in the group displayed markings of allegiance to either side, the question forced the man to answer from his heart, revealing his true allegiance without knowing theirs.

"The true king of England, Richard the Lionheart," Brayson said with no hesitation or fear his answer might cause him to enter a new fight against these three.

"Hail, King Richard," Duchard and Alwain chimed in unison.

"And you?" Brayson posed to Rynhawker. He noticed the knight held his tongue.

"To the Lionheart."

Alwain, ever the scavenger, scampered amongst the dead collecting weapons, shields, rations and anything else of value.

"Where do you ride?" Rynhawker queried.

"To Londontown to offer my sword to the queen."

"Then accompany us," Duchard offered, growing secure enough to return his sword to its sheath.

By this time, Alwain held the blades and shields of the fallen strapped to his charger before regaining his mount. Every weapon and shield could help if they must oppose King Henry's army.

"Perhaps you have food you might share? I have not eaten since the day past," Brayson asked.

"You fight well for a starving man," Duchard commented.

"Then I hope I have earned something to eat."

"That you have, my friend," Duchard said.

He tossed a hearty strip of dried venison to their new comrade.

Duchard wiped the blood from his face as he led the men in a single column clanking through the trees, leaving behind the wounded to die with their fallen comrades.

21

An autumn chill held the air on the morning of the tournament. But nothing would prevent the galleries from quickly filling with nobles traveling from the neighboring lands to view the contest. It seemed every knight within ten leagues under Henry's command chose to participate. Yet none realized the true nature of their participation. No one, save for Roger and the archbishops, suspected they might be going to war against the Brits if Henry's ransom demand went unmet.

Before the sun breached the nearby tree line, Henry arrived with his full retinue to announce the substantial prize for the winner. His proclamation brought cheers from all who gathered on the field. Inspired by the sheer numbers, Henry felt generous this day, believing he would soon receive the ransom he demanded from the queen. So wealth would be his to dole out to the victor.

Ninety-six knights entered the tournament lacking specific knowledge of the prize when they announced their participation. And of course, each believed they would be the winner at the conclusion of the competition. The risk of injury or even death was considerable, but the reward made the risk worthy. Knights lived by honor, loyalty and duty to their king, never by fear of pain and suffering. Now only the reward they might claim with their ultimate victory mattered. Along with the silver came the coveted king's favor. The victorious knight would sup beside his king with his choice of women for three nights following.

Proctors paired participants one against another with the victor each time progressing to face the winner of another pairing until a single mounted knight trotted across the tournament field to claim his prize.

Rothbane cared little for the prize or the competition. He sought only to win the king's good graces as his way to position himself inside the king's court. Only then could he learn with certainty the location of his prey. Henry would keep his prisoner close, so Rothbane believed it only a matter of time before he might learn where they held the Lionheart. His ultimate prize would come when he returned to England to announce to Prince John the deed had been accomplished.

By late morning, Rothbane still waited beneath tall oaks that spread dappled shadows while jousts continued on the field. Iyewebas stood ready to assist his knight before he entered the jousting field. Rothbane convinced himself few could best him in the joust.

"I do not like this," Iyewebas whispered, his darting eyes making certain no one heard their exchange while he tightened straps on Rothbane's chest armor. A single loose strap spelled death on a tournament field.

Knights were paired by their colors, with their banners unfurled at the tournament fence, allowing Rothbane to identify his opponent across the field so he might study his every action while he waited. The man appeared no older than twenty as he paced before his double-belled wedge tent striped in blue and white. Its hierarchy in the tent maze and his appearance indicated an indulgent adolescence. Adding his near constant agitation revealed a knight uncertain of his skills, which bode well for Rothbane. Nervous hands make for faulty grips.

"You suddenly feel the need to speak, mute," Rothbane offered through gritted teeth.

The little man's intrusion banged Rothbane's concentration.

"And if you fall?"

"Your concern for my wellbeing touches me," Rothbane laughed.

"Not you. Our king, our plan," Iyewebas risked, before burying his face in his felt cap.

"When I win, I will leverage my position to locate our king. Then together we will devise a way to reach him," Rothbane explained, smileless.

He needed the serf only until he reached his target. Rothbane never took his eyes off his pacing opponent. He smiled at the man's squire scurrying back and forth offering encouragement.

"You must learn to trust those who know better," Rothbane said, turning for the first time to gaze at his companion.

On the tournament field, a knight in scarlet and yellow unhorsed his opponent on their first pass, with his lance slipping handily inside his opponent's poorly aligned shield.

The crowd vaulted to their feet, raising a thunderous cheer. It appeared the spectators had already selected a favorite. Rothbane intended to usurp the knight's popularity.

Moments later two more flags rose: Black and gray faced green and gold. Rothbane's turn on the field.

"Wish me good fortune, my friend," he said sardonically.

He mounted his blaze-faced black charger, checked his armor once more before setting his helm securely on his head. Iyewebas handed up his lance laced with streaming black and gray banners.

"I will pray you survive," Iyewebas muttered to himself.

Rothbane trotted to the field to face his first challenge.

Iyewebas dashed this way and that to reach the fence, squirming and grunting his desire to view the joust. Few peasants moved willingly, but Iyewebas would let nothing stop him. Much was riding on Rothbane's victory.

When the flags dropped, Rothbane spurred horseflesh with mighty kicks. The beast started slow in the churned-up sward but quickly gained speed. Rothbane had drawn a callow knight, he knew it when he saw his opponent's lance dropping too soon and too low to engage an effective strike.

As the two knights closed, Rothbane shifted his weight askance from the oncoming lance while simultaneously driving his in at the last possible moment. His blunted tip slipped under the man's shield to vault him skyward. Rothbane had drawn one of the many participating knights unseasoned by a real battle. With his first victory, Rothbane tipped his lance in salute to the king before trotting off to the silence of a mostly disinterested crowd.

After observing the first round in its entirety, Rothbane sized up the true measure of his competition. Only two knights appeared capable of challenging him: One of scarlet and yellow, the other gold and blue.

Rothbane had no real squire to attend him, other than Iyewebas, who was too incompetent to benefit him. Nor had he a tent in which to recline until called for his next joust. Instead, like most traveling knights, he lounged beneath the canopy of the sprawling oak with Iyewebas at his side.

"This is too dangerous," Iyewebas whispered while one of Henry's knights unhorsed another with a crack of a shattering lance.

The fallen knight remained motionless for what seemed an eternity. The crowd in unison believed the man dead, until he at last twitched a leg, followed by raising a limp arm. Four attendants scurried to carry the vanquished from the field.

"The king seems pleased," Rothbane commented, ignoring his mute's risky opinion. The knight's smile appeared hollow.

Only occasionally did Henry's gaze stray from the tournament field. Rothbane's opportunity to impress the king grew with each victory he could score. Rothbane and Iyewebas watched as Roger leaned to this king every few minutes to comment on the competition. Roger would be the man Rothbane must befriend once he won the king's favor. He would be the one to divulge what they needed to learn. Men all too quickly divulge their secrets to impress others below their station. While the king would be shrewd, his sycophants would not.

"You will be no help to our king if you are dead," Iyewebas uttered under his breath while he attended Rothbane's saddle.

"I will be a great aid to our king when I win Henry's good graces," Rothbane countered in an equally quiet voice.

It was time.

The trumpeter called for two more flags. The flags rose. Rothbane faced his third joust of the day with his odds of winning improving with each victory.

With a thrust revealing disdain, Iyewebas offered the lance before grabbing the bridle to assist with directing Rothbane's stallion through the crowd onto the tournament field.

Iyewebas hated Rothbane competing. Even short of death, any injury could render the knight useless to his king. And at the moment, Rothbane was the only man fit for fighting. Iyewebas could never defeat any of the soldiers they might come up against.

Secretly Iyewebas prayed his knight would fall without injury and lose his third victory this day.

22

As the last hours of the afternoon drifted away, sixteen knights remained undefeated. Rothbane was one. So was the scarlet and yellow knight. Rothbane sought out the oval marquee pavilion of scarlet and yellow to reconnoiter his opponent. The man rested calmly, shaded from a low hanging sun burning gold. His tent's location relative to the king's proximity indicated the knight to be accomplished, yet not esteemed. If he held higher regard, his tent would appear in the first row rather than the third. He, too, sought the king's favor with a victory to improve his standing.

For many minutes it seemed the tournament had stalled. Nothing happened on the field. The nobles crowding the gallery grew restive. The delay brought concern center in Rothbane's mind. A number of men were conferring with their king, which was at the root of the extended delay. Perhaps the king had decided to alter the tournament at the last moment. That thought sent Rothbane's empty stomach convulsing.

"What is going on?" Iyewebas ground out through gritted teeth while they waited under their natural canopy.

Rothbane remained silent. His throat suddenly went dry.

"Well," Iyewebas risked again, this time making certain no one might hear him.

"I do not know for certain," Rothbane snapped.

"This is bad for us, is it not?"

Iyewebas read the concern upon the knight's face.

Rothbane shifted in his saddle while he waited. Even the galleries began to stir, growing more anxious at the continuing delay.

Maybe they had decided to forestall the upcoming jousts for the following day to allow each remaining knight the opportunity to eat and sleep before next competing.

Then a hulking man beside the king signaled to four men across the tournament field. In moments, six more joined the four on the field to hear their king's declaration. Afterward, the men fanned out to remove the flags used to mark the jousting lanes.

"No," Rothbane muttered in bitter disappointment.

"It is bad?" Iyewebas pressed.

"Very bad."

"Bring both lances to the fence," Rothbane ordered. He tightened his armor straps before nudging his stallion to advance.

The melee. The most accursed form of competition.

Henry's impatience drove him to eliminate the final rounds of jousts, favoring instead to employ a melee to arrive at a victor. The twelve knights would enter the tournament field simultaneously, with unorganized jousting and fighting to ensue until a single knight remained on his mount. Kings favored melees since they most closely resembled the actual battlefield. What better way for Henry to appraise his best in preparation for a battle against the Brits. The twelve best would go at each other. The knights hated melees, since they caused the most tournament deaths.

With the lane flags removed, an attendant hoisted the colors of each remaining knight at opposing ends of the field. Rothbane's flag rose beside the scarlet and yellow. Initially they would ride side by side into the conflict. They would only oppose each other after their immediate opponent had made contact.

Rothbane's toughest challenge would be scarlet and yellow. He could avoid him initially, hoping to see him fall to another before it came down to the two of them.

Paused at the field entrance, Rothbane received his first lance from Iyewebas.

"Remain close to provide me a new lance should I lose mine," Rothbane instructed as the little man stared at the mass of armor and horseflesh assembling on the churned-up turf.

Panic swept through him. He acted like his knight's words had gone unheard. As a deaf mute, he had to make sure it appeared that way to all who cared.

Six knights lined each end of the tournament field. All held lances skyward until the flagman near the king dropped the signal.

Their stallions shuffled anxiously in the dirt, whickering in anticipation of the grand clash set to commence. To the animals, there existed no difference between the tournament field and the battlefield.

The crowd rose in unison when the king's flag dropped. Every serf surged to the fences for the best view of the battle as it began.

Rothbane charged the horseman directly across from him first, his best target being the most direct line. But one had to be on guard in this competition, since knights could combine their strengths to forcing two-on-one confrontations.

Fortunately for Rothbane, no other knight joined his opponent's attack. Rothbane slammed his lance into the opposing shield with a horrible thud, which came just after three other shields deflected lances. The staccato of contact bellowed like thunder.

The crowd cheered when two knights went down. Once riderless, a stallion trampled over the top of a fallen knight, while the other knight regained his feet to scurry haphazardly through the fighting. Horses from the defeated wandered afoot, adding to the chaos. Crushing hooves found many knights during the melee before they might reach safety.

Before Rothbane could drag his stallion fully around for another run at his opponent, a knight on his flank engaged a charge.

Rothbane spun his charger as quickly as he could. He lowered his lance in anticipation. The other knight's lance slid inside his shield—but he missed his shoulder by no more than a hand's width. Rothbane jibbed his stallion sideways into his opponent's. Now within a stride of each other, Rothbane lunged, employing his shield to ram the man askew on his mount. His opponent retained his balance, spurring horseflesh in a clever fading maneuver. He escaped no more than three strides before another lance found him vulnerable. Unhorsed, the knight overturned into the soft earth.

Rothbane allowed himself a brief smile, though undetectable beneath his helm. Another opponent exited the competition.

The moment, however, quickly evaporated. Rothbane needed to locate his next threat. He jerked his warhorse around at the far end of the field. The knight in scarlet and yellow lined up on him and kicked into his charge from the opposing side. Rothbane would have preferred to avoid this clash until the final exchange, but that opportunity was now gone.

Dropping his lance into attack position, Rothbane laid spurs to stallion, achieving full gallop just in time to meet scarlet and yellow near the field's center. Their lances slammed shields instead of armor—but Rothbane's lance splintered in half at its midpoint.

The crowd cheered scarlet and yellow to acknowledge a victory that proved premature.

Panic took control of Rothbane's brain. He rode weaponless. Seeing him unarmed, another knight pivoted his stallion for a charge. Rothbane became the weakest on the field.

Where was Iyewebas?

Rothbane yanked his stallion to point it to the gate, where Iyewebas waited, terror-stricken at the danger. The little man forced through other squires to reach the opening. He hoisted the lance by its handle. His knight had to reach it in time.

Kicking his beast again and again, Rothbane prayed he could gain his weapon before another could unhorse him. He reined hard right, narrowly avoiding another knight's lance.

His panicked jib almost succeeded.

At the last second, he angled his shield to deflect another incoming lance. When the weapon contacted, it slid up and away, neutralizing the assault. But the lance's blunt tip clipped Rothbane's shoulder before angling off his body.

Searing pain ripped like fire into Rothbane's head. Instinctively, he lowered his shield, potentially exposing himself to a deadly strike from yet another knight. Fortune prevailed. No other knight could reach him before he reached Iyewebas.

The exchange of new lance executed smoothly despite Rothbane's weakened condition. He seized the handle while Iyewebas released it in time to retreat before being trampled himself.

Armed with his new lance, Rothbane came around to locate a target. Scarlet and yellow was mounting a charge against him with his lance already in position.

Rothbane angled his shield to thwart the attack, but the pain coming off the movement forced him to lower his protection.

Scarlet and yellow maintained his charge, knowing Rothbane's injury would assist the charging knight.

Rothbane shifted rearward on his stallion, lowered his lance
as best he could to align it with the scarlet and yellow target. He
knew his only chance of surviving the next strike was to slam his
opponent's shield first, forcing him off balance before he might
complete his run.

The lances slammed shields simultaneously. Rothbane's lance
missed its mark. The scarlet and yellow lance rammed Rothbane's
shield high, but sufficient to unseat Rothbane from his galloping
mount.

The darkening sky crossed Rothbane's eyes through the slits
in his helm. He thudded on his back, which took his breath away.
For him the tournament was over. He lay there many long moments
writhing in pain, with light entering his eyes through the eldritch
blur of a collapsing tunnel. He fully expected the next horse by to
trample him.

When he at last removed his helm, he saw three knights still
on horseback bearing down on each other, all vying to emerge the
tournament victor. The pain in his shoulder lessened more than the
pain in his mind at his defeat. His chance of getting close to the
Lionheart evaporated.

Moments later, Rothbane had no idea how many, as it seemed
everything moved slower than real life, the scarlet and yellow
knight trotted before the king to claim his prize.

By the time Rothbane rose, Iyewebas had left the tournament
gate. Even his lowly serf abandoned him.

23

Joanna rushed into Rynhawker's arms the moment he entered her bower. She feared she had lost him forever.

A lone torch lit the vaulted expanse of her chamber, casting a glow upon their faces and the tears sparkling in the princess' eyes.

At that moment she felt so warm and secure in his grasp. So much so, that she hoped she would never have to leave it again. She knew not how to deal with the feelings swimming in her mind. She had never been in the arms of a man she actually loved. She had never felt love for the men her king forced her to wed, be it her father or her brother. To be a princess was the dream of all young women. To live the life of a princess was to sacrifice all for your kingdom.

Rynhawker brought her face away from his.

Her jubilant eyes held his in the flickering light.

Without contemplation for her actions, she kissed him gently on his lips.

Her knight did not resist.

Joanna released herself into his arms, and his passion, as he held her kiss against his lips.

So much confusion swirled inside the knight's head. Joanna was the first woman he had allowed himself to become close to since losing Merewen. A part of him grew angry for kissing her. A part of him warned what he did went against God, and he must draw himself away. A knight and a princess could never be. They could never love each other. King's law forbade royalty from lowering their station.

"I prayed thrice daily that you would return to me," she whispered so only he could hear.

When Rynhawker attempted to draw away, she thrust her arms tighter under his to keep him against her.

"I could think of no other the entire time we were apart," Rynhawker replied.

Feeling his breath against her cheek, the manly air he spread to her and the firmness of his muscled body sent her into a swoon. She so much wanted to share her bed with him. She wanted to feel him in love the way the others had forced themselves upon her. She desired to give herself without reservation for the first time in her life.

Yet she resisted.

"We must not," Rynhawker finally forced out.

"Please. It is meant to be," she pleaded.

"I am not..."

She stopped him with a finger to his lips.

"You are. I can resist my yearnings for you no longer."

Rynhawker kissed her again, to be certain there was no err in what they shared. He thought he would never love another after watching his dear Merewen fade in his arms. He scolded himself when he considered what would come next between them. Could he even go through with his feelings for Joanna? Should he pull away now, leave her chamber before he allowed himself to sin in a way that would burden him the rest of his life?

"Please stay with me," she begged with her words as well as her eyes.

Rynhawker surrendered to her touch.

"My lady," he began.

Her kiss silenced his response.

"It is not your words I must have at this moment," she said when their lips parted.

His touch sparked a fire deep inside her that could only be quelled with his love.

She refused to allow him a response to her request. She knew in her heart what she was about to do was wrong and would bring only pain and heartache. But for the first time in her life of thirty and two years, she wanted to be with a man. For in this moment, she would do anything to feel what love felt like in her heart. She would defy God, her church, her mother and her brother the king to know the swells of true love in her soul.

Rynhawker surrendered to the maddening desire consuming his body. He drew Joanna into his arms, felt her warm hands wrap his neck as he carried her to her bed.

In the dark quiet of the deepest depth of night, Joanna felt the love she so wished for since the onset of her adolescence. She now knew what it felt like to actually be in love with the man who bedded her.

Rynhawker's gentleness brought her to the pinnacle of what she felt inside. Their moments of ecstasy lingered as they slept lightly in each other's arms.

Joanna wished for this night to never end. She refused to release him when he sought to exit her bed before the first rays of a dawning sun might find their way into the princess' bower. At all costs, he must vacate before the light of a new day exposed the sin they had committed. No one could ever know they had shared their love for each other. No one, except God, would ever know Joanna had allowed a man in her bed, at the worst, a knight.

At last Joanna released him, so he might locate his clothes. He dressed awkwardly, groping about like a blind cripple. She smiled when he stumbled in the darkness. His clumsiness seemed the antithesis of a valiant knight. Or did it just make him human?

They needed no words to know how they felt for each other. Their actions in her bed conveyed that without retort.

Before leaving, Rynhawker knelt beside her bed. She came to him so he might kiss her once more before they tore themselves from each other.

A moment later Rynhawker slipped silently away, disappearing into the corridor while darkness still shrouded his departure.

Joanna turned over in her bed, curled herself tightly under her fur wrap, and there, she drifted off into her first deep restful sleep in weeks. Rynhawker would be in her dreams. Her knight would be forever in her heart.

Hours later, with the sun probing through the window drapes to see if she were alone, Joanna awoke with a start. She recalled every moment of the night, had relived it over and over in her dream. But in its aftermath, pain and remorse spread through her like fire through kindling.

Tears took her eyes. She had found someone to love who loved her in return. She had someone to give herself to until he could have her no more. She found someone to share her life with.

Then thoughts of what they were about to do buoyed to the surface. She scolded herself for feeling the way she did. She knew the dangers they faced in the coming months would take each, if not both, to the brink of destruction. Now that she had found Rynhawker, they would face death to save her brother.

For a moment she searched her mind. Was there any other course of action? Could she find a way to free Richard without jeopardizing her life and the life of her knight? Could they negotiate a lesser ransom suitable to the King of Germany? What if they failed? Would Henry follow through on this threat to kill the Lionheart? Certainly, if he failed to deliver on his threat, he would lose face with not only his subjects but also his neighboring rulers.

Joanna could not bear losing her knight, nor could she bear losing her brother. It was her brother who freed her from that tyrant of a king in Sicily. It was he who rescued her from an evil man's pleasure of inflicting pain upon her in their marriage bed.

Her father had arranged that marriage. She was the gift that bound the King of Sicily to the King of England. Chattel, nothing more. A gift the receiving king could treat as he wished, then even destroy if he so desired.

Could she instead remain in England and pray Henry released Richard to return to his crown? Could she ever trust the King of Germany?

Could she trust God?

Joanna spent the entire day in her bower. She refused her servant Althera, postponed her daily visit with Annalise, and instead, she contemplated what she must do, and how her decision would alter her life and the lives of all those she loved.

Most importantly now, she might be deciding the fate of the man she loved. If she continued on the path that took them into Henry's lands, she might lose her knight. If she resigned to allow the queen and God to decide Richard's fate, she might lose her brother. She could never long endure the loss of either in her life.

She vowed to find a way to have both. She would rescue her brother from the evil on the continent, and yet in doing so, still keep her knight safe from harm.

Was that even possible?

24

Without a word of explanation, Rynhawker led Duchard, Alwain and Brayson out the castle gates into the surrounding forest. His cryptic request left them uneasy about what was to come. Could they be going up against John's forces? How prepared with they to fight? They rode for hours without the knowledge of where they were going, why they had departed the castle, or when they might arrive at a destination.

Their grumbling grew more insistent as Brayson and Alwain fell further behind Rynhawker and Duchard. The trailing two rode side-by-side, while the other two maintained single file. While they felt vulnerable along the forest trail, they tempered their fear with the belief Rynhawker would never lead them into harm's way without informing them first.

"Do you think the young knight Thomas is unseasoned?" Brayson queried Alwain, his voice low so the others wouldn't hear.

"He appears too young to have fought in the Holy Lands," Alwain agreed.

"So we risk having one so callow at our sides? I, for one, do not trust him fighting beside me," Brayson pressed.

They clopped on in silence for a few moments.

"We must have each other's guard. You may trust in that, my friend," Alwain offered.

"And what of Sir Rynhawker? I notice he limps on occasion. Tell me, should we trust our very lives to a squire and a cripple?"

Brayson's words set Alwain's mind agitating. What exactly was he enlisting his sword to do? Everyone still refused to divulge the reason they were recruited to the castle.

Falling to last in line, Alwain suddenly stopped, sweeping the expanse of the surrounding trees in a focused glance. They were in the middle of a forest with no obvious destination in sight with the late hour casting long shadows.

"I go no further!" he shouted, his restrained anger overrunning his voice.

A few strides further Brayson reined his charger to a halt.

"Nor will I!"

The other two likewise stopped. Rynhawker nudged his stallion's snout about only reluctantly to face his comrades. He had asked for their trust, which had only taken them this far. But the knight feared if he revealed anything about the nature of what was to come, they would all return to the castle. He and Joanna could be left with nothing.

"We are close now," Rynhawker called.

He read his comrades' eyes. Clearly, they had reached the end of their faith in him. Rynhawker steadied his stallion when the beast drew onto hind legs. Duchard came beside him in a display of unity.

"Do not abandon us. You will understand soon enough. For now, know that I lead in good faith."

"Good faith? Ha!" Brayson shouted. His hand went uneasily to his sword. The surrounding gloom caved in around them.

"We do this for King Richard," Rynhawker persisted, though his words failed to rouse loyalty.

"Before the sun leaves the treetops we shall arrive at our destination," he promised.

"We must go. Our delay only jeopardizes our safety," Duchard injected.

"Our safety from what?" Alwain pressed.

"These lands may be rift with the prince's men," Duchard offered.

"You will see soon enough," Rynhawker added.

Rynhawker wheeled his stallion to renew its slow gait up a rise into the thickest part of the forest. They would be there soon enough, he thought to himself, but will they stay... once they know the truth. The words churned uneasily in Rynhawker's mind. Even *he* began to question that he had taken on a fool's quest—one destined to fail, or worse, one that could never rally the men around them.

Another hour passed before Rynhawker stopped the men in the midst of a wide hollow in the trees. Fading sunlight pierced through the crown canopy to bathe them in warmth as they waited. Their stallions whickered sensing their riders' uneasiness.

Instinctively, Alwain and Duchard fanned out, positioning their mounts so they could control their perimeter. Brayson shifted toward the center for time to react to any sudden attack.

They expected to arrive at an inn or village where they might find food and ale to warm their insides. Their muscles ached from the extended time on their mounts. All looked forward to sleeping in a soft bed this night.

"This is where you lead us?" Alwain griped, his eyes roving the trees in constant agitation. There had to be good reason behind why the knight stopped here. As each moment passed in silence, Alwain grew more uneasy.

Yet Rynhawker remained mounted, as if even he grew uncertain of this place and the dangers that might lurk in its vicinity.

"You have wasted our time!" Brayson snarled.

Duchard remained still without comment. He trusted his friend's pure intentions, even if they seemed misguided.

"I have not. You must be patient," Rynhawker barked back.

Alwain nudged his stallion beside Rynhawker.

"I will not get caught unawares at night," Alwain charged.

He jerked his stallion's snout to return it to the path that had brought them there.

"Your king... thanks you for your attendance," Joanna called unseen amongst the trees.

All heads twisted to find the voice well concealed behind dense foliage.

"What is this?" Duchard called out, now raising concern about the events unfolding.

He took to his sword out of reflex, though he felt no immediate danger in the exchange.

"You find need to levy your sword against me?" Joanna asked.

She breached the clearing. Thomas followed a few paces. They joined Rynhawker at the lead of the group. Her dappled palfrey moved slowly, burdened with provisions.

When she threw back her cowl exposing her face, the knights tightened on their reins to approach her.

"Princess Joanna," Alwain said, bowing with no more than a head nod.

"Why do you summon us to this remote place?" Duchard pressed.

"For the service of your king. Your true king," she replied.

"Long live the Lionheart!" Brayson shouted.

"This is not the time, nor the place, to hail our king. We meet here to prevent those who would usurp Richard's crown from discovering our cabal," Joanna said.

The men looked to each other.

"No one can witness us together, lest your lives be placed in peril. John's minions infiltrate our castle. Only here can I guarantee you, and the secrets we share, will remain safe."

"And what is our intent, my lady?" Duchard asked.

Joanna tossed three slain hares from a lanyard on her saddle to the ground in the clearing.

"First, you have journeyed long. Begin a fire."

Gathered close around the meager light and warmth of the small campfire, Joanna allowed the men to eat and drink their fill before she spoke. Few words were exchanged, each waiting in anticipation. All wished to learn why they had been summoned. Joanna suspected she knew how this night would go, but she hoped somehow she might convince these men to enlist in her plan.

"You have not asked us here just to feed us well," Alwain said.

He seemed the most skeptical of the group. He may become the most difficult to convince. Joanna studied each man around her while the fire hissed and crackled.

"Yes, faithful knight, I have asked you here for a purpose more noble than any in the kingdom that might be asked of you," Joanna replied.

Her words drew questioning stares from all three knights, who looked to Rynhawker. They realized in that moment he was privy to the princess' intent, while they were kept unaware.

"We are going to help our king," Joanna said plainly, watching their eyes. However, she disliked what they revealed.

Their initial reaction would be their most telling, revealing what was in their hearts. Could they be trusted? Would they be willing to risk all for their king? It was a simple matter to recite the oath of knighthood—much harder to live up to it when death faced them squarely.

And that time had come.

At first they laughed at the notion. They were but five knights against an army.

"How will we do that?" Duchard ventured.

Intrigue snared him.

"The details you learn only when needed. Secrecy is paramount to our cause. For now I ask you trust in what I say and what we will do," Joanna answered.

Her response came simple and honest. Yet all sensed from her tone and the weight of the words this would be the most perilous quest they could undertake.

"Milady, you have said we. It is not your intention to lead us, is it?" Alwain asked.

He saw no need to hide the concern in his voice. She suggested the unthinkable.

Duchard shot a sidelong glance to his friend. Inside he fumed at the notion of the princess ordering him. She was no more qualified to command knights than a page is to mount a charge in a tournament.

"I have devised a plan. One that requires your absolute trust in what I command," Joanna started.

Having none of it, Duchard shook his head dismissively, which angered the princess. Her restraint would control the tide of their exchange.

She held back, bracing for the worst and waiting for responses. The men were either too astonished to react or too angry to speak. Her faulty word choice placed them on edge.

"You would need ten score knights, or at least more than I see here," Duchard spoke up.

"The more who know, the greater the risk of exposure to our enemies. Only we who sit before this fire shall be privy to this night and what it means to the future of England."

Alwain tossed aside his flagon of ale.

"You think us fools. You wish us drunk, so we may agree to such foolish thoughts?"

"This is no foolishness," Joanna countered, her voice rising in anger. She knew here and now she must stand her ground against these men. Without their respect, her daring plan stood no chance of success.

"A woman intends to aid our imprisoned king? You do think us fools," Duchard charged.

All three grumbled in support of Duchard's statement. The knight's disbelieving look he cast upon Rynhawker caused him to stir in his place.

"Certainly not fools. I require the bravest, most trustworthy knights in Richard's realm. Are you five stout enough to undertake my quest? I ask you now. For only the bravest will consign to what we are about to do."

"I'll not be led by a woman," Alwain burst in anger. As for himself, he wanted no part of this.

"Nor will I," Brayson rallied beside his comrade.

The two men cast aside food and drink to leave.

"You are bound by your code of chivalry and the command of our queen, are you not?"

"She does not lead us into battle. And you are not the queen!" Brayson charged back.

The men marched two steps toward their tethered mounts.

"You would abandon your king in his darkest hour... in the time he needs most those who believe in him? Because I am a woman?"

The princess faced her most critical moment. They would either choose to follow or all would be lost.

"I will never desert my king," Rynhawker announced.

Those were the first words he had spoken.

"Nor will I," Thomas added.

Silence held the clearing on tenterhooks, shattered only by the sharp snap of an exploding ember between them.

"Nor will I," Duchard finally added, succumbing to the intrigue.

He stabbed his dagger into the ground before him.

"Command me, princess. I stand ready to give my life for my king," Duchard concluded.

While the men looked long and hard at each other, Joanna's eyes never strayed from Alwain and Brayson. She needed every man they could recruit.

Alwain returned to the fire first.

Then Brayson returned beside him.

25

Prince John strode into the court of King Philip with a king's swagger. He convinced himself it was simply a matter of time before he ascended the throne of England. His mother could do nothing to prevent his coronation once Richard had been disposed of. And he would eliminate the Lionheart at whatever the cost.

Philip sat upon his throne with his robes tight across his body to stave off a morning chill. John was surprised Philip granted his audience so quickly. Yet now they shared a common enemy, a bond sealing them together for the good of both kingdoms.

"What news do you have for me this day?" Philip asked, dispensing with the posturing typical between kings.

John held no power to conduct the affairs of England with France. He was a disgraced prince, and as such, a man without a kingdom. He was a traitor in his own land and welcomed here only in as far as he might allow Philip to advance France's agenda.

John bowed out of respect, hoping the gesture might elevate him in his new ally's eyes.

"I bring no news from Henry," John started.

After speaking he realized a better strategy would have been to withhold information from the king. He had no certainty regarding what Philip might do once he learned the deed against the great Lionheart was done. Would he attack England before John might take the throne?

"So your man has yet to succeed... if he is even still alive."

"He is alive, my lord, of that I am confident. But Henry is a cunning fox. He will hide his prize well."

"How much longer then must I wait to gain the advantage?"

"Soon, your majesty. Our time will arrive soon enough."

Philip pressed back in his chair. He found himself disliking the prince the more he listened to his strident voice.

"Perhaps I have chosen a weak ally."

"I promise France will grow strong through our union."

"And should you fail, who then pays the retribution of your angry king?"

John allowed the first glimpse of a smile to grace his face. He had positioned the King of France well.

"There is another reason I come before your majesty. One which may allow us to advance regardless of circumstance. One that eliminates the possibility of our failure."

Intrigue caught Philip's mind. The king raised a hand, dismissing two archbishops standing in attendance behind him. The men dutifully bowed before their king, after which they departed through a side door.

The two were alone to speak unencumbered.

"I am intrigued. Speak freely, prince."

"What if we could ensure the Lionheart never interfered with our kingdoms again, regardless of my mother's decision? Would you align with me?"

Philip shifted forward on this throne. Something that kept Richard from England forever, was that even possible?

"Go on."

Suspicion crept into his response. Could this be a ploy to manipulate him into doing John's bidding? Had John become suspicious regarding the intentions of the King of France? Certainly even the prince understood what was at stake in this conflict between Germany and England. Richard's recklessness had jeopardized his kingdom's very existence.

John witnessed the glean in Philip's eyes that his words had planted. He touched upon one of the king's secret desires.

However, Philip held his smile in check. He needed to understand much more before he might allow excitement to supplant suspicion toward the prince's intentions. And he needed to know the cost of John's cabal to France.

26

Gerand descended the staircase to the stench of dungeon air with Iyewebas in tow. Weeks of loyal servitude to the captain had brought Iyewebas to the point he had been praying for. He had yet to confirm if his king were imprisoned here, but he knew if he had the chance to find out, he could then move on to the next castle if this quest proved fruitless.

The dungeon door unlocked with a clank as the guard inside opened the formidable iron-bound timber for them.

"Someone to clean the filth from the cells," Gerand said with the glint of a smile.

Iyewebas was being promoted from cleaning horse dung. His face held a stone-cold stare while his heart raced inside his chest. His mind churned with a handful of possibilities. He was about to gain access to the prisoners. He prayed silently his king might be here. Cultivating the trust of the captain had brought him here, and all his effort would go for naught if Henry had imprisoned the king in another castle. But Iyewebas' logic held that if Henry were in residence, then there stood a fair chance his prisoner would also.

"This way," the guard snapped, offering Iyewebas no more than a casual glance.

Iyewebas held fast, staring into the dim light flickering off torches ten paces distant. He pursed his lips as if in deep thought, posing unaware that he had been addressed.

"He is deaf and dumb," Gerand informed the guard.

The man grabbed Iyewebas at his collar, which brought Iyewebas' eyes to his.

"Grab a bucket there, and come with me," the guard yelled harshly, expecting Iyewebas to somehow hear him and respond.

Gerand shook his head.

"He is deaf. Yelling does not allow him to hear you," he corrected.

For a moment the guard became lost in what he should do. He never had the occasion to deal with someone deaf and dumb. After a pause, he yanked Iyewebas to the bucket to place it roughly into waiting hands.

"You muck out the cells," the guard muttered. Then realizing the futility of it all, he tugged Iyewebas along with another guard to the first cell in the corridor.

Iyewebas controlled his breathing so as not to appear anxious the moment the cell door unlocked.

While one guard swung the door open, the other drew his sword, tilting it at the ready. Iyewebas half expected the rush of a flailing prisoner from the way the guard postured for battle.

Inside, four men huddled across the cell. So grimy were they that only the whites of their eyes appeared in the darkness. They more resembled frightened rats than men. The first guard tilted a torch in to survey the occupants.

"Against that wall," he ordered the way a king commands soldiers.

The men scurried in response.

Iyewebas noticed the leather whip dangling off the first guard's belt. The thought of his king enduring the whip sent shivers up Iyewebas' spine. Certainly, they would respect Richard as the king he was.

"Remain there," the first guard commanded. He planted both feet inside the cell. The second guard followed, and only after all men huddled in the corner did he temper his sword.

When torchlight landed on the prisoners, Iyewebas could see ashen skin. Who knew they had been deprived of sunlight and proper care. Anger and hatred swelled inside the little man's chest. Not for the treatment of the prisoners, he could care little for what King Henry did to his own subjects, rather for the implication of what he might find when he at last came upon his king.

No one moved for many moments, including Iyewebas.

The guard then pulled the little man into the cell, where he stood dumbfound in the weak light falling off the torch.

"Pick it up," the guard ordered.

Iyewebas measured his response. If he moved, if he responded in any way, he might inadvertently reveal his deception. Certainly, he would not understand what the guard commanded.

The guard lowered his sword to the dung piling up in a corner.

Iyewebas now understood. He had cleaned up so well after the horses that they promoted him to cleaning up after the prisoners. More the better if he were correct in his thinking.

Without delay, he lowered himself before the piles, where he reached with one hand while steadying himself with the other on the bucket.

"Not you, fool!" the guard corrected with a growl.

Iyewebas waited until the guard jerked him back. A silent sigh of relief slipped out unnoticed. He wiped his tainted hand on the leg of his breeks.

Slowly and painfully, each of the prisoners crawled forward to retrieve the waste, which they placed into the bucket Iyewebas held for them. Once complete, Iyewebas waited until the guard jerked him back to retreat from the cell. Standing with the bucket in both hands and enduring the stench of its contents wafting to his nose, Iyewebas waited outside while the door closed.

They moved to the next door in the row.

By the time they had exited the third door, the bucket grew half full. The stench hitting Iyewebas' face was more than he could withstand.

The fourth door brought more of the same with the exception of a motionless prisoner curled in the corner. Dead for days, Iyewebas learned he was also to haul out the corpses. Emaciated from extended starvation, it required surprisingly little strength to drag the body out by its stiffened leg. The sound of the bones snapping out of sockets sent Iyewebas' stomach into his throat. Once out of the cell, the guards locked the door and moved on. Iyewebas wondered who then removed the body from the dungeon. He hoped it was not him. Just touching the dead caused him to cross himself thrice in rapid succession.

Four more doors later they approached the end of the dungeon corridor. His heart sank when he realized his ruse would all be for nothing. On the opposing, he had succeeded in determining this castle did not hold his king. With the morn, he and Rothbane could travel to the next fortress, advancing deeper into Henry's domain, hoping the next would bring success.

Iyewebas waited in the corridor. The bucket grew heavy as the guard unlocked the last door. For this one, though, a third guard advanced into the light. He planted himself beside the others with sword ready. All three now levied blades before unlocking the door.

The very sight caused Iyewebas to leap for joy in his mind. Additional security could mean this cell merely contained more prisoners than the others, he tempered. Maybe there were a dozen men inside and that alone warranted an additional blade.

Or maybe...

The door swung full open. The lead guard filled the frame.

"Retreat to the far wall," he commanded.

At first, there came no movement from within. Then Iyewebas spied a silhouette crawling from them. Then another rose to shield the one moving. A third came up unsteadily.

Iyewebas spied Baldwin's face first, hidden behind mangled hair and the grime of neglect.

The little man's heart leapt. The man standing beside Baldwin, the man assisting him erect was King Richard!

Masterfully Iyewebas buried his surprise. He had located his king! His mind raced in a hundred directions. Was now the time? Should he reveal his true self and attack the guards? He need only give his king time to overpower them so they could seize their swords.

The other guards crowded in, flanking the first.

Only two long strides separated Richard from a weapon. But what if Iyewebas failed? What if he became a prisoner like his king? No, Iyewebas needed patience. He had to plan and scheme to devise a way to help his king get free. Now was not the time.

For a torturous moment, indecision plagued the little man. He could ill afford to err at this critical juncture. He had no weapon. But maybe he could grab a dagger from the guard's belt.

Before Iyewebas could devise a workable plan, the guard thrust him toward the piles in the corner.

Did Richard know it was Iyewebas? What if he failed to recognize his humble servant before him?

Iyewebas lowered the bucket into stinking straw.

"Pick it up," the guard ordered.

No one in the cell moved.

Richard remained defiantly stoic against his captors. After moments of weighted silence, Hugh stepped toward the corner.

"Not you," the guard growled, angling his blade at the Lionheart. "You."

Richard stared into the cold eyes of his nemesis.

Iyewebas shifted into the light, drawing Richard's eyes onto him. As torchlight flickered in, Richard discerned the features of Iyewebas' face. The king's eyes subtly revealed recognition.

Iyewebas' hand twitch acknowledged his king's signal.

Baldwin took that first step past his king to vacate his corner.

"On your next step, you fall to my sword," the guard barked, angry now at their opposition.

The second guard's sword fell in line with his comrade's. Richard pressed Baldwin back with a stern hand to his chest.

"Be quick with it," the guard ordered, relishing his control over the king. His blackened teeth shone in his haughty smile. He wanted the moment to last as long as it could.

Richard lowered to a knee, where he moved the piles from the corner into the bucket Iyewebas held. The action allowed Richard the opportunity to scrutinize Iyewebas' face to fully confirm his identity. Their eyes met before Richard returned beside his men.

Richard's heart raced. It was his comrade from the ship. The king maintained a stone visage for the guards, all the while contemplating the meaning of their exchange.

The three guards laughed in ridicule at first, after which they backed out, posing their swords defensively to ensure a safe exit. No prisoner made any motion toward the guards, nor in any way posed a threat. But the guards knew to treat these three with due caution, lest Richard attempt another foolish escape. No one expected the king to remain a cooperative prisoner.

Iyewebas retreated last, but not before straying close enough to Baldwin so he might also see his face.

"We will call you the Manure King now," the guard ridiculed before slamming the door to plunge them back into the stygian gloom.

Richard surged to the door the moment it locked.

"We are not alone," he said.

"How can Iyewebas possibly help us?" Baldwin asked, defeated. Their last failed attempt had crushed his spirit. He truly believed he would die in this place—along with Hugh.

Richard paused to think. There must be a way to seize this advantage.

"He will provide our location to the queen. Our knights will attack this castle to free us," he said.

Baldwin listened; he also realized the truth. Iyewebas survived the shipwreck just as they had. But if there were no others, Iyewebas may be incapable of helping them.

27

Joanna spent a fitful night sleeping in an overstuffed chair near Eleanor's bed. The grand opulence that was once the queen's bower had become no more than the bare essentials for comfort. Everything went to support Henry's ransom demand.

The queen's fever had raged over the previous forty-eight hours, and though Joanna had no idea what had inflicted her mother, she knew she must remain at her side until she recovered.

The quiet and solitude afforded her time for contemplation. But each time she attempted to focus on her plan, thoughts of Rynhawker took over her mind. She refused to consider what she might have to do if her mother failed to recover. Could this change everything in England? Eleanor's untimely death would elevate John to the throne without anyone to stop him. He would rule until Richard could be returned home.

Eleanor's urgent cough brought Joanna awake and from the chair to her bedside. Her hand went to her mother's forehead, waking the queen. It felt like the fever might have receded, but still her mother felt warmer than she should.

"You are still here?" Eleanor asked, her voice so weak the words slipped out in a whisper.

"I am. You must remain quiet now."

"Have you been here all night?"

"I have."

Joanna rinsed a cloth in a water urn before setting it folded upon Eleanor's forehead.

"Are you feeling better?"

Eleanor withheld her answer. She feared she reached the precipice of death, though she would refuse to pass unto Heaven until she had rescued her son.

"The sun will rise soon," Joanna whispered.

Joanna brought water to her mother's lips. Eleanor refused it.

"Please, you must," Joanna persisted.

Her mother tried, despite the pain it caused upon her throat. At her second attempt, she swallowed, which brought a comforting smile to Joanna's face.

"How long have I slept?"

"Since midday of one day past. Your breathing grew harsh in the night. I prayed you might get better with God's graces."

For a time neither spoke. Eleanor closed her eyes.

"I have begged God to spare me until I may see my son again," she at last replied.

Her hand found her daughter's.

Joanna wrapped her mother's in both of hers.

"God will see us through this," Joanna said.

"God is angry for the things I have done in my life."

Joanna left Eleanor's hand to smooth her thin hair.

"God is not angry. You have served him well, as you have served your husband well in life. You have done all he demanded of you."

Eleanor chose to remain silent. She had hid so many secrets from her children over the course of her years. If they knew, would they be able to forgive her transgressions?

"I will summon the servants. You must eat."

Joanna shifted from her mother to refill the water goblet from a pitcher beside the bed. It gave her a moment to hide the tears welling her eyes. If her mother were to leave her now...

Then she returned to the bed.

"Drink," Joanna offered.

This time Eleanor worked harder to drink, though more slowly, but she took water. When she finished, she turned to face her daughter.

"You can't love him, you know," the queen said once the water had slipped down her throat.

Joanna stared at her, uncertain of how she should respond. They thought they were careful to keep their love secret. No one, not even her mother, was to suspect them.

"It is you we concern ourselves with at the moment," Joanna replied, deflecting her mother's remark.

"I see the way you look at him. And the way he looks at you. We are not meant to love in our life."

Joanna swallowed, considered her response. She could never lie to her mother. Not now, not with the possibility...

"Then I will deny I love him," Joanna offered sharply.

"Your eyes will say otherwise. Have you told him so?"

There came the faint glimmer of a smile from the queen. She knew what it meant to be in love with a man. She knew how Joanna felt and what it would mean to her. She also knew it could never be; the forces controlling their lives would never allow it.

Joanna averted her eyes.

"You must tell him. Do not make the same mistakes your mother has, child."

"And you, my queen, must get better. Our kingdom, our king, and I depend upon it," Joanna replied more pointedly.

"You must say the words, hope he feels the same way in his heart. Even if you can never be together, he must know he has won your heart."

"I am in no need of advice concerning the affairs of my heart, mother."

"If you have yet to tell him, then you are."

"We can never love each other. I understand that. My brother will return, and I will be at his bidding for marriage. But regardless of what Richard does, I will always love Rynhawker in my heart. Neither Richard, nor anyone else, can ever take that from me."

Joanna held the goblet, Eleanor forced another small drink.

A soft rap came at the door.

The first rays of the dawning sun found their way through the windows to shed a glow upon Eleanor's bed.

"Enter," Joanna ordered, though she refused to leave her mother's side.

The door opened slowly with Rynhawker stepping quietly inside. He remained at the door awaiting permission to advance.

The queen smiled when she learned it was him. She observed Joanna's face brighten each time the princess saw him. There was no masking the love she felt whenever she looked at him.

"Yes, come forward," Eleanor said.

"My queen, the Archbishop of Yorkshire has arrived to request an audience with her majesty."

The request seized Joanna. Panic raced through her mind. She had been careful to hide her mother's malady from any outside her bower. It was critical no one discover her illness. Anyone might reveal her condition to Prince John, giving him cause to make another play for the crown.

Joanna had prayed every hour that her mother would recover. Her death could place John on the throne. And once there, he would never agree to the ransom, nor mount an offensive to free Richard.

The princess moved to Rynhawker's side. They shared a look of grave concern over the situation. Could John be using the archbishop to monitor his mother? Was this another ploy to gain information from the castle?

"My lady, can we trust the archbishop at this time?"

His mind told him to deny the archbishop the opportunity to view the queen in her weakened state. But that decision rested not with him, but with Joanna and Eleanor.

"What nature of business does he bring before the queen?" Joanna queried, hoping to devise a reason to deny him.

"He refused to reveal that," Rynhawker replied.

Throughout the kingdom, the clergy could remain secretive regarding their business with the queen. If it involved matters of the church, no one could force them to reveal their purpose. John also knew the archbishop could, at any time, gain a private audience with her. And once alone, he may trick her into revealing information the prince could use.

"We will find a way to stall him," Joanna whispered.

"No!" Eleanor voiced from her bed in a way that seemed too strong to have come from her.

"Mother, John must never learn of your illness."

"Nonsense. I will see the archbishop. I will conduct the affairs of the kingdom as I have done since your brother's departure for the Holy Lands."

"But you are ill."

"Then let us make certain his holy archbishop sees me in a light that deceives him into believing I am well," Eleanor said.

28

Sabine's lilting laugh brought a smile to Thomas' face as they hurried hand-in-hand down the corridor. She led, knowing exactly where they were going, though it remained a surprise for Thomas.

It was their first opportunity together since Eleanor recovered from her illness. Sabine relished her only time free in a fortnight. And for her, two weeks was a long time from seeing her knight.

Thomas' heart stirred at the thought of being with her. He knew what they were doing was dangerous, that if they were caught, he would face the queen's stern punishment. But he also knew in his heart his minor transgressions would easily be forgiven by her majesty when she realized they were in love.

The young knight had never felt such a wonderful emotion before. Certainly, he had loved Merewen, but not in the way he loved Sabine. His heart ached for her every minute of every day. Their days in absence were agony upon his soul. He could only hope Sabine felt the same. What if she didn't? What if this were only her way of toying with him?

The light grew dim as they progressed swiftly and silently down the passageway until they reached a door at the far end.

What was this place? Thomas wondered.

Sabine stole a kiss before opening the door. She pulled him into the darkened storage chamber housing shields and armor and racks of all manner of war weapons.

"We will be safe in here," she whispered, knowing there was little need for men to draw on what the chamber contained.

He felt her hot breath against his cheek. Inside he stirred in a way that shot pleasure into his mind. Excitement swarmed over him. He could think of nothing but Sabine. He wanted to touch her, to feel all she had to offer him, but he knew as a knight he must remain honorable every moment of every day.

The danger fraught in the instant faded as time passed in silence. No one roamed in the hall to encounter or disturb them.

Sabine drew Thomas to her so she could press herself against him. She could wait no longer for his lips to come to hers. She kissed him with all the passion she could bring. Their contact weakened her when his arms brought her even closer.

When after a few moments Thomas failed to advance their passion, Sabine took his hand to place it on her breast.

Thomas, in return, allowed himself her direction. He rationalized there could be no dishonor in touching her when she made the invitation.

His hand felt her breast, craving more.

He felt himself prodding into her.

While Thomas held their kiss, Sabine tugged at her bodice to release her flesh into a waiting hand. His touch sent fire up her spine.

"Thomas, I so much want to feel you," she whispered in gasps between their kisses.

Thomas could restrain himself no more. He wanted to feel love in its fullest. He needed to experience Sabine's love. His hand left her breast seeking the apex of her legs.

Sabine moaned in pleasure when she felt him stroking her there. She was ready for him. Dare she touch him the way she touched Prince John? She knew the pleasure she bestowed upon the prince when she manually excited him.

For a brief instant she considered how Thomas might react to her own actions. Was it wrong for a woman to touch the man? Should she wait until he found the courage the press into her?

As Thomas worked his fingers up and down, Sabine surrendered to the carnal lust ravaging her mind.

She had to have him. She had to have him now.

Maddening desire drove modesty from her mind. Her hand found him poised for her. She worked her digits around him as best she could. When she did, she felt him lurch forward in need.

Her own need grew more intense. Her desire raged out of control. In her mind she begged him to come inside her, to make her feel the bliss of love between them.

Thomas could also restrain no longer. She worked the back of her dress until it fell around her waist, exposing in the darkness both her pert breasts with their taut, excited nipples.

Thomas moved his hand from one to the other. He never knew touching a woman's body could bring such wonderful excitement to his head. Even without training, he knew what he would do. He needed no further instruction than the innate urges of a man.

Sabine tugged at Thomas' belt. She stopped suddenly, realizing its release would cause a clamor that might capture the interest of anyone in the passageway. In the still of the deep of night, sound traveled great distances. So much so, that it might alert others to their location.

Thomas suspended his belt while Sabine worked the buckle free. He understood the same dangers dropping his sword would bring. Once undone, he lowered the belt slowly to the floor, his lips never leaving hers.

Sabine dropped her dress immediately afterward, allowing Thomas to feel her excitement.

"I love you, Thomas," she murmured as his breeks fell.

In the next moment, Thomas found his way inside her.

Sabine clutched his neck with both arms, swallowing a moan, as he filled her with a pleasure she had never known from her master. Her face wore the ecstasy exploding inside. She would relish this moment with her knight for the rest of her life. She knew in that instant she would love Thomas with all her heart.

The rapture of their union slipped away faster than either could want. They wished to linger in the bliss they had just given each other. But danger might lurk beyond their door. If anyone came upon them, Sabine would surely be scourged for her unchristian actions.

Thomas wasted no time locating Sabine's dress to return her modesty. In the next second Thomas raised his breeks and regained his sword. He could not see Sabine's face in the darkness, but he knew her smile was all consuming.

"We must go. I will return to the servants' bower, you to the knights' hall. It is best no one see us together," she instructed.

Thomas nodded in the darkness, stole another kiss before opening the door.

"I love you," he whispered without having to consider his response first.

Then he allowed her to exit alone into the passageway. But before she could get far, he seized her hand to bring her back.

"There is something you must know," he said.

At first the words froze Sabine's heart. They struck panic in her mind. What must she know?

"What is it?" she pressed anxiously.

"Soon I must depart the castle. I will be away from you," he said as if his heart were breaking.

"Why?"

She knew not how to react to his words. It was exactly as the prince had instructed. By pleasuring the young knight, he would reveal important secrets to her.

She remained in place, struggling through her moment of conscience. Could she go through with it? She knew what she was about to do was vile.

"Where are you going?" she found herself asking, despite her mind commanding her to refrain. If she knew not, she could say not.

"You cannot know," Thomas whispered.

Urgency forced her to kiss him again. Then, crying, Sabine dashed out of sight. Her tears erupted not from having to be apart from him; she expected that would come to pass with a knight. Her heart ached from knowing she must report what she learned to her master. If she failed to reveal what she gleaned, and John uncovered her deceit, he would stone her until she breathed no more.

Thomas remained in the chamber a long time, wanting to make certain no one wandering the castle might uncover them in the same proximity and grow suspicious of their time together.

But in those lingering moments Thomas relived the ecstasy he had experienced with her. He wanted to herald his joy, but he knew silence was most appropriate at this time. He would never be able to fall asleep on his pallet after what he had just experienced. Already his stirring began anew. Already he wanted her again. Time would drag torturously by while he waited for another opportunity to be with her. He could only hope she was as excited about their next meeting as he.

At last Thomas threw open the door to slip back into the passageway, heading quickly and quietly in the direction opposite which Sabine had departed. He could still smell her fragrance in the air inside the corridor. Or was it simply inside his mind, the way her face now filled his thoughts?

Inside the knights' hall, Thomas picked his way around sleeping men to locate an open pallet in the furthest corner. There he reclined, only to stare at the vaulted ceiling. He thought about nothing but Sabine—and their love—until finally he drifted into a dreamless sleep.

29

The messenger appeared ragged and unkempt before his king. Henry's face lacked a smile. He had already lowered his expectations when notified a messenger had arrived from the western reaches of his kingdom. The king's lips remained tight and thin across his face.

Henry showed little patience for the soldiers he commanded; only knights garnered his attention, and only the bravest, strongest of his knights gained his respect. Henry cared little about serfs or common soldiers he ruled over. They were his to use and abuse. As long as they obeyed, and provided the king with his wishes, he would allow them to exist in his kingdom.

"Speak man, before I throw you in chains," Henry growled, growing anxious in the silence while the man calmed his breathing.

"There is news you bring," Roger asked in a civilized tone.

The words diverted the messenger's attention from the king, which angered Henry even further.

"Your majesty, I ride from Bruges Forest with news from your knights."

"And that is?"

"None report ship sightings nor an approach from France."

Henry molded himself to his high-backed chair, looked to Roger, who creased his brow in concern. Each day silent from the queen drew Henry deeper into depression.

"Surely I have given her sufficient time to raise the ransom. By now she should have sailed or chosen a land route through France to meet our demands," Henry muttered.

The messenger bowed, signaling the completion of his report. He wished to be dismissed, so he might eat and drink to make up for the many days ride without pause.

"See him well fed." Roger motioned an attending archbishop.

Henry remained lost in his thoughts. It wasn't until the messenger and archbishop departed that his eyes met Roger's.

"How much longer must I wait?"

"Perhaps the queen tests your resolve?"

"Could she be that foolish?" Henry asked rhetorically.

"Could she hope you will fail to live up to your word? After all, you have the King of England in your dungeon."

"And there he remains until she delivers what I demand!"

Henry slammed a fist against the armrest.

"Perhaps, my lord, dispatching another messenger to the queen's court... to demand what she intends is in order."

"Perhaps a symbol of my sincerity is in order!" Henry weighed aloud.

"And what would that be?"

"The head of Richard's servant might convey seriousness."

Roger remained silent. Such a message would do little to motivate the queen. Henry sat indeed helpless to apply pressure. If he killed the king, he forfeits his ransom. And Eleanor will require Henry deliver his captive alive and well to her representatives before any ransom might be forthcoming. A formidable army of knights would surely accompany such a treasure, to be certain Henry remained faithful to his word.

"Perhaps, my lord, we should remain patient until we hear from the English court."

"And if we hear nothing? Or worse, we are greeted by legions of soldiers upon our kingdom?"

"Then my lord's armies will drive them into the sea or to France."

Henry weighed the words of his closest advisor. Certainly, Roger would consider all options before making a judgement.

"Winter approaches. Certainly, the queen will forestall an invasion until the spring, if she intends to free Richard by force. That allows us the frigid months to fortify our defenses," Henry said.

"And France, should Philip align with the queen."

"Yes. We hold my prize in the safest castle. In January I will order my knights to assemble. Let her come. She will face nothing but bloodshed and regret for such a foolish decision.

30

Brayson slipped from the castle in Londontown, exiting just prior to the portcullis lowering and the drawbridge rising. He rode at breakneck speed through the night, stopping only to rest in the darkest part and then only for a single hour. Before the sun broke the horizon, he was back atop his charger heading to the south.

He arrived at Tonnewick castle after the sun had set on the following day. By that time, the portcullis had come down and the drawbridge gone up. He was locked out for the night, though he knew his information was too vital to wait until the morn.

"Hail in the barbican," he called loudly. He was exhausted, starving and his parched throat made it difficult to shout in a voice sufficient to be heard.

For minutes he waited impatiently, wheeling his stallion in a tight circle to keep it from wandering.

"Hail in the barbican!" he called out again.

Certainly, someone was vigilant to watch over the night countryside. The kingdom had become relaxed with the impending onset of winter, and the domain was at a tenuous peace while all waited for news of King Richard's return. If there were battles to be fought, they would wait until spring or until Prince John sought to take control of the Crown by force. And if that were the case, this castle would be considered safe, since John had taken it as his new stronghold against the queen. At any time, only a handful of men ever knew the prince's exact whereabouts, so it was doubtful the queen, or Joanna for that matter, could mount an attack on any castle in the realm, let alone the one where Prince John felt safe.

"Hail! Is there not someone in the barbican?" Brayson called out with all the voice he had left.

"The drawbridge lowers with the dawn," a gruff voice came out the black hole of the narrow gatehouse window.

"I must see the lord of the castle immediately. I bring news vital to the realm," Brayson called up.

A slight smile broke on his face. He knew now he would have a warm place to sleep and the chance to eat and indulge in ale.

"I ride directly from Londontown," Brayson added.

"The drawbridge lowers with the dawn. Be off with you," the voice called down.

A moment later Brayson observed the faint outline of a bearded crusty face staring out the barbican window.

"I am a lone rider. I pose no threat to the lord of this castle. Allow me entry so I may deliver my news to your master," Brayson offered more forcefully.

"Go away," the voice called back down.

"Awaken your master. Tell him Sir Brayson brings news of the queen. He will see me immediately."

Minutes passed without retort from above. Brayson began to believe the guard on duty had dismissed his words with no intention of allowing him entry until the dawn.

"Your delay will only anger your master. I urge you to allow me entry to deliver my news."

Brayson was about to abandon his hopes when the drawbridge began to move. As soon as the drawbridge met the ground, the port-cullis clanked slowly upward. Both Brayson and the guard knew the true master of this castle, and no doubt once that master learned of Brayson's arrival, he ordered the castle to receive him.

Three mounted knights awaited Brayson as he clopped over the drawbridge through the barbican gate.

No one spoke. The three escorts merely wheeled around to take up positions on either side before delivering him through the outer bailey, then the inner bailey to the doors of the keep.

Brayson dismounted to be received by yet another trio of men armed and armored.

While it seemed the mention of his name had gained him access to the castle, he remained under enough suspicion to require an escort of so many armed men.

It had been months since he had departed the castle gates on his master's quest, and during that time the prince had grown more concerned of his safety.

Before entering a small chamber, Brayson surrendered his blade. The chamber was situated off a secluded passage in the keep.

"Perhaps I may be allowed food while I wait?" he asked.

He received no reply from the men who closed the door behind them only to remain in positions in the corridor.

Brayson settled into one of two chairs set at a small table near the room's core. A blazing torch provided meager light and heat against the chill.

After minutes alone, Brayson rose to pace the room. His legs ached from the long hours mounted. Moving might provide relief.

An hour passed before the door opened.

Prince John entered, kept warm by a long fur robe.

"I had given up on you," John said, crossing to the table where he took the chair opposite his knight.

Brayson returned to his chair.

"My eyes inside the castle informed me the knight Rynhawker still protects the queen and my sister," John added coldly.

Brayson could not read John's eyes, as the torchlight fell dim before reaching them. Was John angry? Was he disappointed?

"I dispatched my knights to eliminate one knight... and you failed. I received word two fortnights past my men were found dead in the forest. I expected you were one of them."

"My lord, we did as you commanded. We came upon the knight in the forest, but he had others. We attacked, but their skills were greater than ours," Brayson offered.

"And somehow you remain alive," John said wryly.

He stopped when the door opened.

A servant entered with roasted fowl and wine goblets.

"Eat and drink," John offered with a dismissive wave. "For this may be your last meal if you fail to convince me otherwise."

A lump of fear rising in Brayson's throat kept him from swallowing. But famine took over. He grabbed a capon leg, where upon he tore the meat from bone. The food had grown tepid from its time in the kitchen, but still its taste was glorious to a starving man.

Brayson washed it down with the wine, knowing once he delivered what he knew to his master, he would be regarded as a hero rather than a failure.

"My lord, if you will allow me to explain," Brayson said once he cleared his throat.

"That is the only reason you still breathe," John offered plainly.

Brayson could see his prince remained smileless.

"When I realized the encounter was lost, I came to their aid," Brayson offered.

"You came to whose aid?"

"The men you ordered dead."

The words vaulted John forward in his chair. Brayson clearly saw anger seething in those eyes.

"My lord, I felt it better to learn their intent, rather than sacrifice my life with no gain for my liege."

The words seemed to satisfy the prince, at least for the moment. John receded, awaiting further explanation.

Brayson chewed down more meat as quickly as he could. He was torn between filling his belly and reporting to his prince. If the prince disapproved of his information, Brayson may never have a chance to finish his meal. On the other hand, if he finished his meal, the prince may grow impatient, only to punish him regardless of his news.

"My lord, I came to be welcomed into the inner circle of knights attending the princess."

Those words raised John's eyebrow; not yet a smile, but Brayson grew more confident he would receive one.

"Did you reach the queen? Have you learned of her intent regarding my brother?"

Brayson filled his mouth quickly with wine, swallowing without delay.

"No, my prince, I am not trusted enough to be in the presence of the queen. Each time I attempt to learn her majesty's intent, I am excluded. The knight Rynhawker seems the only one with access to the queen along with your sister."

"What do you hear about the ransom? Has my mother raised the gold and silver?"

"I am not certain, my lord. Many dukes see the queen, but few offer the gold and silver needed to save the Lionheart."

"Good. Good. You have done well. My men have not died in vain. What more can you tell me?"

On this point Brayson paused. Should he reveal all he knew? Or should he withhold something in case he needed to bargain for his life later? John could turn against him at any moment, and Brayson might need something to use in his own behest.

"What can you tell me about Joanna? What danger does she pose to our cause? Surely you must have learned something during your time in the castle."

"I have, my lord. The knight Rynhawker has recruited knights on behalf of the princess."

"How many knights?"

"In her service, as far as I can tell, no more than six, my prince. With me included."

"And what does she intend for these knights? Is she plotting against me? Am I in danger?"

"Your name is never spoken in my presence. But she is careful with every word she speaks. I listen well, my lord, yet still I know not her intentions with her knights. But activity grows around the castle, with men moving in and out more frequently than the day I arrived in Londontown."

"Is she amassing an army?" John spat.

He was growing impatient with his servant.

"Nay, my lord. All her meetings are in private. Only the chosen knights are privy to her thoughts."

"And that includes you?"

"Nay, my lord. Of late she excludes even me from her meetings with Rynhawker and the other knight Thomas. She plans something, but as of yet, I have been unable to uncover her intent."

"Does she suspect you might be aligned to me?"

"I am careful in word and deed. They believe me faithful to Richard. So I come and go throughout the castle."

"You have done well, Sir Brayson."

"Laroque asked me to convey that he believes the princess may be the one moving the gold and silver. Perhaps her knights will escort the ransom to King Henry."

"Then you will be one of them."

"Yes, my lord."

"If that is the case, she will carry it to a seaport. There I will have the opportunity to relieve her of her burden."

"Command me, my prince."

"Return to your duty. Uncover what my sister intends. I will find a way to stop her. And learn what measure of gold and silver my mother holds for Richard's freedom."

Brayson smiled. He had pleased his prince. He would see another sunrise, and with that, receive food and drink for another day.

"You must choose death before revealing your allegiance to me. Do you understand?"

"Yes, my prince. You have my word the queen will never discover what I provide you."

With that John rose, smiled and marched to the chamber door. There he stopped, coming about to face the knight again.

"Use Laroque to relay what you gain in the future. Never appear at my door again."

"As you command, my lord. It was he who dispatched me to find you here."

After John's exit, Brayson completed his meal in quiet satisfaction. He emptied both his and the prince's goblets. The knight's smile shone in the torchlight flickering in the room.

31

Althera assisted Joanna into her scarlet silk gown with a low round neck that laced uncomfortably to slim her waist. Intricate white embroidery trimmed the long flowing lace sleeves. The late-day sun descended a sky crowded with streaming clouds. Underfoot Annalise dashed about, careening into the two women while they worked. Afterward, her servant fitted Joanna with a pearl-rimmed wimple. Tonight was to be a special night. She had instructed Rynhawker to dress for the queen and Annalise would dine with them.

Rynhawker never questioned her request, only spent the afternoon hours completing the tasks she had assigned him and Thomas. Both knights knew from her tone their time neared. Something was imminent, though even they were kept unaware of their destiny.

The evening hour approached. Rynhawker picked up Annalise at Joanna's chamber without seeing the princess. They proceeded to the queen's private chamber, where Margray greeted them at the door, led them to a lavish candlelit table near the windows.

Annalise clutched her father's hand, walking with a quickened pace to keep up. She paused in puzzled amazement at the many items casting light in the room.

Within minutes of their entry, Joanna entered through another door to join them. She wanted to look perfect for her knight. Desire urged her to take Rynhawker's hand, but she refrained. Instead, she whisked Annalise into her arms, so she might kiss her cheeks rapturously. Holding the child brought such joy to her burdened heart. Enjoying Annalise's innocent laugh pushed out of her mind, if only momentarily, what was to come.

"Are you ready to meet our queen?" Joanna asked, though Annalise knew only that the woman she called grandmother was the same person everyone addressed as their queen.

Annalise smiled.

Joanna reluctantly released her to her father's waiting arms.

"Let us sit," she requested of the knight.

He first assisted Annalise into a chair beside him, after which he assisted Joanna into her chair across from him. When he sat he saw in Joanna's eyes more than words might convey. She was troubled, he could tell that much.

"Our men are all accounted for?" she asked.

"I have yet to locate Brayson. He requested time to handle his affairs. I expect his return any day."

"Good."

Sabine entered through the same door Joanna entered minutes earlier to assist Eleanor into the room. The queen wore a full flowing plum-colored gown with gold trim and intricate pearl embroidery accentuating the bodice. Stitching in silver with a meticulous pattern adorned her ruffle-wristlet sleeves.

Eleanor's smile ignited a new vibrant energy in the chamber. The queen hid well her worry and anxiety behind eyes glistening with excitement. She believed from Joanna's request this night to be special. So she anticipated good tidings.

"I am pleased we may sup together," her majesty said.

She paused at her chair while Rynhawker assisted her. In courtly fashion, bowing his dismissal before returning to his place.

"You may begin," she ordered Sabine and Margray, who waited patiently to the side.

Three platters were prepared for this night. Each contained a woodcock, a roasted peahen imprisoned by beetroots and onions, along with thinly carved boar to the side.

While Sabine attended the queen's plate, Margray attended Joanna's. After receiving his, Rynhawker prepared bits of vegetables and boar for Annalise. When Annalise reached for an onion, Rynhawker gently removed her hand to her lap. Annalise looked up with confused eyes but kept her hands in place. Even she understood the ceremony of this night.

Each waited, hands beneath the table, until the queen sampled her first bite. Only then did Rynhawker break away small bits of peahen for Annalise.

At first the three ate in silence, while Annalise played with her beetroots as if they were toys. Only on Rynhawker's insistence did she accept her fowl to chew it down enough to swallow.

"Did you walk in the courtyard today, mother?" Joanna asked when the silence proved distracting.

"Gracious it was too cold for me. With winter so near I shall remain within the warmth of my keep," the queen replied.

"Leave us now," Eleanor commanded her servants once they had replenished the wine goblets.

"Your majesty," both said, bowing politely.

On the servants' departure, Sabine took Annalise to return her to Althera's care. But not before Joanna bestowed one more kiss upon her cherub little cheek.

Eleanor did no more than pick at her food, while Rynhawker consumed every last scrap. He suspected they would be going with little food for a time, if he read Joanna's face correctly. He saw restrained despair in her eyes. She was torn by what she intended to do, Rynhawker could see that much.

Noticing Rynhawker's protracted gaze in her direction, Joanna cast her eyes askance, so as not to meet either her mother's or Rynhawker's.

"Now we are alone. You will tell me why this night has been planned," Eleanor said pointedly.

She lowered her utensils, pushed her plate away before turning to face her daughter squarely. She needed no words to know something dire was the cause of this occasion. Her heart raced as she contemplated the meaning of her daughter's insistence.

"I wished that we could sup together before we departed," Joanna said, looking into her mother's eyes to reveal her anguish.

"This is to break my heart even more than dealing with Richard's captivity. Is it not?"

Eleanor reached for Joanna's hand. Her daughter's was warm while hers was cold. Tears formed in the corners of Joanna's eyes before she could speak.

"I will be leaving you," she said, forcing back tears. She had told herself while she dressed, she would not cry before her mother. She hoped she might still succeed.

Eleanor fought her own erupting tears. She had long suspected this day might come. This could only mean Joanna would be placing herself in danger for her brother.

"When?"

"That you cannot know."

"You tell me this because you know I will suffer dearly from your absence," Eleanor said.

"I wish you to pray for us so we have God's speed in what we must do."

"What is it you intend to do?" Eleanor probed.

Joanna slid her hand from her mother's. Eleanor needed no words to know Joanna's intent. The fire in Joanna's heart would never be extinguished until her brother returned to English soil. The lion in her had been unleashed by her brother John. It would never allow her peace until she had attempted everything possible to bring Richard home.

"I cannot say. But when the time arrives, we will depart in the night. No one can know of our absence."

"But they will probe when they realize you are gone. Silence only fuels suspicion. What if John learns of your departure?"

On that Joanna considered the implications. John must be meant to believe Joanna posed a direct threat to him.

"I will say you journey to Staffordshire abbey to pray for Richard's release," the queen offered when Joanna remained silent.

"It is unlikely John will believe that," Joanna muttered.

"My lady, if I may speak. We provide the prince with words he wishes to believe," Rynhawker injected.

His idea brought Joanna's eyes to his. Though improper for him to speak before the queen or princess without proper address, he knew his words might help Joanna consider more clearly what she must do.

"Yes, we must. We shall lead John away from our real intent. For those who inquire, mother, tell them I ride to the northern shires in search of knights to defend the Crown against John's rebellion."

Rynhawker smiled. Her ruse might force John to dispatch his forces northward away from them and Londontown. That may keep the queen safe until Joanna could return. And John would expect that from his sister.

Eleanor stared at Joanna strangely, uncertain of what might be the result of such a tale.

"If John learns your tale is a ruse?" the queen advanced.

"Then let no men into your keep until I return."

"When will you return?" Eleanor pressed, though she knew she would receive no answer to her inquiry.

"I cannot say. I can only say I will miss you every day I am away. And I wish you to pray for me and my knights in what we must do."

Eleanor's heart sank at the words. They were leaving to face the devil himself, Eleanor knew that much. The queen also knew she could never survive the loss of both her son and her daughter.

"I can command that you remain safe within these walls."

"Then I must disobey, mother."

"I can lock you and your knights away," Eleanor pressed.

"Both you and I know in our hearts that is not your wish. You must allow me to do what I must," Joanna said.

"And if you fail?"

A tear trickled down the queen's wizened cheek.

"I have asked God to watch over us. We will not fail," Joanna replied.

"My heart breaks at this moment, but I will not stop you from what you must do."

With that Eleanor turned to Rynhawker. She reached out so he might take her hand. At first Rynhawker hesitated. Then he accepted it.

"I beg you as a mother, not your queen, to protect and care for my daughter. I love her with all my heart."

"I will, your majesty. I pledge my life to keep her safe."

Eleanor removed her hand so she might wipe away the rush of tears stealing her vision. She could say no more. She rose, along with Rynhawker and Joanna.

"I have but one more request," Joanna said.

Eleanor waited for Joanna to continue.

"Withhold the ransom and all communication from the King of Germany until you receive a messenger."

"And should no messenger arrive?"

"Then deliver the ransom as demanded on the feast of Candlemas. Not a day sooner. And only to save our king's life."

Eleanor found her throat too clogged with grief to speak, so she rushed to the door. Before leaving she returned, wrapping her prayer beads into her daughter's hands.

"Either you or your messenger shall return these to me. God keep you safe."

Then Eleanor departed the chamber for her bower.

Once alone, Joanna returned to the table. Rynhawker had expected to leave after the queen, but clearly Joanna had another agenda.

"Make certain our men remain at the ready. They must know nothing about our plan. If they ask, tell them the princess requires their escort on her journey north. When I say, we will depart Londontown under cover of darkness."

"As you wish, my lady," Rynhawker said.

"Of our men, who do you trust least?"

Rynhawker contemplated his answer.

"The knight Brayson. None knew him before our attack. He came to our aid against the marauders."

"Could he be aligned with John?"

"He has been faithful since arriving in Londontown."

"Keep him close then until we are safely away."

"What do I reveal to the men? They will want answers regarding our departure."

Rynhawker knew he must tell say something. They may wish more time to quiet their affairs before leaving.

"Our departure is imminent. They are to report to you in the castle by sundown three days hence. Tell them no more."

"As you wish, my lady."

Rynhawker started for the door. Joanna stopped him with a gentle kiss to his cheek. The knight responded with a kiss to her waiting lips. His arms swallowed her up to bring her body to his.

"I pray God is with us on our journey," she whispered.

Only reluctantly did Rynhawker release her.

"In the event we..." Rynhawker started.

Joanna stopped him.

"My mother will care for Annalise as if she were my daughter. She will grow up under the watchful eyes of our royal staff. I promise you she will receive the finest our kingdom can offer."

With that Rynhawker bowed before the princess to exit into the silent corridor.

Moments later Joanna exited. She proceeded down the corridor in the direction opposite her knight. While the castle slept, Joanna made her way to the chapel to pray for mercy from her God.

32

Rynhawker grew nervous as events unfolded around him. Althera denied him access to the princess all day, informing him at each request that Joanna was unable to attend him at that moment. The servant refused further explanation even when Rynhawker grew angry, repeating only the words the princess instructed her.

By late afternoon Rynhawker realized Duchard was nowhere to be found. When he searched for Alwain to determine why, he, too, turned up missing, along with Brayson. It seemed they had disappeared without informing Rynhawker as to their whereabouts.

At the supper hour, Rynhawker located Thomas in the stables preparing their stallions. The animals had remained in stalls for three days consecutive, and Thomas felt the need to exercise them in anticipation of their use. He knew no more than Rynhawker, and like his fellow knight, he had been turned away when he sought counsel with the princess. Thomas had been instructed to keep the stallions ready to ride at a moment's notice.

"I will get to the bottom of this intrigue," Rynhawker scowled as he stomped from the stables toward the keep.

He was fuming by the time he reached the doors. It felt to him like their plan was spiraling apart before it even began. Surely the princess must be informed as to the state of affairs engulfing them.

Rynhawker planted himself outside Joanna's chamber door rapping softly yet persistently. He decided he would allow nothing to prevent him from attending the princess.

When no response came, he rapped harder with persistence.

"My princess, I bid you to allow me to speak with you on matters most urgent," he called through the wood when no response came to his knock.

He stood as if unable to move his feet.

Another minute passed. His anger deepened. Then the door unlatched to open very slowly. Instinct drove Rynhawker to draw his sword. Something felt terribly amiss.

Althera poked her head out.

"Please forgive my abruptness, Sir Rynhawker, you may enter now," she offered in apology.

Rynhawker stormed into the chamber, thrusting the door full open until it banged the wall. He scanned for Joanna across the darkened room. The few candles burning gave off a sinister glow.

The princess was nowhere in sight.

"Where is she?" Rynhawker seethed.

Had he been tricked? Had something happened to the princess? His heart hammered at the thought. He took Althera at the shoulder.

"All is well, my knight," Joanna offered from across the expanse. Unseen by her knight, and faceless beneath the shadow of her overhanging cowl, Joanna came into the light from the corridor.

Speechless, Rynhawker gazed at her.

Joanna came to him to allow his arms to take her.

Her lavish strawberry flowing hair had been sheared to resemble a young lad. Afterward, Althera burned the extricated hair in the hearth, leaving no evidence behind of Joanna's metamorphosis. The princess now wore breeks beneath a dark woolen shirt with a forest green tunic often worn by serfs scurrying about the castle. Only her freckles and her proud royal stature betrayed her identity.

"What?"

"No one will see me as a royal," she offered.

Rynhawker released her so he might assess what presented before his eyes. Up close no one would deny she was Princess Joanna, but from a distance, she would garner no attention from anyone.

"It is time," she whispered.

"My lady, I have failed you and our king. I cannot account for our knights," Rynhawker confessed, angry at himself for his inattention.

"They have already departed. They will meet us at our departure point," Joanna reassured him.

"What of Thomas?"

"He has his instructions. He awaits us in the stables."

Joanna motioned for Althera, who moved quickly to the rear of the chamber to retrieve something for the princess.

"But it is too late. The portcullis would be down," he said.

Joanna glanced to a gibbous moon rising into a star-filled sky.

"Not on this night. The portcullis and drawbridge remain until the moon reaches the apex."

"Then time is short."

Althera returned with a stuffed hempen sack and Joanna's crossbow, accompanied by six full sheaths of quarrels.

Joanna handed the sack to Rynhawker, accepted the quarrels after slinging the crossbow across her back. Then she took Althera's hands into hers.

"Do you understand what I have instructed?" Joanna asked.

She could see the tears in her servant's eyes.

"My lady, allow me to attend you."

"You must remain here. You must keep our secret safe for as long as possible."

"Yes, my lady, I will give my life to keep your secret safe until you return," she said, bowing.

"I pray it must never come to that again."

Joanna's months of planning and preparation culminated into this moment. Their time had come to depart.

Joanna hugged her faithful servant, hoping it was not to be the last time they were together.

"Lead on," Joanna said, tightening a cloak around her before pulling her cowl over her head. The nights would be cold, the days only slightly warmer, but it was the most strategic time for them.

33

Thomas had completed prepping their stallions when Sabine rushed into the stables. She wrapped her arms around his neck to bring him close until he kissed her. Only then did she release him.

"Please tell me you are not leaving," she cried.

Thomas read eyes of despair, sensed it in her trembling words. "I must."

He slowly removed her arms from his neck to bring them to his chest. But he refused to release them.

"No, Thomas, you must remain here. You must protect the queen," she begged.

"I am at the bidding of Princess Joanna."

"No, my love, you do not understand. You must remain within the safety of these walls. John and his men wait for you beyond," she continued, more frantic.

Thomas released her hands to check the saddle straps of the third stallion. He expected the princess and Rynhawker at any moment, since Joanna commanded their mounts be ready upon her arrival in the stables after dark.

"Please, Thomas, I beg you to remain with me."

Desperation in her plea sent fear up Thomas' spine. She sought to convey more than words. Her eyes begged forgiveness.

"What have you done?" he probed when she began sobbing in his arms.

The young knight's heart sank. Acid backed into his throat. Thomas read guilt across her face.

Sabine's heart stopped his words. She held her breath, tightening her arms around him, wondering if she could alter the future if she refused to release him. Could she keep him here?

She knew she must confess. She had to reveal everything. If she delayed any longer, she might lose her courage, then he would never know the truth. If he learned it from anyone else, he would hate her all the rest of her life. She had but one option left.

"I must confess to you," she said more boldly so he would listen and understand what she must say.

"Confess?"

"I must say these words before you and God. I beg you to find it in your heart to forgive me for what I have done."

"Even if God fails to forgive you, you have my forgiveness."

He found her lips to bestow his kiss upon them. He could feel tears streaming down her cheeks. She sobbed in agony when their lips finally parted.

"I have never experienced true love before you," she started.

"I will cherish always our love," he replied quickly, too quickly.

"Please, I must expel these words that so hurt my heart."

Thomas backed away. Agony in her eyes preceded her confession.

"I have deceived you."

There was a cry in her voice. The moment hung between them. Thomas sought to understand. He couldn't.

"How? How have you deceived me?"

The young knight's mind raced through the possibilities. What terrible thing had she done?

"Prince John..." she started.

Thomas withdrew. Her hand turned suddenly cold. She moved for his—it was gone.

"My prince commanded I become close to you to uncover Princess Joanna's intent concerning our king," she forced out with all the courage she could find.

Rage and disappointment filled Thomas' mind.

"But I came to love you. I yearn to have your touch against mine. My intentions were dishonorable when we first..."

"You used me... to gain information for the prince!"

"Sir Thomas, please understand. I had no choice. He would kill me without mercy if I disobeyed."

"You came to me to steal what I know and deliver it to our king's enemy," Thomas spat.

Anger seethed in his voice. He retreated until even at her full arm's length she failed to gain his touch.

"I came to love you," she cried. "I tell you this only because I wish to keep loving you. I cannot take back the shame I have caused. You must not venture beyond our castle gates."

Thomas needed to think. So many things raced through his brain at that moment. What had he divulged during their moments of passion? He loved her too much to face what would come next. He must report immediately to Rynhawker and Joanna what he had just learned. They were all in jeopardy. He must tell them John knew everything Thomas knew. That Thomas had revealed to Sabine the things they had entrusted to him.

The young knight's heart broke as he considered what would happen because of Sabine's treason. All they had worked for—all they had planned—was now at risk. Yet he could not bring himself to turn her in. John was the villain here, not Sabine. Did she not understand death was the penalty for treason against the Crown?

"What have you told John? Tell me now before we can no longer speak," he said, swallowing the anger and guilt in his throat.

At first Sabine offered no answer. She knew she could lie and hope he might forgive her. But the guilt she already carried tore apart her insides. She could not bear adding further falsehoods.

"Everything you have told me," she said.

Her sobs erupted into raging cries. She desperately needed him to take her into his arms. She wanted him to tell her she was forgiven, that all would be right once Thomas spoke to Joanna.

Silence she received in return.

"Hate me if you will, but I will love you until my very last breath," she cried.

Thomas could find no words to comfort her. He knew her betrayal placed Rynhawker and Princess Joanna in grave danger. His youthful foolishness may cost all of them their lives.

Sabine ran when voices drifted into the stables.

Thomas wrestled with that moment. Then he decided he could not face his mentor and friend to reveal what he had done. Instead, he would be on his guard and pray no dire consequences came from Sabine's treachery. To speak against her was to sentence her to death.

34

Thomas failed to mask his surprise at seeing the princess. Her transformation was indeed clever. The young knight swallowed his guilt. He knew the right thing at that moment was to inform the princess what had transpired. He just couldn't bring himself to say the words.

Joanna mounted her buckskin blaze-faced warhorse, while Rynhawker took to his chestnut roan charger. Thomas had selected a snip-faced bay stallion. Both knights wore tunics absent any markings which concealed their chain mail and brandished swords. They sought to exit the castle undetected. Joanna worried one of John's minions might track them to report their movements.

The sentries knew only that a small hunting party would depart in the night to gain the advantage before the morning's light. Once the riders departed, the sentries were to raise the drawbridge and lower the portcullis for the remainder of darkness.

The three trotted out the castle gate just as the glowing moon crossed its zenith in the sky. They pounded over the drawbridge without looking back. Once beyond the walls they galloped to hasten their departure on the ancient road leading south. They could only hope their ruse had worked, allowing their departure to escape the prince's spies. If they succeeded, it could be days or weeks before John learned of Joanna's absence. Then he would be forced to wonder where she had gone. She prayed by then it would be too late for him to retaliate against her plan.

They cantered nonstop throughout the next morning, pausing only long enough to gulp some water and chew down twice-baked bread. By their direction, Rynhawker surmised they headed for the port at Dorchester. That was until Joanna steered them to the west. The princess had another destination in mind.

By late afternoon they reached the edge of Wyckshire Forest, where the unwelcome shuffling of nearby horses sent them into a panic. Joanna directed her knights down a wooded slope into the darker shadows of the trees. A tightly packed thicket of oak and ash offered them concealment.

Her heart froze when they peered through the umbrage at five riders ambling along the path. Prince John himself led four of his battle-ready knights.

Joanna pointed out the lead rider to be certain Rynhawker and Thomas also made the identification.

Anger fumed inside her. How could John have discovered their departure? What were they doing roaming this forest at this moment? Had Joanna and her knights been followed?

While they waited in abject silence, Joanna recounted every detail of the previous days in her mind. She remained careful to conceal any details from anyone without an absolute need to know. Even Rynhawker was kept uninformed of their true destination.

She trusted only Duchard with their destination, so he could lead the other knights there. Joanna believed it best to divide her forces, thereby limiting the possibility John's men might determine her strength.

Even after the column passed beyond sight, the three remained ensconced in the umbrage. How much danger were they in if John roamed these forests in search of her?

"My lady, they may uncover our tracks then mount a charge against us," Rynhawker risked in a whisper.

The notion of coming under attack now sent Joanna's mind swimming. They needed to reach the small port at Hythe undetected. Joanna's plan hinged on leaving English soil with no one aware of her movements.

"Do we continue?" Thomas pressed.

Joanna held them another few minutes while she contemplated. There was no going back. Could it be coincidence John chose this forest? Perhaps the prince was only scouting the land for possible locations from which to launch an assault against his mother. Yet Joanna knew she could not take that chance. Had her strategy somehow become transparent to her brother? Had he correctly predicted her next move?

"We head south," she ordered.

Joanna breached the entangled limbs first to assume the lead. She had traveled this journey in her mind twenty times before this day. She knew exactly the best way to proceed in order to provide them with the greatest cover.

Before long they broke into a frenzied gallop, taking sharp turns this way and that along the forest way, hoping their tracks might confuse anyone following their trail. It would take longer to reach their destination, but they might be safer along the way.

As they emerged from the forest fringe along the southern coast, Joanna released a sigh. They had made it... until Thomas threw a glance over his shoulder. He indicated the shoreline to their eastern flank. Less than a league away, five horsemen erupted through the trees.

Somehow John had located them! His men lurched into breakneck speed.

"Ride with all God's speed," Joanna yelled as she kicked her mount to full gallop.

The three raced along the coastline. In the distance, moored in the small harbor, their ship bobbed at the ready. There would be no time to spare.

Rynhawker came beside Joanna.

"We can make it," he called, witnessing her white-eyed terror.

The journey to their ship was intended to be uneventful. They were supposed to be invisible to John's men. How could John have known to hunt the forest for them? Someone had revealed their departure to the prince. Someone was working against them.

Joanna reached the port first to gallop up the ramp and through the open loading door into the darkened hull. Rynhawker galloped up next, halting at Joanna's side. As Thomas ascended the ramp, Joanna dismounted to dash up the ladder to the deck, while the two knights pulled the loading door closed.

"We depart now!" she screamed at the helmsman manning his wheel in the aft castle of the ship.

From the forecastle balustrade she could see John clearly now. They were close. But time and distance remained Joanna's ally.

Deckhands sliced the tethering ropes. The sails rose to catch the wind. With a reluctant groan the ship dipped through the gentle waves slapping her bow.

Joanna removed her crossbow. Employing the oak pull lever Rynhawker had affixed to the crossbow stock, she cocked the weapon against the balustrade. Thanks to the ingenuity of her knight working with the castle's artillator, they created the weapon specially designed for her. She could now cock her crossbow with the aid of any stationary object. As the ship rocked into breaking waves, she fumbled to load a quarrel into the channel. Her hands trembled at the thought of what she must do.

Rynhawker came beside her to lower her crossbow, which brought her eyes to meet his.

"We are safe for now. Your weapon is best kept concealed from your enemy," he said.

He read the fear in her eyes at what had occurred. John knew of their departure. The prince had somehow uncovered details of their plan. Someone had betrayed them.

The ship gathered speed when the frigid sea wind stiffened, sweeping the vessel further from land as Prince John and his knights pounded the timber dock before reining their stallions.

From the balustrade, Joanna and Rynhawker saw fire and hatred in John's face. She risked one more look at her fuming brother then pushed away from the rail.

For now, Joanna and her men were safe, but their quest for invisibility had come to an untimely end.

35

The small ship sliced in loping fashion through the lapping waves. Rynhawker watched the crew scurry about trimming the sails and securing lanyards across the deck.

John and his men reversed their mounts, returning to the forest depths. This was not the last they would see of him. John would never abandon his fight as long as Richard remained imprisoned.

"We must get below," Joanna ordered.

Rynhawker assisted Joanna down the ladder to enter the darkened hull. Moving about proved cumbersome, as the white caps sought to toss them left and right. Once below, Thomas joined them. He had secured their mounts in the makeshift stable at the ship's aft. Joanna led them to the cabin at the ship's starboard.

Inside, Duchard, Alwain and Brayson waited. Rynhawker did not like what he saw in their eyes. Across from the knights, Delphi along with two other young lads huddled beside the same three friars Rynhawker had brought to Londontown to serve the princess.

But Isaac's presence most surprised Rynhawker.

"I see everyone made it safely to the ship," Joanna said without a smile.

She knew time was short and only here in the creaking belly did she feel safe revealing the crucial details of her plan to the men surrounding her.

"Are we the ransom ship?" Duchard ventured when everyone else remained eerily silent.

Without responding, and under the light of hanging lanterns, Joanna assumed a commander's position at the table. There she spread a parchment for all to view. The men crowded, as this would be their first information regarding why they sailed from their home in a time of chaos in their kingdom.

All looked over the map uneasy, and no one dared speak. They needed to assimilate what lay before them: A charcoal map of King Henry's domain. This map, however, only revealed the locations of three castles.

"One of these imprisons our king," Joanna said.

"From your tone I suspect we are not delivering the ransom," Alwain said.

Duchard's eyes narrowed. Rynhawker determined that something troubled his friend. He waited, hoping the knight would be forthcoming. When he was not, Rynhawker pressed him.

"Now is the time to speak your mind, my friend."

Duchard's gaze went to Rynhawker's before sliding off uneasily to Isaac.

"Why is the Jew here?" Duchard pressed with naked disdain.

"I am a Brit, same as you! I am loyal to my king, same as you," Isaac replied.

"Then you do not deny being a Jew?" Alwain added.

"I serve the Lionheart, exactly like us all," Isaac offered in defense.

Joanna remained silent while angry glares shot back and forth across the table.

"I will not tolerate the presence of a Jew," Duchard said.

"Sir Duchard, Isaac is a friend to my brother, one vital to our quest," she offered, her voice too meek for one commanding others.

"A Jew necessary to help us? We are knights. We need nothing from Jews," Alwain protested, growing angry at the discussion.

Anger flashed across Joanna's face.

"If we are to succeed, we need Isaac," Joanna reinforced.

"We need nothing from a damned Jew," Duchard charged, realizing afterward he must tame his voice, temper his anger. His hatred sowed seeds of discord in his comrades.

"Listen well. Isaac can move more freely amongst Henry's subjects. He will learn things we cannot. I beg you trust me in this."

"I stand ready to die for my king, same as you, despite the vile contempt you levy upon my kind," Isaac reaffirmed.

Throughout their exchange Isaac remained calm, restraining the tenor of his voice. He saw mounting hatred in all the knights, yet he refused to reduce his honor to their level. He feared speaking one word ill might get him a dagger in his belly from the very men he sought to aid.

"I ask each of you to trust me henceforth. We who are gathered here are going to rescue our king. I require your loyalty. Richard requires your courage. Isaac will demonstrate his worth to his king as a true Brit, I assure each of that."

Joanna stared at each knight around the small table. In the ensuing silence Duchard swallowed his anger, redirecting his attention to the map.

Only after it seemed all came to accept what was, did Joanna resume her discourse.

"Once we uncover which castle holds our king, we determine how to breach it, free Richard and escort him safely home," she asserted.

"And for this we require three children?" Brayson asked.

"They serve a purpose. I ask you only to concern yourselves as knights with how we get our king safely beyond Henry's reach once he is free."

"And how exactly *is that* to come about?" Duchard pressed, raising a skeptical brow.

"In time I will reveal to each what you must know. For now you each receive a map to our rendezvous location in Henry's kingdom. If we must scatter for any reason, proceed with all haste to that location. Is that understood?"

The knights grumbled their confirmation.

"And if Henry's men take you prisoner?" Brayson pressed.

"Then I command you return to England, report what you know to our queen. She shall direct your course after that."

The waves grew mean and rough as they crossed the deep of the channel during the night, with seasickness ruling until the next day, forcing Joanna to postpone her briefing so all could lie down. Even the lads found travel on the water distasteful.

But they had succeeded in departing England. Once on the continent, Joanna now would have to anticipate John's next move against them in order to prevent the prince from obstructing their plan. They could only hope God remained on their side.

36

Henry paced his throne room while waiting. His mind raced in a multitude of paths once he received word two messengers had arrived seeking an audience with the king. Could it be what he hoped for? Was it possible Eleanor was prepared to pay his ransom? A broad smile consumed the king's face while visions of the gold and silver he would add to his already formidable coffers played across his mind.

He laughed aloud when he thought of that fool Duke Leopold, who so easily relinquished the greatest prize a noble could acquire.

The waiting seemed endless while the messengers were escorted through the castle into the keep. They would be heavily guarded once inside, and Henry had ordered extra soldiers in the room just to be safe. There was no telling what ploy Eleanor might have conjured up against him. The woman could be cunning and ruthless, Henry knew that much. But he had left her with little bargaining power regarding the King of England. She had no choice but to deliver the ransom if she wished her son's return.

"Where is Roger?" Henry growled while pacing.

"I am here, your majesty," Roger called out as he hurried into the room, rushing to Henry's side. "Good, I am not too late."

Henry returned to his seat, where he rubbed nervous hands together. What could be taking so long? Could it be the messengers were delivering the ransom? There was no word that the men carried anything.

"Do you think the Queen of England has agreed to your terms?" Roger queried.

"We can only hope Eleanor fears I will make good on my promise to kill her son if she delays."

Finally, the throne room doors opened, allowing two messengers entry, accompanied by four of Henry's knights.

The men approached unarmed, which initially surprised the king. Surely Eleanor would have sent knights along with her messengers. Clearly, one was a friar and the other an elder with wisping gray hair over speckled skin worn from years of toil in the sun.

What is this? Henry wondered while he waited.

Neither man smiled as they approached. They appeared frightened as they cast their eyes at the floor with each step, avoiding contact with his majesty. They knew not what to expect from this audience. Inside, each prayed they might survive to return home.

"Your majesty, we bring forth information from the king's court," the friar said as they stopped before Henry on his throne.

The man foolishly spoke out of turn, causing him to cringe at the thought of angering the king.

But an optimistic and forgiving Henry merely smiled. This was to be good news.

"You bring news of the ransom I demand for the release of the Lionheart?" Henry shot back, fully expecting to hear exactly what he wished.

"No, your majesty, we journey from King Philip's court."

"Philip? What does France wish from me?" the king shouted. "If you have come to dissuade me from holding the Lionheart, I will return you to your king with daggers in your backs," Henry scowled.

His mind reeled from the information. Philip had no right to meddle in the affairs of Henry's kingdom, or with the affairs of England. Was this meant to frighten Germany? Did Philip intend to announce an alliance with England against him? Maybe this was a ploy by the queen to force Henry into rethinking his demand.

"Speak your words carefully, friar, as I am inclined to gut you myself if your news fails to suit me."

The friar held his tongue for a long moment.

The old man beside him shifted rearward to distance himself from his traveling companion. Little did he realize he would likewise receive whatever the king doled out to the friar. Unless, of course, the king wished one kept alive to deliver Henry's reply.

"Your majesty will be pleased with what I deliver for my king," the friar insisted.

The clergyman's smile grew larger with each word he spoke.

A bold move, Roger thought while watching the exchange unfold between the friar and his king. He inched closer to Henry to better hear what the man would say next.

"King Philip, in concert with Prince John of England, makes a formal request upon his majesty the great and noble King Henry of Germany."

"State their request, man, before I plunge a dagger into you," Roger growled.

"King Philip offers five thousand pieces of silver," the friar started.

Henry's fist clinched on his armrest. How dare Philip... how dare the King of France think he could offer a pittance in exchange for the King of England? Did he honestly believe he could threaten Germany with the force of the French army?

"Ha! I'll not have the King of France involving himself in the affairs of Germany and England," Henry yelled. He slammed a fist on the armrest. His face grew ruddy with rage as he swallowed the full meaning of the friar's statement.

"Your majesty, they intend to pay the silver for each year you keep the Lionheart imprisoned," the friar concluded calmly.

At first perplexed, Henry just stared at the man, uncertain of how to interpret what he just heard. What exactly did the man say?

"The King of France agrees to pay our king five thousand silver pieces on annum to keep the Lionheart in chains?" Roger asked, as if he had heard something other than what the man had said.

"Yes, my lord, King Philip and Prince John wish you to accept their offer, along *with* the ransom from the Queen of England, as long as his majesty agrees to keep Richard imprisoned."

Henry settled back into his chair. Could his ears be deceiving him? The King of France wished to pay to keep the Lionheart a captive? Perhaps Philip harbored desires to invade the English kingdom while Richard was a prisoner. But if that were so, why would he be waiting, and why would he offer Germany silver? So much made no sense to the King of Germany at the moment. What did Philip hope to gain by keeping Richard imprisoned?

Suspicion supplanted reason in Henry's mind. The sum was indeed tempting. But what were the probable consequences of such action? Could he possibly succeed in taking the treasure from both parties, and then doing what he pleased with the Crusader King?

Henry concealed his smile. Greed swarmed chaotically through his mind. Was he strong enough to defy both the King of France and the Queen of England? Perhaps he should find out.

If Henry accepted Philip's offer, he would be bound by honor to hold Richard even if Eleanor delivered the ransom. Once Eleanor realized the King of Germany had no intention of releasing her son, she would surely amass her army to invade. Could he repel her invasion without losing everything in the process?

"Suppose I agree to Philip's terms. When is the first silver delivered to this court?"

"King Philip intends to deliver the agreed upon sum to your majesty within three fortnights."

"Of what purpose does Philip hope to gain from this arrangement?" Roger asked.

"I do not know, my lord. I am only the messenger."

"I will think upon your king's proposal and deliver an answer that you may take to Philip's court. Until then, my men will feed you and provide you comfort in my castle."

With that, the knights guided the messengers from the room.

Henry and Roger exchanged looks of uncertain elation.

"What do you make of this?" Roger asked once alone.

"What plan could Philip have in mind with such a request?"

"Perhaps he intends a play for the English Crown. England is weak in the hands of her queen. Eleanor is no match for either you or the King of France," Roger offered.

"Then if we accept Philip's offer, we aid him in conquering England," Henry pondered out loud.

"That could be Philip's intent."

"Then I indirectly aid France in her conquest, and for that, I receive a mere five thousand pieces of silver."

"Per year, your majesty," Roger corrected.

"And I am to trust him beyond his first payment? He has little incentive to pay once he controls the English Crown."

"As always, you are most astute, your majesty."

Henry considered the ramifications of his actions. Indeed, he could aid France in a conquest. But if France failed, England would come after Germany, if they learned of the bargain Philip struck between the two kings. Yet the messenger spoke on behalf of both the King of France and Prince John. Could it be that John sought the support of Philip to usurp the throne from Richard? Can he ever allow France and England to become allies against him? And more importantly, did Philip secretly have eyes on Germany? With an English conquest, he could become strong enough to defeat Germany in an invasion.

"This could all be a trap, my lord," Roger said to break Henry out of his trance.

"Indeed it may. Philip may use me, my position with the Lionheart to better France."

"My lord, what is the worst that can occur if you do as Philip proposes?"

For a time Henry said nothing.

"If you accept Philip's proposal, and at the same time accept the ransom without releasing the King of England, what would Germany face?" Roger advanced.

Henry had no answer.

37

Rothbane's charger clopped across the lowered drawbridge while Iyewebas crossed minutes later on foot. Neither made eye contact until they progressed well inside the sparse market square.

Already Iyewebas' heart pounded a desperate rhythm inside his chest. He had to convince himself he could go through with their plan.

Few merchants chanted out their wares this chilly morning. Only the more desperate entered the castle square in the hopes of making it a profitable day.

Iyewebas, famished from not eating on the previous day, made his way to an elderly smiling man offering up palm-sized barley bread rolls. They were stale, he could tell that much by the touch, but he motioned for one, though he held out empty hands. He had nothing with which to barter for some food.

"Go away, beggar," the merchant growled, turning away in the hopes of enticing a passing soldier to purchase his offering. The soldier scurried away with head down to avoid them both.

Iyewebas motioned he was hungry, that he could neither speak nor hear. But the man kicked at Iyewebas' leg to move him away.

Then a coin dropped onto the small blanket, capturing both men's attention.

Rothbane said nothing atop his steed, snapping the reins to keep the beast in check.

With a reluctant smile, the merchant delivered the small roll to Iyewebas, understanding the knight's gesture.

"And for you, fine sir?" the merchant pressed, hoping to gain another coin for his salesmanship.

Rothbane wheeled his stallion, proceeding instead toward the keep. There he would find food and ale and a warm place to sleep for the night. Knights were easily welcomed into the castle, while a beggar must find his way to the stables to sleep amongst the dung.

Iyewebas scurried away, chomping on his breakfast, a smile on his face. The easy part of their mission had been accomplished.

Next came the more difficult.

Without looking around, Iyewebas crossed to the stables, where he began his chore of mucking dung from the stalls. No others would perform the tasks Iyewebas performed. But then no one suspected him of being a Brit, nor of his intent to rescue his king.

The morning hours passed painfully slow. Iyewebas found himself flinching at the slightest sound—a very bad sign for someone supposedly deaf. He silently scolded himself for his actions, reminding himself he was capable of serving his king. But he still had things to accomplish if their plan was to succeed.

By now Gerand completely trusted the mute. Iyewebas gained entry to the dungeon unattended so he might move from cell to cell to clear away the waste of previous days. Three times he had seen his king in his cell. Three times he had quietly and dutifully performed his task of holding the bucket while the men filled it.

Tonight, all changed for Richard the Lionheart.

On this night Iyewebas would rescue his king and facilitate his escape by way of a horse in the stables. His plan was to free the king, along with Hugh and Baldwin, with Rothbane's help. They would sacrifice themselves, if necessary, so their king could ride free to France, escaping the clutches of King Henry. If they died, so be it in the service of their kingdom.

Hours dragged on as Iyewebas busied himself, waiting for his opportunity. He needed a weapon, a dagger he could conceal until safely inside Richard's cell. The dagger would allow Richard to overpower the guard to gain his sword.

Iyewebas watched across the stables when three soldiers entered leading mounts. They turned over their reins to Iyewebas expecting him to brush down the lathered beasts before stowing them away in stalls.

The little man watched carefully when one soldier removed his chest plate to stack it on a long table. Next came the belt—with its sheathed dagger. Iyewebas clandestinely eyed the blade. He would need only an unattended moment once the soldiers exited to secure the dagger under his clothes.

The other two soldiers kept their armor on and their weapons at their hips. Iyewebas' heart sank when the first soldier snatched up his belt before leaving.

For a brief moment all was falling into place. Now one elusive piece remained beyond his reach. He contemplated entering the dungeon unarmed, hoping he might secure a dagger from a sleeping guard. But if that failed, his king would be weaponless. Freeing him might become too difficult.

The sun set before Iyewebas completed his tasks in the stables. Throughout the day, soldiers and knights came and went, yet no one left a weapon unattended long enough for Iyewebas to take it.

Concerned and depressed, Iyewebas departed the stables against a cold north wind to make his way to the rear door of the keep. There he would forage for scraps the soldiers and knights left behind. He was surprised when he discovered two platters with lingering strands of woodcock. In moments, he used crusts of bread to sop up the traces of fat before gnawing the few bones discarded. It wasn't much, two mouthfuls at best, but it would quiet his grumbling stomach.

It was, however, more than he had supped on the night before. Rothbane felt no need to share his food with the beggar—that is how he still viewed Iyewebas—even though the beggar had shared his daring plan to rescue their king, while accepting Rothbane's help in its execution. But Iyewebas bore all the risk. If he failed in the dungeon, he would surely die where he stood. Once the guards realized his intent, they would bring him down with a sword to his belly. Iyewebas would have nothing with which to fight back.

Fear swarmed over him as he made his way through the kitchen area. He meandered into the knights' hall to find most of the men had settled into out-of-the-way places in which to fall asleep. He picked his footing carefully amongst the sleeping men, seeking a dagger easy to steal. Most kept their weapons tucked under or in their arms. Weapons were too prized by knights and soldiers to leave lying about. No one parted with one absent a struggle.

Iyewebas realized the hour was growing late. He must proceed to the dungeon to perform his duties before long. If he dallied further, he might anger the guards on duty. The last thing he wished on this night was to draw unneeded attention.

Panic set in. Iyewebas moved through the entire knights' hall. Not a single dagger came within easy reach. In desperation, he lowered to one knee before a barrel-shaped sleeping man with remnants of his supper trapped in his beard. He snored like a grunting hog wallowing in mud.

Iyewebas steadied his hand. He ceased breathing while easing toward the hilt of a dagger extending from the man's side. He could reach the blade to slip it out—if the man remained in his current position. If he shifted away from Iyewebas, the hilt would disappear under his rippling fat.

Indecision plagued the little man. His hand froze short of the dagger's hilt. Sweat trickled into his eyes. He had to move or lose his opportunity. His fingers eased down contacting metal. It felt gloriously warm and hard. It was like gold in his reach.

Then the soldier rolled onto Iyewebas' foot, forcing him to snap his hand away, jerking back to his feet.

For a terrible moment the snoring ceased.

Iyewebas watched the man's eyes. They remained closed. The dagger settled beneath a flopping belly. His opportunity vanished.

His hope of gaining a dagger lost, Iyewebas needed another plan fast.

38

Flickering torchlight illuminated the way to the dungeon. Iyewebas walked neither fast nor slow, knowing his presence would go unchallenged in the area. With each step he reaffirmed he could succeed. He had to free his king. There was no other who could do it in his stead.

Over the previous weeks, most had come to expect his visits. The guards relished the thought that Iyewebas took on the chore of mucking out prisoner cells and dragging away dead bodies without displaying the disgust soldiers and guards always displayed.

Iyewebas pounded the door in anticipation of his duties. He hid the smile crossing his lips. For a moment while he waited, he envisioned the outcome of his bravery. He would be the one to save the King of England. He would be the one who risked everything in service of his lord. The legend of his name would be woven into songs glorifying this night.

After moments of waiting, Iyewebas pounded again. No doubt the guards were sound asleep at the small table they gathered around in the nigh. Having eaten earlier, they would sleep unabated until new guards arrived in the morning. Watching over prisoners during the night came to be desirable for the king. Since no one came to interrupt their sleep, they spent their days as they pleased.

Worry crept into Iyewebas' mind as he shifted at the door. What if they slept so soundly, they never heard his pounding?

Iyewebas grunted loudly, pounding a third time.

Then a sleepy face peered through the small grated portal, and after a fumbling moment, the bolt slid as it had done so many times before. The door opened. Iyewebas swallowed the excitement welling in his throat.

Once inside, the guard quickly secured the door behind the serf before trudging to his chair at the table. His partner never once moved from his sleeping position.

The lethargic guard plopped down, kicked his feet onto the table then leaned his head against the wall.

Sleep well, fool, Iyewebas thought.

Tonight, they would regret their actions.

Iyewebas wanted to rush directly to the king's cell. The sooner there, the more time they had to fight their way to freedom and flee the castle.

Yet he knew better than to break pattern on this night. Everything must appear as it had always been. Every action he performed had to reassure the guards this night was no different than any other that Iyewebas appeared in the dungeon. The guards must witness him working exactly as he did every other time.

So Iyewebas retrieved the buckets from the corner, and with one in each hand, he paused at the first cell. He waited patiently while the second guard pulled himself from the table to join him.

"Be quick with it," the guard grumbled, unlocking the cell.

Iyewebas bowed repeatedly, the way a serf bows in forgiveness before a noble. His gesture fostered complacency.

One by one, the guard moved with Iyewebas from cell to cell while he filled the buckets. The stench proved so vile that twice Iyewebas gagged. The guard, however, maintained his distance, which on this night brought a slight smile to Iyewebas' face.

All the better for his king.

Iyewebas' heart surged when they at last paused at King Richard's cell door. The moment had arrived. Iyewebas could feel himself sweating. The weight of the buckets, both half full, tugged at his arms. His breathing came in gasps. He worried the guard might detect his behavior change, causing him to respond with suspicion.

Would Iyewebas have the courage to go through with this? Could they possibly succeed in escaping the dungeon?

The other guard rose from the table to join them.

No!

That was not part of Iyewebas' plan. He needed the second guard to sleep at the table. In previous nights, only one guard monitored the prisoners. Iyewebas hadn't anticipated this. Then the guard returned to his chair to lay his head back down.

Iyewebas waited while the guard unlocked the door. At first, the man peered in before pulling the door open wider. His hand covered the hilt of his sword just in case. This was a prisoner never to be taken without due regard for his power. After he discerned all three prisoners lay against the furthest wall, the guard swung the door full open so Iyewebas might enter.

Richard rose across the cell. He kept his movements deliberate, so as not to induce the guard into a defensive posture. As long as that sword remained sheathed, Richard held the advantage.

"Remain there," the guard ordered, extricating the sword hilt a few inches.

Richard said nothing as Iyewebas entered with his buckets. He set them near the corner to begin his work.

Hugh and Baldwin sat still in the hay, neither sought to move or stand. But their eyes never left Iyewebas as he crossed the cell.

The next moments were most critical. Iyewebas needed to transfer the carving knife he stole from the kitchen to his king without raising the guard's suspicion. They would have only a few moments to execute their move to free themselves. If it were ill-timed, all could be lost, and Iyewebas would find himself imprisoned beside his king. He had to cast fear from his brain. He had to go through with it. This might be his only chance to serve his lord.

Richard eyed Iyewebas as the little man set on one knee with his back to the guard.

The moment of truth approached.

Iyewebas glanced sidelong at his king with a smile. In the dim light off the torch outside the cell, Richard detected the signal. Hugh also witnessed what Iyewebas sought to convey with his look.

Both men remained stoic, despite exhilaration in their bodies.

Hugh suddenly sprang up, causing the guard to move askance and withdraw his blade. But Hugh made no move for the guard. Rather he diverted the guard's attention while Iyewebas removed the knife from his shirt to lay it in the straw so Richard could see it.

The king acknowledged with a nod.

The guard paid no attention to the gesture, but Iyewebas knew his king now had a weapon.

While Iyewebas dawdled cleaning up the waste, Richard eased to Baldwin to assist him in gaining his feet.

"Give us some water," Richard demanded.

The guard laughed weakly.

"My men need water," Richard said again with more force.

Getting the knife into his king's hands was only the first step of a complicated plan to free the three of them. But it was to be the most critical one. Without a weapon, Richard and the others had no chance of escape. With one, they could control the dungeon.

Iyewebas hesitated. He had completed his task. The next part of his plan had to work, despite an inability to communicate it to his king.

Taking up the buckets, Iyewebas backed toward the open door. When he did, the guard stepped aside, expecting Iyewebas to clear the cell. But Iyewebas tripped at the opening, spilling the buckets onto the guard's boots.

Richard knew exactly what to do.

The guard reacted as Iyewebas expected. Instead of monitoring the prisoners, the guard kicked the excrement from his boots.

During that inattentive moment, Iyewebas fell into the guard, draping his arms over the man's shoulders.

Richard dove to recover the knife. He lunged for the guard. As he did, Hugh surged forward to clasp the man's mouth shut before he might release a scream.

Richard thrust the blade into the man's side, taking the sword hilt with his other hand.

Moments later, the guard slumped into the straw, staring up at the king. Hugh hammered a fist to the man's jaw to make certain he went unconscious. They knew he was still alive; they held no desire to kill him. They sought only to incapacitate him and thus prevent him from sounding an alarm. This guard had been kind to them in the months previous. The last thing Richard wanted was to kill a man for his kindness. But freedom always comes with a price. And Richard had to be prepared to pay the price.

"Follow me," Iyewebas whispered. It was the first time he had spoken in days, and it felt great.

Richard, Hugh and Baldwin remained silent as they slipped from their dungeon cell into the dimly lit corridor. At the far end, the sleeping guard remained at the table. He had not moved.

Richard levied the sword ahead of him. He hoped to take the guard without a fight. If they could advance undetected, it might be possible to relieve another foe of his weapon. With each sword they gained, they improved their chances of fighting their way to freedom. But if any of them were wounded in the fight, freedom could elude them.

As Iyewebas led them down the corridor, they fell under the torchlight above the table. Iyewebas had hoped and prayed the guard would remain dutifully asleep at his post.

Only once they neared the man, did Richard come out from behind Iyewebas. The guard raised his head, opening drowsy eyelids.

He sprang alert the moment he saw what had occurred. But he was far too slow in bringing his sword out against Richard's. Using the hilt, Richard slammed the man's head, knocking him unconscious. The guard's head banged lifelessly onto the table.

Baldwin advanced to gain the guard's sword. Hugh levied the knife, though he wished he might be able to gain a better weapon before they made their ascent out of the dungeon. Neither guard this night wielded a dagger at his belt.

"Hey, what goes?" a prisoner in another cell yelled at hearing the commotion.

Then another indecipherable call came from further away.

"Open the door," a gruff voice growled.

Richard hesitated.

"Set us free!" the first voice shouted.

Richard turned to Baldwin, confusion in his eyes.

"My lord, we are nearly free. What should we do?" he asked.

Richard had but moments to decide. If he freed the others, they could create enough commotion to mask the king's escape. Or they could rally against the Brits to subdue them in the hopes of earning their own freedom. Certainly they could bargain their way out by offering Richard up to their king.

"We must go, my lord," Iyewebas pressed.

"Let us out," another called.

"Do not leave us here," a new voice, older than the others, joined in.

"My lord, what do we do?" Hugh asked.

"Will the halls be clear for us?" Richard pressed Iyewebas.

"Guards man the main doors to the keep. The knights and soldiers sleep in the knights' hall. We can avoid them to escape, but we will need a way out of the castle. I have help waiting for us."

"How long before sunrise?" Baldwin asked.

"Hours, two maybe."

Iyewebas opened the main dungeon door.

Richard pushed it closed.

"We determine how to get free of the castle before we leave this place," the king said.

He recalled exactly what had gone wrong the last time they sought freedom. He vowed never to err the same.

"I can help you," a prisoner called from a door closest to them.

"Tell me how," Richard demanded at his door.

"Free me and I will help you," the voice persisted.

Richard motioned Baldwin to unlock the cell door.

Baldwin hesitated. This could be trouble. Or it could be their salvation.

39

Richard ordered the cell door open while he took the nearest torch to shed light inside. The dancing flames illuminated a lone man propped in the corner.

"Tell us how we escape this fortress," Richard commanded.

The man fumbled through the surrounding hay until he recovered a makeshift crutch from a gnarled tree limb. Once firmly in hand, the cripple jockeyed himself erect then hobbled forward absent a right foot.

"Take me, I will lead you to freedom," he said, struggling with a hand out for the door.

"My liege," was all Baldwin need say.

It was impossible to save this man. He would only retard them, and he lacked any ability to fight.

"We cannot take you," Richard said with disappointment.

"Please," the man pleaded, tears in his red-rimmed eyes.

He reached the door to demonstrate efficacy, but he made no move to advance upon the king. He knew of this prisoner from the treatment he received, and what he represented to King Henry.

"You are a Brit?" Baldwin queried.

"Nay. A soldier of King Philip. Taken during a fight with Henry's knights. I wish only to return home," he pressed.

His tears sparkled in the torchlight.

"My lord, we must go," Iyewebas begged, shifting nervously at the dungeon door.

"I am sorry," Richard said.

He closed the door then turned the lock, sealing the man's fate.

"Damn you! Burn in hell, you whoreson," the cripple shrieked.

"Rot in hell, bastard!" rang out from a distance.

"Move now," Richard commanded.

He made his way as the last man out of the dungeon into the corridor. He remained behind long enough to engage the dungeon door lock. Even if a guard regained consciousness, they would remain trapped in their own stinking hole until someone came. The action could buy time to escape the castle... at least they hoped.

Iyewebas led the string through the corridor to the spiral staircase. There they stopped, listening for faint voices from above.

Silence.

They hoped everyone in the castle had taken to their pallets for the night. Only the guards would be awake as impediments to the king's freedom.

Baldwin ascended first. But Iyewebas stopped him on the second stair when he noticed Baldwin's unsteady gait. The man would have difficulty keeping his balance, let alone fighting off a soldier.

Iyewebas requested Baldwin's sword, which he turned over without retort, relieved to have someone else fighting for his king.

Though Iyewebas' sword skills were weak at best, and he knew combat on a staircase to be the most difficult, he also realized he had no choice. It was either Hugh or him, and Hugh had favored his shoulder upon release from his cell. For now, Iyewebas and Richard were the only two capable of fending off an attack.

Iyewebas understood his duty to fall before his king. Fear spilled into every crevice in his body. He had to pause when he reached the midpoint in his climb to settle trembling hands. He told himself he could fight; he could defend his king; but his mind scoffed at his fragile confidence.

Hugh and Baldwin advanced next, with Richard at the rear to safeguard against an attack from behind.

Fortune shadowed Iyewebas as no sounds found their way down, reassurance they were still alone in their quest.

Iyewebas shifted to the outside wall as they neared the final turn to ground level. At all times, his eyes studied the flickering torchlight splashing down. The slightest change meant approaching men.

Richard, Hugh and Baldwin eliminated the gap between them and Iyewebas on the stairs. They had to vacate onto the first floor and there face whatever opposed their escape from the keep.

Iyewebas drew in a deep breath, felt his heart settle. He steadied the sword, clutched now with both hands, before attacking the remaining stairs. His mouth had gone bone dry—he couldn't speak even if he wanted to.

When the first floor at the staircase remained deserted, Iyewebas released a silent sigh of relief.

"This way," he whispered, pressing into the corridor while holding tight against the far wall. Their best chance would be through the passageway leading to the chapel in the southern corner of the grand four-level structure. Iyewebas recalled two windows from reconnoitering the castle that might provide an exit into the castle's private courtyard. Once beyond the keep they could elude any guards to reach the stables undetected.

Richard joined Iyewebas. He motioned for Hugh, who struggled at the moment to aid Baldwin with an arm as a crutch under his shoulder, to keep pace with their king.

At the first cross corridor Iyewebas stopped.

Richard mistook his gesture for indecision, so he advanced past him. Iyewebas instinctively clutched his king's arm to draw him back. Now was no time for royal protocol. The king could beat him later if he wished for his indiscretion, but he had to keep his majesty safe.

"A watching point in the next corridor. Passing earlier, two men stood vigilant," Iyewebas cautioned.

"Can we take them?" Richard risked asking.

"I think."

Iyewebas' face displayed no confidence in his response. Richard eased back.

"Another way. How do we escape the keep?"

"The chapel," Iyewebas said.

"Then lead us there," Richard commanded.

The four crept quickly down the deserted corridor until they came to another crossing hall. At this one, Iyewebas paused before leading them left. He believed they were drawing close to their exit point. One more corridor and they could gain sanctuary in the chapel.

The first-floor chapel was purposed for everyone in the castle except the royals in residence, who attended private masses in a fortified chamber on the highest floor of the keep. It was customary and proper for the highest-ranking noble in residence to invite nobles of lesser station to accompany them to mass. As such, King Henry attended his masses there. They were secluded from the peasants while they prayed. Their chapel also served as a refuge during an assault. The royals would barricade themselves in against marauders. The first-floor chapel, on the other hand, fell quickly to invaders.

Iyewebas turned the corner into the next corridor. He stopped. Richard moved to the front, leveling his sword to fight.

Rothbane stood a dozen paces before his king, his sword ready, eyes roving the corridor beyond the men. In the dim light, it proved impossible for them to see the knight's features distinctly.

"My king, he is ours. He will aid in our escape," Iyewebas said, motioning Richard to lower his sword.

But Richard resisted. Something about that shadowy face stirred unease deep inside the Lionheart. Richard recognized something familiar about the telltale scar. But his hunger and thirst, and their dire circumstance, kept him from analyzing what drifted through his brain.

Baldwin also stopped dead in his tracks at the sight. He tightened on Hugh's arm, struggling to force himself upright.

"Come quickly, in here," Rothbane urged.

He likewise lowered his sword, turned about to lead them through the tall door into the chapel.

Once all were safely inside, Rothbane jammed the door closed with the nearest bench.

In the darkness they could discern two dozen rows of benches arranged before a small slab altar elevated on a dais at the far wall of the chamber. A simple cross of eight feet adorned the wall.

Iyewebas noticed Richard held his distance from Rothbane as all gravitated to the nave. Hugh's shoulder aching from supporting his comrade's weight, he took the first opportunity to lower

Baldwin onto a bench. He needed to rest. They remained a long way from escaping the castle. They had yet to even egress the keep.

"What now?" Richard posed, raising a skeptical brow. His eyes never left Rothbane, who marched in search of their way out.

"We are not safe for long," Rothbane risked saying from his place near the altar. He waited for his moment to accomplish what he came to do and for what he would be paid handsomely. A smile crossed his face at the thought of slaying the man he most loathed.

Iyewebas had been correct. Two windows allowed sunlight to illuminate the small chapel during the day. But iron gratings secured them against invasion. That fact had somehow escaped Iyewebas.

Richard scrutinized the bars. Stone and mortar held them solidly in place.

"We have no escape here," Richard announced.

The disappointment in his voice infected the others. All except for Rothbane, who rejoiced the revelation. This would be far easier than he imagined.

"How long before sunrise?" Baldwin asked from the bench. Panic erupted with each word. He sought to rise but stumbled back down; he needed Hugh's stable footing to come erect.

"Little time now," Iyewebas offered.

He had failed his king. He berated himself inside for his incompetence. His king needed him to plan a way out of the keep, and he had failed. They were all in dire jeopardy now.

40

"Think, Iyewebas, is there another way out? We just need to reach the stables," Richard pushed, trying to conceal desperation.

Standing before his king, Iyewebas pressed his brain for a solution. None came.

With the sunrise would come a priest and serfs with servants to attend mass. With luck, thirty or more would fill these benches.

"My liege, can we hide here to use the peasants attending mass to mask our escape. All we need do is blend with them on their departure," Baldwin offered as if brilliance had struck his brain.

Iyewebas smiled at the thought. He had not failed after all. They did have a way to freedom.

Richard grew suddenly uneasy when Rothbane retreated from the altar to join them near the center of the chapel. Their distance from the door offered them a fighting chance, should soldiers uncover their location and launch an assault. If soldiers discovered their escape from the dungeon while they still remained inside the keep, their play for freedom would be lost. Their best chance was to reach the stables before anyone realized they were free. Remaining in the chapel now seemed too risky.

"My liege, I offer my sword to fight our way from the keep. You and your comrades make your way to the stables," Rothbane offered.

"That can only work if we time our escape with the opening of the portcullis and the drawbridge. We have no chance for freedom locked inside these walls," Richard responded.

"I will fight with Rothbane," Iyewebas said.

Richard's sword went up. Rothbane! He suddenly realized who he had raised his sword against. Richard lunged toward Rothbane, who jerked back, readying his blade for an assault.

Baldwin grabbed Hugh to jerk him away.

"It is you!" Richard snarled through gritted teeth with narrowed eyes.

"Yes. And your brother pays well to make certain you never see England," Rothbane spat, lunging at Richard, his sword angled for the king's belly.

Adrenaline surging power through his veins, Richard deflected the thrust handily before lunging for Rothbane, who retreated quickly to deflect Richard's parry.

Hugh and Baldwin skirted further from the fray with each in their own way wishing to assist their king. However, only Iyewebas held the other sword, which he, at the moment, seemed too terrified, or stunned, to raise in his king's aid.

"Dare you defy your king!" Richard shouted, slashing hard left to right to find a way through Rothbane's defenses.

The knight proved quicker and stronger than Richard in his weakened state. Thirst and hunger plagued the king. Now he fought for his life against one of his own.

"Let him be. You will never escape," Baldwin commanded from the tenuous safety of an upraised bench.

Without altering his attention, Rothbane charged.

"I will make certain I have done the deed for the prince then slip away before anyone realizes I stole Henry's treasure."

Richard widened his stance to brace against the swinging steel. He weakened with each wild swing of his blade to force Rothbane at bay. The Lionheart retreated out of necessity to the chapel's rear, kicking benches into Rothbane's path to slow his assault enough to better his footing. He needed to launch a coordinated counterattack if he wanted to live.

Rothbane only laughed at Richard's efforts. The king's death was imminent—there was nothing the man could do to alter that.

"You will die this night," the knight said.

"Not by your hand," Richard snarled, drawing strength from the words. He slashed upward, hoping to take Rothbane's shoulder.

Rothbane jerked right, bypassing the strike while deflecting the steel with his own. He then snapped his sword up, forcing

Richard's blade vertical. Richard's midsection opened to a strike. Rothbane angled his sword for the kill.

Iyewebas threw his body and blade between the two to deflect Rothbane's attack. The knight came in with a fierce downward slash to separate Iyewebas from his weapon. Before the little man could retreat, Rothbane's edge sliced across his chest, cracking ribs.

Blood spurted while Iyewebas' blade clanked the floor.

Richard used that precious moment to counterattack, driving his sword up and in with all his strength to rip into Rothbane's side.

Blood erupted from the knight's mouth and nose. He remained erect, though helplessly limp, a moment longer while gasping his last breath.

"Forgive me, my king, I did not know he was your enemy," Iyewebas uttered as he clutched his fatal chest wound.

Richard dropped his sword to kneel beside his servant. He pressed the heel of his hand against the slashing wound in a vain attempt to staunch the bleeding. When he realized all would fail, Richard cradled Iyewebas in his arms.

"You are forgiven."

Iyewebas clutched his king's bloody hand. Darkness caved in around him.

"I give my life so you will be free."

Richard scrambled for his sword.

Feet pounded beyond the chapel. Then resounding thuds erupted from men throwing themselves to batter down the door.

The clashing swords had alerted the nearest guards. The three no longer held hope for freedom.

Richard touched Iyewebas' shoulder with his blade.

"For bravery and courage in the faithful service of your king, I grant thee knighthood. Forever shall you be called Sir Iyewebas."

With a dwindling smile on his blood-soaked lips, Iyewebas exhaled his final breath as a knight for his king.

Their feeble attempt at securing the chapel door splintered against the surge of three soldiers crashing through with blades poised to fight.

Richard regained his feet, spun around ready to respond. He wanted to slay everyone at that moment. Yet he knew all had been lost. They had no chance of escaping the keep, let alone gaining freedom beyond the castle walls.

For an unending minute, no one moved inside the chapel. Richard held his fighting stance. Baldwin and Hugh huddled behind their king with the aid of Hugh's steadying shoulder.

"Surrender your sword or all die where you stand," the lead soldier commanded the king.

He concealed well his awe for the Lionheart. His hand trembled while he awaited Richard's response. The king maintained his fighting edge at the moment, since none of Henry's men wished to be the one responsible for forfeiting their king's ransom.

A second soldier edged in. The two wavered, unable to discern from Richard's stone face whether the Lionheart intended to fight or succumb. Even if he succeeded, he faced an impossible trek through the castle grounds.

Richard surrendered his sword.

Terror swept through Hugh and Baldwin's souls. They knew the penalty for another failed attempt. Death. All that remained unknown now was how.

41

An angry night sea grew treacherous as the small ship slammed white caps in its quest to reach the Continent. Joanna instructed the helmsman his course to steer. They sought a small port in close proximity to the border of Henry's lands. Once there, they would travel swift and silent through Philip's lands into Henry's kingdom.

Joanna intended to be well clear of Philip's domain before the king learned of their intrusion. He would send soldiers once he discovered what they had done. But it would be too late to stop her.

Everyone remained below deck, gathered around the table, waiting for their journey on the water to end. The young boys found their adventure to be exciting one moment, scary the next, yet always difficult on their tender stomachs. Their seasickness lingered with no one, save for the crew, willing to eat during their voyage.

Isaac especially despised the sea, cursed the way she slapped them around, wishing now he had declined the quest. He prayed every hour for this blasted vessel to remain afloat.

Joanna met with her friars privately, assigning each a young lad. Theirs was the crucial task of locating their king. They would face little danger in what they must do, as long as they adhered to Joanna's instructions. Children and clergy roamed unobstructed in every kingdom. As such, they could move about unchallenged, though Joanna prepared for them credible responses should they fall under the scrutiny of Henry's men.

The princess knelt before Delphi and the two other lads in her service. But it was Delphi's hands she took when she spoke. His small ashen face brightened into a smile.

"You three are about to perform a task of vital importance to our king. I bid you to be brave in deed and do exactly as you have been taught. Listen well to your elders at all times. They will keep you safe. For a time, we will be apart on our journey. But do not fear. God walks beside you to protect you from harm."

"I will miss you, my lady," Delphi said, presenting a brave yet frightened face.

"I will miss you all terribly. We have become such close friends."

"Will we ever see you again?" Delphi asked while choking down tears.

Joanna took him into her arms, after which she reached out to bring the others into their hug.

"We will be together again with our king in his castle in Londontown. I promise," she delivered, burying her own sorrow.

"Land ho!" came the glorious call from the helmsman.

For the first time since leaving Hythe, everyone smiled. They would soon be back on land.

The knights jostled up the ladder first, shoving each other, each preferring cold salty air to the stench from the horses below. Once on deck, Brayson dashed to the forecastle balustrade to wretch over the side. Duchard followed moments later.

Isaac was last to reach the deck and the most elated to see land. They would reach the port before nightfall, and all could rejoice at completing the first leg of their journey. Everyone realized this was to be the safest leg of that journey. From here, danger mounted with each passing hour.

"What are our instructions once on land?" Rynhawker asked while he and Joanna remained separate from the others.

"Each friar will reconnoiter a castle. Isaac shall deliver them with his provisioned wagon. Once complete, he will rendezvous with us," Joanna said.

Joanna fully intended to remain in Henry's domain until she uncovered her brother's whereabouts. If her initial attempt failed, she would devise another. If that one failed, she would make a last-ditch effort to locate Richard by demanding an audience with King Henry, during which she would manipulate him into presenting the Lionheart to her. She could insist firsthand witness to the king's wellbeing before delivering any ransom. While such a ruse guaranteed revealing Richard's location, it also heightened suspicions, which in turn tightened security. They may then forfeit any chance of a rescue. No, Joanna convinced herself she would make her initial plan work.

"How will we proceed?" Rynhawker asked.

"Our two groups travel separately to reach the rendezvous. From there we can strike any of the three castles. Until we know which, we remain invisible to Henry's men."

"My lady, the helmsman steers for the port. Do we remain on the deck?" Thomas called.

"Nay. Return below until we receive an all clear."

"As you command," Thomas replied.

Despite their grumbling, Thomas herded everyone out of sight from any loitering eyes on the shore.

42

King Philip sat at the head of his dais with his finest knights supping at plank tables and benches lining either side of the great hall. Jugglers and dancers entertained in the center. The king was in a particularly festive disposition without offering reason why.

Wine and mead flowed like a babbling brook amongst the tables. Women moved deftly about serving the knights food and drink, while sidestepping this way and that to avoid groping hands from those who had overindulged in the previous hours.

Philip began to fully comprehend the advantage he held in his bargain with the prince. His mind drifted to his plan to expand his domain as a result of John's foolish offering.

All the king needed now was to manipulate Henry and John into doing as he bid. Once he fortified his forces, he would take back all of Aquitaine and the Duchy of Normandy. While John and Eleanor fought each other for the Crown, he would seize their lands. It seemed Philip would gain handsomely regardless of who emerged the victor... as long as Richard remained a prisoner.

Before Henry realized what he had foolishly become party to, Philip would have claimed sufficient territory to make him the viable threat to the King of Germany.

For the present, Henry might gain the king's ransom and the silver France provided. But he would not long enjoy the spoils of his endeavor.

Philip brought the nearest serving wench to him as she passed in her duty to keep Philip's favorite knights sated with wine. In his condition, hers was the sweetest smile he had seen in his kingdom. Her innocent youth set the desires in his mind surging. But before he might advance a gentle kiss upon her, the music drifting down from the minstrel's gallery ceased. The jugglers halted as if danger invaded their hall.

Prince John marched in to disrupt the festivities, flanked with two knights in escort. He made his way to the dais with the stature of a king himself. He would take the throne of England soon enough. His mother could do nothing to prevent his coronation once Richard was dead.

Against the ensuing silence, Philip released the serving woman in favor of sitting forthright in his chair. Seemed the unexpected bothersome appearance of the prince had doused his merriment.

"What news do you bring from King Henry," Philip asked.

John bowed out of respect.

"No news from him," John started.

"Then the Lionheart remains his prisoner, alive?"

"Your majesty, another reason, one more pressing, brings me before you. One paramount to both our futures. We must speak in solitude of this matter."

Philip's face turned a frown at the thought. He wanted rather to continue to drink and enjoy the company of the women around him. Yet the concern across the prince's face told him he must delay his desires in favor of matters more important to his kingdom.

"I bid you all to drink on," Philip proclaimed to cheers from his raucous crowd.

Dismissing the two archbishops who had risen to join their king, and with Prince John in tow, Philip marched away with knights in escort to the privacy of a chamber a quiet distance from the revelry.

Only after they came to be alone in the torchlight room and seated in chairs across a table before a blazing hearth did Philip motion for John to speak.

"Tell me what so concerns my kingdom that I must forgo celebration, prince."

"I have gained information that my sister intends to meddle in the affairs of kings."

The words struck a nervous chord in Philip, though he buried it from the prince. So much now depended on John's manipulation. The king had neglected to factor in Joanna's influence.

"She is on the Continent with knights in her service."

"Could she be so foolish as to think she might negotiate Richard's freedom?" Philip asked.

"Her intent at the moment I cannot be certain of."

"How many knights accompany her?"

"I do not know. I only know I narrowly missed her departure from the port at Hythe."

"Could she have uncovered our alliance?" the king queried.

Philip shifted in his chair, growing restive from the conversation. He sensed from John's reluctance that he withheld something.

"There is the possibility Princess Joanna may convince the King of Germany to release her brother."

The words brought concern to Philip's face. His stomach churned. He became vulnerable if Richard ever learned about the bargain he had struck.

"Or to deliver the ransom," John added.

Now Philip grew angry.

"You assured me your mother would never raise the gold and silver."

"I still believe her incapable of gathering such a sum."

That brought Philip's laughter.

"I have a sennight past dispatched my men with the silver we promised Henry to keep the Lionheart in chains. Are you now saying I may lose the advantage of our agreement?"

John swallowed with difficulty. If Joanna successfully negotiated Richard's release, the prince would find himself caught between an ally who now turned on him and his brother. Philip would no doubt abandon him in favor of Richard.

"Then what do you intend to do?" Philip pressed.

The king eyed the prince uneasily. Both knew the answer to that question. But as a king, Philip could never voice the words.

Was it even possible for Joanna to strike a deal for Richard's freedom that favored both kingdoms? What other purpose could she have to travel to Henry's court? Henry could accept whatever

Joanna offered in the way of ransom, take France's silver and still release the Lionheart, if he gained assurance there would be no retribution from England.

Anger seethed inside Philip at the thought of having delivered his silver to Henry to hold the Lionheart captive. Their arrangement might unravel with neither Philip nor John ever gaining from it. Maybe that was Henry's intention all along.

"I could not have anticipated my sister's involvement. Even now I cannot be certain what she intends to do on the Continent."

"Then tell me now that you have devised a way to prevent her from striking a deal with Henry independent of the queen."

Philip raised a brow. What would make Joanna believe she could interfere with his game of kings? Did she actually think she could convince Henry to act in a way that might defeat John's intentions? Richard back on his throne would dash all hopes.

The king took pause at the implications.

Might Joanna offer herself in exchange for Richard? Could there be a grand cabal forming? If Henry chose to accept a lesser ransom and the princess, Richard could return to England, rebuild his army, and in time, invade Henry's domain for the evil he had perpetrated. In the end, Richard may retrieve his sister and the ransom after gaining his freedom. That made it also possible that Richard could end up with Philip's payment of silver to King Henry.

John sensed he had lost his edge in his dealings with the King of France. He needed to salvage a benefit for his own aspirations.

Philip rose to pace before the prince.

"What do you ask of me?" the king pressed, sensing John came with a need only he could fulfill.

"Two score knights in my charge to hunt down my sister, prevent her from reaching the king. Then Henry never learns of her intent, and our position with Germany remains intact."

Philip came around with fire in his eyes.

"You would implicate me in the murder of a royal while at the same time invading Henry's domain?"

"Nay, your grace. I will do the deed myself for the benefit of both England and France. I only ask that you provide the might I need to ensure the deed gets accomplished. Together we preserve

England and France against Germany. Without it, you risk attack by your greatest enemies."

"Can it be done?" Philip asked.

"I will see to it."

Philip ruminated over the words. He could certainly see the advantages of what John proposed. But what disadvantages need he consider? Could harm come to France as a result of John's action? If their plan succeeded and Richard died at the hand of King Henry, then only Eleanor stood in opposition. And John was capable of removing Eleanor from the throne. Their secret would remain safe between the two kings.

"And if, perchance, you recover the ransom before it can be delivered?"

"Then your majesty receives half for his support."

"And should you fail to reach her in time?"

Philip fired off his questions as if firing off arrows.

"All the better for you, my lord. We will pursue her until we find her. Then she dies by my hand, but Henry receives the blame when I return her slain body to England to show his cruelty."

Never was there any hesitation in John's responses. It appeared the prince had thought his plan through against the princess.

"And no one would learn the truth?"

"I will see to it."

Philip smiled at the implications for his throne.

"A single score of knights you will have."

"As your majesty sees fit," John replied, releasing the slightest glint of a smile in the torchlight.

43

Five horses clopped single file through the winter forest bordering Henry's domain. Joanna led. She hoped to make it to the first of the three castles without encountering Henry's forces.

A bright morning sun cast warmth upon them as they rode. The night had been cold, spent huddled together without the benefit of fire. They carried only sufficient rations as would fit on their saddles. The remaining provisions Isaac transported to be certain the boys and friars were well fed and warm on their journey. Joanna's plan hinged on each pair reaching their assigned castle to perform as instructed.

The princess found no reason to suspect those who traveled ahead on their quest. Isaac would remain forever faithful to Richard without question, and each friar had been carefully vetted to ensure they would never reveal the true nature of what they were to do.

Yet mistrust rumbled in Joanna's mind when it came to her knights. One of them must have betrayed her in England. Only Duchard had been told of the port with his charge being to guide the others there without revealing beforehand their destination. She emphasized no one can know their destination. The only way John could have discovered her departure from Londontown was from Duchard? And worse, how had the prince anticipated her journey to the correct seaport? She had been careful to control what information any man received. Yet they may be placing themselves in an untenable position between two enemies. She took solace knowing only she knew all the details of what she intended to do. The others might guess and surmise, but it remained unlikely they could determine her exact scripted moves.

So far most progressed as she planned. They need now only remain invisible to Henry's forces until they located Richard.

Rynhawker loped ahead of Thomas, who trailed Joanna, so he might come beside the princess.

"How far before we reach a position favorable to our king?"

"Five days or more, if all remains well. I worry we will encounter Henry's men before we can reach our destination."

"If Henry believes his prize is safe, he will do little to prepare his kingdom for a threat from our queen," Rynhawker said.

"Then what we might encounter along the way reveals our enemy's state of mind," Joanna surmised.

Rynhawker smiled. Joanna's thinking was evolving to that of a military tactician. Richard would be proud to know his sister could execute as well as any of his knights.

Duchard kicked his steed into a trot to come beside his friend.

"How long before we eat?" he asked.

Joanna paused to survey the landscape, hoping to find a low spot in the woods to allow them sufficient cover so they could rest and eat. When none appeared, she spurred her ride onward.

"When we locate suitable concealment," she ordered.

"How long before we might have something to eat?" Alwain asked closing in on the pack.

Only Brayson held his position at the rear with his eyes mindful of the forest around them. He wrestled with the notion of what he might do next. He never anticipated his ruse would take him this far. Now he felt trapped by circumstance. As a result, he did the only thing he could. Cautiously he marked their trail when opportunity allowed. If John dispatched men to hunt them, they might uncover what he left behind and realize they had an ally in their enemy's camp. He could think of no other way to send information to the prince. At the very best, he hoped to sabotage whatever plan Joanna had devised.

There was no mistaking they had penetrated Henry's domain. From here forward they would be treated as enemies of the king if captured. Even though they wore no markings of the King of England, Henry would determine soon enough they intended to rescue their ruler.

An hour later they crested a rise, below which a ravine ran to the south. Joanna altered their course into the lowest part of the gully. Seven-foot-high earthen walls concealed their heads even while mounted.

The late day sun arced toward the horizon, and with its descent, cold air rushed over their bodies, robbing them of the warmth they enjoyed before breaching the shadows.

After watering their beasts, they sat one beside another, chewing down dried venison and twice-baked barley bread while huddled in blankets. They wore no armor, protected only by their chain mail, and each carried a single broadsword on their hip with a dagger in their belt. Joanna's crossbow, with her sheaths of quarrels, became her constant companion.

"How long before we reach our destination?" Brayson queried after a lingering silence.

No one answered.

In solitude they contemplated their quest. No one knew for certain what Joanna intended to do. Yet they trusted she would inform them when the time was proper.

"I cannot say," Joanna replied, which was met with grim faces from all her men.

44

Shackled hands and feet, six knights escorted Richard from the same dungeon cell he and his men had occupied before their latest escape attempt. The Lionheart came before King Henry, who waited upon his throne. Throughout his captivity, Richard never once stood eye to eye with his enemy king. Henry always used an elevated position over the Lionheart to reinforce his dominance over his prisoner.

Richard said nothing when the lead knight yanked him to a stop before the king. He saw anger in Henry's eyes. Richard attempted to read his face. What possible punishment might this man inflict that could be worse than what he had already inflicted upon the Brits in captivity?

Three more knights joined the six, who also took positions around their king. Could Henry honestly believe a shackled prisoner might pose such a dire threat to him?

Richard cracked a smile at the sight. Perhaps Henry was indeed the coward that the legends of his reign had spread. Richard never believed his reputation could command such trepidation that it warranted nine men in armor stand over him.

Roger emerged from the shadows to take his place at Henry's right. Though merely symbolic, no one believed Richard would be fool enough to attack the king. Regardless, every man stood ready to any threat that might materialize.

"Have I not treated you fairly... for a prisoner?" Henry jested with mock sincerity.

He avoided direct eye contact with the Lionheart, focusing his gaze instead on the king's forehead. Henry knew better than to reveal intent with his eyes.

"Release me and my men from the dungeon, then we shall discuss your treatment," Richard replied calmly.

He knew what to expect from his enemy. He expected retribution for his failed escape. The king could put him to death if he wished, though Richard's value removed that option. But what of his men? Could he expect any mercy from this king?

"A foolish thing you attempted," Henry said with a flippancy Richard found degrading.

"Only a fool remains a captive without attempting to free himself," Richard replied.

Their eyes remained locked on each other as if they were the only two people in the room.

Henry's jaw held tight. To intimidate the Lionheart is to gain the upper hand, though he now suspected that to be the more difficult challenge.

"Did you believe you could overpower my men to fight your way to freedom?"

"Your men cower behind their shields," Richard said, almost allowing a glint of a smile to slip through.

The knights tightened on their swords.

But Henry waved the comment off.

"The great crusader thought he could defeat a dozen soldiers in his reckless bid for freedom."

To that Richard offered no response.

"I applaud your courage, or your foolishness," Henry added.

"My lord, we remain uncertain of the wounded guard's fate," Roger said, as if responding on a prearranged cue from his king.

The words drew Henry away from the Lionheart.

"There stands the matter of punishment for what you have done," Henry said.

Richard knew from here forward he must act with both cunning and trepidation. For failing to satisfy Henry's demands meant one or both of his men might die.

"I could just order your comrades hanged."

Henry's word choice indicated death was not his intent. He had other plans, which he carefully withheld at the moment.

"Since my men still live, I then must be the target of your retribution," Richard said.

"Convince me why I should allow them to keep their heads beyond the next sunrise."

Richard leveraged the silence of the next few moments to collect his thoughts. He knew better than to appeal to the king's logic—for there was no logic to keeping Richard's men alive. They held no value, but they remained very useful to the Lionheart, should Richard attempt another escape.

From Henry's tone, it appeared to Richard that Roger had held to his word of withholding their earlier escape from his king.

"In conflict, all men are duty bound to take every action possible to remain alive. No man of honor shall ever forfeit his courage for the sake of their enemy. I would expect my men to act the same as your knights who stand beside you if their king were in jeopardy. A true king never punishes bravery, rather let him punish cowardice," Richard said.

The words jolted Henry's reasoning. He expected the Lionheart to plead for his men's lives, yet he instead presented an argument citing bravery, honor and loyalty. Exactly what Henry would expect from his knights in the face of an invasion.

"So tell me how to punish you and your men for what you have done."

For that Richard offered no answer.

"How would you punish me and my knights before you if this situation were reversed?" Henry pressed.

"Death is never the punishment for courage."

"On that, Crusader King, we agree. But we have the matter of my wounded man," Henry added.

"A death for a death would be fair, your majesty," Roger added.

"Has your man died?" Richard advanced.

Henry ruminated, during which time Richard maintained his narrowed eyes on his nemesis.

"If he dies, Crusader King, one of yours dies in return."

"If that is your edict, then so be it. I ask in return you allow my man to die in the honor he deserves—on the field of battle by the code of chivalry."

Henry rose on his throne in surprise.

"You propose I risk another life in your punishment?"

"You consider either man capable of defending against any of your knights?"

Henry laughed, followed by Roger. Neither of Richard's men could hold their own against a knight.

"In a joust," Richard added.

This time Henry remained silent to analyze the Lionheart's response. Was Richard attempting to turn the punishment into a spectacle? The notion strangely appealed to Henry. Could Richard have another plan with such a response? Certainly, the competition would be entertaining, and it would afford Richard the ill-fated opportunity to watch his man die at the hands of Henry's finest.

"To the death?" Henry posed.

"If that is your wish," Richard replied.

"Allow me, your majesty, to strike down his man," one of his knights offered, stepping forward to bow before his king.

An emotional charge seized the moment, just as Richard had intended. This pleased the Lionheart. The knights in attendance grew angry at his words. Men who allow emotions into their thoughts become fools. And fools are easily manipulated.

"I assure you, Crusader King, I will provide my finest champion to battle your man. Yours will die in the exchange. Is that your wish, Lionheart?"

"Is it not the truest honor for a fighting man to die in battle for king and country?"

Richard swallowed the smile surging to erupt. Henry's move offered Richard the advantage.

"I wish you to allow my men to live for their courage in attempting to free their king."

"Courage is without merit to a prisoner in the dungeon."

"A prisoner for a crime against a king never committed. You extoll of merit when you imprison us without it."

"Enough of noble pretense, Crusader King. If my man dies, yours shall take to the field of battle against one of my choosing."

Henry's growing anger supplanted his reason. Exactly as Richard had hoped.

"Perhaps your finest knight would rescind his offer if he were to battle one worthy of his skills."

"I will never back down," the knight boldly proclaimed.

Clearly Richard's words destabilized both the knight and his king. But Roger saw through the Lionheart's ruse. He understood where Richard had taken his king. Richard, however, did detect a glint of anger rising on Roger's face.

"Never will a man true to my kingdom back down from a fight with one of my enemies. Like your men, mine pledge their courage in the service of their king."

"Then I propose a true display of the courage from the men who swear fealty to you. I demand under the code of chivalry to stand in for my man on the field. Let your finest ride against me!"

Richard's words trapped Henry. He could never allow the Crusader King on the field against his knights. If the king won, all would attest to the Lionheart's might. If he lost, Henry might lose the most valuable treasure in his kingdom. Was this worth the risk? Richard's death would forfeit the ransom. Henry could allow neither. But to refuse now demonstrated Richard's cunning over him.

The Lionheart had gained the upper hand on his enemy. Henry had no choice but to back down from the competition. Richard had skillfully spared his man from death at the pleasure of their captor king.

"Then it shall be done," Henry stammered, stunning the room.

Even the knight who volunteered now stood silent, contemplating a battle to the death against the fabled Crusader King, who had never been unhorsed in an untold number of battles he fought.

Roger had no response to Henry's edict. How could his king possibly win in this confrontation?

45

Four knights clopped over the drawbridge into the castle, trailing the serfs trekking into the shadow of the barbican for the market square. The cold morning kept most peasants huddled in farmhouses; only the brave and the starving ventured out, hoping to exchange meager offerings or beg for food to keep them alive.

On this day only a few soldiers huddled about. Then a song captured everyone's ear. No one expected a melody in their midst. Rising over the cacophony of hagglers, the voice grew stronger. So much so, that Gerand left the stables to determine the source of the lyric. He pressed his way through a gathering crowd to its core, which seemed near the keep adjacent to the foremost castle tower.

Clearly the voice captivated most, and as time went on, the haggling ceased altogether while others shifted to investigate.

At the center of the gathering Gerand encountered Delphi, who had climbed onto the friar's shoulders to project his young voice above those who gathered. He sang extraordinarily well for a lad his age, and loudly. So loudly that, as he progressed in his rhyme, all in the square drew near. Even the soldiers stationed at the keep threw open the doors to partake.

When the lad paused at what most believed the song's end, some applauded, others cheered, though no one offered anything tangible for the lad's performance.

"A few crusts of bread is all we ask," the friar begged. "We have little to eat on this cold morning."

At first Gerand smiled at their antics, failing to notice how the friar's eyes routinely scaled the adjoining tower to the narrow lancet windows near the top. If Henry had imprisoned Richard in the tower, the king would hear his song and respond in kind. A single returned phrase was all that was needed to confirm their king's location. A second tower of equal height rose a hundred paces distant, but the friar believed his lad's voice strong enough to carry to anyone held in there.

Gerand's smile turned grim when he at last observed the friar's odd behavior while the boy sang. The young industrious lad could indeed earn a reward for his entertaining performance. Yet the song churned uneasy in Gerand's mind. Why would a lad of his age sing a song glorifying a nameless king? Clearly the peasants listening held no notion of the song's true meaning, only that it sounded pleasant as the boy chimed out the words with youthful exuberance.

So what did the friar so diligently seek with his gaze?

With no answers to his queries, Gerand returned to the stables. But reaching the stable doors, concern tugged him around to observe the friar once more. Could there be a sinister bent to those two, other than gaining something to eat? Perhaps they sought the favor of the castle's lady, so they might get out of the cold. Once inside, they could gain food and shelter. Was that their innocent purpose?

"God blesses you, my friends," the friar said even though no one came forward with charity.

Moments later Delphi started the song anew. This time he projected louder than his previous performance. When most determined it to be a repeat, they drifted away. By the time the lad finished a second time, he and the friar stood nearly alone. Yet again, the friar directed eyes to the tower windows. He was indeed watching and listening for something.

Gerand found their activity most peculiar. What response was he seeking to the lad's song? Moments later, Gerand dismissed it all as a silly ploy to get warm. He disappeared into the interior to check his men's progress.

Within the keep, six knights escorted Richard from Henry's throne room to return him to the dungeon. As they marched, Richard heard the first faint words of the song his mother had taught him so many years ago. He immediately understood its meaning, *and* what was expected of him. For a moment the voice sounded almost like his sister's when she would sing the opening verse with Richard delivering the next.

But the Lionheart was trapped deep inside the keep. He needed a window from which to respond. Someone was contacting him.

Richard buried the smile rushing to get out. He had to find a way to signal his presence to those seeking it.

With each step Richard pressed for a way to reply. He could spontaneously shout out the words, but there would be little chance his voice could carry beyond the walls. The voice he heard seemed so faint he thought he might be conjuring it only in his desperate mind. Then the verse started anew—it was indeed real.

Without any inkling of a plan, Richard surged at the two knights before him. He bolted through to race for the end of the hall. He could only hope he might find a window to call out from.

The three knights at his rear kicked into a run in pursuit. Although Richard had no chance of escape in his shackles, he still chose to run.

At the end of the corridor, Richard turned right to the view of a block of sunlight falling in from a pair of distant high lancet windows. He was a mere fifty paces from the opening. The song grew stronger.

He opened his mouth to sing out.

A pursuing knight threw his weight into the Lionheart, driving him to the floor. Richard attempted to deliver his line. It never made it out. The knight's driving fist slammed his gut, expelling the air from his lungs before he could put it to useful purpose.

Richard gasped to breathe. He needed to fill his lungs so he could sing out before it was too late. His body refused his command while two knights yanked him away to the spiraling staircase.

Richard lost another opportunity.

46

They slogged in single file, each maintaining twenty paces between to allow time to respond to an assault. Joanna led the way along the forest path with Rynhawker following directly behind her. Only she knew the route they must travel through Henry's lands.

The wind turned mean and bitter this day, with Duchard cursing under his breath each time it stung his face.

Then the gray sky opened to drench them. Still they trudged in single file maintaining their distance. Thomas was the last in their column, eyes always vigilant on their wake.

Brayson risked slowing to come beside the young knight, watchful that the others remained unaware of his intent.

"Miserable rain," he muttered so Thomas would hear.

Thomas offered no response.

"A fool's quest this is. She will get us all killed before we ever reach our king," Brayson added.

"I trust her," Thomas said.

"Mark my words, we will all lose our heads for this."

Watching the backs of the others, he kicked his stallion into a gallop to place the necessary distance between him and the young knight, never once looking back.

As darkness settled in upon the barren forest, the rain finally stopped. The gray crowded sky drew back to reveal a narrow sliver of moon offering faint illumination for the path ahead, making their trek all the more slow and dangerous. If a stallion came up lame, they would have to sacrifice a mount vital to their quest.

Alwain grumbled they should find a place to rest until sunrise. He shivered in his wet clothing. He also failed to realize his voice carried quite far in the forest still. So much so, that Joanna heard his complaint. She made no retort, only spurred her stallion on through the tree-entangled path ahead.

The night temperature hovered near freezing. It was the safest time to travel through Henry's domain, as few wished to be out on a cold winter's night without due cause. And since Joanna gave the king no reason to suspect her intrusion into his lands, his soldiers and knights would sleep warm in their tents or any other structure they might find to house them.

Each day they progressed undiscovered brought them one day closer to their rendezvous and their king.

Joanna insisted, despite the biting cold, they travel as far as possible under the moonlight then favor gullies and ravines during the day.

"How much further must we go?" Rynhawker asked.

"I cannot be certain, but I believe three more days ride to the fortress we seek."

The first glimmer of the awakening sun made its presence known. Joanna sought the refuge of a ravine. Once there, they tethered their stallions before locating suitable places to sleep in the cold softness of a carved-out hollow along nine-foot earthen walls. They were well departed from the beaten path of the forest way, and only if someone were intent on seeking them out, would they become exposed. They were also out of the wind, which pleased every one of them.

Rynhawker spread his cloak upon the ground before assisting Joanna into a comfortable place to rest. Then he lowered beside her to bring his arm around in close to keep her warm.

"We need a fire to dry our clothes," Duchard complained, shifting every which way to find comfort in his location.

"No fires," Joanna commanded.

"My lady, if illness strikes, we become unable to fight," Alwain offered.

"Then we pray to God this morn to keep us in health until we reach our king," Joanna responded.

She heard Duchard's grumbling, but she fell short of understanding his words.

"If He wishes to help, let Him cease this blasted rain," Duchard said clearly this time.

"I would praise God if His rain were the only challenge facing us on this quest," Joanna said.

Her words played upon her men's minds, causing them to contemplate what lie ahead. Suddenly the rain became the least of their concerns.

Joanna rested her head against Rynhawker's shoulder. Memories of their night together in Londontown found their way into her mind. She relished the sensation of his body against hers while his warmth spread through her. The sun climbed gradually over the horizon, bringing the surrounding forest under the scrutiny of sunlight. Just having the sunlight invade their ravine made Rynhawker uneasy. In darkness they were hidden; in daylight they were vulnerable even though they sought the safety of the lowlands.

"Have you a plan to breach the fortress?" Rynhawker asked.

His question snared Duchard's attention a dozen paces away. Guilt swarmed over Rynhawker for asking it.

Joanna responded by shifting closer with her eyes closed.

"Is one required here in this forest?" she responded a moment later, opening her eyes.

"No."

"Then I do not have a plan." She smiled at him.

"So how do you intend to reach our king?" Duchard intruded from his place.

The knight's question sought to dislodge her confidence. No one wished to accept that the princess might be clever enough to devise such a daring plan.

"We do not yet know which castle imprisons our king," Alwain offered, seemingly in Joanna's defense.

Rynhawker shifted his blanket so he might cover her more fully to shield her from the occasional wind racing along the ravine.

Joanna offered no answers, only closed her eyes so she might sleep.

"Can we succeed?" Rynhawker whispered a while later.

"We must," she whispered back.

The princess slipped an arm around her knight's waist the way a lover would for her mate.

"Hold me closer," she risked.

From the snores rattling the morning air, Joanna believed her knights were all asleep.

Rynhawker tightened his arms so their cheeks, stiff from the biting wind, touched.

"Are you still cold?" he asked.

"Not now," she replied.

"We must sleep," Rynhawker said.

Joanna gazed into his eyes. She wished to kiss him. She wanted to tell him what was in her heart. She wanted him to reveal how he felt about her. It seemed so right being this close to him.

Rynhawker closed his eyes while leaning his head against the exposed tree root overhanging the ravine's edge. Joanna nestled her head into the apex of his shoulder then allowed her eyes to close.

They slept for hours, hidden from the forest while their horses grazed on roots and small branches from surrounding plants.

When her stallion whickered, Joanna awoke with a start. In so doing, Rynhawker bolted up, still clutching her tightly.

"What?" he sought in a low voice.

"Nothing," she replied. "It is time we ride."

Reluctantly Rynhawker released her so he might wake the men. Duchard refused to come awake, wishing instead to sleep on. Alwain and Brayson required no prodding, springing up the moment Rynhawker stirred.

Thomas was already about, returning to the ravine from his place at the ridge.

"All remains quiet," he reported.

The sun settled low in the sky. In a few hours the cover of darkness would assist them as they proceeded toward their target.

They sat in the pairs Joanna had assigned on the ship. No knight would ever travel alone. Rynhawker and Joanna sat together, Duchard and Brayson sat a distance away, with Alwain and Thomas the final pair. Each's primary duty became to protect the other.

Joanna's stomach rumbled in hunger and thirst.

Rynhawker removed the last of their dried venison and a flagon of water from his saddle. He passed them among the men. In silence they supped until the sun left them in darkness. Another day passed. They had penetrated undetected further into Henry's domain.

Each knight harbored questions, which Joanna left intentionally unanswered. Each pair held a small parchment map indicating a rendezvous point should they need to scatter to save their lives.

Tonight might be the night they came upon the fortress that held their king. Tonight might be the night they would learn what they must do to free Richard from his chains.

On this night, a cloud-layered sky obliterated the moon, forcing them to travel slower than they wished. Duchard cursed the thought of another night of rain. The wind, however, had fallen away, leaving behind warmer air, allowing them to travel with their faces uncovered.

Joanna grew anxious when much of the night passed and still they had yet to reach their destination. With the imminent rising sun would come another day of sleeping in cracks and crevices while hoping to remain undiscovered.

All stopped suddenly, snapping reins holding stallions in check.

Horses whickered somewhere ahead.

Joanna's heart leapt into her throat. They had come so far; they were so close. They had to remain undetected.

At the lead of their column, Rynhawker motioned to abandon the beaten path in favor of a thicket of unruly pine capable of harboring them. There they held their beasts quiet while they waited.

Fear took over each heart.

Ahead a jostling cluster of six mounted knights clopped through the trees, moving steadily against Joanna's right flank.

She eased her crossbow off her back to level it while silently loading a quarrel into the channel.

None of her knights dared raise a sword, fearing the scraping sound alone of a blade sliding out might alert their enemy. Yet all held hands ready on their hilts, anxious for the moment when they might have to fight.

No one breathed. The distance between them and Henry's men grew with each moment they passed unaware of their presence.

More tense minutes expired as the riders made their way through the forest.

Joanna's arm ached from holding her crossbow ready. Then her mount grew anxious, shuffling toward the opening of the copse. It released a telltale whicker.

Panic swept through her. Rynhawker snared her reins, jerking the beast back under the overhanging foliage.

It was too late.

The last knight in the string wheeled about. Instantly sensing danger, he went for his sword. Before he could bring it out, the quarrel thumped into his chest on the right side of his heart.

Rynhawker drew his sword to lead the charge from the pine thicket. Startled, Henry's knights were slow to respond to the charge, allowing Rynhawker and the others to engage them before they could fully position themselves to fight.

Alwain engaged the two closest.

Rynhawker unhorsed the third knight, stabbing him handily in his gut. Thomas met the fourth to charge, which he fought back long enough for Duchard to advance to aid Alwain.

Spying Joanna holding the deadly crossbow, the last of Henry's knights charged unengaged, heading for the princess.

Brayson shifted to shield the princess while she struggled with the pull lever against the closest tree. Once cocked, there came the welcome click of her quarrel sliding into place.

She lowered it against the last of Henry's charging knights. Her aim true, the knight felt the quarrel pierce his throat before tumbling backward from his mount, landing dead on the forest floor less than a dozen horse strides from her.

In minutes, the clangor of battle ceased, returning silence to the forest. None of Henry's men survived—not one of hers suffered an injury.

"My lady, there will be others," Rynhawker warned.

"When these are found, Henry will dispatch his knights in search of us," Duchard added.

"Then hide them well. Take everything useful. Make it difficult to find these bodies. Alwain and Thomas, drag them to the nearest ravine."

"As you command," Alwain responded.

"Then scatter in pairs. Make it impossible for Henry to know our force and intent," Joanna commanded.

The men stared at her, uncertain how to proceed.

"Duchard and Brayson, ride south to the east-flowing river. Use it to find your way to the rendezvous. Thomas and Alwain, ride north to the hills but remain west before proceeding to the south."

"Do you think Henry might suspect us?" Rynhawker started.

"Yes," Joanna replied, needing no more words to understand his question.

If King Henry learned of their intrusion he would move his prisoner, or at the very least fortify his guard over him. It was vital now they reach Richard before Henry learned of their presence in his domain.

The dawn came. Joanna insisted they ride throughout the day forgoing sleep and food. Within an hour of sunset, they came to the edge of the forest and there on a grassy rise Strigaarde castle stood.

Twin conical-capped towers and jutting spires rose up as a beacon for others. The fortress appeared exactly as annotated on the map, so Joanna was confident she had located one of the three castles most likely to imprison their king.

"Now we need a plan," Rynhawker said quietly.

"Come we must go," Joanna replied, turning her stallion's face to return to the forest.

They skirted the woods, careful to remain beyond the sight of men walking the parapet while Joanna studied the fortifications. In her hasty surveillance she sought the castle's weaknesses, one especially that might provide their way in, should this be the castle they must breach to rescue their king. Satisfied she had gleaned all knowledge possible from a distance, they receded into the trees until they reached the river that would guide them to their rendezvous. Strigaarde castle would be difficult to breach, but not impossible.

47

Duchard stared silently at the parchment map for a long time. He never acquired the skills necessary to navigate by them. Brayson waited patiently beside him, scanning their surroundings. Now was not the time to pause exposed to determine which way to proceed.

Despite having no inkling of where they were, Duchard refused to admit to either himself or Brayson they were lost. Besides, he was a knight. His job was to fight. They used others whose specific duty it was to deliver them to the fight. The system worked well. They delivered Duchard to the battlefield and Duchard kept them alive.

Now the system broke down. Somehow it had to be Joanna's fault. She had ill-planned this part of their quest. Duchard required assistance but refused to reveal that fact to his companion.

"Which way?" Brayson pressed at last. His patience with Duchard wearing thin.

"I believe if we remain in this valley we will encounter the river's end," Duchard offered with little confidence in his voice.

"Are you certain?"

Duchard nodded; his eyes reflected the negative.

"There!" Brayson said, indicating a distant cluster of trees.

Knights on horseback.

From their location Duchard and Brayson spotted the knights before being discovered themselves. Duchard kicked his stallion into a trot twisting it into a low spot in the forest. Brayson followed.

The knights strode casually through the trees unaware of Duchard and Brayson in their path.

Neither spoke while they threaded their way through barren limbs desperate to locate harborage before Henry's knights came upon them.

Duchard trotted behind a slope suitable to keep them out of the knights' sight... if the knights failed to detect their tracks and the two remained close to the ground.

Had the riders uncovered their dead brethren and now sought their killers?

Both Duchard and Brayson dismounted, tethered their mounts then fell to the ground near the apex of the slope.

Henry's knights drew closer, still riding with determination, talking softly amongst themselves. They were so close Duchard and Brayson heard every word.

Silently, they extracted blades to be ready. They were outnumbered three-to-one, but if fortune were with them, they might find a way to fight their way past them.

The lead knight in the string slowed as they neared the slope, though he never once glanced in their direction.

Duchard and Brayson held their swords against their chests with their backs to the ground, waiting. At the first sign of attack they intended to spring up and take each knight as they charged.

Moments ticked off.

The sounds grew clearer.

Duchard tightened both hands around his hilt. His mind reeled with defensive maneuvers he might make to take on two in one offensive. He sucked in a breath and held it, praying.

Brayson closed his eyes, crossed himself hastily.

Duchard signaled the men had past their location; they were proceeding away. Still neither breathed for fear they might be heard to bring the knights back.

The forest fell silent around them. Duchard exhaled in relief. When Brayson sought to move, Duchard held him in check. They needed the men to clear the area before resuming their journey.

"We are all going to die in this frigid, godless land," Brayson protested.

"I did not journey here to die."

"Nor did I. But you know in your heart as well as I that the princess lacks the ability to command us."

Duchard glared at his fellow knight.

"I came here to save my king. Why did you come?"

"Not to die. Say the word, Sir Duchard, I stand ready to bring my charger about. We ride to the nearest port in Philip's land to take us home."

Duchard remained silent. Their knight's code forbade them from any such cowardice. Never in his life would he retreat from a fight. If his king needed his sword, Duchard would deliver it.

The knight snared Brayson's arm in anger.

"A knight never abandons a brethren," he scolded at last.

Duchard regained his mount, spurring the beast to resume their journey. Brayson remained stationary, hoping his fellow knight might come to see the folly of such a quest and join him.

"We owe our allegiance to our king, not his sister! She will lead us to our death."

Duchard never looked back. Instead, he kicked harder to force his charger to a trot.

Moments later Brayson abandoned his resistance to spur his beast to trail his companion. At least they would protect each other. All Brayson could hope for now was that the princess realized the folly of her quest and directed them back to the safety of English soil. Or Brayson would need another way to disrupt the princess in her quest to rescue their king.

48

Isaac performed his tasks exactly as the princess had commanded. He delivered each pair of friar and lad to one of the three castles Joanna designated on the parchment map provided. The friars would guide their lads into the market square on three consecutive days, using the boys' performances to signal their imprisoned king. It was imperative that each day the friars listen between performances for a response from Richard inside the keep.

After three consecutive days in the castle square, the friars would lead the boys to the neighboring forest to await Isaac's return. Isaac would travel nonstop from castle to castle to retrieve all three pairs, after which he was to rendezvous with Joanna.

The friar and lad from Strigaarde castle were the first to report their failure. No response came from their performances, so they concluded it unlikely Henry held their king there. Strigaarde was the smallest of the three possibilities, and as such, should have easily revealed their king's presence.

They spoke little as they journeyed in the hay wagon to Brucken castle, situated furthest from the rendezvous.

Holding at the forest's edge on the road to the castle gates, the three huddled in blankets to stave off the late November cold. At last they watched the friar and his young companion exit the gate against peasants making their way inside. This morning's air seemed colder than the previous day, causing the lad beside Isaac to shiver on occasion. Isaac tucked him under his blanket to warm him. The lad smiled in response to Isaac's smile.

Only after the friar and lad made their way down the road did Isaac venture out to meet them.

Isaac held his smile until he read the disappointment in the friar's eyes, which came well before they reached the wagon. The

Jew's heart sank at the thought that again Joanna's ruse to locate her brother produced no results.

The friar assisted his lad into the rear of the wagon before climbing clumsily in himself. The two then shared the friar's robe for warmth.

"Nothing?" Isaac had to ask. He knew the answer, yet he needed the words to confirm his suspicions.

"Never a sound from the keep on any day," the friar reported.

Isaac slowly brought his beasts around to return to the forest. Had Joanna erred in her knowledge of her enemy? What if Henry chose another castle than the three she targeted? How could they hope to locate their king in such a vast domain?

"Did you perchance discover King Henry in attendance in the castle?" Isaac pressed, hoping their reconnaissance might bear at least something useful.

"I did as you instructed. The kitchen servant where we begged said she had prepared no feasts for their king. She also revealed there were few knights in this castle to serve," the friar said.

The report ignited a new idea in Isaac's mind. In anticipation of the ransom delivery, the king would keep his prize close. That required a full contingent of knights in the king's retinue. The clergy would also gravitate to wherever the king decided to spend the winter. Therefore, Henry's refuge had to house a large number of men. Isaac reasoned he might be able to locate Henry by uncovering the increased activity in the countryside surrounding the king's castle. Isaac could query serfs in the neighboring villages and inns. Locating Henry, which should be far easier than locating Richard, could gain them their king's location.

There existed no way Isaac could think of to confirm his logic concerning the King of Germany, short of seeing Richard in the same castle as Henry. But regardless of which king they serve, people liked to talk, and getting them to reveal details about the royals might allow Isaac to confirm which castle held the Lionheart.

Filled with renewed excitement, the wagon traveled throughout the day against a fierce wind, finding a hollow in the forest in which to rest at night. The fire at the core of their small camp warmed the boys as they slept fitfully, well fed with lentils cooked into a soup, some dried boar and stale barley bread that Isaac had squirreled away for them. He hoped to use the food as the reward for the pair who succeeded, but so far both sets had come up without learning their king's whereabouts.

Even before morning broke, an excited Isaac prepared his stallions for the day's journey. He clung to the hope that if neither of the previous castles held their king, Henry might then hold Richard in the third castle, Trifels, which remained still two days away.

The boys awakened slowly and reluctantly at their friar's calling, and before long, the wagon journeyed through the forest to their next destination. Isaac spoke little, silent while he devised a way to confirm Henry's location.

49

Joanna and Rynhawker tethered their mounts in the low of a valley so they might forage in the surrounding vicinity. The night had been cold, the recent rain allowed them to collect water to quench their thirst.

Joanna settled into a shallow in the ground, one that allowed her to rest her crossbow across a fallen log. From there she watched for movement. If luck were with them, she might catch a rabbit or deer within her sights.

The hour grew late with dusk rapidly approaching. Soon darkness would fall, and they would abandon the hunt in favor of continuing their journey to the south. Hunger plagued their bellies. Neither would sleep until they had gained at least something to eat.

Larks and crows fluttered in the trees, but Joanna lacked the confidence in her aim to try for one of them. Even a blackbird, though scrawny, would provide some nourishment.

When the forest floor remained still, Joanna shifted her aim to a bevy of blackbirds cawing in low branches ten paces distant.

Could she make the shot? She wondered.

Perhaps she could turn over her weapon to Rynhawker; maybe he could bring down a bird so they might eat.

Rynhawker lowered to a prone position beside her. They had strayed from sight of their mounts, but the still forest allayed any fears that might arise from being separated from their escapes.

"Perhaps we go for the largest bird," Rynhawker suggested.

"Can you make the shot?" Joanna asked without taking her eyes off the undergrowth.

Rynhawker studied the movements of their prey. It might be possible if they remained in their present location while Joanna transferred the crossbow to him. More likely the action would send them to the treetops to languish out of range.

Then Joanna spied rustling in the midst of a dense thicket fifty paces out. Her stomach rumbled in anticipation.

Rynhawker flattened against the cold ground to prevent any his body from revealing their presence. A stag would be too much to ask for. He would settle for a plump hare under the circumstances.

"There is something there," Joanna whispered, shifting her crossbow in preparation to take her shot.

Moments passed. No further movement came from the thicket. Joanna's heart dropped at the implication the animal had moved on. She relaxed her finger on the trigger, waiting.

It came again. More persistent this time in the growth. Could it be one or more of Henry's men crawling through to maintain cover against them? Had they been detected?

Rynhawker carefully and slowly drew his sword in case it turned out to be human.

Joanna's heart quickened. She prayed for a fawn or doe she might be able to bring down.

Then a furry little head popped out from the bushes, staring in their direction. The brown bear cub sniffed about cautiously before poking through the branches, foraging amongst the winter bracken.

"What do I..." Joanna risked saying.

Concern spread. Rynhawker checked the wind. Terror took over. They were downwind of the young. And a cub is never alone...

Rynhawker rolled to his back as the mother brown bear charged out of a thicket at their rear. The beast rose up in a snarl ten paces away, releasing a mean growl meant to strike terror into their souls. Viscous drool hanging off her fangs, she attacked.

Joanna had a single moment to roll, raise her crossbow to brace against her hip and fire into the wall of fur towering over her!

The quarrel tore into the bear's chest, but the beast continued. Joanna saw only white teeth and dark eyes coming at her.

With no other option, Joanna rolled to the side as Rynhawker gained his feet in time to drive his blade into the mother bear's gut.

Joanna held her scream as the beast lunged at her on its fall. The beast's extended claws brushed her crossbow arm above the wrist before the princess could clear its path. Rynhawker plunged his sword in again as the beast flattened at their feet.

On its charge the brown bear towered above them by at least an arm's length. It weighed thrice Rynhawker's girth, and bleeding, it struggled momentarily while its last blood drained beneath it.

Rynhawker posed motionless over the beast, ready to stab again. Its unseeing eyes gazed out at the now orphaned offspring.

The cub wailed at the sight of its mother before scampering into the thicket that had given it cover.

Rynhawker aided Joanna to her feet, hastily checked her over before taking her into his arms to settle her trembling.

"You are uninjured?" he pressed.

Joanna nodded her head, her skin the pallor of parchment.

"Did it harm you?"

"No," Joanna lied in that desperate moment to prevent the pain in her arm from reaching her face.

The bear claws had ripped into her sleeve during its fall. She refused to examine it, fearing acknowledgement might induce Rynhawker to alter their quest. She would allow nothing to deny her brother's freedom... not even an attacking bear.

"Gather the horses quickly. I will cut away our supper. We must be gone before the wolves catch the scent on the wind. We will never fight them off."

His hands covered in blood, Rynhawker secured three cuts of bear meat to his saddle while Joanna took the lead to guide them south. In the middle of the night, they located a place of refuge to prepare their supper. The cold night air preserved the meat well until they roasted it. By now the carcass of the mother bear would be stripped by hungry wolves. There remained only a slight chance the cub could survive the night.

Their flight forced them to sacrifice a valuable food supply, but they would be safe until they reached their rendezvous. At least Joanna convinced herself as they continued through the night forest aided only by moonlight passing in and out of clouds.

50

Now Rynhawker led the way, with Joanna following close behind as they threaded through entangled branches. Dense fog allowed them to continue their journey well into the morning hours. While they could see no more than twenty strides ahead, neither could Henry's soldiers see any better. If they remained quiet, they could travel until the fog burned away near midday.

The princess clung to her saddlebow with both hands to remain atop her mount. Her illness began hours after they had supped on the bear meat. She knew serious trouble had found her. At first, she suspected the bear meat to be the cause. But Rynhawker displayed no ill effects.

Glancing back, Rynhawker noticed Joanna's gaze unfocused. Sweat beaded her cheeks stiff from the cold. Fear swam into his head. He halted to bring her beside him.

"Something is wrong," he said.

"No! I can go on." Joanna refused to succumb to what had become certain.

Rynhawker knew better. Seizing her reins, he brought her stallion beside his to examine her.

Joanna recoiled in pain when he grasped her arm. Tears welled in her eyes. She jerked free. The knight would be angry if he knew. Rynhawker seized her arm once again, observing for the first time her torn sleeve. He knew what he would find even before he drew the material up.

He stared at three spaced claw marks of torn flesh, swollen and red now, festering with infection. The knight knew what the sight meant. Men died on the battlefield from superficial wounds left untreated.

"Scratches, that is all. I can ride. We go on," she demanded.

Joanna separated her arm from his grasp, needing her hand to steady herself in her saddle.

"We need someone who..." he demanded of her.

"No! Nothing will jeopardize our quest. We proceed to the rendezvous."

"And how shall we proceed when you die?"

Joanna knew the cause of her sickness. She needed to rest, she needed to eat and she needed water, but they also needed to reach the rendezvous. The longer they delayed, the greater the chance Henry's men might discover them.

Rynhawker steadied her when she slumped forward in her saddle. He restrained his beast beside hers long enough to adjust her on her mount. Joanna had grown too weak to continue.

"We must stop," Rynhawker issued with the force of a command. He understood well the princess' stubborn nature. Unless he forced rest upon her, she would forge on.

"No!" she shot back, bolting up perfectly straight. She commanded herself to fight this. "I will make it. We ride on," she scolded in a wilting voice.

Rynhawker refused to budge. He took her hand, not in anger but in concern. She felt on fire. He knew in that instant she needed care as quickly as they could gain it.

"Why do you wait?" she snarled breathlessly.

Still Rynhawker refused to move.

"You will not ride alone."

Joanna said nothing, gazing as if contemplating her response. None came. He was right—they needed someone with knowledge of how to treat her.

Rynhawker tore his shirt to create a makeshift bandage, applying it to the wound after cleansing it with their remaining water.

Afterward, he nudged his stallion against hers. Without retort, he drew her into his arms. He feared she might tumble unconscious from her saddle, killing herself even before she reached her brother.

"What..." she started.

Rynhawker silenced her, cradling her against his chest as they shared his saddle.

After securing her reins to his saddle strap, he spurred his beast into a clumsy slow walk. But they were moving, and with that, they would reach the rendezvous despite Joanna's incapacity.

With an orange sun glowing below the horizon, Rynhawker and Joanna arrived at the river they must follow to reach the rendezvous. They were close now. Joanna, however, had grown worse. Rynhawker prayed they would find the other knights already in position. With Joanna in his arms, they would fall without a fight if they encountered Henry's men. There was no way Rynhawker could abandon Joanna to fend off an attack.

Joanna grew increasingly weak, falling in and out of a light sleep. Though she never said as much, she appreciated Rynhawker taking her into his arms. Clinging to him brought her comfort despite their perilous location.

A gibbous moon shed sufficient light to continue journeying through the lifeless forest until they reached the confluence of three rivers, exactly as Joanna had indicated on her parchment. It was the middle of the night, but they had arrived at the rendezvous.

Rynhawker searched in all directions.

They were alone.

He guided the stallions to a halt in the hollow of a thicket less than fifty paces from a riverbank. The hollow provided harborage from anyone traveling the forest. To be discovered, someone must approach within a dozen paces of their location. In addition, the hollow appeared spacious enough to conceal their entire party when they arrived. Rynhawker refused to think in any more dire terms. They would all arrive safe.

Joanna had selected a perfectly strategic location from which to operate. They had yet to learn which castle imprisoned their king, but regardless of which, they need only travel a few days from the rendezvous to reach it.

As hours passed and they remained alone, despair crowded into Rynhawker's heart. Not one of their comrades had arrived. What if they fell to Henry's men during their trek? What if Joanna and Rynhawker were now alone in their quest?

Rynhawker awakened Joanna still clinging to him. She winced at his touch on her injured arm. Slowly Rynhawker removed the makeshift bandage to examine her wound. It had worsened since his last examination.

Supporting her weight for so long, his own arm, his sword arm, now ached.

"We have arrived," he whispered softly, the way a lover entices a woman.

Joanna drew her eyes open reluctantly to stare at him in the faint moonlight. She attempted a smile.

With great difficulty, Rynhawker assisted Joanna from his mount. She clung to the saddle while he dismounted then set about the task of providing her a place in which to rest. Their horses tethered nearby, Rynhawker arranged blankets on the frozen ground to create a suitable bed. He used the remaining blankets to warm her.

Joanna curled immediately into a tight ball as she shivered from the cold. After determining that her fever still raged, he tried to give her water from the river. She refused, instead wishing to remain in her position to shield her from the wind.

A fire now was too dangerous, though it would benefit the princess. She would be angry if he placed her well-being above their quest. So Rynhawker did the only thing left to do: He curled his body around hers, spreading his warmth onto her. There he settled into a tenuous sleep, praying she would survive the night and that help would arrive with the next sunrise. Being alone would mean certain capture if they were discovered.

51

Isaac maneuvered his wagon carefully through the ruts of an infrequently traveled road leading deeper into the forest away from Trifels castle. He had to hope he would not find himself alone at the rendezvous. Once he located the river, he altered his direction to follow its flow to the confluence. He had been given no other instructions on how to proceed should he arrive with no one there.

Joanna and Rynhawker would be waiting for his arrival and his news, he convinced himself of that. The princess would be excited when he revealed to her what he had learned.

Isaac retarded his beasts, departing the beaten path into the sparse barren trees clustered at along a small rise. The location gave them a vantage point with which to watch over the surrounding woodland. Isaac had no reason to believe others might be following him, since an old man in a hay wagon offered nothing of value.

On the day previous, as Joanna had instructed, Isaac delivered the friars and the lads to the nearest nunnery, where they could seek sanctuary and gain comfort until they journeyed into France. Once in King Philip's domain they could travel to the coast, locate a ship and return to England. Their task in the quest had been completed, whether it succeeded or failed. It was up to Joanna and her men to complete their quest from here.

Rynhawker emerged from a gully to not only greet Isaac, but also to allay his fears. He indicated with a wave where to steer the wagon to conceal it in the winter forest.

"Where is the princess?" Isaac queried immediately when no other body greeted him. He expected her smiling face at his arrival.

"She is here. Hurry. We need help," Rynhawker said.

Concern swarmed over the old man even before he saw the princess. Her coughing preceded her in the low of the gully.

Joanna sat wrapped tightly in a blanket with her head covered against the wind. Her face was reddened from the cold. She curled against the bole of an oak, covering her mouth to muffle her cough.

Isaac rushed to her, falling to his knees.

"My lady, you are burning up," he said, testing her forehead and placing his hands to her cheeks.

"A bear. We were attacked.... The princess was clawed. You must do something," Rynhawker pleaded.

Isaac never looked back at the knight. Instead, he located the wound to find it infected.

"How long has she been..."

Rynhawker read Isaac's face. Fear took over.

"Two days," the knight answered.

"I will be better if I just rest," Joanna offered.

Isaac shook his head, muttering while examining her wound more closely.

"We need a poultice. I have some in my wagon. Then we get you someplace warm."

"No! We cannot risk discovery. If they uncover our presence our advantage will be lost."

"My lady, you will die if you remain here. I will not allow that before you have the chance to rescue your brother. I will secure a place, you will get better," Isaac said sternly, the way a father scolds an obstinate young daughter.

"No!" Joanna forced out weakly.

"You will do as I say," Isaac responded.

Joanna knew better than to argue further. His eyes informed her he would refuse to abide by her wishes. She needed him to keep her alive.

He rose with a creak in his bones to return to his wagon. From his burlap sack, he removed a small leather pouch from which he extracted what he needed.

"Start a fire," Isaac commanded.

"No," Joanna shot back.

"Start a small fire," Isaac corrected.

Rynhawker complied despite what he saw in Joanna's eyes.

Next Isaac cleansed the wound as best he could with water.

"Place your dagger in the flame," he commanded the knight.

While the blade heated, he wrapped a branch with a cloth he held, afterward placing it between Joanna's teeth.

"Bring me the dagger."

Rynhawker knelt beside her. He knew what was to come.

"Forgive me, my princess. This will hurt greatly," Isaac said with an equal pain in his eyes.

At his heated dagger's first scrap of her festering wound, Joanna screamed uncontrollably. The cloth kept the sound from traveling into the surrounding woods. She had never experienced such agony. Try as she might to recoil her arm, Rynhawker held it in place until Isaac completed scraping each of her injuries. Tears flowed without restraint. Joanna teetered at the edge of consciousness when the fire suddenly retreated.

Isaac applied his poultice before wrapping her arm in a fresh bandage, after which, he tucked her arm beneath her blanket. He checked her eyes, saw she had survived the ordeal.

"Keep her warm. She needs water, much water," Isaac commanded on his rush back to his wagon.

"Where are you going?" Rynhawker demanded.

"Force her to drink if you must. I will return with a solution."

Isaac climbed into his wagon, where he slapped the reins to wheel his beasts back onto the path.

Rynhawker stopped him.

"Out of my way!" Isaac snarled.

"Take my charger. You will be faster."

At first Isaac was stunned—a knight offering his stallion to a Jew!

"Take it and hurry."

Isaac gladly abandoned his wagon in favor of Rynhawker's charger. He spurred the beast as best he could to carry him into the forest. It would take too long to return to the nunnery, but Isaac remembered a place on passing that might be able to help them.

52

Rynhawker cradled Joanna to set her into hay piled inside a narrow structure adjoining a stable beside a small inn. The hour was late, darkness concealed their entry from the few patrons inside, and the innkeeper never laid eyes on either Joanna or the knight.

Isaac's search had turned up a sympathetic innkeeper who shared the same faith. It took four inns before Isaac located the one he desperately sought. Though he and the innkeeper were loyal to different kings, they shared the same God. It was that bond that secured Joanna a dry, warm place to sleep and recover.

With Joanna safely inside and warmed by horse blankets, Isaac returned to the rendezvous point. He would remain to inform the others of the situation. It would be a day or two at least before they knew for certain if Isaac's poultice had worked. If it failed, there would be nothing further they could do for the princess.

For the present, only Isaac and the innkeeper knew the location of Joanna and Rynhawker, and Isaac had led the innkeeper to believe Joanna was his daughter who had taken ill.

Rynhawker lay beside her in the hay, bringing her body against his so she might share his heat. She shivered uncontrollably for a few moments before succumbing to his warmth.

Within the hour she lay curled with her knight fast asleep.

Rynhawker gently kissed her forehead. Her fever had yet to abate, but within the span of another hour, the small, covered alcove felt as warm as if a fire burned in a nearby hearth.

The dreary winter's day wore on. Both slept in each other's arms. When Rynhawker awoke the following morning, he realized Joanna's coughing had subsided, she breathed softly and easily beside him. Still he kept her close.

An errant thud from the adjoining stable brought both Joanna and Rynhawker bolting up. Joanna's hand went instinctively to the dagger hidden beneath her cloak. She vowed she would never allow herself to be captured by any evil men again. Suddenly the notion of having a warm place to sleep came at too stiff a price. She wanted to flee. Rynhawker brought her into his arms to gently recline her back into her hay mattress.

"We must remain still. We are safe here," he convinced her, hoping that would allow her muscles to untense.

"How long have we been asleep?" she queried.

"One day. You are feeling better?"

Joanna attempted to exercise her wounded arm. The pain had lessened to a dull ache.

"A little. We must go. They will find us here," she persisted. Yet she made no move to leave her knight's arms.

"What of our mounts?" she pressed after a few moments.

"In the stable beside us. The innkeeper's son tends them."

Rynhawker took a flagon of water to share with Joanna, allowing her to drink her fill first. Then he offered her lentils cooked soft, followed by a crust of twice-baked barley bread. She began to eat, slowly at first, then chewing aggressively to get the food down.

"What of the innkeeper?" she pressed.

"He asks no questions. Isaac assured me of that."

"Then we must go."

"We must stay," Rynhawker insisted.

When Joanna sought to gain her feet, Rynhawker brought her back beside him.

"You must rest. We remain another night."

"It is too dangerous," she countered.

"It is you who convinced us to trust Isaac. Now you must do the same."

Joanna succumbed, returning to his side in the hay while Rynhawker spread a blanket reeking of horse dung to keep her warm.

While she lay beside him, the memories of her imprisonment in Sicily flooded into her mind. Never since those days had she allowed herself to become unclean for so long. She had been forced into months without bathing and scant food when she refused to bow to her husband's cruel will.

She recalled that glorious day when Richard appeared at the castle gates, demanding her release before nightfall. Word spread like fire throughout the castle to reach her in her tower prison. She never saw Richard from her location, but she knew her days of imprisonment and suffering had ended. Richard would have sacked the castle, burning every building to the ground to rescue her.

In the end, the king ordered her release and without ever laying eyes on her again, knights escorted her to the castle gates to reunite with her brother.

She knew in her heart her life would have ended had Richard not come to her aid. Now she would return the favor. She dreamt about that moment when she would stand face-to-face with her brother. Would he be elated she had come to free him? Or would he be angered that a woman would attempt such a dangerous and desperate quest? His response would matter not at that moment. Just having him free was all she needed to fill her heart with joy.

"If you improve, we leave before the next sunrise," Rynhawker whispered.

Lying with her so close muddled Rynhawker's mind. He knew what he desired, but he also knew he must never allow himself to become weak. His code forbade such actions.

Joanna turned to him, kissing him when he least expected it.

At first Rynhawker resisted. It was wrong for her to feel this way about him. It was worse for him to feel the same for her. Even if they survived this quest, Rynhawker knew they could never be together the way he was with Merewen.

But his urges raged out of control at having her beside him. Her kiss filled his head. Rynhawker could no longer keep himself from her. He slid his arms tightly around her to kiss her with a passion that matched hers.

Joanna felt herself surrendering to her desires for him. She opened herself to draw him in, so he might feel her nakedness.

"If we only have this night between us, then I will have loved the moments given me. Do not deny me this, my knight, please."

"You are ill, my lady. I cannot..."

"You must. I can resist you no longer. I must have you. Please love me while the opportunity surrounds us."

Rynhawker caved in to his desires. Within moments he shed his clothes, along with hers to press their bodies against each other. Neither had been able to feel this thrill in such a long time that they exploded with passion in the darkest hours of the night.

Joanna clung to him long after they finished and remained in each other's arms. Rynhawker slept fitfully, turning to press against her to force his arm over her. At one point he thrashed, caught in the throes of his own terrible nightmare.

At the rooster's first crow, Joanna awakened to locate her clothes and dress. She felt stronger. She wasted neither time nor movement to stave off the morning chill with her garments.

Rynhawker was slower in rising to join her.

"We leave now," Joanna ordered while she peered through the slit in the makeshift door of the hovel.

Outside all remained quiet.

Rynhawker came to her, pressed his lips against her forehead in a kiss, meant to determine that her fever was no longer.

"Can you ride?" he asked.

"I can. We must go. To remain jeopardizes our cause."

No one stirred outside the inn, nor could the shuffling of horses be heard in the shack where she waited for Rynhawker to bring their mounts.

"Let us hurry," she whispered.

She wanted to run into his arms to feel his strength against her. Yet she knew time was critical.

Joanna remained inside, watching for the first signs of life coming from the inn while Rynhawker saddled their rides before quietly delivering them from the stable.

The first rays of a dawning sun found their way through the hibernating trees as they galloped into the winter forest. Joanna threw a glance back in their wake. All remained placid at the inn.

They were safe another day, as long as they carefully removed their tracks to prevent anyone from tracking them. In the day next, they would rendezvous with the others and prepare for their infiltration of one of Henry's castles.

53

Joanna and Rynhawker ensconced themselves in the forest fringe in a way that allowed them to watch over the imposing outline of Trifels castle from a safe distance. They remained concealed from anyone venturing in their direction. Coming upon the castle during their return journey to the rendezvous, Joanna determined it wise to surveil the fortress while opportunity existed. According to her information, Trifels was the most fortified of Henry's castles.

By midday, Joanna convinced herself she had chosen well. The drawbridge came down and the portcullis went up with the rising sun, allowing a few handfuls of serfs to flow in and out. The dreariness and cold of winter settled over the land; a time when few strayed far from blazing hearths to venture into the countryside.

Joanna and Rynhawker could make their way to the castle unabated, but at the same time, they were unable to blend in amongst the locals.

"Can we be certain our king is within those walls?" Rynhawker asked.

He yawned, rubbing his eyes from his lack of sleep.

"More importantly, can we find a way in to confirm Richard is a prisoner there?" she asked.

"My lady, we must rest if we are to continue our journey this night," Rynhawker pressed when neither had an answer.

"We will rest once we reach the rendezvous."

"Perhaps we should sleep until the cover of darkness aids us."

Only reluctantly did Joanna retreat from the ridge concealing them. She settled into Rynhawker's arms to share his warmth. Her hand slipped naturally into his before she realized her action.

When she attempted to draw it out, Rynhawker tightened his fingers to hold it there. Joanna looked up to him, he was smiling with his eyes closed.

Could she find anything wrong with what she was doing? If they were to die tomorrow, would she not give everything to share her last hours in his arms?

Thoughts of their intimacy lulled her into a shallow sleep. Even in slumber she kept her ears alert to the forest around them.

Hours passed. They slept in each other's arms.

Joanna's cold nose awakened her with a jolt. She sprang up to gaze in every direction at once. A moment later, Rynhawker awakened to rise beside her.

"Did you hear something?" he asked.

"No," she replied in a whisper.

Her stomach grumbled. They had forgone eating since the morn and now needed something to quiet their rumbling within.

Joanna lifted her head enough to peek over the ridge. The castle remained a tapestry of still life against a drab lifeless sky. No one moved through the open gates or over the drawbridge. She surmised they had but two more hours before darkness fell upon the land. With darkness their aid, they could exit the forest to study the castle close up. After a few moments, Joanna returned below the ridge to settle in beside Rynhawker.

"Have you a plan?" he asked with a smile.

They huddled to share their last bites of twice-baked barley bread. Their water flask provided each a simple gulp. Rynhawker so wanted wine to warm his belly. But that would wait until they had achieved what they came for.

The faint clanking of chains brought them up to witness the drawbridge rising. The moat stretched no wider than ten strides, which meant it could be forded by a few men. But the frigid temperatures could make the wet clothing unbearable.

"How do we cross the moat?" Rynhawker queried.

The drawbridge reached full vertical as they listened to the portcullis clatter down. Sentries appeared in the narrow tall windows of the barbican's two half-round towers.

"I have no answer at this time," Joanna said.

She cleared her stallion's tether before mounting it.

"We will have darkness. It is time," she said.

"Time for what?" Rynhawker muttered.

Without an answer he dutifully untethered then pulled himself into his saddle against an aching back from sleeping on the ground.

"Time to learn how we rescue our king," Joanna offered with a smile.

Her unshakable confidence infected Rynhawker. So much so, that he surged to get astride her before abandoning the security of the forest fringe. A shroud of evening mist muted their forms as they risked venturing closer to the castle.

They proceeded carefully, since soldiers in the bartizans and barbican would be watching. However, if Henry's men were similar to the Brits, they would soon huddle in the corners gathering warmth off the torches rather than scanning the countryside.

Knowing that, Joanna and Rynhawker chose to ride in a wide sweeping arc around the castle's circumference, keeping the forest always at their back, which allowed them to remain invisible... as long as they progressed slowly, and the clouds prevented moonlight from glinting off their steel.

Trifels castle's northern face indeed proved impregnable. No windows nor outcropping in the stone walls existed to allow scaling to the parapet.

However, the fortress inhabitants would never expect a small force of knights to breach their security by invading clandestinely during the night. So Joanna fostered her confidence that if they could find a way in, they could invade the keep without detection.

"What do we hope to see?" Rynhawker asked as they advanced to the eastern face. Like its opposing side, there, too, existed no exploitable security flaws.

Joanna paused. Motionless for a long moment, she gazed at their greatest obstacle. Then she identified the castle's first flaw!

A cold wind bit at her face, reddening her cheeks. Rynhawker warmed his with his hands while he waited, unaware of what Joanna uncovered.

"What do you see?" she asked of him.

Rynhawker studied the curtain wall, scrutinizing every stone in its structure.

"Nothing useful to us," he responded with a head shake.

"Look beyond what you see to what you do not see," she offered.

"I still see nothing to aid us."

"No sentries prowl the battlements," she commented.

Rynhawker trained his eyes along the upper line of the castle wall. After a few moments, he understood.

No men roved about. The entire castle had taken to slumber for the night. Joanna knew this would be most helpful when their time came.

"Then that is good," he said.

"Or is it bad for us?" she queried aloud.

"My lady?"

"Would Henry leave his parapet unguarded if he held our king within its walls?"

Her question unsettled Rynhawker's confidence. If Richard were a prisoner inside, surely Henry would remain diligent in keeping his prize safe.

"Or does Henry not expect a rescue in the dead of winter?" Rynhawker reasoned out loud.

"We are fools to play Henry as a foolish king."

Her eyes scrutinized every nuance of the castle wall before them. After minutes of remaining stationary, Joanna abandoned any hope of finding a way to breach the eastern face. The walls were unscalable without detection.

"Come," she commanded softly.

They advanced to the southern face, the curtain wall opposite the drawbridge and barbican. The moat protecting the castle's rear face grew wider than on any other side. The wall was also absent a postern gate. So, at first, Joanna believed they had no way of silently entering the fortress in search of their king. Then she spied the garderobe outcropping near the top of the wall just below the parapet. No one else would have considered it a structural weakness, but the longer Joanna studied the fixture, the more she realized she uncovered something valuable.

"It is time," Rynhawker said quietly. He nudged his stallion to turn it to the security of the night forest. The receding fog would leave them exposed to sentries in the turrets.

Before joining him, Joanna stole one last look at the castle.

"Tell me, Sir Rynhawker, do you pray before you ride into battle?"

Rynhawker offered no response.

Now she needed her plan to get them inside whichever castle held her brother.

54

Joanna and Rynhawker returned to the rendezvous to be greeted by Duchard and Alwain. Brayson and Thomas had also arrived, but at the moment were foraging in the trees, hoping to add to their rations.

Butchered goat roasted on a makeshift spit over a small, sheltered fire. As expected, overcooked meat with charred edges.

Isaac remained in his wagon isolated from the others. No one spoke to him after arriving at the rendezvous and learning the fate of the princess and Rynhawker from the Jew.

"Who takes responsibility for this goat?" Joanna charged with angry eyes.

"Would you rather we sup on the badger I encountered along the way?" Duchard confessed. He held his smile, seeing the dismay it brought to the princess' face.

"You dare place your comrades at risk over hunger?"

Duchard contained his growing frustration with her. At the time, he saw no harm in absconding with a single goat from a farmer's pen. Hunger drove him to his impropriety. He believed when he did it he performed an act worthy of praise rather than condemnation.

"And if you were discovered? If the local regents were informed of your act?"

"My lady, I was most careful. I acted in the darkest hour of night. I escaped detection, I swear. I would never risk our king," Duchard found himself pleading against his will. He despised answering to a woman, even if she were the princess.

He sliced off chunks of meat to pass to the princess and Rynhawker as his peace offering. She accepted it smileless. Joanna hated goat but was grateful for something to fill her empty belly.

"Come, we all eat," Duchard announced, waving Isaac to join.

"So, how do we intend to free our king, now that we are here? If we even have the right place," Duchard said while tearing flesh from bone.

He tempered anger and frustration out of his voice. He knew speaking without control would only anger the princess, though he never believed she could succeed in such a foolish undertaking.

Joanna remained silent, choked down the goat until Thomas and Brayson returned and all were seated close enough to the flames to indulge their warmth. The night had been bitter cold, and only the bright sun shedding light upon them would take away some of the misery they had endured.

While everyone waited, Joanna ceased eating, staring into the flames, unspeaking.

"Was all as you expected?" Alwain ventured to ask when the silence tore at his very nerves. Silence meant uncertainty, and uncertainty spelled death to all of them before they might succeed.

"Trifels castle is the most fortified of Henry's castles," she said, speaking slowly as if she needed to think further before offering more to the others.

"But do we know for certain our king is in there?" Duchard pressed.

Joanna turned to Isaac for help.

"I have no direct knowledge of our king's location."

All eyes dropped at Isaac's words. They needed to know which castle held Richard or their treacherous journey to the rendezvous had been for naught.

"My lady, this we know. Richard is not imprisoned in a tower, or he would have responded to the lads' song. He is most likely held in the dungeon, since allowing the Lionheart any level of freedom may allow him opportunity to escape. He is also being held in solitude so he cannot recruit others to his cause."

"You claim much for one who has seen little," Duchard said.

"And if you are wrong, Jew?" Alwain added.

Isaac directed his response, and his eyes, to Joanna, who weighed his every word.

"My lady, I can only tell you what I believe. Richard would never be placed in the oubliette, since his death by any means would forfeit the ransom."

"Since you know so much, Jew, tell us which castle holds our king," Brayson said.

Isaac smiled. No one was expecting that. Then he straightened his lips fearing arrogance might become evident on his face. They were knights, he a Jew, yet he had gathered more intelligence than any of them realized.

"I spoke with men who frequent Trifels castle. They believed King Henry to be in residence for the month past. Two months previous, the king presided over a tournament there. This I have confirmed from two who participated," Isaac offered.

"And how did you come by that?" Duchard asked with a raised brow.

"When men drink, they brag. I listen," Isaac reassured them.

"But is the king there now?" Brayson charged with a skeptical edge toward Isaac's claims.

"That I cannot say for certain," the old man replied.

"Does that mean Trifels castle holds our king?" Alwain persisted.

"In truth you have no proof Trifels castle imprisons our king," Brayson charged.

"King Henry will keep Richard close. If Henry is in residence, Richard is there," Joanna said.

"And if you are wrong?" Duchard advanced.

His words set fire to Joanna's emotions. Rather than lash out, she measured the distrust she witnessed on their faces.

"We will die for nothing!" Brayson said.

"We breach Trifels castle first to determine if what Isaac says is true," she advanced.

The men, it seemed, wanted none of it.

"And how do you propose we breach such a fortified castle with only these men?" Duchard snapped.

"Getting in is little concern," she reminded them.

The men flashed looks at each other before staring at her as if she spoke with words they could not comprehend.

"We enter through the gates with the serfs. If we are clever, we will pass unchallenged."

"Not with swords at our belts," Alwain corrected.

"Yes, swords will raise the suspicion of the guards in the barbican for certain. We are greatly outnumbered once inside the castle. I would suspect at least two score knights attend the king."

"So what foolishness do you propose?" Duchard shot back.

Rynhawker rose at the words.

Duchard rose in response.

"I pledged to serve my king, but I will not be led to my slaughter unarmed by the foolishness of a woman," Duchard pounded out.

Joanna needed a way to prevent their faith from unraveling. They had to believe in her to have any chance of freeing Richard.

"And I would never ask that you should die without the honor of your code," she responded calmly.

For a long moment, Rynhawker stared into Duchard's angry eyes. Duchard believed Rynhawker's heart now controlled his mind. The knight thought not about the good of his men, nor their king, but rather for the wishes of the woman he had come to love.

"We enter through the barbican on foot without swords, but we carry daggers under wraps."

"And you would have us fight the knights without our swords?" Brayson commented.

"That is not my intent. You will have your swords. You will only not carry them into the castle."

Intrigued now, Rynhawker and Duchard returned to the ground beside the others.

Both Thomas and Rynhawker remained dutifully silent while Joanna spoke. They had come to trust in her and what she intended to do. They knew only trust could see them through this perilous endeavor.

"Your swords will await you once inside the castle walls," Joanna said, breaking a glint of a smile.

"And how will that be?" Alwain asked.

Clearly, he took no faith in Joanna's words.

Joanna looked to Isaac at the fire's fringe.

Then all eyes turned to Isaac, who held his smile in check.

55

Joanna emerged first from the forest fringe, following the road to Trifels castle. Over the course of two previous days they had relocated their rendezvous to a place suitable for an incursion into the fortress.

Isaac's task, after delivering his hay wagon, was to return to the forest to tend the tethered mounts until they returned with their king.

This day began like any day previous with peasants walking to the castle in anticipation of their day's activities. A brilliant sun shed warmth upon those who braved the cold wind for another day.

Joanna scrutinized the flow of people to time her approach to the castle drawbridge so she might become lost in the crowd anxious to enter the square. Morning mass would begin in the castle chapel on the hour and many around her would enter the keep for the service. Joanna planned to be amongst them. If all proceeded as expected, she would remain out of sight of her knights throughout the day.

The drawbridge began its clattering descent as Joanna shifted closer. When the bridge met land across the moat, the portcullis screeched its way up. Joanna knew those two structures would prove the most difficult to overcome on their exit. The peasants flocked into the barbican once the portcullis cleared their heads.

Joanna, however, waited until the structure had reached its apex and locked into place.

She needed deep calming breaths before marching through the barbican shadows into the outer bailey. So far, everyone viewed her as just another serf, as she expected. She appeared no different than those rushing by. Yet she felt vulnerable without the crossbow that had come to feel like part of her.

With each step, Joanna studied the lay of the castle grounds. Once inside the inner bailey, she began to catalog the structures on her flanks. The stables were left and tucked away in the far corner of the inner bailey. That would be good for them. They were large enough to accommodate at least four score horses. She immediately saw the benefit to her plan. Isaac should have little trouble making his way in to position his wagon as the day wore on.

Joanna trailed the flow to the keep, where the huge timber doors opened. Two soldiers stood silently by while everyone made their way inside. Joanna followed, flowing toward the chapel at the first-floor rear. Everyone appreciated the warmth of being out of the wind.

Joanna positioned herself in the midst of three women accompanying two elderly men as she made her way through the dimly lit passage. When one of the men stumbled, she leveraged her uninjured arm to provide him stability. He smiled at her assistance before continuing. Another soldier leaned against the wall waiting for the last few stragglers to get inside before closing the doors.

Joanna drifted away once inside the chapel to sit on a bench in the furthest corner. Her cowl hid her face while she prayed with her head bowed, hoping no one might approach her. As long as they left her alone, she could remain unchallenged.

Fortune continued with her after completion of the mass. A group of departing women turned down the corridor toward the main halls of the keep, as opposed to the majority who exited the chapel to return to a freezing castle square.

The sounds ahead indicated they were approaching the kitchen. Joanna slipped unnoticed into a room near the kitchen entrance, where she hoped to remain out of sight until later in the day. As long as no one spoke to her, she could go undetected in the keep.

She knew soldiers manned all keep doors at night, so she needed another way to gain her knights entry. But for now, she needed to go unnoticed and surveil possible entries and exits.

Arriving at varying hours throughout the day, Rynhawker, Thomas, and Duchard made their journey to the castle, strolling through the gate into the inner bailey. Each sought an out-of-the-way place which allowed them to remain within view of each other.

If one were challenged, the others would come to his aid. The crowds in the castle square thinned as the sun crossed the sky.

Rynhawker took to worrying when only a few hours remained, and Isaac had yet to enter through the castle gate. A rescue attempt might then be out of the question.

Duchard signaled Rynhawker from across the square. He held a position near the main entrance of the keep, hoping to glimpse inside whenever the doors opened. Unfortunately, few sought entry to the keep this day. Duchard had hoped for a moment of inattention from the guards, which might allow him to slip unnoticed inside. Once inside, he could locate Joanna to provide her protection should anything go wrong.

Thomas wandered to a group of children dashing about at play. He positioned himself to lend the appearance he tended them. Seeing him there rekindled thoughts of Annalise in Rynhawker's mind. He knew she would be well cared for by the servants attending the queen. Yet a pang tempered his heart as he thought of the possibility of her growing up without a mother and a father.

The sight of Isaac's wagon rumbling through the barbican shadows brought Rynhawker back to the present. The knight hid his smile at the sight of the old man slapping the reins to keep his beasts moving, despite a flow of peasants coming at him.

Isaac never looked directly at any of the men in the square; though he made it a point to locate each should danger arise. His contingency, if things went awry, was to divert his wagon to support them. Despite their hatred for him, Isaac thought of them as his men and would give his life to save them.

Once inside the stables, Isaac abandoned the hay wagon out of sight then walked out of the castle with the remaining peasants. He had to be clear before the portcullis came down. He was never meant to be part of the rescue team.

Thomas signaled concern when he watched Isaac exiting through the barbican. Brayson had yet to appear. The knight was supposed to be in place before Isaac entered the castle.

Moments after Isaac passed beyond the gate and across the drawbridge, the timber began its slow climb to vertical. A few moments later the portcullis shuddered down, securing the castle until the next morning. No one was to enter, or exit, until sunrise.

Brayson failed to make it inside.

Rynhawker swallowed his anger at the thought. There was no plausible reason for Brayson to have squandered his opportunity. His absence placed the other knights in jeopardy. How this would alter Joanna's plan, Rynhawker had no idea. He prayed Joanna had thought her plan through sufficiently to allow for success with one less man. Could they afford to lose another in a fight? Their fate rested in Joanna's hands, as did the fate of their king.

Each man retreated into the shadows of the night square after the sun left the sky. Only a few mangy dogs roamed about foraging for anything to eat. The temperature dropped; the night sky remained clear. No rain or snow would impede their plan this night.

Thomas was the first to approach the hay wagon, which Isaac had positioned on the far side of the stables beyond the sight of soldiers in the barbican.

A few voices could be heard inside the stables from men attending horses. It seemed the occupied horse stalls neared capacity, which boded well for them. If circumstance allowed, they would steal mounts for their escape from the castle with the sunrise. If circumstance turned against them, they would have to find another way out.

A few minutes later Rynhawker came beside Thomas, watchful of eyes from above. Together they dug through the hay to retrieve their swords, which were hidden in the bottom of the wagon. Both spun in panic when Duchard approached.

"It is me," he whispered.

Rynhawker pulled up the first empty sheath.

Frantically, they all scattered the hay.

The swords were nowhere in the wagon.

Panic set in.

"Damn you for convincing me to trust a Jew!" Duchard snarled, his eyes locked on Rynhawker.

"What now?" Alwain stammered through gritted teeth when he joined them. "Where is Brayson?"

Rynhawker handed out the sheaths.

"And what do you expect us to do with these?" Duchard asked.

"Fill them," Rynhawker replied.

For now, daggers beneath their shirts were their only weapons.

"We proceed," Rynhawker said.

Duchard snared his friend's arm.

"Proceed where? They will cut us down before we even reach our king," he spat back.

Thomas waited no longer. He left the feeble safety of the stables, advancing along the inner bailey wall to reach the windward side of the keep.

Moments later, Rynhawker and Duchard followed. Alwain, racked with indecision and mounting fear, departed last. The rising moon crept over the treetops. It was time to breach. They had to hope Joanna had found a way to get them inside the keep. Now their next challenge became securing swords.

56

Joanna flowed quickly and quietly up the spiral staircase to the second floor. There would be windows there she might use to gain her knights entry. She moved deftly along. By now everyone had finished supping and retired to their pallets in the knights' hall.

They would be alone in the corridors, save for the guards along the way.

Joanna knew it would be near impossible to breach the king's floor, always the highest floor of the keep, so she decided to use the second floor to get her knights in. The greater the distance between them and the king, the less likely they might encounter the king's guards. Soldiers stationed on the fourth floor virtually guaranteed no one could approach his majesty unchallenged.

Joanna moved from door to door listening for sounds from inside. She focused her efforts on the wing facing the stables, hoping when she found a location, she could signal her knights.

Absent her ability to observe the moon in the sky, she had no idea how much time had elapsed since sunset. Time worked against them if they failed to free Richard and egress the castle before Henry realized the Lionheart had escaped.

At one door, Joanna listened to moans of pleasure seeping under the timber. She quickly moved on. Luck was with her—the next door was silent, and after a few moments she risked opening it.

Darkness welcomed her, along with a tall window on the wall opposite her entry. She crossed only after scanning the room for occupancy. The chamber appeared vacant, used presently to store armor and weaponry for the men of the castle. Three long rows of spears lined one wall, war hammers and maces rested against another, while chest plates, chain mail, and helmets occupied a third.

Joanna picked carefully amongst the accoutrement to avoid causing any noise that might betray her. The room offered relative safety since there would be little need during the harsh winter.

Reaching the window, Joanna leaned out to spy the moon's position then locate the stables. She discerned midnight was upon them, the moon crossing its apex in the night sky. She also spied the stables in the distance to her right.

Her knights would be awaiting her signal.

Joanna gazed down to assess the difficulty involved in reaching the window. Even if her knights stood on another's shoulder, they would fail to reach it. She needed a way to assist them.

The princess crossed back to the door. There she listened for sounds in the corridor. When silence remained, she slipped out long enough to remove a torch from its stanchion a few paces down and returned to the room.

At the window she stuck the torch into the night for the count of five, drew it back for a count of twenty before thrusting it out again for the same count before snapping it inside.

She waited before leaning her head out. First, she scanned the bailey. Nothing. Her knights failed to appear as expected. Had something gone wrong? As a matter of fact, she observed no movement at all in the castle courtyard.

Joanna withdrew back into the chamber. She feared a soldier on the parapet or a guard in the barbican might see her signal. As hard as she tried to make the light seem innocuous, she couldn't be certain someone opposing them might see it and investigate.

Panic cluttered her mind, muddled her thinking as she worried. She had to wait before signaling again. She understood her knights would have no idea where her signal would be coming from, only that they must be watchful and move quickly when they saw it. After her torturous wait, she thrust the torch out for another count of five. When she brought it in, she prayed they had seen it.

She risked leaning out again.

Across the courtyard, three figures skulked along the wall, flowing toward her position. Her heart raced with excitement. She watched Rynhawker and Thomas arrive below her window.

There were only two? No, then she spotted Duchard and Alwain. Brayson was missing.

No one spoke.

The knights remained against the wall of the keep with Duchard watching the inner bailey for signs of movement. The castle would be fully manned at the outer bailey walls with guards in the barbican. But there existed no need for men at the inner bailey.

Alwain motioned Rynhawker for guidance on how they should proceed. Rynhawker responded by leaning toward the wall with his arms braced. Thomas understood the position. He slowly worked his way up with Alwain's assistance onto Rynhawker's shoulders.

Even stretching arms full length, Thomas still came up short of reaching the window ledge. He groped for anything to gain sufficient leverage to pull himself further up. The wall offered no such handholds, since that would allow marauders to breach the keep in an assault.

In the next moment, Joanna appeared at the window. Stretching her arm down as far as she could, she failed to reach Thomas' outstretched hands.

The window's strategic position forced the use of ladders to gain entry, which were easily defended from inside by soldiers dumping boiling pitch down upon the climbers. Since they had no ladder, and forming a human ladder proved impossible, Joanna returned to the room, seeking anything to assist.

She grabbed the closest spear before returning to the window. Within a moment the shaft came out to reach Thomas' hands.

Using the shaft to steady his balance, Thomas walked up the wall to grasp inside the window. Joanna quickly withdrew the spear to assist Thomas inside.

The first knight was in. Joanna swallowed her smile. Neither spoke. Thomas replaced her at the window, lowering the shaft while Joanna came with another.

While Duchard assisted, Alwain ascended upon Rynhawker's shoulders to reach the extending shafts. Following Thomas' lead, Alwain walked the wall to reach the window.

"One of us will not make it," Duchard whispered.

Rynhawker thought for a moment before removing his sword sheath from his hip, turning it over to Duchard.

"Bring all the straps together to make a rope to pull me up," Rynhawker offered.

Duchard smiled. Taking Rynhawker's sheath around his neck, he worked his way onto Rynhawker's shoulders. Rynhawker needed to lower himself to make it possible for Duchard to reach his shoulders unaided. Then pumping his legs with all his strength, Rynhawker returned upright. The knight's legs wobbled under his comrade's severe weight. But they held stable long enough for Duchard to reach the extended spears. Slowly his weight came off as Duchard rose to reach the window.

Only one knight remained outside the keep.

Once inside, Duchard instructed in gestures what to do. They needed every man inside the keep, since Brayson had failed to get into the castle in time. After the leather straps from the knight's sheaths were fastened to form the long strap, Duchard extended it out. It came up short of reaching Rynhawker. Despite repeated leaps at the dangling strap, the knight failed to grab it.

"How do we extend it further?" Joanna risked when she realized they were consuming vital time attempting to breach the keep.

Duchard instructed Thomas and Alwain to grasp his legs while he extended out the window to lower the strap further. The leather came within a hand's length of Rynhawker when he leapt.

Duchard squirmed, able to shimmy even lower down the wall, praying Thomas and Alwain could support his weight.

Rynhawker jumped.

He caught the strap in both hands. For a moment he fortified his grip before beginning the torturous crawl up the wall. The first two steps were the most difficult. But with each successive stride, Thomas and Alwain inched Duchard further into the chamber. Once Duchard returned halfway inside, Joanna squeezed through the crowded opening to lower the spear. Rynhawker wrapped one hand around it, using the strap in his other to steady himself during his final three strides.

Four knights circled Joanna in the room. The torchlight flickered off sweated faces despite the frigid air pouring in.

"Where is Brayson?" she risked in a whisper.

"Never made it in," Rynhawker responded.

"We have no swords!" Duchard griped in a voice too loud for their circumstance.

"What happened?" Joanna asked.

None of them could answer. But clearly Isaac failed in his task to deliver the swords hidden in the hay wagon. The presence of their sheaths indicated something had gone terribly wrong. Either soldiers had gone through the hay wagon to uncover the blades, or... Joanna had no more time to contemplate. They needed to move.

They had breached the keep. Now they needed to find the dungeon, hoping above all hope that Richard would be at the end of their quest. If he wasn't, Joanna's plan was to then escape the keep and hide until morning when they might ride out of the castle undetected by Henry's men. No one need ever know they had even been there.

57

Lacking swords, the knights felt vulnerable. Joanna led them down the staircase to the castle's dungeon level. The few torches along the way allowed them to advance unseen in the foreboding gloom of darkness. Having only daggers against the guards meant they must get close to attack before suspicion sent the men into a defensive posture.

Joanna clutched her blade so tightly her fingers ached. Her breathing came in gasps with each step toward the dungeon door. She told herself to do whatever necessary to save her brother. Even if it meant killing.

How many guards might they encounter? She could not know. She would have only Rynhawker and Thomas inside with her to free Richard from his cell. Duchard and Alwain needed to remain behind to fend off a response from soldiers if anything went wrong. With Brayson gone, they were left with no one to monitor the staircase.

They were so close now.

Rynhawker stopped Joanna with a gentle hand to her shoulder. In response she came around to face him.

"I go first," he whispered, more an order than a request.

"No. For me, they will open the door," she shot back harshly.

One of them must convince a guard to release the dungeon door latch or all their effort would amount to nothing. If they failed to breach the dungeon, they had no chance of locating their king.

The next torch ahead splashed flickering light upon the dungeon door. Joanna watched for signs of movement inside. For a long moment they listened. As they hoped, the guards were most likely asleep. They would have one opportunity to get inside the dungeon to seize the men in control. If they erred, they would end up beside her brother, if he were even being held in there.

Joanna gestured her intent. Rynhawker eased beside her to take his position beside the door.

All remained eerily quiet inside.

Silently Joanna peered through the small portal in the timber slats—two guards slept around a table. Joanna surmised they had at least four more hours of darkness with which to execute their daring escape. She never considered what they might have to do if the dawn rose before they cleared the keep. They needed to be safely inside the stable stalls with mounts ready when the portcullis went up with the sun.

Joanna nodded readiness to Rynhawker, who nodded in return, followed a moment later by Thomas, who hovered at the fringe of darkness against the wall with his dagger. A fight meant death, and death meant no mercy if they were caught.

Joanna redressed her cowl slightly back so they might easily see her face, then she pounded the door.

She watched the men inside jerk awake. Stumbling in response, the closest guard came to the door.

"I bring food," Joanna said crudely, hoping the guard would react instinctively by unlocking the door.

He gazed at her for but a moment before placing the key into the lock without thinking. His sleepy mind had not registered his duty, or else he would have asked to see a platter before exposing them to the breach.

Rynhawker eased closer. They only needed the man to throw back the bolt holding the door secure. But they had to wait. If Joanna appeared anxious, that might arouse suspicion in the guard, causing him to keep the bolt in place.

The guard stopped. He gazed beyond Joanna into the darkness of the corridor. Satisfied she stood alone, he threw back the bolt while his companion lowered his head back onto the table.

The door burst open when Rynhawker threw his full weight against it. The surge threw the man off balance against the dungeon wall before he could draw his sword. His blade rose no more than halfway when Rynhawker seized his wrist, angling his dagger into the chest with a lethal driving thrust. The man chortled blood before slumping to the floor.

Thomas burst in next, skirting Rynhawker to attack the second guard, who rose clumsily while fumbling to extract his sword. Abandoning it for close fighting, the guard found his dagger before Thomas could reach him.

"Now!" Joanna yelled to the corridor.

Thomas snared the guard's dagger hand before he could reach the young knight's belly. With a series of quick, fierce jabs, Thomas gutted the man through his side.

Time stopped. White-eyed, the guard stared into Thomas' terrified eyes. His killer appeared more a lad than a knight.

"Damn you to hell," the man muttered with his final breath.

"Please, God, he must be here," Joanna said.

She worked her way beyond the slain men to the darkened corridor with cell doors on either side.

"Here!" Rynhawker called, tossing the ring of keys extracted from the first guard.

A moment later, Duchard and Alwain surged into the dungeon with daggers poised to fight.

"Good work," Alwain said with a smile at seeing Thomas' victim. Until that moment, Alwain held serious doubts that Thomas could kill.

"Indeed, you are as skilled as your master has proclaimed," Duchard said, seeing Thomas standing over the man's body.

"Guard the door," Duchard ordered the young knight when Thomas appeared unable to move.

Rynhawker relieved the first guard of his sword, tossing it to Duchard, while Thomas withdrew the second sword for himself. The two with blades stood watch at the dungeon door while Joanna and Rynhawker worked their way along the cell doors.

Alwain used the time to drag the guards out of sight.

"Richard!" Joanna called in a harsh, fearful whisper.

He had to be here. This had to be the place where Henry kept his prize. If they erred, they would have to hope they could escape the castle before detection. Their punishment for killing the guards would be death.

"Richard!" she offered louder, now angry that they may have failed in their only chance to free their king.

"Here!" the Lionheart called from the cell furthest away.

Joanna ran to the door, her heart pounding. Tears of joy stole her vision; so much so, she paused to wipe them in order to focus on the door's lock.

Seeing Joanna struggling, Rynhawker took the keys, and wasting not a second, he unlocked and threw open the cell door, allowing Joanna first entry.

King Richard stood three paces away. She pulled back her cowl to reveal her beaming smile in the torchlight. Rynhawker joined her to provide support.

Joanna rushed into her brother's waiting arms. Then she saw Baldwin and Hugh hobbling to stand behind their king. She had not expected other Brits. She thought—and planned—all along that she would be rescuing only her king from Henry's dungeon.

"We are taking you home, your majesty," she said.

58

Joanna's tears kept her from witnessing the smile on Richard's face. His rubiginous hair a mass of long tangles, his face grimy from captivity; but he looked majestic as he held her in his arms.

Alwain and Rynhawker crowded the doorway.

"Your majesty, we must go. Time is short. We must be clear of the keep before the sun betrays us," Rynhawker said.

Both he and Alwain bowed before their king. Elation beyond description filled their hearts at that moment. They had located their king. In a matter of hours Richard would be free... if they could escape detection inside the castle.

Alwain advanced to help Baldwin from the cell, who placed his weight on the knight's shoulder so he might walk faster and straighter.

Rynhawker assisted Hugh into the torchlight beyond their cell.

"Have you a plan to get us out?" Richard asked.

"Trust that we can get you free, my lord," Joanna said.

She refused to release her brother despite the need to move quickly down the corridor to the dungeon door, where Duchard and Thomas bowed on Richard's approach. Both had swords ready.

"Your majesty," Duchard said, his smile so broad it consumed his entire face. "Time to go home."

Richard paused to appraise the situation in that tenuous moment while they gathered at the dungeon door.

"How many men have you?" he asked.

Joanna at first held her answer.

Richard's face turned grim. He counted four knights to rescue the king. Fear swelled into Richard's throat.

"Have you a sword for me?" the Lionheart asked.

"Nay, my king, your knights will lead us out," Joanna responded.

"How many swords have we?"

"Let us out!" someone called from deep in the dungeon.

"Free us also," another strident voice yelled.

"Can they be of service to our king?" Joanna asked, hoping for assistance.

The princess felt suddenly alone. How could she hope to save her brother with so few men?

"No. Most are sick and dying. We abandon them," Baldwin said hurriedly.

"Are they fellow Brits?" she pressed.

"We cannot know. Nor can we consume precious time finding out. We go," Baldwin insisted.

Terror struck in his eyes. He knew the consequences of what was transpiring. Only if they escaped could they remain alive.

Baldwin wished desperately to be free from the dungeon and away from the castle as swiftly as possible. If they were caught, all but the king himself would be killed. Henry would punish everyone for attempting to steal away his treasure yet again.

Richard assumed the lead as they exited the dungeon single file into the darkened corridor.

"Extinguish all torches," he commanded as their first action toward escaping.

Thomas complied, moved quickly ahead to take down the torches to stomp out their flames.

Total darkness consumed the corridor end to end. Only the faint flicker of torchlight emanating from the open dungeon door infiltrated the corridor.

"Where are we going?" Joanna asked.

Inside, she was thankful Richard took control of their plan. She had to pray he would know the best way out. For now their best chance of escape would be to return to the chamber with the window through which they entered to make their way to the stables.

"We need more swords if we intend to fight our way to freedom," Richard said without looking back.

Joanna stopped him.

"Fighting Henry's men will never gain your freedom. We must escape before anyone in the castle realizes you have been rescued," Joanna offered.

Her words forced Richard to reconsider. Each man in the string stopped when the body before them halted.

"Why do we stop?" Duchard pressed.

He used that moment to come beside his king.

"Your majesty, let my sword be the first to carve your path to freedom," he offered.

Richard offered no response; rather he turned to his sister, fumbling about to secure her hand in his.

"You have a plan?" he asked.

"I do, my lord, we exit the keep through the window that gained us entry."

"Then lead on," the king replied.

At first, Richard failed to comprehend her meaning. There would be only one escape from the castle, and that required gaining swords from any who crossed their path inside. He had no idea how they would get through the gates before sunlight. Then Richard realized he must trust his sister. She had found him, made her way through the castle into the dungeon and released him from his prison cell.

"Then what?" he pressed.

He encountered difficulty relinquishing his control to someone as untrained as her. He knew Joanna could be clever and wise, but he never believed she held the skills in battle to assist him. Now he would have to find out if she were indeed capable.

Overcoming fear, they began moving, slowly at first, then with more determination as they neared the staircase. Faint glimmers of torchlight from above found their way to them.

They would be exposed, vulnerable on the staircase. The one holding the higher ground commanded the advantage.

Richard motioned for all to pause before making their ascent. To move ahead without due caution could destroy all they had accomplished to this point. And they were a long way from freedom at the moment.

"My liege remains in darkness until I and Alwain control the staircase," Duchard said.

As they waited, their order in the line shifted. Rynhawker moved beside Joanna. Thomas advanced to place himself beside Richard. Each held daggers ready, knowing against a sword they would surely fall to any armed foe.

Joanna's hand trembled while she clutched her blade. So much so, that in the darkness, Rynhawker needed to steady it. Memories of that terrible night in Griswalt's castle flooded her head. She envisioned the image of her dagger plunging into Griswalt's belly for stripping her of her life's joy. She would never be the same again. For a brief instant, Joanna held doubts if she could plunge her blade likewise into the chest of Henry's soldiers. Then she reaffirmed she would deal with the Devil himself to guarantee Richard's freedom... even forfeit her life if it came to that.

"Move on," Richard commanded in a whisper.

Duchard took the first tenuous steps up the winding staircase built wide enough for two men to pass at the same time. His sword led the way, glinting off the torchlight as he came to the midpoint of their climb. Alwain remained four steps behind to afford both the distance to fend off an attack if they were discovered.

Footfalls forced Duchard to pause. He thought men approached. Alwain stopped, angling his sword to protect Duchard.

Moments passed. No one breathed. If Duchard and Alwain could reach the top of the staircase undetected, they could, at the very least, hold off Henry's men long enough for the others to reinforce the fight.

Silence reigned again in the castle. It seemed everyone had taken to their beds on this cold winter's night, resting in the secure thought that no one would dare attempt to rescue the king in the dead of winter during the bleakness of the night.

Duchard advanced one more step. He held his position. Likewise, Alwain advanced one more step to hold his position. Duchard swung to the opposing side of the staircase so he might glimpse around the turn to determine if any had detected their movements.

In that moment, Duchard trusted God to watch over him as he rounded the final turn to race the six remaining stairs to the top. He gazed down a long stretch of corridor motionless. His heart hammered at his chest. He felt the sweat taking over his brow. Only his deep breaths helped to fortify him.

They were still alone.

Duchard retreated to wave Alwain beside him.

They now controlled the staircase. They could protect their king if attacked.

It became vitally important to move their king up the stairs beside them. The more blades they held together, the greater became their chances of fending off soldiers.

"Advance," Alwain whispered.

Seconds later frantic footsteps pounded up. Thomas rounded the final turn first, followed by Richard, Joanna, Rynhawker, Hugh and Baldwin.

Duchard and Alwain journeyed from the staircase down the long corridor to provide a safe distance between the others on the ground level.

"Is the armory close at hand?" Richard pressed.

No one knew. Joanna knew where they could find spears, but no swords.

"How do we gain weapons? We will fall if we cannot defend ourselves," Richard pressed against their silence.

In his mind he still saw only one way out of the castle—through force. Yet he needed to trust that Joanna might get them out without having to lose any of their men in a fight. Freedom was still a long way off even after they egressed the castle.

Richard motioned to a corridor on their right as they approached the first crossing corridor.

Joanna motioned they shouldn't.

"I've been led through these halls many times over the last months. We follow this one to a door that leads us to the stables."

"No," Joanna countered. "Soldiers sleep in a hall near here. We cannot risk alerting them."

"Is Henry in attendance?" Richard chanced to ask.

The words stopped them in their tracks.

Dare they go after the king? Taking Henry hostage would guarantee safe passage from the castle—or death if they failed.

"We have not seen the king inside the castle. When was the last time you saw the king here?" Joanna said.

Going after the king was counter to her plan. She wanted them out of the castle, not in greater jeopardy inside it.

Yet Joanna struggled with her decision. They could not proceed with her plan until a decision had been made as to whether to escape the castle or go for the king.

Richard paused for a long moment. The burning desire in his heart to go after Henry to gain revenge for the king's deeds clouded his thinking at this crucial time. Yet he was so close it would be a simple mission to overpower his guards and take him while he slept, no doubt in his usual drunken stupor.

With the King of Germany in their possession, they could command a ransom far greater than any Henry had sought from England. But if they failed, all would be lost. There was no army of English knights and soldiers advancing on this castle as they worked their way through the halls. There was no fighting force poised to assist them in extricating the king from his stronghold.

"I know what you are thinking," Joanna whispered.

She read his eyes, knew how his mind worked. She also knew what he felt in his heart at that very moment. But he had to think beyond the moment they were trapped in. He must consider the consequences if they erred.

"We go for the stables to secure mounts for our escape. That is what is most important at this moment," Joanna pleaded.

Her eyes met Richard's. She could only hope her words swayed what she read in his.

The moment lasted an eternity while they awaited Richard's decision. Joanna remained dutifully silent. She must wait, and accept, her king's decision. She must obey him. She could only hope he would make the right choice.

Richard turned to Baldwin, his friend and advisor since he had ascended the throne years ago. Baldwin knew he would be expected to read his king's mind to provide him with the correct advice.

"We are stronger as free men. And we are not yet free."

The logic seized the king, who turned to Rynhawker.

"Lead on. Get us free of the castle."

"As you command, your majesty," Rynhawker said.

They had not progressed far when they came across the first of their resistance to their escape.

Two soldiers stood before a door leading into an open hall of the keep. They had either to find a way past the soldiers unnoticed or remove the soldiers from their path. They needed to reach the next staircase to reach the keep's higher floors.

With his fingers, Rynhawker indicated two as they waited out of sight in a side corridor. Hugh slowly slid along the wall to reach Rynhawker.

"I will lead them away so you may reach the door," Hugh whispered.

At first no one spoke. Hugh seemed willing to sacrifice himself for his king. But that was never Joanna's intent with their escape. She would find a way to get them all out safely. No one need sacrifice himself if they executed her plan.

"No," she whispered back.

There had to be another way out to reach the stables.

59

"Is there another way?" Joanna queried her king.

"No. That door may lead us out of the keep," Richard responded.

Joanna removed her dagger.

"Then I will handle this," she said.

Rynhawker took her arm. She saw anger in his eyes even in the faint light from the torches burning twenty paces distant. Rynhawker signaled Thomas and Duchard to take the lead of the column. Richard, Baldwin and Hugh huddled behind them.

"We will remove the guards," Rynhawker whispered.

But even his faint sounds had reached the guards in the still of the sleeping castle. They sprang alert. One soldier advancing toward their location. Then the other shifted to follow.

They were out of time to plan. Rynhawker and Joanna had to act before it was too late.

He drew Joanna into his arms, and together, they stumbled into the corridor. He supported her as if she were a drunken lover. Immediately Joanna fell into her role, tripping convincingly.

The soldiers paused, lowering their weapons, and their concern, as the two approached. One even allowed a smile to slip through his hardened exterior.

Joanna giggled as she clung to Rynhawker with her left hand, while her sweated right concealed her blade behind her back. They paused as if noticing the soldiers for the first time.

The closest soldier spoke, but neither Rynhawker nor Joanna slowed their stride.

The men stopped five strides away. The second soldier retreated a step, as if to take up a defensive posture, while the first approached.

They became suspicious, but not so suspicious that they drew swords, though the second soldier shifted his palm to his dagger.

Rynhawker's laughter faded as they slowed their approach.

The soldier furthest away smiled.

Rynhawker and Joanna advanced to within two strides of the lead soldier, who barked for them to stop.

Neither listened.

Without communicating her intent to Rynhawker, Joanna deduced she must take the closest while Rynhawker took the other. Her heart pounded inside her brain. She knew she must act. Her slightest hesitation could cause her knight to fall.

Joanna's hand came around fast—quicker than the first soldier expected. He saw the dagger. He now understood their intent. He went for his blade.

Joanna's strike ripped through chain mail, driving deep into his flesh. The tip deflected off the breastbone missing the heart but tearing into lung. In response, the man struggled to gain his dagger. When it came out, Joanna curled her fist over his to drive his own blade into his belly. She watched his eyes as he gurgled his last breath.

The first soldier's body shielded the strike from the soldier behind, who failed to react quick enough to draw his sword before Rynhawker seized his sword arm.

Rynhawker's dagger sliced into the soldier's unprotected neck while he fumbled to extract his own blade from an uncooperative sheath. Blood sprayed when Rynhawker twisted his blade to open the artery.

Joanna held the first soldier's mouth tightly closed until he slumped to the floor.

When they turned, Richard and the others were two steps in their wake with their swords ready. Securing two additional swords gave Rynhawker and Thomas each a fighting blade. They could now attack full force any who opposed them. They intended to let no one stop them from freeing their king.

Rynhawker pressed through the door first. It opened into a vaulted silent hall. He scanned the breadth of the room to be certain they would not have to fight their way through more guards.

Moments later, the others slipped in, closed the door. They had no idea how much time they had before the slain guards were discovered.

They crossed the room single file, with Rynhawker and Duchard leading. Richard and the others followed, all keeping at least two sword lengths between them.

The king never believed Joanna capable of killing to save him. They placed another hurdle behind them. No one knew for certain how many more existed before reaching freedom. Richard understood the imperative of evacuating the castle before the king realized they had escaped. They needed time on their side once beyond the castle walls. Even a half day's advantage could be sufficient to reach safety before the king could mount a pursuit.

"We must get to the exit point in the castle. Duchard and Alwain, gain us more swords then join us at the staircase," Joanna said. She sounded as commanding as their king.

Duchard and Alwain looked at each other without speaking.

"Who will protect our king?" Duchard protested against Joanna's command.

"We have our daggers. Rynhawker and Thomas will vanguard our escape."

Both Duchard and Alwain looked to their king. Instinct warned against abandoning the Lionheart at such a critical time in their plan. First and foremost, they had to ensure Richard escaped the castle. Gaining weapons could jeopardize that.

"I have a new plan. We will get him safely to the garderobe on the third floor. You must find weapons for the fight afterward."

Bound by confusion, the knights stared at each other. What Joanna said made no sense. They needed to reach the window to escape the keep and get to the stables.

"My lady, we will never reach the stables from there."

"I beg your trust. There is another way out... a safer egress for our king."

Even Rynhawker grew nervous at the princess' words. She was instead leading them deeper into the keep and further from the horses necessary for escape.

"My lady," Rynhawker started.

"Time grows short. Listen well to me. Once the bodies are discovered, the portcullis will remain down. We will have no exit. I have the only way out left to us. All must trust me."

"What happens after we escape the castle?" Richard pressed with a skeptical eye toward his sister.

"We have horses waiting, though we did not anticipate more than you."

"We double up on the mounts until we can secure more," Rynhawker added.

They had no choice but to trust her. Even if they reached the window and made it to the stables, they had no guarantee the portcullis would go up and the drawbridge down in time for their escape. Being trapped inside Trifels castle meant certain death for all except the Lionheart.

Moving quickly, Alwain led the way down the corridor to the opposite end, where they would find the next winding staircase to take them to the third floor. There they would find the garderobe. It became their only means of escape now.

Alwain ordered all stopped when sounds arose. Men were speaking somewhere in the corridors. From the faintness of the sounds, it appeared they were distant. But they still needed to be factored. They could be moving toward them, or they could be stationary watching over the corridors.

At the first crossing corridor, Alwain poked his head out slightly. The cross corridor remained empty, yet the voices persisted.

Duchard came alongside, motioning to the right. They would have to take that corridor to reach the next staircase.

Without speaking, Duchard motioned for Richard and the others to move toward their destination. Using gestures, he indicated he and Alwain would track down the source of the voices, with the notion they might gain one or more swords. Richard and the others were to proceed down the other corridor to wait at the staircase.

Duchard and Alwain moved painfully slow down the passageway to reach the next crossing corridor. By now Richard and the others were out of sight.

Alwain indicated two men. The lengthy distance to reach them ruled out the advantage of surprise. Instead, Duchard began tapping irregularly on the wall with the hilt of his dagger.

The odd noise snared a guard, who approached the sound without regard for safety. Their swords remained sheathed as they sought only the source of the noise without concern for its cause.

Time had made them careless. Neither guard suspected a threat.

Duchard seized the first soldier entering the cross corridor, while Alwain lunged out to stab the second. Within a few moments, both soldiers lay mortally wounded and dying; and most importantly, relieved of their blades. Alwain located the nearest unlocked door to stash the bodies out of sight.

Now they held four swords, each carried a dagger. Moving quickly back, they made their way toward the second staircase. As expected, Richard and the others waited at the base.

Duchard handed Richard a sword; Rynhawker accepted the other from Alwain. Now only Thomas was without a long blade.

Duchard and Alwain assumed the lead up the staircase with Richard and Joanna nestled between the other men, affording the royals the maximum protection under the circumstances.

They stopped midway. Sounds drifted down.

Duchard took the best possible fighting stance on the stairs. He waited, sweating, holding his breath in anticipation of the fight.

Alwain took to the opposing wall of the staircase.

Instinctively, Thomas drew his dagger, placing his back to his king to protect him from anyone climbing the staircase.

Moments passed.

Joanna clung to Richard's side, squeezing her dagger. She would have little need to use it but wanted its heft if they chanced upon the worst.

A lone soldier approached the staircase to start down without regard for what awaited him. He called back to a comrade further from the staircase, diverting his eyes from the stairs when he turned.

Duchard's fist to his jaw took him immediately unconscious. Rynhawker lunged to catch the man before he could clank to the staircase, thereby alerting whomever he had called out to. A series of dagger thrusts to his chest eliminated him as a threat. They couldn't abandon the body on the staircase. Once discovered an alarm could be raised before they escaped, trapping them inside.

Thomas slid quickly around Baldwin and Hugh to drape the man's arm over his shoulder to drag him along, after relieving him of his sword.

"We are fully armed now," Rynhawker whispered to Richard.

The king motioned to proceed, though Duchard held them back while he reconnoitered the third-floor corridor.

One-by-one they crept up until all reached the third floor. Whoever the soldier had called back to before descending the staircase had moved on and now presented no threat to the group.

Joanna assumed the lead; she knew exactly where they had to go to escape undetected. She would lead until they were free of Henry's fortress.

They traveled single file, extinguishing the torches in their path. The darkness behind them offered a modicum of security, though the two torches ahead illuminated their forms, allowing anyone to easily distinguish them.

As long as they progressed undetected, the odds of success remained in their favor. Reaching the end of the corridor Joanna checked the next. All were asleep on this floor of the keep. Fortune remained on their side.

Joanna found the next corridor. They were close to their exit. They need only make it to the far door to slip unnoticed inside.

Richard followed Hugh and Baldwin, along with Rynhawker and Thomas, by a dozen paces to allow the king the opportunity to flee if trouble found them.

Joanna reached the garderobe first. Silently she prayed they would find the room empty. She made her way inside. The acrid smell of waste fouled her nose. A moment later, Thomas entered with the body to dump it into the corner. Richard, Hugh and Baldwin entered. Duchard and Alwain remained outside until Rynhawker reached the door. Then they entered.

The room was small, meant only to be used by a few people at a time, so they squeezed in. Initially, Joanna had believed Richard would be alone, which made this escape route viable. Now she was no longer sure. She had to account for the two others. They would be difficult on the mounts also, but they would find a way to make it work.

"What now?" Richard asked.

Uncertainty crowded his voice.

"We exit through there," Joanna commanded, pointing to the iron-grated rectangular opening in the stone floor. It was wide enough to allow a man to slip through—if they could remove the grating holding it secure from invaders.

The knights looked at each other.

The iron grating covered a section of floor overhanging the exterior castle wall. It was the castle's waste disposal, and as such, no one would think to use it to escape. At least Joanna hoped.

Below the moat glistened silent and still. At twenty foot distant, the water would provide a soft landing if anyone missed the berm. However, their splash might alert sentries in the turret—if they were awake. The other concern was they would be soaking wet in the night cold while traversing an open field to reach the forest.

"How do we remove the grating?" Baldwin pressed with an edge of anger to his voice.

His breathing came in heaving gasps. He felt trapped inside the room. He believed escape was impossible at the moment. In a few short hours Henry's men would wake, they would all be captured once again. They could never fight their way free from here. This was a foolish plan to get them all, save for the king, killed for their boldness. Baldwin locked his jaw. He fought down the urge to push his way out. There was no alternative but to trust the princess.

"How will we do that?" Duchard snapped.

Clearly this stage of Joanna's plan angered the knights also.

But Richard squirmed forward to kneel beside Joanna. There he began jabbing at the mortar securing the stone blocks that encased the iron grating. After a few attempts, a stone chipped away, revealing the grating could be pulled loose if they chipped away enough stone.

Rynhawker knelt beside his king, began stabbing another joint holding the grating. Thomas joined, while Duchard and Alwain remained vigilant at the door.

"Stop!" Duchard ordered. His harsh whisper commanded immediate response.

No one moved.

Duchard readied his blade to slay whoever entered.

They waited.

Sweat trickled down Duchard's face. He adjusted his grip.

All remained silent. Duchard listened at the door. Nothing. Only their frantic breathing.

"Proceed," he said with relief slipping out.

Now four men chipped at the stones securing the grating.

Richard took hold of its center. He yanked. The grating yielded... but only a little. The king shoved the grating right then pulled again. Mortar cracked, giving way a little more.

"Chip that stone there," Joanna instructed with an insistence that would not have her denied.

Rynhawker and Thomas shifted dagger hilts to work the area Joanna indicated. A larger chunk of stone fell away, falling through the grate to splash into the moat below.

All stopped, fearing the noise alerted sentries on the parapet. They needed to exit the castle unseen to have any chance of reaching the forest.

"One more hard pull," Richard whispered to start the men working again. He saw success at hand but refused to allow a smile to crease his face.

Another fist-sized chunk of rock split away into Rynhawker's hand. All withdrew to allow the king to position over the grating. He took hold of the iron, and with both hands, wrenched it in its mooring.

The grating cracked the stone holding it fast on the right side. Rynhawker squeezed in beside his king to take hold of the side that still held. Together they pulled with their combined strength. Another stone cracked, the grating broke free from its mooring. A moment later it came away in Richard's hands.

Smiles of victory circled the room. Baldwin and Hugh silently cheered as all gathered to stare out their portal to freedom. Each made a rushed sign of the cross. They still needed God's assistance.

60

"Who goes first?" Rynhawker asked of Richard and Joanna.

They looked at each other, deciding.

They needed swords on the berm to fight off any attack that may materialize. They also needed swords in the garderobe.

Lowering to his knees, Thomas poked his head through the hole. He scanned. Moonlight glittered off the moat. A breeze luffed the waist-high dormant grass crowding the water's opposing bank. Nothing else moved. No soldiers on the ground waiting for them; no reason to believe anyone had discovered their escape. But from their inverted location they could not determine if sentries roamed the parapet. Yet the harsh winter temperature should likely keep them inside the turrets at each corner of the fortress.

The turret and barbican windows were designed to watch the countryside. They weren't meant to observe the castle's rear wall.

Now they prayed no soldiers were diligent in their duty this night. They needed to reach the waiting horses in the forest.

Joanna motioned for her knights to remove their cloaks. One by one she strung them together as best she could.

"That will never reach the ground," Duchard growled, watching Joanna work.

Urgency tugging at her mind crushed her concentration. They had to make it work.

"It extends far enough. We lower halfway, drop the remaining distance silently," Joanna replied without looking at her men.

In fact, she had no idea if what she proposed would even work. She also knew they had but a few feet of berm between the moat and the wall on which to land.

With four cloaks knotted together, Joanna fed the makeshift rope through the opening. It ended less than halfway down. She removed her cloak despite the cold to lengthen their lifeline. It dangled another foot closer to the ground.

"Duchard goes first," Joanna ordered.

After she spoke, she realized her words would likely anger the knight. Before their king, it was improper for her to bark commands to his knights.

"Alwain first," Duchard countered. His words leveled his distaste at her command.

"You shall..." Joanna started.

"The best sword remains to protect our king. Our greatest danger is beyond that door, not on the ground," Duchard delivered with a mean finality.

They would discuss it no more.

Both he and Joanna turned to Richard for the final decision.

"I have no time to determine the greater swordsman. Alwain, descend first," Richard commanded.

Joanna acquiesced without retort. She needed Richard's knowledge of fighting to aid them.

Alwain merely smiled before making his way carefully through the opening with Rynhawker and Thomas securing the makeshift rope for his descent.

In moments, Alwain shinnied down to rope's end. He dangled precariously a few seconds, allowing his swing to abate. Needing to drop straight to avoid the moat, he sought the widest strip of berm and released.

He landed in a squat position with his toes teetering at the bank. At first, he dared not move for fear his momentum would tumble him into the water, creating a telltale splash. Once his confidence returned that he could avoid the water, he edged back against the castle wall.

Alwain waited with sword still in hand. He expected no confrontation, but if they were discovered from the parapet, they would have very little time to make their way to safety. Nonetheless, he took a defensive position a short distance from his landing spot.

Richard came through next. He eased himself slowly down— his hands quivering in his weakened state. Sweating palms made clutching the rope more precarious. Nearing the rope's end he gazed down to focus on a target best suited for his landing. His towering stature made his drop more dangerous. If he hit too near the bank, his own force would send him into the water.

Joanna whispered a prayer while watching his descent, hoping he could hold onto the end without tumbling into the moat. While she had carefully analyzed each step of their escape, she could never account for mishaps forcing alterations to the plan.

"I stand ready to assist, my king," Alwain risked in a low voice, hoping only Richard would hear, and meant to settle his king's anxiety at having to free fall such a distance.

Alwain scanned the parapet as best he could from his position, and though he saw nothing, he could not know if sentries roamed.

Richard clung to the rope's end with a faltering grip as he banged the castle wall. He suspected his worst response to be kicking away from the wall when he released. The resulting arc might surely plummet him into the freezing water.

Richard needed deep breaths to steady his hands before releasing. His arms grew weary from the strain of his suspended weight. He issued a silent prayer for God's aid at his moment of release.

The king landed less than two paces from Alwain, who quickly snared his arm as Richard teetered at the bank. Both lurched back, using the castle wall to arrest their movement.

For a long moment no one inside the garderobe breathed. Only Rynhawker and Joanna had witnessed Richard's drop to freedom.

"He is free!" Joanna exclaimed in an almost silent voice.

She had completed the first stage of her rescue, getting Richard outside Henry's castle. She believed that not to be the most dangerous part of their quest; but with each small success, her confidence grew that Richard would reach England alive.

Baldwin's face for the first time turned a smile. He grasped Hugh's forearm in a gesture of success. They had endured so much since their shipwreck and lived each day with the fear of knowing King Henry could end their lives on a whim. Even now, both still harbored a wrenching belief that they would never see their beloved England again. They were still too far from her shores to instill faith in them.

"You go next, my friend," Baldwin said to the man he had shared captivity with over the long enduring months.

"No. You require assistance. It is better you go first," Hugh replied.

Joanna held them both back. Baldwin would need assistance when he hit the ground due to his bad leg. But she needed fighting men beside her in case they were discovered. She could still become a captive and so could any of her knights. She needed to get Richard beyond the reach of Henry's soldiers and knights. And for that, she needed every fighting man she had.

"Duchard and Rynhawker remain behind. Thomas, you go next to assist them when they reach the ground," she commanded.

"I desire to remain with you," Thomas countered.

He delivered his response with an insubordinate sharpness that would deny argument.

"I command you, our king commands you go next," Joanna ordered equally as sharp.

"My sword is to protect you, my lady," Thomas countered.

"Your sword must protect our king," Joanna corrected.

"Thomas, delay only jeopardizes our king's safety. Go now. Trust that I will protect the princess," Rynhawker said.

Thomas studied them both. He wanted to protect Rynhawker and Joanna. He needed to be there if anything went wrong. The last thing he wished was to leave them vulnerable inside Henry's fortress. Once he exited through that opening, there was no way to return to save them.

Duchard, still listening at the door, motioned for silence. A voice reached his ears. He held his breath, pressing his cheek against the wood, hoping to discern if it were a single voice, or more.

The voice stopped.

No one in the room breathed.

All clutched daggers, ready to attack if the garderobe door opened.

Moments passed torturously by. They had come this far. They were so close to freedom now. They could not allow anything to stand in their way.

Duchard motioned the voice had faded.

"We move now. We have no more time," he said.

Joanna motioned Thomas.

Without retort this time Thomas lowered himself through the hole then took hold of the rope. He shimmied himself quickly to the end. There, he dangled for only a moment before dropping to land a few feet from Alwain. Richard had strayed off a dozen strides from the landing to allow space for each to land without disturbance.

Thomas stepped away to take the lead position with his king. If any were to come now, they would encounter Thomas on one side and Alwain on the other.

Hugh came through next. His arms quivered with each hand hold as he progressed unsteadily down the rope. But he never reached the rope's end. In his weakened state, his grip failed halfway down, plummeting him toward the moat.

Alwain had a single moment to react. He snatched Hugh as he fell toward the water. With all the force he could muster, he latched onto Hugh's dangling arms to yank him toward the castle wall. Hugh's left foot, however, missed the solid ground, plunging into the freezing moat past his knee. Yet Alwain kept Hugh steady long enough to pull him out. A moment later, Hugh rested safely against the castle wall. He gazed up at what had been his prison. Although wet, hungry and spent, Hugh the Merchant, after many long difficult months stood free of Henry's fortress.

"You remain there until we are in position," Alwain called up into the hole in an angry whisper.

Hugh's escape had come too close to failure. Had he tumbled into the moat, the resulting disturbance could have drawn sentries from the turret.

Joanna realized they were also running out of darkness. They had to reach the trees before the sun broke or risk detection.

Rynhawker and Joanna assisted Baldwin through the hole, where they held him in place until he could grasp the rope.

"Can you hold on?" Duchard questioned when it seemed Baldwin might slip off before even clearing the opening.

"I will. I must," Baldwin said.

Seeing Baldwin coming through the hole, Alwain motioned for Hugh to move aside, away from the landing spot, and for Thomas to join him to aid with Baldwin's landing. Both expected the worst. But despite the danger posed by the two additional men, no one ever considered abandoning Baldwin.

Thomas turned his sword over to Hugh before taking up a position beside Alwain. He no sooner reached his position when Baldwin lowered himself unsteadily down. He paused halfway to better his grip, praying God would help him maintain hold of the cloth until the proper time came to release. He refused to look down, fearing that might cause him to drop at the wrong moment.

"Now," Alwain whispered up, hoping to time their actions with Baldwin's. Without delay Baldwin released, placing his trust in the knights who braced to receive him.

Baldwin swallowed an agonizing scream when he landed into the waiting arms of both Alwain and Thomas. But his leg jammed the ground, sending fierce pain into every corner of his head. Initially, he thought he would go unconscious. He could see nothing around him.

For many moments the knights held Baldwin without moving while Alwain clamped a hand over his contorted mouth. The rictus on his face told them he had made it—but with severe payment.

"Can you support your weight?" Alwain pressed.

The pain firing inside Baldwin's head proved so intense he could find no way to respond to the knight's question.

With their answer, Alwain and Thomas remained rock steady until Hugh came to lend an arm under his comrade's.

"Come, we must move away," Hugh said.

He coaxed Baldwin into that vital first step. Then he shifted his weight so Baldwin could take another. As they hobbled to reach the aid of King Richard, Thomas reclaimed his sword and resumed his defensive posture.

In the garderobe, Duchard held the rope so Joanna could make her way through the hole to its end. Thomas awaited her with open arms. He snatched her up the moment she touched the ground.

They were all almost free of the castle.

Rynhawker gazed through the hole to confirm Joanna's safe landing.

"Who's next?" Duchard asked as he waited.

"That would be you," Rynhawker replied.

Both knew the dilemma facing them. One had to hold the makeshift rope for the other. The last one in the garderobe had no choice but to drop the entire distance to the ground. The chances of landing uninjured from that height were so slim that to try would jeopardize the safety of the others.

"I will hold the rope for you. And take good care of the princess until I may join you again, my friend," Duchard whispered.

"Then what of you?"

Duchard read the agony in Rynhawker's eyes. He hated to leave his friend behind. They still needed Duchard should they face attack from Henry's men.

Both looked to the slumping body. Could they somehow secure the makeshift rope to it so Duchard might descend safely? They brought the corpse close enough to try but abandoned the plan when too much length went to securing it around the man's girth.

"We have no more time. I will find another way out. Our king is free. You must see him safely back to England," Duchard said.

Rynhawker knew they had no time to debate. He lowered himself through the hole, where he grasped the rope while Duchard braced himself holding it steady. Hand over hand Rynhawker lowered himself until he reached the end. He looked back up to see Duchard's straining face smiling down on him. Then he dropped to land beside Thomas, who used his arm to angle Rynhawker toward the castle wall.

Standing in a line against the castle wall they waited for Duchard.

"He's not coming," Rynhawker said.

"What?" Joanna asked.

"The drop is too dangerous. He will find another way out. We must go now," Rynhawker said.

From the garderobe, Duchard realized they would need the warmth the cloaks provided. So, he released the rope, allowing it to drop into Rynhawker's waiting arms.

Joanna shifted beside Rynhawker, where she unknotted the cloaks she had strewn together.

"Duchard, do not become foolish now. You can jump. We will break your fall," she risked ordering him.

She pushed the end of a cloak into Rynhawker's hands before shoving him to open it.

Duchard stared at the makeshift target they had formed. Thomas joined in, with now three holding the cloak outstretched to break Duchard's fall.

He had but two choices before him. He could drop from the hole, hoping they could keep him from breaking his legs, or he could remain in the castle to work his way to the stables to steal a horse and ride away when the portcullis came up in the morning.

Escaping the castle meant evading Henry's men until morning. If he were caught, he would be killed as soon as the king realized he had aided the Lionheart's escape. He considered if he were meant to die, what might he do to disrupt the pursuit Henry would order the moment the king learned his prize was gone.

"Do not be foolish, Duchard. We can spare you from injury," Joanna called up. Forced to keep her voice no more than a whisper, she was uncertain whether Duchard had even heard her.

After a moment's contemplation, Duchard decided to give his life for his king. He would remain behind to confound King Henry's pursuit. Accepting his fate, Duchard set about returning the iron grating over the hole in the stone floor. For a time, the king's men would believe Richard was trapped inside the castle as long as the portcullis remained down. As a result, they would waste hours in a fruitless search of the fortress, after which they would accept that Richard had indeed escaped. That in itself provided time to ride into Philip's lands... as long as Duchard evaded capture.

61

Joanna and the men sidestepped along the castle wall to the far corner, stopping beneath the turret facing the northern forest. The moat appeared shallow and narrow, allowing them to cross with the least difficulty. That location was also a blind spot for soldiers in the turret and on the parapet. Darkness still offered benefit, but their time was limited. The only advantage they owned at the moment was the forest fringe towered a short distance once they crossed the water.

"How do we cross?" Richard asked.

All the factors opposed them. The water remained unfrozen, but a thin layer of ice had formed. Its temperature clung near freezing. The only way was to cross through the water.

"We determine the depth at this point. As long as we cross here, we remain out of view of the sentries in the turret."

"Then what?" Rynhawker asked.

"Crawl through the tall grass on our bellies, in a single line, thirty paces apart to reach the forest."

Richard sized the distance from the opposing bank to the forest fringe. It seemed far away, but they had no other options.

Alwain waited no longer. He slipped into the water first, shattering the ice sheet, to plant his feet firmly on the silt bottom. Frigid, waist-high water attacked his legs.

"Keep the cloaks dry," Joanna ordered.

Their movements progressed painfully slow and deliberate to keep them from losing their footing on the slick bed.

Once Alwain reached the center, which entailed six stout strides, Hugh entered the water to begin his trek. He needed no assistance, and by the time Alwain rolled out on the other side to flatten in the high grass, Hugh reached the midpoint of his crossing. At no time had the water risen above Alwain's waist.

Thomas assisted Baldwin in, and when he proved unstable with his injured leg, the knight entered beside him. Together they eased their way to the center.

At the other end, Alwain assisted Hugh onto the bank before both disappeared into the tenuous safety of the entangled grass. Hugh immediately crawled away to attain a dozen strides between them. As long as they remained apart, the sentries would have difficulty discerning exactly what slithered through the growth.

The biting cold air invading their wet clothes sent them shivering out of control. But they kept moving.

Alwain threw a glance back at the turret then along the parapet. No bodies moved along the wall, nor did any faces appear in the turret window. While the sentries slept huddled in a corner for warmth, they were escaping their fortress.

By the time Thomas and Baldwin reached the bank, Alwain had progressed fifty paces in the direction of the forest fringe. And at that same time, Richard slid into the water to begin his trek.

Only Joanna and Rynhawker remained on the berm. When Joanna advanced to the water, Rynhawker held her in check.

"They need more time to disperse. We wait until our king is safely hidden," he said.

"We must go," Joanna pressed, growing frantic. They were minutes away from disappearing into the forest. They had to keep the sunrise from fouling their plan. Sunlight heralded their doom if any failed to reach the trees in time.

"No. We wait," Rynhawker countered.

Something Rynhawker observed made him feel ill at ease at that moment. Maybe it was the way the grass moved as the men squirmed through it, or just intuition that they proceeded too quickly without due caution. But something warned Rynhawker to allow more time for his king to escape.

At the lead, Alwain reached the forest fringe to assist the others when they arrived.

Richard slithered from the moat, rolling into the high grass where he waited, shivering so violently that his teeth chattered. His eyes never strayed from the turret. Joanna had been correct. From their position, it became impossible for sentries in the turret to detect any movement in the high grass, as long as they traveled in a direct line from their exit from the moat to the forest fringe.

Lying perfectly still, Richard watched the grass ahead as Thomas and Baldwin worked their way through it.

Joanna and Rynhawker continued to hold their position on the berm until Richard began his slow crawl through the unruly vegetation. The greater the distance between bodies, the less likely the sentries might detect their movement.

As thrilling as the sight of her brother free was, Joanna knew a smile was still premature. Only after all were safely ensconced in the forest could she allow any elation to enter her head.

Rynhawker slid into the water first, where he assisted Joanna in beside him. They could cross without detection, and they measured each step carefully, while each held the cloaks head high.

Though the frigid water bit her legs with each step, Joanna could think only of reaching the trees and the waiting horses. On the other side, she watched Baldwin and Thomas crawl into the forest fringe.

Rynhawker held back a step as they approached the opposite bank to steady Joanna while she negotiated the difficult maneuver of slipping unseen out of the water into the grass. Less than a minute later, Rynhawker pulled himself into the grass a distance from her. From here forward, they must remain apart while each took disparate paths to reach the trees.

Rynhawker maintained an eye on Richard's location. His king had reached the midpoint in the meadow. The trees beckoned him in the night breeze.

Joanna cast her gaze east. The first rays of an awakening sun peeked over the horizon. They were out of time.

Alwain came to his feet but only after reaching a barrel-width bole of a sleeping oak. He shivered in his wet clothes awaiting Hugh's arrival. By penetrating twenty paces into the forest's shadowy depth, they hoped no sentries might detect their location.

So excited was Hugh to be finally free that he lifted off his belly to his knees before reaching the low hanging limbs.

"Remain down," Alwain scolded loud enough to be heard. They were distant enough from the castle that their voices should not betray them, if they remained careful.

Hugh responded immediately, flattening to his belly. He squirmed into the forest proper until he reached Alwain's outstretched arm. The knight pulled him to his feet behind the tree trunk before easing forward to anticipate Baldwin's arrival.

Then Alwain captured the movements of his king in the high grass. Freedom stood at their doorstep.

Baldwin and Thomas crawled beyond the two men in waiting to pull themselves up behind the next suitable tree trunk. The pain in Baldwin's leg exploded when he sought to place his weight upon it. It gave way immediately, forcing him against the trunk to remain upright. But he cared little for his pain as he stared at the walls of Trifels castle.

"We are free!" he chimed in a low voice, yet loud enough for Hugh to share.

Alwain fought down the urge to leave his concealment to assist his king. He could see Richard's eyes as the Lionheart crawled the final twenty strides needed to gain cover inside the forest. He motioned for Alwain to remain in check while he squirmed over gnarled exposed roots to reach yet another tree bole to conceal him.

Each waited behind their respective shields for movement in the grass, shivering out of control in the bitter cold. No one spoke, waiting for Joanna and Rynhawker to complete their slow crawl through the meadow.

Rynhawker had lost sight of Joanna but had seen his king rise up to gain refuge behind a tree. King Richard the Lionheart was safe... for the moment. The worst of their escape was back at Trifels castle. Once they gained their mounts, they could carry him beyond Henry's reach.

Concern clouded Rynhawker's mind. He failed to detect Joanna moving in the grass. She should be reaching the forest to join the others. Rynhawker had intentionally held back to protect her.

Then the grass parted. Joanna crawled into the forest, rising up to blend with the curve of the tree trunk concealing her brother. Richard assisted her to her feet, where she immediately wrapped a cloak around him to stave off the vicious cold. In moments Richard's shivering began to wane.

She risked tossing a cloak across the way for the others. It fell short, forcing Hugh to retrieve it. When he returned, he placed it around Baldwin and tightened it the best he could.

"You will be warmer now," he said.

Baldwin's face had paled. He stared at nothing.

"Rynhawker, where are you?" Thomas pressed.

Their delay, and the thin line of sunlight drawn at the edge of the eastern horizon brought concern.

The field of high grass became visible from the fortress. Faces appeared at the turret windows.

"I am almost there," Rynhawker said.

The voice came from their right flank. But it seemed a distance away. Rynhawker chose to breach the forest thirty paces to their west. Once Thomas spotted his movement, he motioned to the others to recede.

One by one they peeled back from their hiding places to retreat deeper into the forest proper, placing them completely out of sight of any sentries. They came together only after descending a woody slope, thereby guaranteeing no eyes from the castle parapet might discover them.

Rynhawker took Joanna into his arms, holding her against his frame to stave off her violent shivering. He tightened a cloak around her while rubbing her arms. Alwain did likewise for Baldwin when he realized the man teetered at the edge of consciousness. They could ill afford to carry an unconscious man to the horses.

"Your majesty, you are free," Rynhawker said.

"How far are the mounts?" Richard asked.

There was no time to rejoice. They had no idea how long they had before Henry discovered his prize missing.

Instinctively, Richard roved the forest between them and the castle. He would not rest until they had reached a safe refuge.

"I lead," Joanna said. She still believed a smile premature. But she had rescued her brother just as she had said she would.

62

Duchard listened at the garderobe door. Few would suspect a lone man wandering the halls of ill intent. But it was imperative his presence not alert anyone as to what had occurred. Richard and the others needed time to reach the forest.

He needed to focus on one thing at the moment. And that was how to escape the castle before King Henry learned of Richard's escape. As soon as the dead bodies were discovered, the entire castle would spring into frenzied activity. Duchard needed to remain out of sight until he could find a way out. He wished he had some way of checking on his comrades' progress from his location. He knew for certain that had their escape already been detected, all available soldiers and knights would be scrambling. A silent keep meant Richard had succeeded. He was free.

Duchard eased the door open a crack. He held it there for what seemed an eternity. The first morning rays seeped into the room. Faint light spilled across the corridor beyond the door.

At the present all remained clear.

Soundlessly, Duchard abandoned the safety of the garderobe. He would make his way down the staircase, where he might find an escape from the keep. With the courtyard and inner bailey deserted at this early hour, his presence might trigger suspicions from the parapet. Still the cold air should force all unnecessary men inside the array of buildings on the castle grounds.

Servants would be the first to rise, working in the kitchen to prepare the king's morning meal. The bodies and commotion could allow Duchard to blend in among the serfs. But to do that, he must ditch his weapons.

Circumstance forced the knight to banish all worrisome thoughts concerning his king. He must focus on getting himself free of the castle. At the staircase, he paused with hand covering his hilt. A prematurely drawn sword identified him as the enemy. It was possible he could traverse the corridor to reach the staircase without attracting attention. He might even be viewed as another of Henry's men getting an early start on the day.

Panic set in at the staircase. Voices? Were there voices coming from the floor below? He couldn't be certain. Maybe his mind triggered his panic. Duchard had to press on. He remained close to the wall while slowly descending. Surprise would be on his side against anyone he encountered. No one expected an enemy of the king wandering the halls of the keep.

Duchard paused before backtracking up a few steps. Below two armed men marched by. He listened to their exchange and their clanking swords, concluding from their tone and unhurried pace that no one had yet discovered Richard's absence. By now Richard and the others were concealed well inside the neighboring forest.

When the first-floor corridor returned to silence, Duchard abandoned the staircase. He proceeded quickly down the main corridor without running. Moving too fast might draw the attention of any roaming the corridors.

The aroma of baking bread enticed him toward the kitchen. There he would find the door used to bring in fresh game for butchering. That exit led to a courtyard which opened into the inner bailey and the stables. He chose facing angry women over a handful of soldiers.

However, he did not advance far.

Armed men jostled down all the corridors at once. The absence of talking coupled with their frantic surge on the first floor indicated the alarm had been raised. They knew Richard had escaped.

In panic, Duchard located a storage room down the second crossing corridor he came to. He slipped inside unnoticed. His heart pounded inside his head. His breathing came tense and forced. The moment he most dreaded had arrived. He might become the focus of an intense search inside the keep.

The maddening flurry of chaos began.

He leaned against the door, listening as feet pounded by. For now he was safe, but his time would be severely limited. He expected at this very moment one of Henry's aides was angering their sleeping king to inform him of what had transpired during the night.

Alone and now concerned he might fail to find a way out, Duchard tightened his grip on his sword and reassured himself he still carried his dagger in his belt. However, fighting his way out became an impossible option. He reasserted in that moment he would die before revealing anything that might cause his king's capture.

63

A persistent knock rattled Roger's door, jarring him from his restful sleep. Curled beneath his fur blanket with an arm tucked around the nubile naked woman beside him was where he wished to spend the next six hours. Being dragged into the cold to deal with petty issues for his king was the last thing he desired.

The knock's growing insistence, however, could only be seen as a bad omen. Another day of misery, Roger thought, drawing himself from under his blanket.

"Enter," he barked, shoving the servant woman to force her awake against her will. She reluctantly pulled sleepy eyes open. The sun was barely awake. Why was someone disturbing them?

"Leave," he commanded her with an equally severe bark.

She wasted no time slipping from his bed to snatch up a badger-fur robe, which she hastily tightened about her sinewy body. Her pale skin glowed in the faint light radiating off crumbling embers in the hearth. The chamber's temperature had dropped severely once the flames died. In moments she was gone out a side door in Roger's bedchamber.

"My liege, we have trouble," the knight said even before reaching the bed.

The man exhibited his relief at knowing he need only deliver the terrible news to Roger de Argenton, rather than the king himself. Roger owned that dubious responsibility.

"Speak man, why must you disturb me before the sun?" Roger scowled.

He fumbled beside his bed for a robe. Emerging unclothed into the cold morning air did little to improve Roger's now soured disposition.

"The king has escaped," the knight rattled softly, his fear undeniable at having to speak the words.

Roger snapped alert. Again, he thought at first. His sudden jarring movement sent his mind spinning, and for a brief time, his brain undercut the severity of what he had heard. Why would Richard continue his futile folly of trying to free himself? Trifels castle was impossible to escape from. Now Roger had to return the errant king to his cell.

"The dungeon guards are dead. King Richard and his men are gone."

"What say you?" he stammered, hoping in some strange somnambulate state he had misunderstood the knight.

"Dead?" Roger muttered, hardly believing his ears.

Roger needed to swallow. This was the worst possible news to be dealt upon him. Henry would fly into a tempest when he learned. It was one thing to attempt escape; Henry even expected such from the Lionheart. No king was worth his salt if he succumbed to imprisonment without struggling to be free. But to kill in the process was unforgivable. Richard's men would pay with their lives, if they were still alive when Henry's soldiers retook them.

"The castle remains secure," Roger commanded.

The knight nodded acceptance of the order.

Henry's treasure was gone? How could that be? No, Henry's treasure was not gone. It remained inside the secured fortress walls so Roger could return it to safekeeping.

"Organize the search. Keep them trapped inside!"

"Yes, my lord. I have knights searching every corner of the castle. But someone must inform our king," he said.

Now Roger found it impossible to swallow. A sudden sick feeling swelled inside his gut at the thought of informing his king.

The knight retreated to the door while Roger fumbled about the chamber to gather up clothes to dress. He instructed himself not to panic, rather to think clearly before he said, or did, anything he might regret. He had to find a way out of this without serving up his own head to his king. He convinced himself he would have

Richard back in chains in the dungeon before the sun reached its apex in the sky.

Roger knew it was his duty alone to disturb the king to inform him of what had occurred while he slept. Unless... Roger considered withholding the information until they at least had an opportunity to retake the Lionheart. If they acted swiftly and quietly, they may even locate Richard and thereby withhold the escape from Henry. It may even be possible to hide the fact two guards had perished in the attempt.

Roger was uncertain why he felt the way he felt, but his stomach churned uneasily at the thought of having to put the two comrades of the King of England to death for their foolish act. Roger always believed he provided the compassionate side to King Henry's rule. Roger's efforts had spared countless men from punishment and death over the years, through reasoning with his majesty at times when the king's anger took the best of him. Was now another of those times? After this, could he possibly save either of the men from execution?

"Go now, find me the Lionheart!" Roger commanded through gritted teeth.

The knight pulled the door to exit.

"Tell no one. And pray they have not escaped the castle, or you will likely lose your head for this," Roger growled while he sought boots to shove his freezing feet into.

The knight departed while Roger strapped sword to hip before attaching his dagger. He must assume the errant king was now armed with at least two swords. If the guards brandished daggers, Richard would have them also. Armed men would likely put up a fight, unless so outnumbered they realized the folly of resisting.

Inside, Roger smiled at Richard's resourcefulness. The Lionheart had proven he is never to be taken without due regard for his might. Even the great King Henry lacked the fortitude to keep the King of England in chains.

Roger consumed the next hour pacing voraciously from end to end inside his chamber. The sun had broken well over the horizon, and by now, all the halls of the keep were fully illuminated. If Richard and his men had taken refuge inside, they should be easily captured. If they had per chance escaped the keep to wander inside the castle walls, it was only a matter of time before others spotted them and hailed the soldiers.

Richard was doomed to be retaken, Roger convinced himself while stomping back and forth. His stomach growled in anger, begging to be fed. His throat had gone bone dry from the moment he heard the knight utter the words the King of England might be free.

Roger held hope that at any moment someone would bang his door to report the Lionheart was safely back in the dungeon. But minutes passed and still no knock came. His time was running short. Soon Henry would be awake and proceeding to his throne room to attend to the business of the day. First on that agenda must be a plan to recapture the King of England.

As Roger ruminated over his situation, he began to realize the folly of withholding such vital information from his king. He could blame the captain of the guard, or the other knights for failing to inform him of the incident. Would a knight then be willing to take responsibility over Roger? He thought not.

Roger ceased pacing long enough to stare at the door, as if doing so might force the knock that would end the misery of the uncertainty he endured. Most of all, Roger knew better than to panic.

He marched to the door, throwing it open, hoping to see a knight standing there. Nothing. He could wait no longer, lest he anger his king even further and thereby place his own neck in jeopardy.

64

Roger paused for a long calming breath outside Henry's private chambers. The guardsmen stood aside, sensing something dire from Roger's worried stare. His king could be vicious when disturbed. Roger would rather face a cobra than this. His news would send Henry into a tirade. Roger decided to step delicately through the situation to keep his majesty from lashing out at him. He would dole out information sparingly, so as to minimize the risk of Henry actually losing his prize. Above all else, he must reassure his king there existed no way Richard could remain free for very long.

Yet hours into their fervid search, they still found no sign of the Lionheart.

He chose not to knock. Instead, he pressed open the door slowly to slip inside. The room remained darkened save for the heap of flickering ashes casting off an amber glow. Hunting tapestries hung from every wall, while damask wool drapes cocooned the fire's warmth and excluded a morning sun so Henry could sleep into the day.

Roger shivered. Was trepidation the cause?

"Your majesty," he said slowly, calmly poised inside the door.

Henry slept like a huge, rounded lump beneath a mound of brown bear fur, snoring twenty paces across the spacious chamber in a bed wide enough to sleep four. With his face hidden, he resembled the bear more than a king.

"Your majesty, it is Roger. I must speak," he offered louder, more confident in his plan to manage this unfortunate situation.

"Roger, only word of the ransom's arrival will keep me from biting your head off," Henry growled without opening his eyes or shifting in his bed.

Heart thumping in his chest, Roger wished he could deliver such wonderful news to offset what he really must inform his king.

After a lingering silence, Henry rolled to face the door.

Roger's face held no smile. His brow creased in concern while his eyes revealed such despair that it jolted Henry fully awake. No, it surely was not the ransom's arrival Roger came to announce.

"Approach," he added when Roger seemed uncharacteristically hesitant to advance.

That uncertainty brought Henry up from his pillow. He was alone in his bed, which surprised Roger, since Henry regularly selected a bed mate from the bevy of exquisite women who served him in the great hall. No woman in his kingdom dared refuse a king's bed request.

"Speak your reason for this cruel disturbance," Henry said.

The way he uttered the words revealed Henry already suspected the worst.

"My lord, I have just been informed Richard has attempted another escape," Roger lied. Hours had elapsed and still the Lionheart remained at large.

Instinct drove him two steps further from his king.

"Richard has escaped *again*?" Henry responded in exasperation and disbelief.

He had hoped the Lionheart would have learned the simple lesson that escape from Henry's clutches was impossible and mindfully foolish. Henry now regretted the leniency he showed Richard's men after their last foolish attempt.

"How did he escape our dungeon this time?" Henry shot back.

Then the king considered more deeply. A sudden urge for clarification rushed his brain.

"He has only escaped our dungeon, right? He has not fled the castle?"

The latter became paramount in Henry's mind.

"Our men search as we speak. Our fortress remains secure. I am confident Richard remains trapped inside your walls, my liege."

"How long ago?"

"Sometime during the night."

Slowly, Henry began to grasp the full gravity of what he had been told.

"You will find him," Henry stammered more as an order than a statement.

The king refused to believe his prize could have escaped from his charge. No. Richard was hiding somewhere in his castle, and sooner rather than later, his men would turn up the foolish royal and his two minions to return them to the dungeon. This time they would find their master unmerciful. This time every one of them would suffer.

"The drawbridge remains up and portcullis down until we locate your prize."

"Because you are certain they are trapped in my fortress? Tell me that is so!" Henry's hollow words reflected a sudden lack of confidence in his men.

"Yes, my lord. There is no way they can escape your castle."

Henry pulled himself from his bed so he might locate a fur robe to wrap his rotund belly. The cold morning air forced a shiver.

"You will deliver to me the men responsible for this transgression against their king," Henry ordered while he tightened the robe. He refused to look directly at his aide.

The next moment hung between them.

Roger vacillated. He contemplated finding some way to keep what he must say from his king. But if he erred in his judgement, he might also pay dearly for his transgression.

"Your majesty, they killed two guards during their escape."

The words froze Henry where he stood. Rage spread like a wildfire inside him. Men died at the hands of the Lionheart—his men. Richard had gone too far in his desire to be free. He would pay for that.

"How could this happen?"

"I do not know, my liege, but I will find out, and I will bring you any who dare aid in the king's escape."

Roger bowed to bid his leave, though Henry made no motion to dismiss him. For a brief instant, Roger believed he had side-stepped the king's wrath over what had occurred.

But he was not to be so lucky.

Henry snatched a three-legged stool to launch in fury. He spun about without warning to fling it at Roger, who ducked, but not in time. The stool cracked the side of his head.

"Leave me. And find the Lionheart! If he escapes our castle, everyone who has failed me hangs!" Henry screamed. The veins in his forehead bulged in anger.

Roger backed out as quickly as he could, using the heel of his hand to staunch the bleeding. He held no doubt if the Lionheart had indeed escaped Henry's clutches, hangings would follow upon the gibbet. Roger could only pray he might locate the King of England before it became too late to keep his own neck out of a noose.

65

By afternoon Richard and the others arrived at their horses tethered in the forest in a dense thicket of hazel trees. Isaac smiled when he watched his king emerge with the others. However, before he could utter a congratulatory word or embrace his friend, Alwain clamped the old man's throat to throw him to the ground fully pre-pared to run him through with his blade.

White eyes stared up at the knight.

"You wished us to die in there!" Alwain snarled through bared teeth.

Isaac jerked to squirm free, but Alwain refused to withdraw his sword until his king intervened.

"What did you do with our swords?" the knight charged.

None of the other knights sought to restrain their comrade. Isaac should feel fortunate he still gasped for breath.

"What are you saying? Please, I am not at fault. Sir Brayson..." Isaac stammered.

He scanned, realized Brayson was unaccounted for.

"Sir Brayson did not trust me. He, himself, buried the swords in the hay wagon as the princess instructed."

Isaac turned to his king with eyes bulging in terror.

The fire in Alwain's eyes intimated Isaac's death was close.

"Please believe me. I would never do anything to bring harm to any of you."

Alwain retreated, withdrawing from the old man's throat. He recognized the truth in Isaac's words.

"Then what happened to them?" Rynhawker charged more calmly than his comrade.

"Please, sir, I do not know. I never actually witnessed the knight hiding the swords. He said he had completed his task while I slept. I had no reason to distrust him."

With the tension ebbing, Joanna assembled the horses for their departure. Time was precious. For all she knew, Henry already dispatched knights in pursuit.

"Did you observe Sir Brayson on the road to the castle?" Joanna paused to ask.

"No, m'lady, he was to depart hours after me. I never saw him again. Where is he?"

"He never arrived at the castle," Thomas said.

"And what of Sir Duchard, did he fall?" Isaac asked.

Joanna held her horse in check while she extracted an object tucked beneath her saddle before turning her mount over to her brother. Then she realized Brayson's stallion was also gone.

"We have found our traitor," she whispered to Rynhawker away from the others."

"Can he harm us?"

"He knows no more than any of you," she assured her knight.

She returned her attention to Isaac.

"He remains trapped inside Trifels castle."

"Command me, my lord. I will find a way to aid him," Isaac offered, bowing.

Richard looked to Joanna instead. At the moment, she was in the best position to command her men.

Joanna considered how she might use her friend to help their king. Isaac could remain safe in Henry's domain as long as no one associated him with those who aided King Richard. They remained a long way from reaching safety. And each minute's delay afforded Henry an improved opportunity to retake his prize. After a pause, she drew Isaac from the rest. Even now secrecy remained paramount to their success. Once beyond the others Joanna spoke.

"Find a secure place nearby. Await Duchard. He will come here once he escapes. Do not journey to the castle to aid him. He will find a way out himself."

"For what purpose, m'lady?"

"Inform him we are safe, and we head for the coast."

Joanna extracted the parchment taken from beneath her saddle. She unfolded it to share with Isaac.

"Tell him we will arrive here, where this river empties into the sea in Henry's domain. We may need his sword."

"And what of me?"

"Travel with all haste into Philip's domain. You will be safe there. Find a ship to return to England."

"I will do as my princess commands."

When Joanna joined the others, all were mounted, anxious to depart. Hugh and Baldwin doubled up on Duchard's charger. Isaac sought refuge in a thicket a short distance away.

Alwain led the party through the winter forest, keeping to the lowlands as much as possible. Sooner rather than later, Henry would realize Richard had escaped his fortress and was racing for the safety of France.

Baldwin teetered on his mount, trailing behind his king and Joanna. Hugh steadied him as best he could with his damaged shoulder.

Hunger plagued them as the day wore on. Joanna's emergency provisions provided for only her men and Richard. Now they needed to feed two additional, both coming off months of starvation. Brayson and Duchard's share would go to them now.

Richard nudged his stallion closer to Joanna, who rode with her crossbow slung across her arms. Her quarrels were attached to her saddle so she might load her weapon most quickly.

"You are not the sister I rescued from the King of Sicily," he said with a smile that proved irresistible.

Despite the grime of his captivity, he still appeared a king to her. Goose flesh rose on her arms at the sight. Her brother was free.

"Nor am I the sister you grew up with in our father's court," she commented back.

He reached across to take her hand. She allowed his warmth to flow into her. His touch brought a shiver. For so long she believed they would never see each other again.

"I suppose you brandish that weapon to fool others into believing you a lad," Richard said.

"My aim is as true as any in your army," she countered.

Rynhawker, trailing the formation beside Thomas, loped ahead to come alongside Joanna.

"How do we keep Richard free from Henry's pursuit?" he asked.

He and Joanna believed they shared a bond known only to them as they looked upon each other—one, however, that could never escape an attentive king's notice.

Richard hid his reaction to what he witnessed.

"This way," Joanna ordered, directing the column off the path to their right flank. They altered their course to head north.

Alwain, the last to receive her command, had allowed a precariously large gap to exist between the rest. So much so, that attackers could isolate him from the pack to slay him before he might gain another's aid.

"Why?" Richard questioned.

"We have been too long under the sun's scrutiny. We shall rest in that gully until night brings us cover," Joanna said.

"Your majesty, we must ride. The longer we remain in Henry's lands, the more we risk capture," Baldwin pleaded.

"No. We obey Joanna's command," Richard replied, surprising everyone in the column, including his sister.

Exhausted and hungry, Richard wished only for Baldwin to gain time off his mount to help his injured leg. Even Hugh seemed to smile when he received Joanna's directions.

They weaved their way down a wooded slope onto a craggy path in a gully paralleling their desired course. One by one they dismounted, tethering beasts to nearby barren branches.

"Alwain, Thomas, guard our king," Joanna ordered.

She cocked her crossbow before counting her quarrels. Thirty-seven, each vital to survival.

"Rynhawker and I will forage."

No one opposed her command. All were relieved to be sheltered from the biting wind, and in a secluded place where they might gain some rest. It would be impossible to truly sleep knowing Henry would dispatch his knights the moment he learned Richard was nowhere inside his castle. But those hours of fruitless searching beforehand would give them a precious lead on their pursuers. Now they needed to be clever enough to keep that pursuit confused as to their intended course.

Hugh assisted Baldwin to a place suitable for laying his head in a pile of leaves before covering him with a cloak.

Richard settled beside Alwain and Thomas, situated a few feet away. Each held their sword ready to respond to the slightest disturbance that might indicate they had been discovered.

"My liege, you must rest. I will remain vigilant," Alwain said.

At first Richard did nothing, gazing at the surrounding forest. Then he leaned against the cold ground to cover himself with his cloak. Within moments the king fell asleep.

Thomas spread his cloak to cover Hugh before working his way to the top of the ridge. There he scanned the breadth of the woodland. In the distance, he spied Rynhawker and Joanna disappearing over a rise.

Joanna advanced ahead of Rynhawker with a quarrel ready, as her eyes studied the surrounding forest tangle. She decided it wisest to remain stationary until the sun turned to dusk. The twilight of the day favored hunting forest creatures. In the faint light, deer, boar, and rabbits rallied the courage to emerge. Winter brought scarce feeding, which Joanna hoped might force creatures to reveal themselves out of desperation. Hunger drives all creatures to unwise risks. While that could provide them something to eat, Joanna had to be certain they avoided falling prey to the same flawed thinking.

"Here is a suitable place to wait," she said, settling into a low spot on the forest floor. From their location, she could watch over the others while monitoring the nearby landscape.

Rynhawker held her hand so she might sit without losing her balance. However, he refused to release it after she found comfort on the ground. Then he settled beside her.

"You have rescued our king," he said with undeniable admiration on his face.

She smiled at him.

Her cold hands caused him to remove his cloak to provide her an additional layer of insulation against the winter. A shivering hand makes for an errant shot.

Joanna placed her hand over his.

"*We* have freed our king," she corrected.

Rynhawker cradled her hand with his. Then he slipped an arm around to bring her closer.

"You still shiver," he said.

Was this the right moment to share a kiss? They were alone and distant enough that Richard would never witness it. Is that what Rynhawker wanted also? She wondered. She studied his eyes, saw that he wanted her.

"Placing our faces cheek to cheek will warm us further," she invited.

Rynhawker needed no further prodding. He brought her so close that her warmth spread over his face. He could feel her breath upon his cheek.

When he turned to face her, he knew what she wanted, so he obliged her. Their kiss was soft and enduring but lasted only a few moments before his shivering severed their contact.

"We lack sufficient men to see our king to safety," Rynhawker risked saying. He knew the impact those words would have on her.

They had lost Brayson and Duchard. They could nary afford to lose another.

"Our dire circumstance forces us to outwit our enemies. That is all."

Silence allowed both to contemplate her words.

"Will we make it back to England?" he asked.

The moment returned them to the forest, the cold and the hunger from a day with nothing to eat.

"You mean if we do not starve first?"

"I trust you have a way for us to escape."

"I will soon," she said, revealing uncertainty in their future.

"I..." he started.

Her finger silenced him.

It was not what he at first thought. She motioned into the forest. Picking its way carefully through a barren thicket forty paces distant, a doe emerged, desperate for anything edible.

Rynhawker eased away, allowing her to prepare her shot. Neither spoke, fearing sound would drive off their supper.

Joanna eased her crossbow to level it at her prey. She had always relied on something solid and stationary to steady her weapon. Now she had only her left arm.

The unsuspecting doe brought her head up, sampling for predators. They were upwind of the animal. Joanna thought she was on the verge of losing her opportunity. Yet she was not ready to fire. Releasing now would only cost them a quarrel.

Rynhawker's face turned a frown as moments passed with Joanna holding her weapon in check. He wanted to command her to fire. He wanted to eat so badly that he would have taken the crossbow from her to make the shot, if he believed his action would not frighten the animal off.

Then Joanna ceased her breathing.

The doe returned to grazing brown sparse bracken.

Joanna released. The quarrel caught on a breeze, whizzing past the doe, errant of its shoulder to disappear into a piney thicket.

The doe lurched off the ground, loping into a thicket before Joanna could reload.

Neither spoke. Joanna's shivering had betrayed her. But she refused to be defeated. Calmly she removed a quarrel, used the pull lever against a tree to cock her crossbow, then clicked her projectile into the channel. She asked God to provide them another opportunity to eat before night fell full upon them.

66

Seeking only the abyss of a dreamless sleep, Richard found slumber tenuous at best in the cold. The looming threat of recapture pulled him awake each time he sought to release himself to his exhaustion.

Across the way Baldwin moaned while attempting to shift his legs. Hugh remained close to provide aid. No one knew what might exist in the next moment. Their freedom could be fleeting at best.

"How long can we remain free without food or a way to reach safety," Richard said. His eyes remained closed.

Thomas remained silent. He never expected the king would address him. After a few moments, Alwain switched his attention from the forest to his king.

"We will find a way to get you to France, your majesty."

"How far are we from Philip's lands?"

"Five days ride at best, my liege."

For a few moments no one spoke while Richard assessed their chances of reaching King Philip's domain. At the moment it seemed the only logical course left to follow.

Alwain bolted up, bringing his sword around to fight when crackling branches underfoot stole his attention.

"It is us," Rynhawker called to allay his fears.

The knight entered the gully before assisting Joanna down the frozen slope. She carried a gutted plump hare, which she tossed to Thomas for roasting.

"Build a small fire so we all eat this night," she commanded.

"It is too dangerous," Alwain warned.

"It is vital we eat. Alwain and Thomas, make your way down the ravine to a place suitable to cook the meat. Douse the fire immediately afterward and return. We will watch from our position to warn if danger approaches."

The two knights slogged through the low of the gully to travel beyond where the gully turned toward the south. They would be dangerously out of sight of each other, but Alwain and Thomas would draw their enemies to them, allowing time for their king and the others to escape.

"I missed a doe," Joanna confessed as if just saying it crushed her spirit.

"Rabbit will suffice then," Richard offered.

Rynhawker strayed from Richard and Joanna to a place along the ridge which allowed him to watch over the forest for both them and Thomas and Alwain. He had to tamp down his urge to claim a position that allowed him to protect the young knight. His first duty fell to his king. He may fail Thomas if trouble erupted.

After a few minutes he glanced back at the others. Hugh and Baldwin slept fitfully curled beside each other along the earthen wall. Joanna sat with Richard while he warmed her with an arm cloaking her.

They had succeeded. Joanna's cunning had found a way to rescue her brother. They had but one more task to face: Get Richard off the continent.

The ensuing minutes were crucial to all. Alwain and Thomas needed to roast the meat and return without detection. Once they doused the fire, they again became undetectable in the forest.

Rynhawker allowed his mind to drift. Had Henry learned of Richard's escape by now? Surely, he must have. Soldiers and knights must be swarming the countryside in search of lost treasure. Had Duchard remained free? Or had he fallen to Henry's men? The king would be unaware of how many were involved in the rescue... unless Henry uncovered Duchard. He would torture him ruthlessly to extract all he could. Thoughts of his friend's suffering caused a cringe. Maybe Duchard had ended his life before allowing the enemy to take him.

"We must reach France before Henry's soldiers get to us!" Richard said after many moments of silence.

His long, entangled hair covered much of his face, along with a beard grown wild over the past months. Henry evidently saw no need to keep his prisoner groomed despite his royalty.

"No, my lord, your difficulties are more severe than you might know. I believe Philip is in league with John. I fear he has conspired to seize the crown in your absence. Placing you in Philip's hands will only guarantee your death and John's ascension to the throne," Joanna replied.

Richard's face at first turned grim, then angry.

"Philip betrays me?"

"I suspect they act in concert to keep you from returning to England."

"Have you substance to these charges?"

"No, my lord."

"Then maybe you err about the King of France."

"Richard, my lord, we cannot risk that I may be right. I can never allow Philip to take away what I have gained. You are free. Before God I swear I will keep you free until we reach England."

For a few moments neither spoke. Richard needed time to accept that even his friends, driven by greed and lust for power, had become his enemies.

Joanna worked her arm around his waist to gather more of his warmth. Her shivering had finally subsided. Her heart was at peace.

"Henry will assume you to make a run for France. He will concentrate his forces along the critical points of his frontier where you will seek passage. As long as he remains unaware of our assistance, he will believe he chases three escaped Brits."

"Then how are we to proceed?" he asked.

Those words felt wonderful in Joanna's mind. Richard trusted her. He accepted her as capable of completing what she set out to accomplish. Never did she expect her king to listen to her.

"We use the forest, travel north to the sea. It is the longer, more treacherous journey, but one Henry least suspects."

"And when we reach the sea?"

"A ship, moored beyond sight from land, awaits my signal. Only then does it approach Henry's coast. We will see you safely onboard," Joanna said.

Richard hated to accept that his friend the King of France would dishonor his faith to England. But then Philip had angered Richard with his refusal to fight in the Holy Lands.

"I believe John has struck a bargain with the King of France to keep you from your throne."

"John is ever the fool," Richard muttered.

"Then, my lord, we must not become foolish by trusting anyone now."

"Henry's men will never invade France in pursuit of us. We need only seek refuge in his lands without his knowledge," Richard offered.

"My lord, I will not allow another vile ruler to take you from us. The sea is our best play for freedom. I fear Philip may even strike a bargain with Henry to return you once all learn of your escape."

"What of the ransom? Surely Henry demanded a ransom for my return."

"More than our queen could collect. I have instructed her to withhold it until the deadline, or until I return."

"Then England has given Henry nothing?"

"Nothing, my lord. Henry still awaits our queen's decision. We have given Henry his answer. Now we must get you out to sea."

Richard laughed, unable to recall the last time he had done so. For all Henry's effort, the man gained nothing in hand. No ransom, and now, no king.

The Lionheart tightened the cloak around his sister. Then he kissed her cheek.

"I trust you never intend to cut your hair this way again."

For the first time since departing Londontown, Joanna laughed. She drew closer for more warmth.

"We *are* going home," she said, holding back tears.

Rynhawker withdrew from the ridge when he spied Thomas and Alwain threading down the ravine's center with cooked meat.

"Tonight we feast," the king said.

The aroma of rabbit brought Baldwin and Hugh awake so they might cluster with the others. Tomorrow they renew their flight to freedom.

67

Duchard moved deftly about the castle throughout the hours of daylight, always narrowly avoiding soldiers rushing through corridors in desperate search of the escaped king and his two comrades. None of Henry's men ever thought to question anyone out of place in the castle. Duchard surmised from their frantic actions that all still believed no outsiders were involved in Richard's escape.

That one fact allowed Duchard to keep moving and concealing his identity from Henry's subjects. But he needed to egress the keep to secure a hiding place closer to the stables until he could escape the castle. Sooner or later, the drawbridge would come down and the portcullis raised when Henry realized Richard was no longer inside his fortress.

Duchard counseled himself for patience. He needed to blend with the others in the castle to have any hope of surviving this frantic time. And that meant abandoning his sword and donning clothes that made him less conspicuous.

Late in the afternoon, he risked entering the knight's hall, hoping to find it empty. His hopes were confirmed. Not a single knight or solider loitered about. The frenzied activity had swept through the castle onto the grounds. But Duchard could only wonder how long he might evade the men.

Hunger rumbled through his belly, triggered by the aroma of boar roasting in a kitchen hearth. He hoped to abscond with some nourishment to settle the anger within. He had gone much of the day undetected, and despite salivating, he needed to maintain his strategy of avoiding contact with anyone in the castle.

As he roamed the corridor leading to the kitchen, he formulated a way to fill his belly while still maintaining his ruse.

Wandering into the buttery, Duchard located a blood-stained leather apron servants wore while slaughtering animals brought in from the forest. He would appear less a knight, more a servant, clad in the apron. He replaced his jacket with the garment then hid his sword behind a cask of ale in the corner. He would leave the room unarmed, as even his dagger must be abandoned. Someone might become suspicious seeing a servant wielding a sword or dagger while working the kitchen.

There would be others to contend with there, but Duchard decided he would risk exposure for a chance to eat and maybe even gather news regarding the errant king.

Duchard sucked in a deep breath before exiting the chamber. He threw a glance back at the barrel concealing his sword one more time. Surrendering his sword made him vulnerable, though he believed he could attain what he sought with his ruse.

The knight entered the corridor leading to the kitchen with its two flaming hearths and an array of tables against the far wall used for preparing meals for the royals and the castle's fighting men.

As suspected, he received no more than a cursory glance from the workers before returning to their duties. Warm bread just out of the hearth lined the first table he approached.

He struggled with the urge to snare a loaf for himself. It would be too soon. On his exit he might find an opportunity to steal some.

A succulent roasting boar sizzled on a spit in the second hearth. Flames occasionally flared to lick the drizzling fat. The beast was nearing completion. Duchard suppressed his smile.

Carefully he inched toward the boar, looking this way and that for a carving knife with which to test the animal. He figured if he acted like he knew what he was doing, no one would challenge him.

At the table furthest from the hearth he spied a knife waiting for use once the beast came off the spit.

Duchard approached the meat to examine it closely. Without touching it, he tilted his head this way and that to view the exposed sides. Yes, roasting was nearly complete, certainly sufficient for Duchard to slice away a taste. If he looked like he belonged, no one should question him.

Ignoring others scurrying about with beetroots, leeks and onions from another storage chamber, Duchard retrieved the knife before returning to the animal.

Slicing into the boar's shoulder released a stream of fat into the fire. As the flames flared up to brush his hand, he risked extracting a chunk of the pork. At present it was far too hot to taste, but Duchard remained in place, never allowing his eyes to stray to ascertain if anyone were watching. After blowing across the meat, he sampled a finger-sized bite.

He had to resist stuffing the rest hungrily into his mouth. It must appear to all that he only tasted to certify the dinner met with the king's expectations.

A large scowling woman draped in black with her hair under a wrap and apron shielding her bodice glared at Duchard.

Glaring back, he popped the remainder of the slice into his mouth, flashing her a smile to indicate he approved of her diligence in preparing the meal.

The woman's lips remained tight and angry across her face, expressing displeasure that Duchard opened her boar. But dutifully she returned to her work, placing her back to him.

The food, though scant, tasted glorious as it made its way into his grumbling stomach. The knight remained at the hearth a few moments longer. He wanted to take the boar's ear, but he must do it only when no one watched. Such an inappropriate action might raise suspicion.

Moments ticked by while Duchard loitered, appearing as if he were inspecting the dinner more closely. When he felt confident all the women were engaged in their duties, he sliced quick and hard. The ear dropped into his waiting hand. Despite burning his palm, he clutched it tightly, knowing it would be worth the pain to sup on that tasty morsel.

However, it became time to take his leave. Duchard returned the knife where he found it, crossed the room to exit while passing the table with the loaves. His hand swept down to snatch the last in the string, whereupon he slid it beneath his apron. Three quick strides and he entered the corridor for the storage room.

What he had gained must satisfy him until he could find a way out of the castle. That was if, and when, the king decided to lower the drawbridge and raise the portcullis. The knight would have little chance of escape until people again flowed in and out through the manned barbican.

Huddled in the corner of the lightless chamber, Duchard consumed his meager supper. After regaining his weapons, he spent a long time listening at the door. Remaining anywhere too long could get him caught. Hearing nothing, he eased the door open enough to slip into the corridor.

A dozen strides later, a surge of soldiers pounded through the knights' hall. Something had warranted a new flurry of anxious activity.

That could be bad for Duchard... very bad.

68

Night brought security as Joanna and Rynhawker led the others through the forest to the north and west. Having consumed their rabbit and filled their bellies with water from a stream, all were anxious to continue their trek.

"I do not know how much longer they can ride," Rynhawker commented, indicating Hugh and Baldwin.

So consumed was Joanna in her thoughts she never heard him.

"We double back now," she ordered.

Joanna had grown comfortable in her role as leader. The more confidence she demonstrated, the more she expected her men to abide by her will.

"Why?" Rynhawker asked, confused by the tactic.

At first Joanna offered no response. She simply wheeled her stallion off the beaten path to face the others.

"Come about," she commanded all who stopped.

They stared at her confounded.

"Proceed back into the forest?" Alwain questioned, initially wanting none of it.

"Why?" Richard pressed when it seemed their efforts would only lengthen their journey making it more treacherous.

"We must continue toward France," Baldwin insisted.

His outstretched arm stopped Hugh and Richard from wheeling their beasts in response.

"My lord, we have left sufficient tracks to convince Henry's men you race for France. Now we turn toward the sea."

"The sea! Have you lost your mind?" Baldwin asserted.

"You think it wise to remain in Henry's domain?" Thomas ventured.

Joanna posed her responses to her brother instead of the men who pressed their questions.

"My king, it is wise for Henry to believe we are going for Philip's aid. He will overcommit his forces to secure his border. That leaves the sea unguarded."

"And once we reach the sea?" Thomas shot, restraining his growing agitation at Joanna's intent.

"A ship awaits. We will all be safe. No one, save for the captain himself, knows I have arranged this, so neither John nor Philip can mount an offensive against us, my liege."

Richard analyzed the moment. Then he smiled, broke into laughter. Seconds later, Hugh and Baldwin laughed with their king.

Rynhawker, Thomas and Alwain remained stoic, knowing Joanna's chosen path would not come without peril. Henry could still dispatch men to the coast to thwart the Lionheart's escape.

"Come, we go now," the king said.

Rynhawker spurred his stallion to the lead as the column retreated slowly through the trees the way they had come. Dreary hours passed in the cold night as they trekked north, where they would come upon the sea safer than if they had made a play for France.

Joanna trusted no one, save for the men who surrounded her at that moment. She had to pray the man she trusted to bring his ship to their aid would be faithful. If he failed them, they could become trapped at the coast with no means of escape. Joanna had spent months considering the risk involved in this part of her plan. Henry had not expected her to free her brother, nor would he expect her to guide him to the sea for his escape.

Baldwin swayed unsteadily in the saddle. When it became apparent Hugh could no longer assist Baldwin on his mount, Thomas volunteered to switch horses. He rode with Baldwin while Hugh rode alone on Thomas' stallion.

The first rays of a new day crept over the horizon to light the barren trees, stretching in every direction as far as they could see.

First came the wind whistling through the branches, then the clatter of hooves. Rynhawker was first to detect riders in the distance. The thin fog shrouding the forest made locating the source all the more difficult. The commotion seemed to bounce off the trees. All heads twisted, desperate to uncover the source.

Panic swept over the column. They halted abruptly, with every man peering through the mist into the surrounding umbrage, not for the men coming after them, rather for harborage to hide them.

Tense moments passed without solution. They were exposed. They had only four viable swords with two men incapable of defending themselves.

Joanna sought the lowest point in the forest and led them into a thicket offering partial concealment.

They quickly dismounted, tethered their animals to trees before finding places where they might hide. There was a chance the riders were nothing more dangerous than errant men returning home from a journey of their own. They were, however, more likely a hunting party dispatched to find Henry's prisoners.

Joanna removed her crossbow to set a quarrel in place before lowering herself to the cold ground. She leveled the weapon over a fallen log. Listening carefully for the next sounds, she hoped to determine their location before the riders sprang upon them.

Hugh and Baldwin huddled in a thicket away from the others to avoid the attack when it came.

Richard flanked Joanna on one side, Rynhawker on her other, both with swords ready. None yet knew the extent of the danger the shuffling noise in the forest posed. Joanna, however, readied herself to drop the lead soldier when they appeared.

Alwain and Thomas found defensive positions upwind of the other three. Richard ordered Thomas and Alwain to vanguard their defense against the riders. They would engage the first wave, allowing Richard and Rynhawker crucial time to assess the onslaught and respond to keep everyone alive.

Fear and panic seized every body in the thicket.

The first pair of riders emerged in the trees a distance away. They rode leisurely—unaware of the escapees—as they clopped in a meandering path. Moments later, three more knights emerged over the slight rise trailing their comrades.

Save for the riders, nothing in the forest moved. Their colors and armor deemed them Henry's knights. Sooner rather than later, they would uncover the tracks Richard's horses left to realize they were close.

Joanna waited, expecting more men in the hunting party. When none appeared, she realized Henry must still believe Richard had escaped without assistance. If he had suspected aid, the king surely would have doubled the number of men in each party to make certain they held superior manpower to retake the king. It would seem Henry still believed Richard and his two wounded comrades had somehow escaped his castle to roam the forest in a futile attempt to be free. That fact boded well for Duchard. He must have eluded Henry's men inside the castle.

Joanna suppressed her fleeting smile at the thought of outwitting the King of Germany. But now was no time to gloat—they were not free yet.

Joanna leaned in close to her king.

"At this range, I can take two. You and Rynhawker must unhorse at least two others when they charge," she whispered.

Richard stared at her incredulously at first.

"Prepare for their assault," he whispered.

Joanna shifted her crossbow right to focus on the trailing horseman. Their best chance for survival came if Joanna eliminated the last knight in the column followed by the first. That order provided her with sufficient time to reload, if the others failed to see their comrade drop. Richard and the others would have to handle the other three.

Joanna tightened on her crossbow, sought the upper chest of the last rider while steadying her hand. She was terribly nervous, yet she convinced herself she could make the shot.

As the riders neared, she ceased her breathing, confirmed no wind to confound her.

She fired.

The quarrel whipped silently through the air puncturing the base of the rider's neck. The man clawed at his bleeding throat while groping wildly for his sword and an attempt to control his stallion. The beast immediately strayed from the path with the four horsemen never looking back to see their comrade struggling.

There was no time for celebration. Joanna stood to cock her crossbow against the log before setting her next quarrel in place. Her action exposed her to the riders, now less than a hundred strides distant, who drew swords to charge.

Richard and Rynhawker sprang into a fighting stance as the riders spurred their stallions to full gallop.

As they closed, Joanna dropped to her position behind the fallen log, leveled her crossbow to take aim on the lead rider in the string. She had but a moment to plan everything she needed for her shot. If she missed, it might mean Rynhawker or Richard took a sword from the rider.

Thomas and Alwain charged the second rider to come within range.

The other riders were only strides away.

Joanna ceased her breathing, focused her eye on the rider and banished all other thought from her mind.

She fired!

The quarrel took the lead knight in his side, leaving an out-stretched sword arm vulnerable.

Three riders clashed with Rynhawker, Richard and Thomas. Alwain drew away from the attack to protect Hugh and Baldwin should a rider break through their defenses.

But Joanna chose not to cheer her victory. She evacuated the area in favor of a position on higher ground from which to launch another quarrel. She had to be ready to assist her brother.

As the king attacked the third rider to encounter them, Rynhawker charged the other to maintain a one-on-one confrontation.

Seeing that the tide of battle was shifting in favor of Henry's men, Alwain joined the fray, which frightened one of the riders. The knight yanked his reins to steer his stallion into retreat.

"He must not escape!" Richard commanded the others. But none were positioned to launch an assault on the fleeing knight.

Cleaving the knight's shoulder, Richard took the man from his horse, and once on the ground, the king drove his blade cleanly through his armor into his belly. The man ceased breathing. His horse bucked to gallop off into the trees.

The retreating rider was too quickly escaping.

Richard spun in search of Joanna.

She was nowhere in sight.

Thomas raced to untether his horse. He had to mount a pursuit. The rider must not return to the others to reveal their location and strength. They had to keep their secret safe as long as possible. Henry would concentrate his forces effectively against them based on what that lone rider could report.

Joanna tracked on the fleeing knight with her crossbow. She fired. The quarrel held true, burying its tip into the fleeing soldier's back at the joint in his armor.

For the first few seconds the stallion maintained its frenzied stride. Then it slowed when the man lost consciousness, no longer commanding his beast.

They watched the stallion slow to a walk just before the soldier toppled headlong into the forest.

All cheered as Joanna slung her crossbow over her shoulder.

"You have trained my sister well," Richard said to Rynhawker.

Rynhawker only smiled.

"Move quickly before others learn we were here," Richard commanded.

Thomas and Alwain collected up weapons, water and rations before tumbling the bodies into a ravine where they might remain out of view at least for a time. Hopefully, time enough for them to reach the sea.

69

Duchard entered the deserted stables to a handful of horses in the stalls. Henry must have realized his prize had escaped his fortress, since the castle opened up, allowing soldiers and knights to spill into the countryside in search of their escaped prisoners.

Richard and the others had obtained a vital lead over their pursuit. With luck they would reach France before Henry's knights could overtake them.

With the risk of capture inside the castle minimized, Duchard occupied an empty stall. He decided to remain hidden until just before the drawbridge came up for the night. Then he would steal a mount to pass through the baileys to the barbican. Timing his exit with the departing serfs, he could slip away undetected to return to the rendezvous. He had given little thought to what he must do after that. His only alternative seemed to travel to France to secure passage back to England.

Only a few men came and went in the stables. Two were stable keepers cleaning stalls, and two were soldiers late to join the hunt.

Duchard curled into the corner, which had already been cleaned. He expected to go undisturbed.

He wished now he had taken more to eat, for he knew it would be a long night in the forest without food. He had nothing with which to hunt, leaving his only option to steal.

He idled away time contemplating the status of his king. Richard and the others could, by now, be a day's ride away, or they could have found refuge in a safe location.

Then an idea prodded that overturned his plan. What if his king and Joanna were captured? If he remained inside the castle, he could further aid them. If he departed, he might forfeit any opportunity to return to rescue them. However, he was but one man.

Certainly, Henry would make it impossible for anyone to aid them if he were fortunate enough to gain back his prize.

No, his best strategy was to flee as intended then track his comrades or failing that, enter France. He had their starting point for tracking. They would leave their trail from the rendezvous. Riding hard, it might take but a few days to reach them. They would need his sword.

The thought of rejoining the others invigorated his spirit. Richard and the others could fight for themselves as long as they were free and armed. The Lionheart would never allow himself to be retaken. He would surely die in his quest for freedom.

Silence surrounded Duchard while he waited. The cold permeated his horse blanket to chill his bones. Darkness approached. The men left behind would be supping in the knights' hall. Only those in the barbican and turrets would be watching over the castle.

Thirst drove Duchard from the stall. He crossed to a watering trough for the horses. A few hurried gulps sated his thirst, but he dashed back to cover when voices drifted in.

Clutching his sword with both hands, he prayed to avoid the need to fight his way out. He would kill if necessary, but he would rather escape without further bloodshed.

He held his breathing until the voices faded. No one entered the stables. It was time to egress. Waiting any longer could cost him his freedom.

Abandoning his empty stall, Duchard dashed from one to the next until he came upon a dappled gray stallion with an unblemished white snout.

"Easy," he soothed, approaching from the side to stroke its mane.

He needed the beast calm while he bridled and saddled it. If detected, he could forgo the saddle, but a bridle was essential.

The beast luffed when Duchard slipped the bit into its uncooperative mouth.

"Remain calm, my friend," he offered in a soothing voice.

The beast seemed to understand, as it immediately settled down for him.

Next Duchard secured the saddle before guiding the stallion from the stall by the reins. He would mount when he reached the doors, in case the stallion whickered or raised a commotion that garnered attention.

Duchard swung the stable door open enough to ride through. He wanted no more than that.

All progressed well. Slowly and carefully, Duchard pulled himself into the saddle then spurred gently through the crease.

He departed the stables at a retarded pace, ambling through the castle square into the inner bailey. A cluster of peasants lugging sacks made their way through the outer bailey. Duchard slowed to flow amongst them.

The barbican guard monitored Duchard's movement from his window. Was he watching for anyone resembling the King of England? Duchard avoided eye contact, instead nudging his beast closer to the men exiting, hoping to make identification more difficult... if the guard were at all interested in Duchard's movement.

Emerging through the barbican, Duchard spurred his stallion into a trot. He had cleared the castle gate. Even the peasants, it seemed, cared little for a lone rider departing the castle. He remained but a few strides from freedom. It would take minutes to raise the drawbridge, even if the guards sounded an alarm. The portcullis could drop in seconds, the drawbridge required much more time. And the portcullis was behind him now.

Duchard smiled as his stallion pranced over drawbridge timbers. He so much wished to turn back to wave good-bye. But discretion won out. He simply swallowed his gloat bursting to get out.

King Richard the Lionheart was free, and Duchard, the last of the valiant men who achieved such a feat, had just escaped Trifels castle. With luck, the King of Germany would never learn about the knights—and the woman—who invaded his most impregnable fortress, freed their king and fled without a single loss of life.

70

Henry paced ferociously throughout the evening. As each hour fell away, his rage grew. By midnight he wanted to lop off heads. Roger entered to report their search of the castle had failed to uncover the Lionheart. And that his knights at this moment were scouring the countryside for the king's prize.

Wisely, Roger hovered beyond throwing distance in the throne room, mindful if he strayed closer, he might receive another attack from a flying object.

"All search parties have departed," Roger offered.

"Tell me, Roger, how could he escape my castle with the portcullis down and the drawbridge raised?"

Henry's mind, and gaze, drifted off.

Roger chose to avoid speculation. The very notion seemed impossible. No one—not even the Lionheart—could accomplish such an incredible feat. All his previous attempts failed. This one should have also.

"If I were a prisoner in Richard's castle, how might I escape?" Henry muttered, returning to his chair.

"Your majesty, it would be impossible for a single man to escape the dungeon, find his way out of the keep then scale the walls," Roger offered.

"Impossible! Impossible! You buffoon! Richard has done it, has he not?" Henry screamed, his veins pulsing in his neck.

"My liege, we do not know for certain Richard has escaped. Perhaps he and his men hide within. We may uncover them groveling in a darkened corner," Roger offered in his own defense.

Henry vaulted from his chair to resume pacing.

"Richard had assistance. That is how he achieved his freedom. Just like his last attempt."

"But, my lord, the penalty for aiding a king's prisoner is death. All would realize that."

"Evidently my subjects have defied me. Perhaps Richard convinced them with a handsome reward for their betrayal."

Roger seized the opportunity. He could reconcile himself. Deflecting blame onto another might exonerate him.

"Your majesty, your cunning mind has no doubt solved the mystery of Richard's escape. The guards believed he would reward them for their betrayal. So foolishly they released him only to be cut down by the very man who promised riches."

"Indeed, Richard's smooth tongue has persuaded others to follow him to their deaths. He almost tricked us into his foolishness about the crusade."

"You were indeed much wiser than the Lionheart," Roger offered with the glint of a smile.

The more he shifted responsibility onto another, any other, the less Roger would suffer. He might yet escape the noose.

"If I am so much the wiser, Roger, how then did he escape from me?"

"My lord, we will hunt down the Lionheart, and he will be returned to your dungeon. He will never see the light of another day until you wallow in your ransom."

"Report to me every hour until we have him in our clutches. And see that anyone witnessed aiding the prisoners is killed."

"As my king wishes."

Roger bowed while backing out of the throne room. Once in the corridor he leaned against the wall, where he stared at the heavens through a vaulted window.

"Please bring him back," he whispered to no one.

If the Lionheart were lost for good, only suffering and death would come, and Roger might still be marched to the gibbet.

71

Ahead, crowded gray trunks thinned to reveal the rocky coast of King Henry's domain. Uncertainty clouded Joanna's every thought as she guided the lead stallion through the forest. Would the ship be there when they arrived? If Tobrin failed her, what must she do next? They survived the escape and the trek to the sea. They needed but one more element in place for Richard to be truly free.

Joanna anticipated the king might deploy men to secure the coast against what she intended. Yet that notion hinged on Henry having discovered that the Lionheart had English aid. It was beyond hope to believe they might make it through this next day unscathed.

Seeing the sea sent her mind back to Duchard. How had he fared inside the castle? She could only hope he had evaded capture and torture. That was why she kept everyone ignorant of her true intent once Richard was free. No man can be forced reveal what he did not know.

The sea was Henry's last chance to recapture his prize. She would have Richard on English soil well before her mother must release the ransom.

At the cost of her own life, Joanna was determined to prevent Richard's recapture. They were too close now to allow anyone or anything to keep Richard from his throne.

White caps crashed angrily against the shore as they breached the forest, pausing before the open expanse confronting them. Joanna disbursed Rynhawker to the west, Thomas to the east, to scout the shoreline for signs of Henry's men.

Richard and the others remained ensconced in the umbrage as best they could. They had no idea how Joanna would accomplish what came next, only that they would trust she could evacuate them from danger.

After minutes of tense waiting alone, Joanna returned to the others inside the forest's edge.

"What occurs next?" Richard asked.

At first Joanna said nothing, contemplating her response. Then she scanned for the high ground. Less than a league away a hill rose in prominence. It provided the elevation she required.

She pointed north and west.

"Safely beyond sight, a ship awaits my signal. Once received, it will approach. Men are waiting to transport you to England."

Richard stared at the sea for unending moments in search of any sign to confirm what Joanna said. He could find none. Was that good, or was that bad?

Joanna wheeled her mount back into the forest with a wish to see Duchard galloping up to greet them with that smile he so often displayed. She could only hope he had fled Henry's castle to find his way to them. If not, he would surely be dead, or imprisoned and tortured in the king's dungeon.

Joanna had promised herself at the onset of this quest that she would save her brother while never having to sacrifice the men she had come to care for so dearly. But already one went unaccounted for, a second left behind, and they still needed to reach the ship. Once Richard was aboard and sailing into open sea, the King of Germany could no longer reclaim his prize.

"How long must we wait?" Richard thought to ask.

Before Joanna could answer, Thomas galloped up at full pelt. At first Joanna's heart leapt into her throat. Was he evading a pursuit? Had a new obstacle appeared between them and freedom?

"My lady, all is clear," Thomas reported, breaching the forest.

Their horses whickered nervously, causing Hugh trouble in controlling his beast. Only with Thomas' aid did the mount calm.

"Hold her steady!" Thomas scolded.

"I'm doing what I can," Hugh replied.

"We fortify a position close by and find something to eat," Joanna said.

Her eyes never left Rynhawker's tracks in the sand. He was still beyond her sight, which worried her. What if he were taken? What if they had been waiting in ambush?

Joanna edged out from the forest fringe for a better vantage point to observe the shoreline. Each passing minute heightened her concern. Still nothing came into view. Richard came beside her. For a time both scanned the shore, hoping to see the returning knight.

"What you are doing is wrong," he said without his eyes straying from the crashing waves.

"I know. I love him."

She turned to her brother. She wanted him to see into her heart through her eyes. They were royals. Love mattered not. The kingdom and its future were all that could matter to them.

"I cannot, will not, change what is in my heart," she said, turning her gaze back to the water.

"I see he feels the same about you," Richard said devoid of the expected emotion in his words.

"I seek only to see you safely to your throne."

"You have rescued me. I am in your debt."

Joanna took Richard's hand.

"My brother, my king, I give my life for you."

Richard's horse grew nervous, shying to break their contact.

"I will stand aside for your desires. I offer my aid and comfort for you and your knight. No one shall come between you, as long as I control the throne."

Joanna nudged her horse beside his. It was the closest they could get to hugging each other under the circumstances.

"I must find him," Joanna said, lurching forward on her steed. She spurred into a full gallop.

"No!" Richard commanded in a resounding way.

His command went unheard. She would never abandon Rynhawker.

Richard spun to face the others.

"You, assist her," Richard commanded Thomas.

"By your leave, your majesty," Thomas said.

Thomas, however, needed no command to spur his gallop. He would have darted out on his own without Richard's insistence.

He left his king under the guard of only Alwain. It seemed the young knight might be committing to a fatal decision, but he would not abandon his mentor.

"My king, we must retreat further until we can assess the situation," Alwain said.

Richard paused for a moment, watching his sister gallop along the shoreline. Then he wheeled his stallion in a tight arc for the safety of the forest. Moments later, Richard, Alwain, Hugh and Baldwin disappeared.

72

Joanna's charger pounded wet sand at full pelt, following the curve of the shoreline. She passed quickly out of sight of the others. Only then did she throw a glance to Thomas racing in her wake.

They reached a rocky outcropping running from the forest's edge to a few strides into the water without seeing Rynhawker. Fear turned to terror when her mind raced through the possibilities.

"My lady," Thomas called out frantic. "Wait!"

Thomas drew his sword, cautious over what they might find rounding the boulders to reach the other side.

From the jagged rock's edge, came the clanking of iron against iron.

Tears rushed Joanna's eyes. Her knight was in trouble. She slowed as Thomas galloped past into the crashing waves, which dangerously retarded his progress.

Joanna reined her stallion to a jarring halt. She crawled over the rocks to the top, where she peered from the apex as Thomas pounded out of the water to increase his speed in the wet sand.

Two hundred strides distant, Rynhawker, still mounted, battled a horseman accompanying two ground soldiers. One body already lay slain in the sand. Rynhawker slashed mightily at each as they charged him with spears.

Joanna removed her crossbow, laid it on the flattest rock she could find. Frantically she fumbled to get her quarrel in place.

"Please, Jesus God, please help me," she uttered, knowing she had to call up her courage to control her sobs and the panic raging. Above all else, she had to keep her vision clear.

It took critical seconds to settle her breathing, lock onto the charging horseman, who she believed was Rynhawker's greatest immediate threat, then release her quarrel.

The tip came in low, caroming off the shield and right of the man's shoulder.

But her shot distracted the man! Rynhawker drove his blade around the shield to pierce ribs.

A ground soldier whirled about, leveling his spear in panic against Thomas. He threw up his shield to hit the slicing blade.

Thomas snapped the shaft in two; then delivering a hard driving backward slash, he relieved the man of his protection. His next thrust stopped the man where he stood.

Another mounted knight charged from the forest fringe, flailing his broadsword against Rynhawker.

"No!" Joanna yelled when she realized Rynhawker faced an onslaught from two at once.

Her hand trembled, trying to position her next quarrel. Time raced against her. She begged for God's assistance. She had to eliminate one of them before both engaged her knight. An errant shot during close fighting could mistakenly bring down the man she loved.

Joanna settled her cheek against the crossbow stock. She swiped at her tears. Uttering a single syllable could force a failed shot. She pulled in a breath and held it, shifted the crossbow slightly left. No time to check the wind. Only time enough to pray.

The mounted knight's sword came down to engage Rynhawker's blade.

Joanna fired!

Her quarrel tore into the mounted knight's shoulder just above his shield. Her strike made his sword arm useless.

Rynhawker lunged, cleaving into the knight's opposing shoulder, which immediately went limp before he toppled from his charging stallion.

With his closest threat neutralized, Rynhawker pivoted his stallion just in time to heave his sword against the spear driving at his chest. The spear tip shattered. The ground soldier retreated a step. Rynhawker lopped off his head with an efficient blade sweep.

Only then did Rynhawker wheel about to the rock outcropping.

Joanna rose tall upon the rocks vaulting her crossbow to Rynhawker. He brought the flat of his blade before his face in salute.

"Did any escape?" Thomas asked.

"There were only these. They came from the forest to attack from behind."

"There may be more prowling along the sea."

"Our king is unguarded? You left our king vulnerable?" Rynhawker said with an angry scowl.

"He hides in the forest," Thomas defended.

The words backed acid into Rynhawker's throat. No one was safe from Henry's men. Rynhawker had to make a decision.

"First we hide the bodies. If they are discovered, they will know we are here," he said.

One by one they consumed precious minutes dragging the bodies into the forest fringe. Would they remain out of sight long enough for the king to gain the safety of the sea? Only time would tell. For now they had to trust they might remain safe in the forest. They now had confirmation soldiers lurked in the area, so they needed to be cautious in their every move. Their small force could never outfight a score or more.

They no sooner returned to the shoreline when Joanna galloped around the rocks to join them. Her fervent pace indicated yet more danger.

"Riders! We cannot return that way," she called out in panic.

They were cut off from their king.

"What of the king?" Rynhawker pressed.

"They moved inland for safety. We go this way," she said, indicating the forest where the soldiers had launched their attack.

The three stallions pounded sand as swiftly as they could, with Rynhawker remaining behind momentarily to grind his stallion's hooves into the red-stained sand to erase it from Henry's men.

Joanna breached the trees first with Thomas right behind and Rynhawker reaching the fringe just before riders broke the rocks.

The three held their mounts in check, watching four fully armored horsemen canter along the wet sand near the breaking waves. Never once did they glance toward the trees, nor did it appear they discovered the bloody sand.

Joanna motioned Rynhawker further into the forest proper. They would be out of sight should the men come about to return.

"We must get to the king," Rynhawker charged.

Without speaking, Joanna led them down into a ravine before wheeling her mount in the direction they had come from earlier. They hoped Richard had taken refuge in the forest cover without straying too far away. They needed to remain near the coast until Joanna could signal the ship.

"We should have joined them by now," Thomas muttered, following the two moving slowly ahead.

Joanna returned to the place where they initially breached the forest for the coast. Within minutes she located what she hoped to be their tracks leading deeper into the woodland.

73

Joanna, Rynhawker and Thomas followed the tracks to a low-running, dried-up stream bed.

"We are here," Richard called, excited to see them unharmed.

Several moments later the king emerged from behind large boulders. He held the reins of Hugh and Baldwin's horse steady with Alwain beside him, his sword ready for a fight.

"How many were there?" Alwain asked, seeing the blood splatter on Rynhawker's tunic.

"Four. Now there are none."

"This place is not safe," Rynhawker said.

"We remain until darkness. I signal the ship in the night. On the morrow, they will come to take us away," Joanna said, as if all details were perfectly in place and nothing could go wrong.

Confidence proved a reckless ambition in these difficult times. Joanna tempered her excitement. They needed to reach the ship.

"And if Henry's army searches this forest?" Richard posed.

"They may discover their comrades' bodies in due course. They will know we are here," Alwain pressed, much to his king's dismay.

"We do as Joanna instructs. But we need food to keep us until the morn. It will help us fight our way to the ship," Richard added.

For a time no one spoke, each looked to the other for an answer. Joanna was the best suited to fulfill their need. However, that meant abandoning them in favor of hunting. And hunting could lead to their exposure.

"Rynhawker and I will forage. Thomas and Alwain protect our king. Conceal yourselves well from your mounts. We will return as soon as we can."

No one countermanded her order, not even Richard. Instead, Alwain led them deeper into the dried-up stream bed to seek refuge in the deep fissures lining the banks. The knight then walked the animals a hundred paces north, hoping if soldiers came upon the animals, it would allow the men a chance to slip away on foot.

Joanna hated leaving her brother in the woods guarded by such a small force. If what Alwain said held true, they should only come upon four riders and still have a fair chance of winning in a fight.

The two meandered through the forest until they came to the slope that carried them to the crest of a forested hill. From their vantage point they could gaze a far greater distance out to sea than anyone along the shoreline. She buried her concern that even from her location they failed to locate the ship awaiting her signal. What if it had been delayed? Or worse, what if John learned of her plan and he prevented Tobrin from departing the port?

She refused to consider such dire circumstances. She had to believe the ship had sailed from the coast to the point she indicated on Tobrin's map. The helmsman had to be able to discern the curvature of the shore she now towered over. It was unique along the coast, and thus, provided both a suitable landmark to rendezvous.

"Is the ship out there?" Rynhawker asked after staring blankly at the rolling sea.

Joanna held her answer. Her silence sank Rynhawker's heart. They had made it against all odds to the sea. Now their safety depended upon a seemingly non-existent ship.

Shaking off her inertia, Joanna scurried about, gathering dead branches and dried grasses as she worked her way back to an open hollow in the trees.

If she started her fire where they stood, there was a chance her ship could see it. But there also existed the chance they might fail to see it. The way to be certain her ship received her signal was to advance to the edge of the cliff facing north and west. She had instructed Tobrin to remain at sea but watch for a signal from on high.

Rynhawker busied himself aiding her effort to collect kindling when he suddenly stopped.

Something underfoot cracked nearby.

Joanna brought her crossbow around, groping for a quarrel, fearful of what danger they faced next.

Instead, Rynhawker pointed to fleeting movement in the trees. A stag had wandered up the hill downwind of them. It vanished before Joanna could even prepare her weapon.

74

The blaze grew as Joanna tossed on branches while Ryn-hawker stoked the fuel with his sword. Needing maximum flame height, they had no idea if their creation would be sufficient to be seen by a ship bouncing out at sea.

Once the fire roared, they advanced to the cliff's edge. Ryn-hawker could see the hope in Joanna's eyes. They could ill afford to face the coming days without the ship.

A night sky absent of clouds allowed a silver sliver of moon to cast a glow upon the waves.

Rynhawker brought Joanna close to stave off the cold wind whipping through the trees at their back. She took his hand into hers. He read disappointment growing in her eyes the longer they waited absent a response from the sea. Maybe difficult weather forced the ship to turn back to spare the crew from disaster? Maybe the man she charged to command the ship betrayed her out of loyalty to Prince John? Rynhawker had to consider an alternate course of action should the ship fail to materialize on the coast.

How long do they wait? How much do they risk in the hopes of seeing the ship? The longer they remained near the fire, the more dangerous it became.

Joanna refused to abandon hope, even after the flames at their backs withered. Despite the warmth Rynhawker provided, she abandoned him in favor of collecting more wood.

They must be out there. Somewhere down below, Richard huddled in darkness waiting to be carried safely away.

Rynhawker went to Joanna, drew her from her gathering.

"We must go now. If any see this fire they will investigate."

Joanna released the branches, threw herself into his arms.

"We must wait. It will come. The ship is there," she whimpered, desperate to silence her cry. A knight would never cry—her brother would never reveal emotion despite dire circumstances engulfing them.

Joanna pulled herself from him to return to the cliff. The sea sparkled against a spectacular canopy of stars shimmering overhead. Yet no signal emerged from the ocean to announce her ship.

"Do not fail us, Tobrin," she pleaded to the night.

He must be somewhere out there waiting.

"It is time we abandon this place," Rynhawker said more insistently.

Joanna complied. Together they doused the remaining flames with dirt carved up with Rynhawker's sword.

She knew her signal was grand enough to be seen far out at sea. If her ship waited at its location, they would have seen it and responded in kind. Yet she spied nothing but dismal water.

Rynhawker led her through barren trees down the hill to return to the darkened campsite, where the men restlessly slept.

Richard awoke with a jolt at the sounds of approaching horses. He brought his sword up to fight, though the riders were still a distance away. When he realized it was Joanna, he returned his sword to his side and settled back into his slumber. Exhaustion and hunger had stolen all strength from their king.

Joanna dismounted first, Rynhawker scanning to be certain they remained undetected. Then Rynhawker dismounted to tether their horses with the others.

Thomas awoke.

"Tell me good news," he whispered to his master.

"We have none," Rynhawker replied.

Alwain turned to Rynhawker. In the darkness, the fear in his eyes went unseen.

"Will there be a ship?" he asked.

He received no reply.

"Sleep now. We have but a few hours before the sun comes up to betray us," Rynhawker said.

After Thomas and Alwain settled back to sleep, Rynhawker crossed the expanse to join Joanna at the base of a dormant beech.

"We must sleep now," he said.

Joanna knew she would never sleep. She had trusted a man to provide them a way out of Henry's reach. Had she erred? For the moment she knew she must discard all thoughts of betrayal in favor of devising a new plan to gain Richard's safety.

Visualizing her parchment map in her mind, she discerned how far they needed to traverse to reach King Philip's lands. It would take many days of difficult riding.

But it was possible.

And she had no idea what to expect when she reached France. Would Philip stop them from returning home? Would Philip take them all prisoner only to return them to German hands?

"What will we do now?" Rynhawker whispered so only Joanna would hear.

"You are unable to sleep?" she whispered back.

"Sleep is difficult without knowing what tomorrow will bring. Do we remain in the hopes your ship exists? Or do we depart?"

"Can we make it to France?" she asked.

Joanna wished to sleep, knew she must to keep her mind sharp for what the next day might bring. Yet when she closed her eyes, only thoughts of their dire situation came to mind. She shoved them away, only to have them return moments later.

As the first rays of a new sun filtered into the ravine where they slept, Joanna finally succumbed to her exhaustion.

Thomas was the first to awaken to take up a position where he could watch over their surroundings. Frost blanketed the forest. He shivered in the cold morning air. Their horses whickered in the distance, but save for their noise, the woods remained silent and still. So much so, that Thomas chose to allow the others to remain asleep.

Vigilant, Thomas maintained watch over the others. He wondered what this day would bring. Would they still be free when the sun set again? Maybe they would be aboard a ship sailing for England. Or might they be attacked and die this day?

Hunger gnawed at Thomas' belly. First and foremost they needed to eat and find water. Afterward, they could determine what they might face in the rest of the day.

After an hour of solitude, Thomas gently shook Alwain wake. The knight bolted up ready to fight. Thomas clamped a hand to the man's mouth to prevent the release of any telltale noise.

"What?" Alwain asked, trying to assess the danger.

"I need you to watch while the others sleep," Thomas said.

"Why?"

"I am going to forage."

A short distance away, Richard came awake to stare at the two knights.

"My king," Thomas said, bowing before taking his leave.

Richard surveyed his surroundings, exhilarated they were still free.

The desolate hours of the day dragged on with Thomas and Alwain foraging while everyone else remained hidden in the ravine. No one spoke as each contemplated the next steps in their plan.

They were free of the castle, but yet to be free of Henry's reach. When Thomas and Alwain returned, Joanna and Rynhawker left to travel to the coast. Joanna prayed that when they arrived, they would see a ship sailing toward land.

Rynhawker had little faith the ship would appear to save them. He wanted to say so many things to Joanna but knew at the moment her sense and sensibilities were fragile. She had freed the king, but could she keep him free until they reached England?

They retarded their stallions as the breaking waves became visible through gray skeleton limbs. They paused just inside the fringe at a place where they could monitor the shoreline in both directions and yet gaze out at the sea.

If her ship had seen her signal and only failed to respond in kind, they might still be sailing for the coast, directing their course to rendezvous where the fire signal originated. They had no other way to communicate with each other. Joanna had to trust that the man steering the ship knew where they were to meet.

With the sun disappearing from the sky, Rynhawker turned his stallion to nudge Joanna's mount to bring her about. They needed to return to their camp.

"We will have no ship to carry us from here," Rynhawker said.

Joanna refused to hear his words. Wheeling her stallion about, she needed one more lasting look along the coast—hoping. She saw only waves crashing over the sand.

Now she needed another way to get her king beyond Henry's reach. On their journey back, Joanna considered options that might be available to them. They could travel south to find a way into France, or they could follow the coast west until they reached the end of Henry's domain. Either choice meant they must get through Henry's defenses.

As the final rays of a dying sun cast upon their faces, Joanna discerned a faint smoke swirl rising from the ravine where they hid. Anger surged into her throat. If they saw it, so could their enemy.

They spurred stallions into the ravine in the hopes of extinguishing the fire before it was too late.

They arrived to discover the charred remains of a small camp fire. Freshly gnawed bones scattered the ground, yet there were no bodies. Joanna and Rynhawker followed the ravine around a sharp bend to find their king and the others, huddled within thick pines.

No one smiled when she breached their location.

"Who left the fire?"

"I did," Alwain confessed.

"You wish our king back in the dungeon?" she spat.

"We erred, but we were able to feed them," Thomas offered.

Rynhawker grew agitated at Thomas' words.

"You would sacrifice your king for scraps of rabbit," he scolded.

"Actually, hedgehog," Alwain corrected much to Rynhawker's anger.

Alwain offered up a roasted leg.

Joanna's face softened at the sight of the meat. Her stomach begged to be fed. She had ignored it most of the day.

"We must now move," she commanded between bites.

It took moments for Rynhawker to devour his meat. He gulped the water Thomas offered.

Minutes later all trekked west from the ravine. They would travel only an hour, using the dusk to illuminate their way until they came upon a hollow in the woods which provided suitable concealment. The new location was less acceptable than the ravine, but remaining near the fire could only bring trouble.

In the silent still of the night they settled in amongst the trees to stay warm and sleep another night.

Joanna, however, rose an hour later to prepare her mount for departure.

"Where are we going?" Rynhawker pressed.

"To signal the ship," she replied.

"The ship that is not there?"

"There is no ship, is there?" Alwain asked, keeping his voice low to avoid disturbing the others.

Joanna said nothing. Instead, she mounted her stallion, turned it about in the direction of the hill they had climbed the night before and spurred the beast into motion. But she paused when Rynhawker took up his mount to join her.

75

Joanna crested the hill overlooking the sea. They encountered no fresh prints to indicate others had discovered their signal fire. Rynhawker dismounted first, whereupon he gathered branches to set the blaze anew. If Joanna believed the ship was there, then Rynhawker would support her. He would risk igniting the fire again.

Neither spoke as they gathered kindling. In a short time, the first sparks set the kindling to smolder. If nothing else, they would be warm while they signaled the vacant sea. But would they be safe? Each time they ignited their fire, they risked revealing their location. Rynhawker took solace believing that even if they were overrun here, their king would remain safe from capture.

Joanna turned to the sea in the distance.

"Please be there," she prayed to herself.

Panic swept through her. Something shifted about in the trees! There were men buried somewhere in the dark woods. She distinctly heard someone crunching dead branches. They came to investigate her fire.

Joanna removed her crossbow, cocking it in one smooth motion against the closest tree trunk before setting her quarrel in the channel. She would get one of them before they took her or her knight.

Rynhawker came beside her with blade drawn. He had heard the same noise. They peered into the black beyond the fire's glow.

A figure skulked amongst the trees. Both clearly saw it. Rynhawker pulled Joanna behind him, advancing to face the charge from their enemy.

"Hail, friend," the voice called.

Duchard emerged into the glow off the fire, his hands empty, his smile lighting up the night around him. Behind him, Isaac poked his head out.

"You survived!" Rynhawker chimed as the men shared a hug.

"God has answered our prayers," Joanna said.

She shared a spontaneous hug with the knight and then with Isaac. She had believed the worst of Duchard's fate.

"How did you locate us?" Rynhawker asked.

"Isaac conveyed Joanna's instructions, and your tracks led us to the sea. If we could find you, so can Henry's men. Your backtracking was indeed clever, but once I determined the ruse, we continued on your trail."

"Our king remains hidden in the forest," Joanna said.

"How did you know to come to the fire?" Rynhawker pressed.

"I asked who would be so foolish as to set such a blaze where it can be seen. When we approached, I saw it was you."

"We pray no others have seen our flames," Joanna said.

"I fear our king is not safe for long. We have witnessed armor gathering in this woodland," Isaac said.

Joanna stared out to sea while Duchard and Isaac warmed themselves at the back side of the flames.

"We acquired water, lentils and boar a peasant kindly surrendered at my beckoning," Duchard said.

"At the beckoning of your sword," Rynhawker corrected.

"Yes, that did improve the man's generosity."

Duchard offered strips of dried boar from inside his shirt. Rynhawker divided the rations, providing Joanna the most.

The men joined Joanna at the cliff to view the sea. No one spoke. Each prayed.

"It is time. We must leave now. The next man to approach will be our enemy," Rynhawker said.

She looked at him with desperate hope. The fire had lost its flames. He cradled Joanna's hand. She jerked it away. The ship had to be there. Their very lives depended on it now.

Duchard returned to the fire, where he scraped earth to extinguish the remaining flames. Rynhawker, however, refused to abandon Joanna.

"We must go. God will see us through this," he offered.

At the moment, Joanna wondered why God had abandoned them when they most needed His aid.

Then the first light streaked low across the sky in a parabolic arc. It might have been mistaken for a shooting star until they realized the light originated out of the sea. There came another, followed by a barrage of six flaming arrows arcing low across the night sky to enter the sea moments later.

Tears stole Joanna's sight. She threw herself into Rynhawker's arms.

"We are going home," she said. Then she cried.

God had seen them through their terrible ordeal.

Without thinking, she kissed Rynhawker in the dwindling light from her dying signal fire. Duchard stopped kicking dirt long enough to witness Tobrin's signal from the ship.

King Richard the Lionheart was going home.

Or was he?